SHELL GAMES

A JOHN MARQUEZ CRIME NOVEL

SHELL GAMES

KIRK RUSSELL

CHRONICLE BOOKS
SAN FRANCISCO

First Chronicle Books LLC paperback edition, published in 2004.

This is a work of fiction. Names, places, characters, and incidents are products of the author's imagination or are used fictionally. Any resemblance to actual people, places, or events is entirely coincidental.

ISBN: 0-8118-4111-1

The Library of Congress has cataloged the previous edition as follows:

Russell, Kirk, 1954–

  Shell games : a John Marquez crime novel / Kirk Russell.

    p. cm.

  ISBN: 0-8118-4186-3

1. California. Dept. of Fish and Game—Fiction.

2. Government investigators—Fiction. 3. Abalone fisheries—Fiction.

4. California—Fiction. 5. Smuggling—Fiction. I. Title.

  PS3618.U76S47 2003

  813'.6—dc21

                        2003009590

Manufactured in the United States of America

Designed by tom & john: a design collaborative

Composition by Suzanne Scott

Cover photo by William R. Curtsinger

Distributed in Canada by Raincoast Books

9050 Shaughnessy Street

Vancouver, British Columbia V6P 6E5

10 9 8 7 6 5 4 3 2 1

Chronicle Books LLC

85 Second Street

San Francisco, California 94105

www.chroniclebooks.com

For Judy Rodgers and Kate and Olivia Russell

1

When Marquez saw the forested ridge at the end
of the canyon he knew he was close. He rounded the last curve and
lowered the driver's window, smelling pine pitch and dry grass as
afternoon heat swept the truck cab. As he slowed to a stop near the
steel posts at the campground entrance, Davies stepped out onto
the road and started toward him, a smile on his sweat-streaked
face as though they shared some joke played on the dead men.

"Guess they weren't as smart as they thought, Lieutenant,"
Davies said.

"Guess not. Where are they?"

"About half a mile up the creek trail."

Marquez drove over the entry chain and the quarantine sign
attached to it. He parked near a rusted iron barbecue at one of the
campsite slots and sat on a picnic table, his fingers tracing initials
carved in the top as he phoned the sheriff's office in Mendocino.
He identified himself as the patrol lieutenant of California Fish and

Game's covert SOU, the Special Operations Unit, telling the detective he was with a Mark Davies, who'd found the bodies of two men along the canyon wall northeast of the Guyanno Creek campground, south of Fort Bragg. The detective drew a breath and Marquez heard a pen scratch paper.

"And when did this Davies call you?" the detective asked.

"Roughly three hours ago."

"Why did you wait so long to call?"

"He said if I didn't come alone he'd leave."

"Who is he?"

"An urchin diver. He works out of Noyo Harbor in Fort Bragg. He's helped my team a couple of times."

"An informant?"

"More like a concerned citizen."

"Right. Your name again, officer?"

"John Marquez."

"Hold for a second, Marquez."

When the detective got back on the line he wanted to confirm it was the campground that had been closed by a bubonic plague outbreak and then said they were on their way and not to leave, not to touch anything. Marquez hung up guessing it would be more than an hour before detectives arrived, at least twenty minutes before a county cruiser. He folded his phone and walked up to where Davies stood cleaning his sunglasses with his T-shirt, near a car parked at one of the campsites, an '80s model with faded black paint, a salt-rusted body, a beater with a set of new tires that were probably worth more than the vehicle. He saw dive weights and flippers in the passenger foot well, a yellowed newspaper on the back seat, a sweatshirt turned inside out.

"The owner of this got the shady side of the tree," Davies said. "Somebody really did a number on them."

"You knew him?"

"I recognize him, but I didn't know him that well. Knew his dive partner better."

Marquez decided he'd run the license plate of the Supra after Davies showed him what he'd found. They started up the creek trail, skirting waist-high greasewood and taller poison oak with red leaves curled and drying. He smelled creek mud and the dry oaks, and for a third of a mile the trail shadowed the water and then climbed into sunlight where a yellow two-man tent was pitched on a patch of grass and thistle, its flap open, two sleeping bags visible, rumpled clothes, a battery-powered lantern with a shattered light. No blood, no sign of violence.

"Did you toss their campsite?"

"Yeah."

"Why?"

"Messing with them, letting them know they weren't alone up here like they thought."

Marquez nodded as though that made sense, but it didn't. Why tip the poachers off that you were here? He felt Davies studying him as he looked over at the campsite. Bottlenose flies rested on the tent sides. A cooler lay in the dry grass nearby with an open package of hotdogs spilling out. A jar of mayonnaise had its lid off and the ants had found it. He pictured Davies tearing up this campsite in the early morning.

"They didn't cook up here," Davies said, as if somehow that was important. "They probably cooked down at the barbecues or ate in town."

He knew Davies easily could have left without making any calls. He could have burned everything he'd touched in a barbecue pit, left it smoldering and taken off, and with the campground closed there was no saying when these bodies would have been found.

"How did you know to look further up the trail?"

"I figured they were shucking it up here somewhere. I looked all around down at the main campsite before I ever came up here. You ready to take a look?"

Marquez picked a couple of bay leaves as they passed through a stand of trees. He folded the leaves, bringing the pungent smell close to his nose before letting them fall to the trail. Nervous anticipation started in him. Something didn't feel right in Davies's story, not that he was lying, but leaving something out. When they came out of the trees he studied the terrain ahead, remembering how the canyon narrowed as it funneled toward the mountains, the country steep and thick with brush. The path didn't go much farther and you had your choice of a deer trail or staying in the rocky creek bed. He heard a faraway police siren like an animal calling from down the canyon and turned his back on the sound, looked upstream through the brush and trees, trying to spot the poachers' setup. He saw a flat table of dark rock and a flash of orange in the brush. He pointed at it.

"There?"

Davies nodded but didn't move, blocking the trail instead, the long muscles of his arms rippling as he folded them over his chest. His face carried white streaks of dried sweat and he was unshaven, his whiskers black, eyes bright with urgency.

"I know you're wondering about me, Lieutenant, but I didn't kill them. I was done with anything to do with killing when I left the navy, but I did get in a fight a couple weeks ago with one of these guys and that's going to fuck things up. It was a bar fight; he got a lawyer to sue me. Supposedly, I fucked up his eye with a chair leg."

"What else haven't you told me?"

"I was going to tell you that."

They started moving again, working their way down to the creek. He left his shoes on, but rolled up his pants and the water felt cool and smooth against his calves. Rocks turned and slid underfoot as he walked up the stream bed with the light current pulling against him. When they reached the work area the poachers had built he put a hand on a flat boulder and stepped out of the creek.

A wood plank had been laid across two aluminum sawhorses to make a table to shuck on, and a pile of abalone shells was at one end, hundreds of them spilling under the brush and into the creek, their silvery green and pink interiors iridescent and reflecting underwater. Flies buzzed around the pile and as he flipped one of the bigger shells with his foot they swarmed around his ankle. White, green, red, pink, threaded, and black abalone had once been plentiful up and down the coast, but only the red were left in any quantity, and Fish and Game was fighting poachers for those, losing a quarter million a year to the black market and to divers who ignored the state limit of twenty-four. There'd been twenty grand in abalone here. He slapped at a fly on his neck and decided he'd get his camcorder and notebook from the truck and come back up here alone.

"There's someone with cash to burn who wants it all, Lieutenant. He's paying fifty, sixty dollars an ab. You've got to be hearing the same thing."

Marquez stared at the shell pile knowing the truth in that. It was the main reason he'd driven up here before calling the county. The global black market in animal parts was second only to drug running, but until now California had dodged the commercial poachers. That they were up against one he didn't doubt at all. They hadn't been able to touch him and biologists and recreational divers were reporting abalone beds that looked like they'd been vacuumed. Bars and docks were boiling with rumors of big money. He pictured the pair here lugging their catch up the creek trail, then carrying shucked abalone back out to the parking lot packed on ice in coolers. Deals going down in the campground, the chain dropped, coolers of abalone transferred under headlights, and then sitting around afterwards near their tent, drinking and smoking under the long arc of the stars, feeling like they had it all figured out.

When they got back to the creek trail the siren was much closer. They climbed and Marquez saw a clearing ahead. His eye followed the trampled grass and thistle to a man's body on the far side of the clearing, sitting against a large oak, head tilted slightly up, as though he'd been resting in the shade waiting for them to arrive. As they got closer and he saw the wound in the man's abdomen a buzzing started in his head. Davies's voice floated in the distance.

"That's Ray Stocker," Davies said. "He was a grade-A asshole."

Marquez looked at the knife buried in the tree above Stocker's head and an image from another killing rose in his memory, one from his DEA years.

"What else do you know about Stocker?"

"He hung with a guy named Danny Huega you'll want to talk to. I don't know for sure Huega was working with them, but there's a pretty good chance. He's another urchin diver."

"Does he have a boat?"

"The *Coney Island*."

Marquez knew the boat and had an idea who Huega was, pictured a brown-haired diver with a coffee-colored birthmark on one side of his neck. They'd find him and talk to him, if not today, then tomorrow.

Davies pointed. "See the tattoo on Stocker's right arm?" The bluish blur was hard to make out at this distance. "That's the constellation Orion. Stocker called himself Orion. That's the kind of bullshit he was. The guy around back of the tree is the one who owned the Supra. Name is Peter Han. He showed up in Bragg about seven or eight months ago and was probably selling dope with Stocker. No one is making a real living off the water or anything else around here anymore. That's why there's more poaching. They're closing the Georgia-Pacific plant in October so there's not going to be shit left of Fort Bragg. They talk about tourism but who's going to stay in Bragg when they can stay in places like Mendocino."

Even with the heat, decomp had barely started and Marquez guessed they'd died last night. The second man sat with his legs splayed, right arm falling to the side, but Marquez couldn't get a good look at his face without getting closer, and didn't see a way to do that without contaminating the crime scene. He could make out abrasions on Han's face and wondered if he'd had answers beaten out of him. Was this a robbery, torturing them to find out where money was hidden? Why take it to this degree? He took in the broader scene again, Stocker facing out toward the clearing, Han toward the brush and steep canyon wall. A heavy link chain had been wrapped around the tree and their necks, then ratcheted tight with a rusty come-along that looked like an old coyote trap. Wrists and ankles bound with wire.

Stocker's intestines had sagged onto his groin and Marquez looked again at the knife stuck in the tree above his head, a military blade or a knockoff of one. He'd been a big man, heavy-boned, tall, about two hundred-fifty pounds. Both wore boxer shorts, so maybe they'd been asleep in the tent. That would be the time to take a man Stocker's size. Hold a gun to his head and tell him to get up very slowly. Bind his wrists before backing him out and walking him up here.

The siren closed in now and then shut down abruptly. Marquez guessed the county cop was just reaching the campground entrance and looking for him, probably thinking about the quarantine, the young girl who'd contracted plague here a month ago in August. The girl had survived but the media had played it up and the cop was probably wishing he hadn't caught this call.

When they hiked back down there were three county patrol cars parked in the lot with their lights still spinning. Marquez showed his badge. He could tell the uniforms had been told to sequester Davies and after they sat him in the back of a patrol car, Marquez got his video camera from the truck and walked back up to film the shucking table and shells. He'd wait for the detectives to clear him before removing any evidence, but he documented and made a rough count. He wrote his notes and made a sketch of the setup, putting the creek in his drawing, the brush and the flat rock, reasoning that the poachers had carried the abalone up here in case anyone visited the campground, though they'd also cut the entry lock and put on their own.

Two detectives had arrived while he was filming and had gone up to look at the bodies. They had put an end to the sightseeing, confining the county cops to the paved area, ordering crime tape strung across the upper end of the campground as though they could close the canyon off. When he returned from the shell pile, Marquez sat on the table near his truck and finished his notes as the cops running the yellow tape behind him agreed that this had been a drug hit and that it was no surprise. One cop said the last case of plague had been in Ukiah, you never saw it this close to the coast and that probably it was because of global warming. He said last winter's rains were proof, and then their conversation went sideways into the poor quality of tires on county cruisers nowadays.

Marquez watched the two county detectives come down off the trail and start toward him. Detectives Ruter and Streatfield. They shook his hand, listened, and took notes, their eyes offering neither acceptance nor judgment, their smiles a formality. The taller one, Streatfield, had a tired brown mustache and eyes that looked like they wanted to sit in a porch chair and get out of this heat. The other, Ruter, was clearly in charge. He exchanged cards with Marquez and wanted to know about the Fish and Game covert team, but Marquez said little by way of explanation, which was his habit because they were often working small towns where word traveled fast and cops gossiped as much as anybody, maybe more.

They took his statement, working it chronologically, moving slowly up the timeline from Davies's first phone call this morning, an edge creeping into their voices as he admitted not following protocol by delaying his call to them. They wanted him to say he was a friend of Davies and kept coming back to it.

"He's helped you before," Ruter said. "Isn't that right?"

"It is."

Poaching tips were the rainwater that nourished the Fish and Game system and Davies had helped his team without ever asking for CalTip money, the fund used to pay tipsters. Marquez had a lot of respect for that, but this was something else and he wasn't sure what he thought yet and wasn't going to speculate with the detectives.

"And he was here for you today. He hiked up the creek last night on a mission for Fish and Game."

"We don't run missions."

"He talks like he's on a mission and he's an ex navy SEAL, did you know that?"

"Yeah, he told me once."

"He reported in to you and maybe you said you'd handle us. You're fighting a war to save the abalone and he's on the front lines."

"I think I already saw that movie, Ruter. Why don't you cut to the chase?"

"All right, I will. You ought to be full of apologies for giving the killer or killers an extra three hours to get away, but you're not and Davies talks like what he did was the right thing to do, calling you first. So I'll be calling your chief this afternoon and asking him when shellfish became a higher priority than murder."

"I'll give you his phone number and my cell. That's the best way to get ahold of me."

"You're not leaving yet. You stick with your picnic table a little longer."

Marquez made phone calls. He picked up his voice mail and listened to a message from Jimmy Bailey, a ponytailed informant out of Pillar Point, near Half Moon Bay, thirty miles south of San Francisco, a man his team had nicknamed "Docktalk." Next, he called Fish and Game dispatch and ran the Supra, got the name

Peter Han and a Bay Area address, Daly City. He asked dispatch to check Stocker's and Han's names for boat registration and they came up negative. It was another hour before Ruter came back to him.

"What kind of money is in abalone?"

"Roughly fifty dollars a pound."

"What do poachers take a year? Give me a dollar value."

"Ten million."

"And what do these divers make on urchin?"

"A dollar fifty a pound."

"Fifty a pound for abalone, a dollar fifty for urchin," Ruter repeated. Marquez nodded. Ruter continued, "I guess you do need help if you can't keep a lowlife like Stocker from pulling that many abalone. You're not covering the base and you're worried about it? Is that it? Davies called and you jumped in your truck without thinking about procedure."

Marquez let it slide and Ruter pointed at the camcorder lying on the picnic table.

"Did you take pictures of the victims?"

"No."

"You don't mind if I look at the tape, do you?"

"Go ahead."

Ruter talked as he watched the video playback. "I wish we had equipment like this, but we had to fight just to get cell phones. That's our big victory this year."

Marquez knew what tight budgets were about. The SOU budget had been halved this year. His team had been cut to six. He watched Ruter run through the video, then lay the camcorder down.

"Thank you," Ruter said, hitched his pants, and walked down to his partner.

Marquez waited a few minutes then drove down to where they had Davies. Both rear doors of a county car were wide open and Ruter sat next to Davies with one arm up on the seat back. He was a short, bullet-headed man, salt-and-pepper hair parted on the left side, red in the face from walking up the slope repeatedly in the heat. He sat with his trousers hiked up, one foot out the door, left hand covering his inside holster.

"I'm taking off," Marquez told him.

"Stay available," Ruter said. "Don't get too far undercover."

Marquez touched Davies's shoulder, said, "Give me a call, I want to talk to you more about this."

"Where are you going to be tonight?" Ruter asked.

"In Fort Bragg."

"If I want to talk to you, where do I find you?"

"Use the number I gave you."

Ruter turned back to Davies. "Is that the number you called this morning?" he asked, and Marquez never heard the reply.

A couple of hours later, he was driving between Mendocino and Fort Bragg. The sun was low on the horizon, its last light streaking the water. His phone burred softly and he looked at the number showing on the screen, then matched it to Ruter's card.

"Your friend killed them," Ruter said, his voice hoarse now. "And this isn't about abalone. Stocker was suing him and Davies saw a way to use the poaching as a cover and take care of the problem." Ruter paused, waiting for a response, but Marquez had gone as far as he was going to go with the detective today. "Davies went berserk in that bar and Stocker was going to win the lawsuit. Stocker's lawyer says the case was a no-brainer and Davies was going to lose his boat."

"Everything is a no-brainer for a lawyer."

"Davies told me this afternoon that someone should have turned Ray Stocker's lights off a long time ago."

"I don't think Davies is your man."

"You've got a lot of opinions for a game warden."

"And you solve cases faster than any detective I've ever met." He heard Ruter's hard exhale. "Look, Ruter, I'm sorry I didn't call you sooner."

"So now you're sorry? I'll tell your chief that for you. If I was your superior officer, I'd—"

Marquez pulled out his earpiece and clicked the phone off. He drove slowly north looking out over the darkening water as DEA memories invaded him again.

2

Marquez got into Fort Bragg after dusk and met Sue
Petersen at a pizza parlor in the old part of town. A red neon sign
arched over the entry of Carlene's and she was standing in the softer
shadows to the side, wearing jeans, a white T-shirt, and brown
leather loafers. Her black hair was cut short, her face animated as
she smiled. They'd worked together for eight years and she was
the only warden left of those he'd started with in the SOU.

"You ironed your T-shirt," he said, as he walked up.

"I figured you were buying dinner, so I went all out."

Before Davies called this morning, Marquez had bought yellow
onions, garlic, basil, canned tomatoes, and spaghetti. His truck
smelled like wilted basil. It had been his night to cook at the SOU
cold house in Fort Bragg, but after leaving Guyanno he didn't have
it in him and called Petersen suggesting Carlene's. He dropped the
basil in a trash receptacle on the sidewalk before they walked inside.

In the back was the cedar-paneled room Carlene's called the party room, and they asked for a table there because it was empty. A waitress took their order of salad, pepperoni pizza, and a pitcher of beer almost as soon as they sat down.

"No beer for me tonight, John."

The waitress was still there, but he didn't change the order, and after she left, he asked about Tran Li, the Vietnamese immigrant they were building an abalone poaching case against. They had more than enough to take him down, but so far, Li hadn't led them to anyone else. Li had either outsmarted them or not sold any of what he'd brought home. He had a big freezer in his garage, they had a search warrant in place, but Marquez had been holding off because he figured Li was the best lead they had to the buyer working the coast. Li was diving every day, taking as much as he could, and it was Marquez's gut feeling that Li was connected to their bigger buyer. He knew Petersen didn't agree with the decision to wait. She thought Li would plea-bargain and give up the buyer and that they should have taken him down today.

But she gave him the day without comment. Li had gotten into Fort Bragg near dawn and dove with his older son for six and a half hours. The SOU had videotaped them in coves and rock gardens and then later in Noyo Harbor as they unloaded the Zodiac and loaded their car. The rest of the team was camped outside Li's house tonight in Oakland.

"Li and son got gas at the Chevron and stopped at the Sea-Lite Motel on the way out," she said. "We went in after and I talked to the manager. They ate in the little restaurant there. She remembered Li's kid having a hamburger and she found the ticket and showed me."

Li had stayed in the motel twice since starting this poaching spree and Marquez was sure the motel was a meeting place.

"The kid must have wolfed the burger because they weren't there twenty minutes," Petersen said.

Li was wearing the team out running, sometimes twice a day, between Fort Bragg and his house in Oakland, a three-and-a-half-hour drive. He'd get in the fast lane and sit on eighty miles an hour. He was a compact, hardworking diver who'd argued his own case in front of a Santa Rosa jury when they'd busted him three years ago. The jury had been barely interested in abalone poaching and the judge sympathetic to Li's immigrant roots and his desire to better his family. He'd been lectured by the judge, given a suspended sentence and reduced fine. Marquez had hoped he'd never poach again.

A week and a half ago they'd recognized him at Noyo Harbor, like a bad bear coming back, Petersen had said. They'd tracked him eight out of the last nine days. Committing the same offense within three years would make him much more likely to get a prison sentence this time around. It would add to the leverage they'd bargain with.

The waitress arrived with a plastic pitcher and slid it onto the table, beer sloshing over the sides. She put down two salad bowls, wiped her fingers, and walked away. Marquez offered beer to Petersen again and when she shook her head he filled his glass. As he tipped his head back and drank he saw an image of Ray Stocker's head and heard Davies' drawling comment that Stocker was looking up at the sky for his home planet in the constellation of Orion. They'd run Davies's name through NCIC, the National Crime Information Center, and had come up with two minor arrests, nothing significant. The drawl was Georgia. They'd have to find out more about him now.

"Tell me more about these killings," she said. "You said on the phone Davies hiked up the creek canyon from the beach lot. That's a long walk."

"That's what he claims he did. Parked his van at the beach and walked through the culvert under the highway and used night vision goggles to get up the canyon."

"Why does that creep me out?" Petersen asked.

Marquez reached for his beer and knew what was coming.

Davies had made Petersen's permanent list when he'd surprised her and another warden during a surveillance in Eureka five years ago. He'd thought they were planning to steal from a boat and had bumped the van they were hiding in with his truck. Petersen ended up with a bloody nose and wounded pride and had never forgiven him. She still claimed it had given her a chronic sinus problem.

"He's a loner, John, he lives on that boat to avoid people. I'll bet part of him misses military life. Not so much that he wants to go back, but enough to like the connection with you. He needs that action with purpose and wants your respect because it validates him. To keep you talking to him he has to produce information. No information, no contact with you."

Marquez scratched the poison oak rash on his left arm and ate a couple forkfuls of oily lettuce. Though he couldn't generate a real appetite, it was nice to be with Petersen and to hear the voices of people out in the front room. Good to be near normal things after the killing scene.

"He gets a rush out of making a problem for poachers, which is not the same as protecting abalone," she said.

"Leave it that we don't really know that much about him," he replied. The waitress slid the pizza and their check onto the table. He watched Petersen lift a piece of pizza, the strands of cheese stretching before she tore it with her fingers.

"Are you going to eat," she asked, "or just drink beer?"

He drained the rest of his glass thinking about what came next. "Tomorrow, you and I will try to find this Danny Huega. We'll go up the canyon first and I'll show you where they were and what they had going."

They left the pizza parlor and drove back to the cold house at the outskirts of town, a nondescript brown-painted house with a sizable back garden that had long gone to seed. The department rented the house from a relative of a warden and Marquez was careful how many wardens he had here at one time. Before the last round of budget cuts, when his team had still been ten wardens, it was harder to control the flow. Now, with the SOU down to six, including himself, it wasn't as hard to keep the neighbors from being suspicious, although they'd already had to decline a request from a schoolteacher neighbor who'd asked that one of them come to her third grade class and talk about the food chain because their story was that they were government biologists studying kelp beds. Lately that had become the joke. When you were late getting somewhere it was because you were teaching class.

Tonight was the first time in years he'd been here alone with Petersen. She made tea and walked into a bedroom, talking on her cell with her husband, Stuart. She was a long time on the phone and Marquez checked Shawn Cairo and Carol Shauf, two of the SOU wardens staked out down the street from Li's house. Li was done for the night, had backed into his garage and lowered the door, but given the way he'd been at it, they assumed he'd dive again tomorrow. When he hung up, Petersen sat down across from him on the couch. She cradled her tea mug, leaning forward, her eyes on his, ready to say something but still hesitating.

"This is really hard for me."

"Something happen at home?"

"In a way." She smiled then looked down at the coffee table. "Stuart wants me to resign tomorrow."

"Let's catch this guy first."

"John, I'm pregnant."

He reacted slowly, then it began to hit him, and he smiled and felt genuine happiness for her. "That's great. Congratulations. That's really great. How much pregnant? When's the baby due?"

"I know it messes everything up."

"It doesn't mess anything up."

"The timing couldn't be worse, could it?"

"There's no good timing for having a kid. You just do it, I think."

"What do you know about that?"

He remembered a conversation she'd had with him years ago, telling him she wanted to have two kids someday. That was before either had married and in the weeks when they'd slept together, and briefly imagined having those kids together. He'd never told anyone and doubted she had either. It had all come and gone one fall and what came after was a familiar banter and they'd avoided situations where they were alone together for a year or more. He tried to remember Petersen's exact age. Thirty-two, he thought, and could see the emotion crossing her face. She didn't need to explain. He knew how much her job meant to her and he knew already how much he'd miss her.

"I'm only ten weeks, but Stuart has been waiting five years, John. This life has been really hard on him and I've kept putting it off. He's never liked me being away so much, never has liked the whole SOU thing." She reached over and punched him on the arm. "Can you believe it, me, a mom?"

He could see the happiness in the back of her eyes and it touched him. It pushed the killings back. It held the DEA memories at bay.

"And Stuart's big case settled," she said.

"The railroad thing?"

She nodded and he remembered her husband, whose self-employed existence as a lawyer had made their finances sometimes rocky. Stuart had confided to Marquez at a Christmas party that he had a case that was going to make them rich.

"Did it work out like he thought?"

"Better even. It totally changes everything."

He started to ask again what the lawsuit had been about, then stopped himself because it didn't matter. The railroad lost and Stuart's client won. What mattered was she wanted to tell him it was time for her to move on and that she was pregnant and going to raise a family.

"You'll have to name those kids after the railroad." He looked at her hands. She'd had to put the tea down and press her palms flat on her thighs because she couldn't stop the shaking. "Yeah, how am I going to make this work without you?" he asked.

"Like you make everything work."

Nothing was working lately, and he was waking at night having trouble breathing. Except for the case against Li, everything was running hard the other way, and by now, they should have something. They should have a lead to this big buyer and they had nothing.

"I want to stay on another month and you need me to," Petersen said.

He studied her face. They both knew that the department required a shift to light-duty status with pregnancy and keeping her on meant not telling anyone and assuming the liability himself. As her direct supervisor it was his responsibility.

"A month from now it's over for me. I'm not coming back as a uniform," she said. He nodded but hadn't answered her request, though they both knew he'd do it. "I don't need light duty, at least not yet."

Then, as if she had to because they were here alone or to even things up, she asked about his marriage, how it was going, were Katherine and he getting it worked out.

"We're talking." Tomorrow, it would be exactly five months since he and Katherine had separated.

She waited for him to say more and when he couldn't find an easy way, she said, "I don't mean to pry, John."

After Petersen called it a night, Marquez put on a coat and took a walk. The murder scene had left him more emotional than he'd expected and he played it back in his head, the creek trail and clearing. He walked several miles and after getting back to the house wrote out details of the case that seemed too familiar to him. He read for a while trying to lose the uneasy feeling and went to sleep around one.

Before first light the next morning he headed down Highway 1 with Petersen. They bought coffee at the Chevron station in Fort Bragg and she was lighthearted and easy as though talking last night had lifted a weight from her. When they took the Guyanno Canyon cutoff the sky was streaked pink with dawn, the road empty and pale in the early light. A new lock secured the chain across the entrance. They stepped over it and over crime tape that had either been taken down or had fallen in the night. He walked up the creek trail with her and his chest tightened as they walked out the trampled grass across the clearing to the oak tree. He had to say something about what he was feeling, to Petersen, at least.

"This is going to sound hard to believe, but I've seen killings like this before, a lot like this, so much it's kicking up memories."

"Where?"

"In Mexico in the '80s when I was undercover with the DEA."

"What do we do with that?"

"Nothing, right now."

"But you're telling me for a reason."

"The man behind those killings was named Eugene Kline, a contract killer working for the cartels. As far as I know, he's still operating and he used to run dope from Humboldt County up here."

"He's a dope smuggler, too?"

"He had an organization of his own. I've got some stuff at home I'll show you."

They drove back to Fort Bragg and into town, stopping at the convenience store first, asking for the clerk Davies had named as Stocker's doper friend. He got a blank face from the woman behind the counter until they pressed her, then made it clear they'd keep coming back. At the surf shop, the owner and his friend standing near him had heard that Ray Stocker and Peter Han had been chained to a tree and gut slit. Marquez identified himself as Fish and Game and asked what they knew about Stocker diving. They didn't know anything. They thought he dove occasionally. Or maybe he didn't dive at all anymore. They weren't sure. If he did dive, he might poach a little ab, but he didn't surf anymore and looking at each other, passing some signal about law enforcement, they remembered he'd given up diving and weren't sure about him selling dope. Did they know what he did for a living? No, because they didn't hang with him. In fact, they hardly knew him, but if there was any possible way they could help they'd like to because they were pro-environment.

After the surf shop they split up and worked the town. Marquez walked into the bar, Hadrian's, where Davies had fought with Stocker. The bartender was a heavy-bellied bald man missing two fingers on his left hand who wanted to see ID before he'd say anything. Marquez flashed his badge, pocketed it.

"Sure, I knew Ray Stocker. I didn't know his friend, but Stocker practically lived here. He drank and smoked every dime he made."

"Were you working the night he fought with Mark Davies?"

"I called the police when Davies went nuts." He added, "It's mostly losers that come in here."

"Is Davies a loser?"

"What's he doing with his life?"

What are you doing with yours, Marquez wondered. He looked around the dingy room, a couple of salmon lacquered on planks on the walls.

"There are hundreds of abalone shells up at the Guyanno Creek campsite," Marquez said, watching the bartender's eyes. "We're trying to figure out what boat Stocker was working off of."

"I'd like to get those shells. My girlfriend makes jewelry."

"See what you can do for me and I'll see if I can get her some shells. Call the number on the back of the card."

Marquez hooked up with Petersen again and they checked Noyo Harbor, walked the dock, and met with the harbormaster, who told them the *Coney Island* had pulled out early that morning.

He'd heard that Stocker and Huega had both been staying down at
Albion River Campground.

They dropped down the road to the campground and looked at
the campers of the more permanent residents, an American flag
flying from one, the river bridge holding the highway with its galvanized steel and concrete supports towering overhead. Scanning
the field Marquez saw few temporary campers. He checked
with the office and the young woman told him Danny Huega had
stayed there until yesterday. She didn't know where he'd gone and
didn't know who Ray Stocker was. As Marquez left the office he
saw Ruter's sedan dropping down from the highway.

"Called you twice this morning," Ruter said.

"I haven't had a chance to call you back yet."

"Busy morning checking fishing licenses?"

"Something like that."

Both detectives got out. Streatfield engaged Petersen, saying
"I understand you've got a poaching problem along the coast."
Marquez heard Petersen take him up on it, and Ruter motioned
him to walk over and talk privately.

"I've got that report I was going to fax you."

Marquez took the copy of the police report and leaned back
against the detectives' hood. There were statements from Davies
and Stocker and several from witnesses. He read a statement from
a woman.

*"My husband and I were at the bar seated three stools down
from the man who started the fight. One minute he was sitting
there and then he kind of jumped up and went straight over to a
table where there were I think four men. He flipped the table over
and hit one of them in the throat. I was watching because of the
way he got up from the bar. It was very weird. I thought it was
some kind of martial art or something the way he jabbed at his
throat. Then he hit him in the eye with the leg of a chair. It was*

*very fast and one of the other men tried to stop him and he started
attacking that man. It was so out of control it was scary, but I
couldn't tell what was happening after that because my view got
blocked. We just wanted to get out of there."*

"That's your friend," Ruter said.

Marquez glanced at the detective's eyes, saw his pleasure in
the reaction he'd gotten. Then he read the rest of the report.

"Does that sound like the man you know? Davies was sitting
at the bar talking to someone about the Middle East. There's a
statement from that man, too," Ruter said.

"I just read it."

"He might have killed Stocker that night if he'd been allowed
to." Ruter paused. "This morning, when he came down to meet us
we put him in an interview box and he talked for an hour just as
calm as could be. He didn't have a problem with anything, said he
understood we had to do our jobs and agreed it didn't look good,
and by the way he said he was sorry he involved you. Then he
wanted a bathroom break, but instead of going down to the bathroom he hauled ass out of there. That blue Econoline is parked
down at Noyo. Must have driven there and got on his boat. Not
charged with anything, but he's the hell out of Dodge. What do
you think about that? Where's he headed, Marquez?"

"As far from you as he can get."

"You haven't talked to him?"

"No."

"We need some of your time this morning."

"Let's get a cup of coffee and talk."

"Not here. We'd like you to come in to the sheriff's office. If
you want, your warden can take your truck and you can ride with
us and we'll drop you afterwards."

"We'll follow you."

"Your partner could be sitting around for a while."

"Why are you doing this, Ruter?"

"Because like your friend, you're not telling me everything you know and I'm going to be with you until you do." Ruter smiled. "Does that make it clear enough?"

3

"There was something you wanted to find before we got there," Ruter repeated.

Marquez was past being angry. He was over it. He'd brought most of the problem on himself anyway. He glanced at Ruter scratching his nose, then at the door swinging open, Ruter's partner coming back in carrying three coffees in small Styrofoam cups, dropping one on the floor and swearing as it splattered across the wall. Neither Ruter nor Marquez watched him clean it up.

"Two men had been murdered and you needed to see a shell pile before calling us?"

"Give it a rest, Ruter." Marquez opened his notebook, found the name of a fisherman who'd been attacked by two men in a pool hall bathroom last week in Eureka. They'd blinded him in one eye with a fork because he'd told them he planned to report them to Fish and Game. He flipped the notebook around and slid it at Ruter. "Read that. He was in the hospital when I tried to talk to him and his phone number is there. Maybe you'll have better luck. He's a little sensitive toward Fish and Game, right now. But I think he brushed up against the same people we're looking for and maybe Stocker and Han did, too." He leaned forward, chest touching the table, eyes on Ruter. "Wouldn't it be very hard for Davies to pull that off alone? Or are you going to tell me I helped him?"

Streatfield interrupted, coming in as the middle guy again, the amiable peacemaker, explaining the scenario they must have been kicking around.

"Davies rousts them at gunpoint sometime after they went to sleep, and maybe he's disguised and they don't know who he is, but he reassures them nothing will happen as long as they cooperate. Let's say they think they're going to get robbed and then everything will be okay. Maybe that story is believable, maybe it's not, but he has a flashlight shining in their faces and a gun and he has Han bind Stocker's wrists before he lets him stand up. Neither Han nor Stocker know they're taking a walk yet, but now he starts them up the trail. He keeps the flashlight on their backs and he's got the gun. Han had some serious facial bruising so let's say he's had to be convinced before he'll start walking, but they both go up the trail. Davies walks them out across the field to the tree and they don't have a clue because he's stashed everything up there ahead of time, the chain, the knife, everything he's going to use in addition to the gun in his hand. When they get to the tree he has Stocker sit down with his back against it and Stocker does it because he's scared and Davies keeps telling them everything will work out okay if they cooperate. Okay, so then Han ties Stocker's ankles, but Han is real scared and he knows they've got to do something soon, so he decides he's going to run for it and when he does Davies shoots him twice, once in the lower back and once in the left leg. He drops him about twenty feet from the tree."

"Han was shot?"

"Yeah, he was shot. His left knee was shattered and he bled heavily. He was still alive but didn't have much blood left when he got the final knife wound. We've got bloodstains off the grass being analyzed. We think we know where he was shot. Anyway, he goes down and Davies pounces on him and runs the wire around his ankle, twists it tight, then drags him back over to the tree. You with me?"

Marquez nodded, though he didn't buy it.

"Okay, now Davies retrieves the chain he's hidden nearby and runs it around their necks. Now, it's question-and-answer time, except maybe Han is moaning because he hurts, so Davies starts with him, starts asking where the money is hidden. Maybe he gets an answer or maybe he makes an example out of Han, since Han is fading anyway. He rips up through Han's gut with the knife and Stocker can hear it all, he's just a couple feet away. Probably had to stand over him and use two hands to bring it up through his gut like that." Streatfield raised a hand as though Marquez was going to interrupt him. "Han died as much as four hours ahead of Stocker and Stocker may have died within eight hours of when you got there. Stocker's knife wounds occurred while he was in a sitting position, but you can bet it wasn't until he gave up the location of the money. When Davies came for him it looks like he struggled and tried to twist to one side. The body was probably repositioned afterwards." He paused a beat. "No more lawsuit and he gets some money out of the deal." Streatfield stroked his mustache, adding, "An irony."

"You know anything about rigor mortis or body temp?" Ruter asked Marquez.

"Yes."

"Pretty good chance only his head had locked when you got there. You weren't that far behind the killer, and Davies was either holding the knife or right on their heels. Real close, too close in my book. That put more perspective on it for you?" Ruter pushed his chair back and stood up with Marquez's notebook. "Okay, if I make copies?"

"Go ahead."

Streatfield unfolded a California map, then asked him to identify harbors where he'd met with Davies in the past. Marquez marked Noyo, Crescent City, Half Moon Bay, Pillar Point. They talked about urchin diving, Davies's habits, and Ruter came back in. He'd copied most of the notebook and wanted to go through the pages, reading as he did. Ninety-foot black pickup boat. Anecdotal threats of violence. Possible Hispanic suspect and a description. Possible caucasian suspect and description. Rumors of abalone transfers from one boat to another done out on the open ocean. When he finished he stacked up the papers, handed back Marquez's notebook, and slid his chair back, arms folded over his chest.

"I tried to learn something about you this morning, Lieutenant. I talked to your deputy-chief, Ed Keeler, and he was unwilling to give us any records on you, but he did say you'd been DEA before Fish and Game, so I called a friend at DEA. Did you ever know a Bob Cook at DEA?"

"No."

"Well, he's high up and works out of D.C. He did some research and told me you left the DEA in 1989 after your team went down in Mexico. Everybody except you in one night and then you quit and went looking for the killers. You were obsessed with finding a man named Eugene Kline and at some point he came after you, or maybe he was already looking for you. Is that correct?"

"In a loose way."

"You didn't find him but you had a close call that put you in the hospital. It scared you and you came home."

"Is scared his word or yours?"

"Probably mine, and if it's the wrong word, no offense."

The only reason Marquez could think of for Ruter to have made the call was that they considered him a possible suspect.

"What I'm getting at is you went after this Kline on your own and it cost you your job at DEA. They warned you off him several times. Cook read your file to me. He also said and I quote, 'you had a habitual disregard for procedure.' His words."

"My first thought when I saw those two chained to the tree was Kline."

Ruter smiled at his partner. "So now he's here? From Mexico to Mendocino, huh. Is he following you?"

"We got close to him up in Humboldt once. You could check that with your new friend and he'll probably tell you Kline is more diversified now."

"Oh, I see, you still keep tabs. Do you do that through Fish and Game?"

"I haven't talked to anybody about him in a couple of years."

"Until today."

"Until yesterday, Ruter."

It would have been better to have said nothing about Kline. He waited them out now, regretting having said a word. He pictured Kline's long pale head, the deep-set eyes, and returned Ruter's stare. Abruptly, Ruter pressed his palms onto the table and stood.

"All right, Lieutenant, we're done here today."

Marquez left the detectives sitting there and when he got outside Petersen was arranging stuff in the back of her truck. She'd been in touch with the team, but nothing had changed with Li. He hadn't moved today. They picked up lunch and Marquez told her he'd head south now to hook up with the Li surveillance. Petersen would watch Noyo and check further up the coast for Huega's boat.

After he'd left Petersen and was driving back to the Bay Area, coming through slow traffic in Santa Rosa, Marquez took a call from Italy.

"I tried you earlier," Katherine said, her voice low and husky.

"I was in a meeting."

Separated after seven years of marriage, he didn't go two hours of any day without thinking about her and his stepdaughter, Maria. They'd been apart now long enough to have some distance. Katherine's friend, the marriage counselor who'd suggested it, had insisted that separation helped couples talk things through and break "patterns of conflict." Katherine and Maria had moved back into the house she'd owned since before they'd married. Every other weekend or so, they'd come up to his house and stay the night as though they were guests. Sometimes they'd come for dinner during the week and then leave, and all of it felt completely unnatural and ate at him. It didn't seem to him that the separation had allowed them to get any nearer to sorting their problems out, and if anything, it had created a new distance in him. Hurt pride, perhaps. The counselor's idea that they talk on the phone or meet for coffee seemed more a slow breaking away than anything else.

He knew Katherine was throwing herself at expanding her business. She had a coffee bar on Filbert Street in San Francisco that both the tourist magazines and the locals liked. She was close to opening another one in a little space south of Market on Spear Street. He still hadn't seen the new place. An Italian manufacturer of espresso machines had paid for a hotel stay in Rome and she was over there for five days. He didn't doubt what the manufacturer wanted, all she'd had to come up with was the airline ticket. And he knew Katherine was trying to build a life that was financially secure and gave Maria a fair shot at a good college. Fish and Game paid one of the lowest salaries in law enforcement. You had to do a lot of interviewing and work hard to find a lower salary. You could do it, but only if you found a small enough city or went to work for one of the bankrupt Sierra counties and though Kath might say all day long that money never figured in, it did. It affected quality of life and it affected Maria's chances.

He glanced at the dashboard clock, realized it was after midnight for her. She was in her hotel room with the windows wide open looking out over a piazza on a warm night.

"I've got this big bed, but no you," she said.

He didn't know how to answer, unsure whether she even meant it. They hadn't slept together in three months. He changed lanes without commenting. It looked like a fender-bender slowing traffic, two young guys scuffling on the highway shoulder.

"How's my Maria?" she asked. "Have you seen her?"

"No, we've been talking on the phone. She had a sleepover with Alice last night."

"Is she eating?"

"She says she is." He added, "She's going to a movie tonight with her friends."

"She shouldn't be doing that on a school night."

"One night won't kill her grades."

"Have you been home at all?"

"No."

Call waiting interrupted her response and then she wanted to hang up, telling him first that Maria was losing too much weight, that there was a problem that needed to be dealt with, now. He rolled to the incoming call. The reception was poor, the connection crackling with static, Davies's voice fading in and out.

"That fat fuck of a detective is trying to figure out how to charge me with murder."

"Then come back and defend yourself."

"In the navy they taught us to be ready for anything."

"Did they teach you to run away?"

"You can be pretty cold, Lieutenant."

"You're starting to look like a man hiding something."

"You were in the service, weren't you?"

Marquez stared out through the windshield, still thinking about Katherine. He figured he was about to get Davies's justification for taking off.

"I was in the marines getting ready to ship out of Oakland to Nam when the war ended," Marquez said.

"You stayed in the world?"

"That's right."

"Lucky, man."

But there wasn't much about that year that was lucky. He remembered having a shaved head and getting spit on for wearing the uniform.

"I was a SEAL until I hit a kid on a bike when I was driving home one night," Davies said.

"Where was that?"

"Georgia. Where'd you go when the marines let go of you."

"Africa."

"Africa?"

"You need to come back and keep talking to these detectives."

"I didn't kill Stocker."

"Then what are you afraid of?"

"I'm out here getting answers."

"Yeah, what answers? Where are you?"

"North of Shelter Cove up off the Lost Coast with that diver I told you about, Danny Huega. I'm going to drop him on the beach up here when I'm done with him."

"What's he doing on your boat?"

"He's helping me put it together."

"Put him on the phone."

"He can't talk right now, Lieutenant."

"Don't make another mistake."

"Hey, it's his mistake. He lied to the detectives."

"Why would he lie?"

"Those detectives offered him a deal. See, he's got some old beefs with the county they can help him on, but we're just getting to those details. After I get some answers he'll be humping it down the beach toward Gitchell Creek. I think he can help you out, but I'd get to him before that fat fuck and his sidekick."

"Don't hang up."

Marquez tried to keep him on the line. He was pulling over onto the shoulder when the line went dead.

4

Marquez called Ruter and related the Davies conversation, said it sounded to him like Huega would be dumped somewhere south of Punta Gorda, beyond the abandoned lighthouse, maybe between Sea Lion Gulch and Randall Creek. There were stretches where the cliffs were on top of you and the beach was a white ribbon that sleeper waves could cover completely. You had to keep your eye on the ocean, but there was no fog tonight and Huega would see a big wave well before it happened. He'd see a black hump rise and roll toward him with moonlight glistening off its shoulder.

"You might ask the Coast Guard to take a run up there and see if they spot him on the beach," Marquez told Ruter.

"Is he hurt?"

"He may be."

"Thanks for the call."

"Let me know what happens."

Ruter never answered. Marquez was in Oakland, a block and a

half from Li's house, parked alongside an empty house for sale. A half-eaten burrito, two chicken tacos, and a thermos of coffee were on the passenger seat. The food would carry him until another SOU warden, Cairo, took over after midnight. Lately, he'd been living off Mexican food; fish tacos, burritos, tostaditos, guacamole, and chips. Since Katherine and Maria had moved out he'd barely been to the store, other than for the most basic staples and for dinner on the nights they came over. He had tomatoes growing on the deck, wrapped in chicken wire to keep the deer off. He'd make a dinner out of bread, tomatoes, peanut butter, and rum or beer.

He had all his gear with him tonight, two guns, the takedown vest, all the cameras and night vision equipment, everything he needed if Li rolled, though the team reported that Li hadn't left the house all day. He thought more about Davies as he sat in the darkness. Davies had gone over some edge and the question was whether it was before he'd called from Guyanno or after. He reached over and closed up the bag with the tacos, lowered his window, and leaned back in his seat. Another hour went by and then his phone rang.

Davies's voice was remorseful, slowed, and thick. "He slid against a knife, Lieutenant, but he's fine. He's onshore. I dropped him. He got cut when the boat pitched, but it was no big deal, maybe a couple inches long, a quarter-inch deep. He's walking out to Gitchell Creek. You'll want to pick him up there. That's going to be a good time to lean on him."

"How much farther do you want to cross over the line?"

But Davies didn't seem to hear him.

"I got some information from him and he got on the phone for me. We made some calls to his friends. You sit Danny down, Lieutenant, and he'll talk to you. Put his feet to the fire, though. That's the way to get results."

"Bring your boat in, Mark." He hoped this Huega was okay, figured he probably was, and felt a quiet regret for Davies, who'd be looking at prison time for this. "You're blowing it; they've got an all-points bulletin out on you."

"If I come in I'll be sitting in a cell with some dweeb-ass county defender trying to tell me to plead guilty because he's never won a case in his life. You don't have to tell me I fucked up today, Lieutenant." He hung up.

Marquez stared at Li's house after Davies clicked off. He phoned Ruter, left a message, and was surprised by a call back two hours later.

"We got him," Ruter said, "and we're looking for Huega. You ready to admit you were wrong about Davies? Maybe you ought to check out your informants more carefully."

"Do you have anything tying him to the killings?" Marquez asked.

"No one is going to teach you anything about denial, Marquez. You could write the goddamned book. I'll call you after we sit down with him."

5

Marquez took another call from Ruter while watching a teenage kid with his hands buried in the pockets of his sweatshirt, shoulders rolled forward, hood all but covering his face, walk past with a Doberman on a leash. The dog sensed his presence, but the kid's head bobbed only to the music piped through his earphones and never looked over. Marquez listened to Ruter's certainty as the kid disappeared down the street.

"Davies has taken his last boat ride for a while," Ruter said. "But I need to get with you again and tighten up the time frame. When are you north again?"

"Could be tomorrow."

"Call me, it can't wait."

Marquez slid the phone in his pocket and lights started winking out at Li's. It was either bedtime, or else Li would use the darkness to move. Nothing happened and the street was quiet until after midnight when a tricked-out Honda Prelude with a spoiler drag ran a "sideshow," racing a Subaru Impreza. They blew past Marquez and he guessed they went through the stop sign down the street at close to eighty. He watched their taillights and then sporadic house lights coming on, dogs barking. When it quieted again he replayed the saved voice mail messages from Davies, the calls made before Davies had gotten through to him from Guyanno Creek. There were two of them, the first at 7:55 yesterday morning.

The first went, "I'm up at Guyanno Creek campground, Lieutenant. There's a bad scene up here. There's a ton of abalone shells, but the divers who were doing the poaching are dead. Give me a call, okay? I don't want to do anything until I hear from you, but call me soon, all right? It's a bad situation, I mean, these guys were carved up. I don't know about hanging around here." There was a gap now, a long silence, then, "Okay, Lieutenant, I'm waiting here for your call." He'd left his cell number.

The second call was more controlled, but equally anxious. When he replayed them yet again it was still hard to picture Davies staging it all as Ruter believed. Davies wasn't who Marquez had thought he was. That much was obvious, but still it didn't fall together for him the way Ruter wrote the script.

At around 1:30, Cairo and Alvarez took over the surveillance and Marquez checked into an Oakland motel along the frontage road just off 880. He lay on his back on a squeaking motel bed, smelling the dust in the room, listening to heavy trucks rumbling past on the freeway and to his heartbeat. He thought about Katherine and Maria, the silence on the other end of the phone when he'd tried to talk to Maria tonight. He missed her a lot and he'd have to find a way to spend some time with her tomorrow. That might mean driving down late in the afternoon from Fort Bragg. Couldn't get there before her school let out, but maybe he'd take her to dinner and talk over this food thing.

He didn't remember falling asleep but awoke anxious and momentarily unsure of where he was. The red numbers of the nightstand clock glowed 4:37. He sat up, thinking he'd shower and get breakfast somewhere before hooking up with the team, and was dressing when the phone rang.

"Lights are on, looks like we're a go," Alvarez said. "He's in the garage."

"All right."

"Are we going to do it today, Lieutenant?"

"We are."

He made a quick stop at a convenience store, bought a bagel he could barely bite into and a large black coffee. They gave Li plenty of room, hanging way back, closing some as he came up the east shore of the bay through Richmond and across the Richmond/San Rafael Bridge. He had both sons with him and was loaded with dive gear. He drove a steady seventy-eight miles an hour up Highway 101, then broke for the coast on Highway 128 where he could see any lights well behind him. The road rolled and climbed and then ran past Boonville and through tall stands of redwoods before reaching the coast.

In the predawn Marquez called Ruter's cell, figuring the detective would have been up all night questioning Davies. But it sounded like he woke him up, got a bleary, "Ruter, here."

"It's Marquez. Did they find Huega?"

"Shit." The phone clicked off and Marquez smiled, punched in the numbers again. "No, they didn't." The phone went dead again.

Li was almost to Fort Bragg. The dark shapes of three heads were visible in the truck's front seat, Li's younger son in the middle nearest his dad, the older boy slumped against the passenger window, styled haircut getting crushed flat, shoulders buried in a baggy camouflage jacket. According to Alvarez, the kids had shuffled like zombies to the truck, barely awake when the drive started at 4:45. Marquez was sorry the kids were along. He was okay with charging the older son with poaching, they had enough on videotape to do that, but he regretted that the kids would see their dad get busted, particularly the younger son. He keyed his mike, talking to his surveillance team as Tran Li dropped down to Noyo Harbor. Marquez wondered how he'd take it this time. Last time they'd busted him he'd acted as his own lawyer, arguing his case, his pale gold face animated by determination as the jury leaned forward and tried to connect his broken English.

Li loaded equipment into his black Zodiac and Petersen joined up with the team. She spoke quietly as the kids lugged dive equipment from the back of the pickup.

"He's taking a chance with the weather. We had thunder cells last night."

"He's got a couple of hours," Marquez said. "Water is still calm."

"A couple of hours at the most."

Depending on how Li played it. Marquez checked the horizon again. Close to shore the water was slate smooth in the calm of early morning, but a heavy band of rain clouds lay along the horizon and cirrus had begun to fan overhead. Isolated thunder cells were forecast, unusual for this area, squalls, periods of high wind. Li left the harbor, his wake rocking off the concrete jetty. He cleared the gray rock of the breakwater and turned north, the Zodiac looking small, dark, and vulnerable as it moved out to sea. The boat was well offshore as it passed the town and Marquez's covert team on land drifted with it. They followed Highway 1 and spread out along the cliffs where they could trace the silken line of its wake. Sooner or later, he'd come in because the abalone beds were all in the first sixty feet of water.

Roughly a mile north of Fort Bragg he turned shoreward, and Marquez adjusted the positions of the SOU wardens. He had let everyone know they'd take Li down today and he could feel the excited tension, and yet, he wanted to play it as far as they could. Maybe Li would return to the Sea-Lite Motel after diving, maybe today they'd take down his connection, as well.

Li skirted the coast, moving from cove to cove, several times reversing direction, and Petersen observed, "He knows he's taking too many chances. He may feel us."

Marquez agreed. "I called Hansen from Noyo, didn't get him though."

He was trying to reach the skipper of one of the Fish and Game boats, the *Marlin,* working out of San Francisco Bay. He expected a call back soon enough, though Hansen's crew was doing a lot of homeland security patrols and was less available. He'd also had another call from "Docktalk," the Pillar Point informant, Jimmy Bailey, claiming his lead was worth five thousand dollars.

Fifteen minutes later, Li had on scuba gear and was sliding into the water. The wind was rising and the Zodiac rose and fell on oily rollers. Marquez watched the two black-haired sons riding the swells, the younger boy's fingers tightly gripped around a rope. The sky had been blue overhead after sunrise, but was milk-colored now and Petersen was right; Li should have sat out today. But he'll try to get it over fast, Marquez thought. Li was a capable enough diver and he had his sons with him.

They waited for him, ready to videotape whatever happened next, expecting an urchin bag with a float attached to bob to the surface. They'd confiscate his dive equipment and impound his boat. Last time, he'd been selling to restaurants and out the back door at card games, taking twenty, thirty red abalone a week, netting a grand in cash, putting the money in an education account for his sons. He'd brought bank statements to court.

This time would be different. It would be harder to lean on cultural differences, much harder to argue ignorance. But poaching was low-level crime in California, not exactly a hot-button issue for the public. Counties rarely had the money to prosecute or supply public defenders and judges were reluctant to give poachers prison space that could go to a three-strikes shoplifter.

An orange float surfaced. The boys maneuvered the Zodiac over, and wrestled the bag aboard, then Li hooked an arm over the gunwale and his older son pulled him up. He rested and ate. He unzipped his wetsuit and smiled and joked with his boys while his eyes scoured the cliffs.

When it was time to dive again, the older boy, Joe, suited up with him. Marquez watched them disappear under the surface and then picked up his phone.

Bailey had called again and left a message as though he'd forgotten their prior conversations. Listening to it reinforced that he was on the make. Bailey drifted, repeating himself, droning on as though his stream of consciousness made a message, but finished with "I might have something on the dude you're looking for."

Marquez called Bailey back, left a quick "Got your message, let's meet tomorrow."

Li and son surfaced with another urchin bag and climbed on board. A puff of blue smoke rose from the engine and the Zodiac moved out and then circled, as if he was trying to decide whether to continue north and dive another bed. With the wind rising he was probably gauging the weather. Petersen sung a corny, "Should I stay or should I go?" as the Zodiac did another loop, a big donut on the water.

He went farther up the coast and dove again, Joe going in with him. Then it began to look like rain. Wind gusted along the cliffs and the light flattened as the seas rose. The young boy alone in the boat looked frightened and Li must have felt the change, because he surfaced with only a partial bag. After they were on board and Li had shed his tanks, he reassured his younger son, tousling his hair, and it occurred to Marquez that the boy might not be a swimmer.

The Zodiac turned south and the team started back toward Noyo Harbor. Not much doubt that he'd run straight there, though it would be a slow ride in these swells. Two wardens, Cairo and Melinda Roberts, were already waiting at Noyo. Marquez drove through Fort Bragg, bringing up the rear, a nervous anticipation vibrating in him as he waited at the stoplights. He played back Bailey's message again and took a call from Nick Hansen on the *Marlin,* who deadpanned their old, running joke.

"Sorry, guy, I'm going to spend the day with my girlfriend. You'll have to take him down without me holding your hand," Hansen said. Marquez smiled, some edge taken off the morning. Hansen went on, "I got your message and we're already on our way to you. We'll be another thirty minutes. You're going to want us to stay clear, right?"

"Yeah, we'll call you if we need you to close, but it should go down in the harbor."

"Check with you in half an hour."

Hansen clicked off and Marquez took the little jeep out onto the flats above Noyo. He watched the Zodiac slow and hold up before entering the harbor, a small black boat rolling on the swells. Li was on his cell phone now, but didn't seem to be talking to his wife. She was in the passenger seat of an old maroon Nova parked in the lot beyond the businesses and the bridge reconstruction, right out along the harbor mouth where Roberts and Cairo had a good view of her. She was staring out at the harbor. She wasn't holding a phone.

"He's not talking to her," Cairo said.

"Who's on the dock?" Marquez asked.

"A couple of locals."

"Anyone else on a phone?"

"No."

"He's holding up and he's on his phone. Someone is tipping him off. Are you sure it's not his wife?"

"Roger that, we're positive, and we're scanning the cliff, but we don't see anybody from down here. Unless they're in a motel room."

They knew the watcher could be in one of the rooms on the bluffs above the harbor. They'd look for light, a reflection off binoculars, but a watcher could sit ten feet back in a room with the window open and Marquez's gut told him it was someone in the motel, in the Sea-Lite. It had to be and he tried to work his way along its windows as the Zodiac rolled off a swell and faced the open sea. Lightning flashed at the horizon as Li took control of the Zodiac from his older son, backed away from the harbor and started down the coast. Marquez was unable to hold the disappointment from his voice because he knew Li had been warned off and would likely dump the catch at sea.

Melinda Roberts repeated again that it didn't look like the woman in the car was talking, but she was definitely Li's wife. They'd just run her plates and gotten back an Oakland registration address, a different name, not Li, not Li's address, but maybe a car borrowed from a friend or relative, and Marquez returned his focus to the Zodiac. Li had kicked his speed up and bumped south through rain showers and heavier swells. Marquez checked in with the *Marlin,* talking to Hansen.

"What's your position?"

"Two miles south of you."

"He spooked and is headed south not far offshore, moving slow, and could be looking for a place to beach. We've got one of these rain cells moving through."

"Do you want me to close?"

The *Marlin* was a relatively new department boat, a stainless, high-speed catamaran built by Kvichak out of Seattle. Would Li recognize it? Hard to say, but with the heavy seas and curtains of rain he had his hands full and probably wasn't as watchful.

"Yeah, to within a quarter mile, and I'll keep talking to you."

Marquez hopscotched along the road shoulder as rain hammered the windshield. Petersen was furthest down and had the best view. Gusts shook the jeep and he knew Li didn't belong out there anymore. It looked like he was running scared and without a plan.

"Definitely looking for a spot," Petersen said. "He may be suiting up again. It looks like he's putting on his mask and fins."

"What about the older son?"

"He's steering or trying to, but they're bouncing around out there. The younger one is using an air tank to reinflate the floats on the urchin baskets."

"Then Li is going to try to float the abalone in," Marquez said.

"Yeah, he just got in the water. Can you see him yet?"

Marquez had cut over to the shoulder and parked. He saw Li in the water, the younger kid struggling to get the urchin bags overboard and the older son leaving his position steering the boat and going to help. When he did, the Zodiac drifted closer to the rocks and Marquez read it the same way Petersen did, heard her calm but worried voice saying, "This is no good, John. No good."

He got out of the jeep and the wind stripped her words as he left the shoulder and started picking his way down, keeping his eyes on the boat, wary still, not wanting Li to spot him, then realizing it didn't matter anymore. He told Petersen he was going to get down there as fast as he could and to call the *Marlin;* tell them to close and not worry about whether Li saw them or not. Just get here.

He scrambled onto the black shore rock, all of it slick with rain and he slid down, fell, got up again as the Zodiac stalled and one side rose against the rocks. He saw the younger boy catapulted face forward out of the boat and tried to keep his focus on where the boy went. His head showed briefly, a blue parka rose on a wave, then Marquez was sliding again, tearing his palms open on the drop down the last steep face to the sand. He couldn't lose sight of the boy's parka. Had to spot his head again. He kicked his shoes off and the Zodiac rose against the rocks and flipped as Marquez ran and dove through a breaking wave, swimming hard underwater as the cold hammered his chest. When he surfaced he swam toward where the parka had been, eyes blearing with salt water and rain as he scanned the sea. But the parka was gone and the boy nowhere on the surface. He looked toward the Zodiac trying to see if a kid was hanging from a gunwale rope, couldn't tell and swam toward it, circling wide of the rocks, fighting the swells and aware the current would take him, but seeing Petersen on the beach, trusting she had an eye on him. He spotted Li now, close to the rocks.

The Zodiac slid along the surface as though greased, Hansen finally bringing the *Marlin* in close, nosing into the debris that floated away from the Zodiac. A cooler top and plastic bottles went past as Marquez swam out. The cold reached deeper into him, he felt time going and kept hoping that somehow the kids were hanging onto the boat, off the rope ringing the gunwale, that the older boy had gotten a hold of his brother and that somehow they'd stayed with the Zodiac. He swam for the Zodiac, was close enough now to see two then three sides, and as it spun, the fourth empty as the rest, and then Hansen's voice came over the bullhorn as the *Marlin*'s lights washed over him.

"John, grab hold."

They pulled him on board and continued searching, Hansen running as close as he dared to the rocks and beach. They could see Tran Li onshore with Petersen and then the lights picked up a swimmer and Marquez saw it was the older son, fifty yards offshore and struggling to get in.

"I need a wetsuit and flippers," Marquez said. "I'll go get him."

Hansen pointed at an approaching Coast Guard boat. "They're closer," Hansen said.

"Keep the light on him, let him know we're coming for him," Marquez said, and he took the bullhorn. "Joe Li, hang on, we're coming for you." He had no idea whether his words carried, but kept at it, and then they saw the kid stop fighting the current and let the tide carry him as they kept the light on him.

"He heard you," Hansen said.

Marquez scanned the water again for the other boy as the Coast Guard reached Joe Li. Petersen reported Tran Li was with her, but injured, had a possible broken collarbone and she was having trouble controlling him. He wanted to go back in the water and look for his younger son, and had told her that the boy couldn't swim. She needed assistance holding him and Hansen confirmed that help was on the way. Marquez put on a weatherproof coat. His pants stuck tight to his skin and he'd started shaking so hard it was difficult to talk. He heard a helicopter, saw it coming at them with a spotlight on the water. It was too late but they kept searching with the *Marlin,* as well, Marquez working the light.

A half hour later, Hansen turned the wheel over and crossed the deck to Marquez. They were too close to shore and the *Marlin* was his responsibility. He had to make the call, but that was hard with Marquez on board, something about the presence of the guy, Marquez still acting like they'd find him alive. He put a hand on Marquez's shoulder.

"John, we've got to back away," and Marquez nodded, but didn't take his eyes from the ocean. "We're going to run you back. You did all you could."

"The boy is dead."

"You did what you could to save him."

But Marquez didn't see it that way, at all.

6

Li's wife was in her car, sitting at the end lot out near the mouth of the harbor when Marquez and Roberts drove past the construction equipment assembled under the bridge. Two Fort Bragg police cruisers followed and parked nearby, but it was Marquez who walked across the wet asphalt to her car. His body trembled with cold though the wind felt strangely warm. As her pale face turned toward him he read her apprehension and fear through the rain-streaked windshield. His heart hurt for her, but he didn't show it now, raised his badge instead as she opened the door. He couldn't find it in himself to tell her so bluntly.

"Mrs. Li, your husband is down the coast on the beach. There's been an accident and we'll take you down to him."

She pointed past the rock jetty out into the opening of the harbor. "He come soon."

"He's already onshore."

"No, no, he come now."

The Fort Bragg officers walked up to help and Roberts stayed in the van, scanning the cliffs, trying to find who else might be watching this. They escorted Mrs. Li to a patrol car, helped her into the backseat as her limbs went weak, and Marquez and Roberts waited until the police units crossed under the highway bridge, then followed, climbing back up to Highway 1.

The memory of another woman came at him, the wife of a federal prosecutor, her expression freezing in horror and disbelief as Marquez told her that her husband had been murdered. He remembered a beautiful woman on the cusp of middle age, the lines beginning to deepen around her mouth and eyes, a word forming and reforming on her lips but no sound.

"They've found the boy," Petersen said, sighing. "I'm rolling with them. He's on a beach about half a mile south of where they flipped."

When Marquez and Roberts got there firemen and Coast Guard personnel were grouped together on the rough-pebbled beach. Li and his wife arrived a few minutes later in the back of a CHP cruiser. Marquez watched Mrs. Li run down across the rocks to the beach, to her son. She dropped to her knees, pressed her face to the boy's, cradled his head, wiped sand from his face, ignored the hands reaching to restrain her, the voices trying to be firm with her as tears streamed down her cheeks at what had been taken so unfairly. She straightened her son's clothes and scolded him, admonishing him to get up off the sand, and Marquez had to turn away.

When he looked back, a fire captain had squatted near her and put an arm around her shoulder. A white coroner's van was just arriving and turning off the highway onto the tiny parking lot. Li was still up in the CHP car, had never gotten out. His head was bowed, unmoving. Marquez looked back at Mrs. Li, saw her rise to her feet and two firemen grab her arms as she crumpled to the sand. He felt Petersen touch his arm.

"This is terrible," she said.

"I want to get everybody to the house and meet," he said.

"Now?"

"We're not needed here anymore."

"Okay, but I heard something we're going to want to find out about." She pointed at one of the Search and Rescue people. "They're talking about a body a camper found this morning up near Gitchell Creek."

"You just heard that?"

"Just before I walked over to you, the guy in the blue cap over there."

He walked over to Search and Rescue to find out, asked if they wouldn't mind getting on their radios and trying to get more information since their people were with the body. A call was made and he listened to the back and forth. It was an adult male, north of Abalone Point and Black Sands Beach, close to Horse Mountain Creek.

"You know where that is?" the Search and Rescue leader asked. Marquez said he knew the area and thanked the man. He drove back to Fort Bragg following Petersen, trying to call Ruter from the road and getting dumped into voice mail. But he'd gathered from the radio chatter that some cooperation between Humboldt and Mendocino counties was underway in identifying the body. He tried Ruter again as he got to the cold house, and someone answered the phone, then clicked off after Marquez identified himself.

Five or six cans of Campbell's chicken soup bubbled slowly in a pot and the humid smell filled the living room. They pushed the couch back, brought a couple of chairs over from the dining table, and opened the slider to let in some air. Everyone was shaken by what had happened and they talked out the sequence of events first, and then about Li's wife, what her role was today, whether it could have been her that Li was on the phone to when he made the decision to back away from the harbor entrance. Marquez was determined that they focus on what they'd missed.

He looked at Cairo's lean, dark face. Cairo and Roberts had been in Noyo Harbor. They'd been positioned to watch.

"Can you account for every boat in the harbor?" Marquez asked.

"We tried to."

"Tried to?"

Melinda Roberts cut in and he felt the same tension he got off her earlier in the van. "We know, Lieutenant, and we're sorry we missed whoever was there. We picked up his wife as soon as she got there and we had every vehicle run."

There was silence in the room, no sound but the soup bubbling, a chair scraping as Carol Shauf slid hers back. They were shell-shocked and Cairo and Roberts felt like he was laying it on them, because they'd been at the harbor in position watching everything. But one way or the other the team was getting burned and Marquez figured he had to push to find out how and why.

"Li was at the mouth of the harbor when he took the call," Marquez said. "It may have come from the motel. It may have come from a car parked on the road or someone standing on the bluff." He looked at Alvarez. "Brad, why don't you and Carol see if you can find any witnesses, anyone working in one of these places that might have been looking down on the harbor?"

"He may have gotten scared on his own," Roberts said.

He stared back at her, irritation starting in him though she was free to throw out any idea. He felt frustration at his own failure, anger at the pattern of the past two weeks. She was new to the team, relatively inexperienced, and he listened now without concentrating on her words as she defended Cairo and herself, exploring the idea that Li had turned away from the harbor on his own. Marquez knew he'd kept everybody too often in similar positions during the days Li had been out, and given the repetitive nature of Li's diving he should have adjusted more. That was apparent now and should have been this morning. What he wanted from this meeting was the clue they'd seen but missed. He wanted someone to remember something they'd seen and dismissed. Most likely, that was Cairo and Roberts.

"We accounted for every boat and we've got a list of all vehicles," Roberts said. "There were a couple of fishermen shooting the shit, that's about all, and they weren't watching us. There was one old boy scraping his boat." She turned toward Cairo, broke eye contact with him. "We had a good view of Li's wife and we had the harbor covered. She wasn't on the phone."

Marquez leaned forward. He sketched out the dock, the ocean where there'd only been one fishing trawler well offshore, and the slope across the harbor. He glanced back at Roberts, trying to take a different view of her input. She was heavily into tech and maybe that was the answer here. She was tuned into ideas he wasn't, such as using sensor nets with cameras that could be strung along the abalone beds and would broadcast on the Internet, computer programs that let Net surfers become guardians. He wanted her to turn that part of her mind to considering how someone found them and how the other side might be tracking the SOU and possess better tech than they did.

Brad Alvarez, who'd said little so far, spoke now. "There was a black BMW pulled over on the shoulder about the time the *Marlin* picked you up. It might have been a seven series model, I couldn't tell, I wasn't close enough. They were gone when I got there."

Petersen nodded. She'd seen them, too, and figured they'd pulled over out of curiosity. She said the occupants were two middle-aged men and a young woman in the back seat. Marquez looked at Alvarez, his goatee, the wiry frame. Alvarez shrugged. There was nowhere to go with the BMW and none of them really believed they'd be followed in something as conspicuous.

They talked about Li now, Marquez saying they'd have to sit down with him sooner than later and it was likely to be rough. Roberts opened her notebook and ticked off a list of vehicles that had been in the harbor in the early morning. She wanted to make the point again that she and Cairo had accounted for every vehicle.

"You had it covered," Marquez said, "but as a team we got beaten. Our problem going forward is to figure out who made us and where they were. Whoever they are, someone else saw them. Someone else must have seen them. Maybe they were in the motel, or parked on the road, whatever, but we need to get out and ask questions." He paused a beat. "We're up against an organization, a network. The murders of those divers could easily connect to whoever made us. Don't forget that when you're out there."

He ended the meeting by throwing out an initial list of places to check and those quickly got divided up, and then he looked at the faces around him. He knew they were stunned by the death of the boy and not much would get accomplished today.

Petersen rode with him to Gitchell Creek after they'd confirmed that police were still up there. They went north from Fort Bragg out to Highway 101 at Leggett and he drove hard to Garberville. Not far from there they turned back toward the coast and Shelter Cove. The little jeep didn't handle well once they were on the beach, but Marquez stayed on the hard-packed sand, dodging the waves. He knew it was less than four miles to Gitchell, though the soft sand further up the beach could make it tough with the tires on the jeep. They weren't near as wide as they wanted to be.

"You all right?" he asked Petersen. Her face was green.

They'd talked very little on the way up, both trying to figure out what had gone wrong and Marquez trying to come to terms with the drowning, at least temporarily. He couldn't escape a feeling of responsibility, though rationally it had been Li's decisions that led to the accident.

"I need to stop here," she said. She opened the door, took a step out and vomited. He scrutinized what might be vehicles up ahead while he waited for her and as she got back in he handed her a water bottle and then started forward slowly. "Going to need to stop again now," she said, and after he'd slowed to a stop he pushed his door open so the full breeze came in off the ocean. She had her eyes closed and tiny beads of sweat had formed on her forehead. For ten minutes they sat and then she opened her eyes again, smiled, and he started the engine. "Sorry, John."

"Don't be," he said, pointing ahead. "There they are."

Marquez saw Ruter standing with an older Humboldt County detective, a white-haired man that Marquez thought he recognized as a Shelter Cove resident. He knew he'd seen him a few times before. Ruter pointed their direction and shook his head, but Ruter was out of his jurisdiction up here, he wasn't making the calls. The Humboldt detective walked over, offered his hand and Marquez introduced himself and Petersen. The detective's name was Al Fields and the name clicked. Fields was older with sun-leathered skin, a slow confidence about him, none of Ruter's bluster.

The body lay on its right side near a low hump of sand, its face lying in shore weeds. A white male with black sideburns, a pug nose, overweight, wearing a frayed wetsuit that was too long for him, one that would fit Davies's six-foot-plus frame. He looked more closely and recognized Huega, saw the birthmark. There was a long knife wound similar to Guyanno Creek and he was able to look at it more dispassionately, able to turn ideas with more clarity. Humboldt crime techs had made a plaster cast of vehicle tracks and he overheard Ruter saying Davies had docked his boat, driven up here with Huega and killed him.

"Walk me through the phone call you had with Davies," Fields said, moving off to the side with Marquez, treating him warily but with curiosity in his eyes, wanting whatever Fish and Game had. "Why do you think he called you after dropping Huega on the beach, if he did drop him?"

"He knew he'd made a bad mistake and needed to talk about it."

"Murdered him?"

"I wouldn't go there yet."

"Detective Ruter tells me that when you were undercover in the DEA you saw something like the Guyanno killings."

"That's right."

"Willing to talk about it?"

Marquez realized that Fields and Ruter had worked out this routine before he'd arrived. He saw Ruter frown at being excluded, but it was an act, and Fields motioned him toward the body, for another look at it together.

Now, Marquez leaned over Danny Huega. The wetsuit had been unzipped before he was killed. His shorts had been lowered and the blade had touched only skin. He saw where the cut started on the lower abdomen and smelled blood and the stink of Huega's organs, felt sweat start under his arms, and when he straightened he gave the Humboldt detective a shorthand version of his knowledge of Kline.

"Too much is familiar," Marquez said. "This one less so, but definitely the killings at Guyanno." He ticked off parallels on his hand now, giving Fields a verbal list.

"Did you ever talk with Mark Davies about these Kline killings, ever exchange war stories?" Fields asked. "I understand that once or twice you've had a beer on his boat with him. Maybe you talked about your DEA days."

"I put my Kline file away. I don't talk with anyone about Kline other than the FBI, and I don't call them more than twice a year and they don't call me back."

"Kline's not new to California," Fields said, catching Marquez by surprise. "I was a lead investigator in San Diego for twenty-two years. He touched us there, too. But this Davies was around both circumstances up here. In my experience that usually means one thing and the simple answer is usually the right one."

Fields stared as if he had another thought, but didn't say anything. If Davies was telling the truth, Huega swam in and walked down the beach roughly ten miles. His body might show higher lactic acid levels and other indicators. Marquez asked Fields about that, then thanked him for letting them see the body and offered to help in any way he could. He'd seen what he'd come to see and had wanted Petersen to know what they might be up against. He made a point of shaking Ruter's hand. He turned the jeep around and Petersen glanced in her side mirror as they drove away.

"He's watching us."

"Who is?"

"Ruter."

"He's thinking it over. He doesn't know what to make of this anymore. No one does."

She was quiet for the rest of the ride back down the beach and it was nearly dusk when they got close to Shelter Cove. Large cumulus clouds sat out over the ocean and the air was cooler, but his skin burned as though he had a fever. It felt like something was crawling on him. At sea the light seemed to reflect with a peculiar intensity.

As they hit the paved road, Petersen said, "It seems as if you've been expecting Kline. I don't mean that exactly like it sounds, not that he was coming here specifically for you, but like you've been waiting all these years for him to come into your life again. Maybe that's because it was left unanswered for you, John. You had to give up without finding him and you feel guilty about being the only survivor."

"I agree everything points to Davies," Marquez said.

"But you believe it could be Kline."

"Like I was saying when we went up to Guyanno." He realized she must not have taken him seriously at Guyanno. "About six months after I married Katherine she said that either the file left the house or she would. I put the Kline file in the crawl space under my house and stopped making calls. I thought I'd buried it." With grim humor he thought about Katherine leaving anyway, and when he turned to look at Petersen the skin of his face felt tight as a mask. He went on. "The scale of this operation we're up against fits with Kline. He was doing contract work for the cartels, mostly hits, when I was DEA, but he already had a criminal network by then. He was associated with kidnappings and drug running outside of the cartel sphere. That's what brought him up here in the first place. He didn't want to cross paths with any of his cartel clients so he moved dope out of Humboldt. I know he did some trade in animal parts in the late '80s. It wouldn't surprise me if he kept at it."

"He's a businessman."

"Yeah." Marquez remembered a roundtable discussion where they had psychologists sit in and offer their opinions. "We thought the stylized killings were to make his name and instill fear and then later some of the experts began to think there was a sexual element, as well."

"I believe that."

He gestured at the ocean. "This is not a small deal we're up against. It's not a handful of former commercial divers disgruntled with DFG regulations, scheming to get rich. Divers are just the pawns in this. This is someone with a network and the experience, people, connections, equipment, the will to pull it off."

"You talk like they're going to."

"Maybe we've got a situation similar to South Africa."

Operation Neptune, a combination of South Africa's Department of Environmental Affairs, the national defense force, and local police, fought Chinese triads and gangs, but was still losing. After South Africa the next best abalone was in California.

"Translate that from Marquezese for me."

"It's someone with a network who's comfortable with violence and not intimidated by law enforcement, the type of organizations cleaning the abalone out of South Africa. If it's Kline he'll do everything he can to find out who he's up against. He'll try to buy his way into SOU computer files and once he finds any one of us he'll try to find out where we live, about our families, everything he may need later. That might sound exaggerated, but I've seen it happen. That's what happened to my DEA team."

"You really believe he's here? You're looking at these murders and drawing that conclusion?"

"Something is too familiar."

"Well, if he's here we'll handle him."

The simple certainty in her voice reached him and he looked over. "That's right."

"Whoever he is, John, we'll take him down."

Marquez looked out at the ocean. He thought of a Mexican Federale captain who'd told him about rumors in the mountain pueblos that Kline wasn't really a human being, that he was the devil himself. "Diablo," the officer had said, and then smirked.

7

When they got back to the safehouse in Fort Bragg, Marquez sat down with Melinda Roberts. She'd work with him tomorrow as he met with Jimmy Bailey, the Pillar Point informant. It would be a chance to work one-on-one with her, something he hadn't done enough of, a casualty of budget cuts. But with Petersen leaving in a month there was more urgency. Integrating a new warden into the team was easier when the SOU was a ten-person unit, but he didn't know when those days would come back, if ever. Roberts was a natural for covert work, very observant, very aware, and blended easily—very quick to assimilate, but she was also willful and there was a perspective issue that showed itself again now.

"Bailey is a flake," she said.

"He is, but we're not going after his parents."

She frowned at the obscure humor, not finding anything funny in it. A lot of their informants were flaky and had no more ambition than to leach CalTip dollars for beer money, get even with an ex friend, or take out a competitor. Tomorrow he'd meet Bailey, alone, but figured Roberts would drive down to Pillar as well and they could evaluate together what to do with the information Bailey delivered, if he delivered anything. From the numerous messages he'd begun to believe Bailey might have something, but he didn't say that now, and didn't really want to allow himself that hope yet. They left it that Roberts would meet him in San Francisco and they'd drive tandem down the coast.

Marquez left Fort Bragg, cut through the coastal mountains on Highway 20 and followed 101 back to the Bay Area. He was tired and the ride felt longer than usual, the glare of headlights hard on his eyes. When he got close to home he called Bailey. A young woman answered.

"Jimmy is here, but he's partying," she said.

"Any chance he could take a break? I really need to talk to him."

There was a long delay and he heard her ask somebody nearby if they knew where Jimmy was. Then she came back on.

"He's in the hot tub."

"Tell him it's Banner. He's been trying to get me all day." The name was an alias he used with Bailey, but it sounded odd tonight, like the name of somebody's dog. The phone dropped on the counter and he didn't really know whether she'd gone for Bailey or not, but he stayed on the line, listened to Santana playing in the background. Five minutes later, as he was coming across southern Marin and close to hanging up, Bailey coughed into the phone, said he was getting water everywhere and couldn't talk right now anyway. Marquez confirmed 8:00 tomorrow morning. He'd found that you had to make these final phone calls with Bailey or you got a shit-eating grin and an excuse about forgetting the next time you saw him.

Now he exited into Mill Valley and climbed the steep road up Mt. Tamalpais. His house was two bedrooms and a study and looked like a cedar-sided cabin from the outside. It had a stone chimney and a deck on the backside and the gravel driveway was narrow and dipped and then rose to the knoll where the house sat. A wooded shoulder of Mt. Tam fell away to the right of the house and below there were stands of trees, open flanks of dry grass and folded ravines with oak and brush, then the ocean. In winter he watched the leading edge of storms approach and in the clearest months, April and November, there were mornings when the ocean was the blue of a sapphire. He had a partial view of the top of the towers of the Golden Gate Bridge and the pinnacle of the Trans-America building and the taller buildings of the city, and still, it was dark enough at night up here to where you could see the stars.

His grandfather had deeded ten acres of the land below to the county in exchange for permanent release from property taxes and on the agreement that it would never be built on. Marquez had inherited the house but there was a funny disconnect to that because it wasn't property that anyone with his job could afford. The joke within Fish and Game was they always backed the wrong candidate for governor, so their budget increase requests typically got blue-lined and their pay now was well below what a highway patrol officer made. He never forgot the luckiness of having this house or the perseverance and hard work of his grandparents. It was his thought that he'd leave the house to Maria one day, and had made a will to that effect and had resolved that if the separation from Katherine turned into divorce he'd still leave the will alone.

He parked and reached for the light switch as he got inside the door. Six months ago Katherine and Maria would have been home, the lights would have been on, and maybe he would have heard them talking or Maria's laughter as he walked up. He felt the emptiness and wished he could have the moment back and could talk it out with Kath. He wished he'd been more open-minded and less stubborn and hadn't withdrawn hurt and angry so fast.

He walked into Maria's room. She lived or had lived in the study, the room that had been his office before he married

Katherine. A lot of her stuff was still there and they had an awkward thing going where she was still spending a certain number of nights here as he and Katherine tried to get things worked out. On the nights they'd been able to pull it off they'd have dinner together, and then the next morning he'd drive her to school. They'd gone along okay that way in the spring, but since school let out in the summer she'd been here less and not at all, lately.

He poured rum in a tumbler, dropped in a couple of ice cubes, then wrote his report to Chief Keeler on his laptop and e-mailed it. When the rum was finished he searched around for something to make a sandwich, settled for peanut butter, poured another drink and sat out on the deck and thought about tomorrow. He felt tired, tense, too wound up from lack of sleep and hoped the rum would loosen him, free him for a couple of hours, maybe even help him see things differently. His team thought he should have taken Li down sooner and that unspoken judgment weighed on him tonight. They'd had Li on commercial trafficking, which in addition to impounding his boat, dive equipment, and car, allowed a judge to fine up to $40,000. They should be able to get him to talk.

Now he turned on the TV, looking for late-night local news, and found a report on the drowning and then a longer piece on the Huega murder, including a headshot of Huega, whom they described as having a minor criminal history and known drug ties. They all but called it a drug killing, didn't name Davies, but said police had a man in custody they were questioning. The report ended and he flicked through other stations. His nerves hummed and yet he knew he should get some sleep. He thought of the younger Li boy's face pale in death, his blue parka rising on a swell before the ocean took it. The TV reporter had cited the unusual weather, the thunder cells on the north coast, an area that didn't usually see that. He clicked the TV off and went out the front door with a flashlight.

Low on the western side of the house was the crawl space

door. He unlatched it and stepped over the foundation grade beam. There was maybe five feet of clearance underneath and he had to stoop below the floor joists. Cobwebs brushed his face as he made his way over to the base of the stone fireplace his grandfather had built out of rocks gathered from the property. He'd mixed aggregate, cement, and sand in the old iron-handled wheelbarrow that Marquez still stored under here. He'd hated banks and had embedded an iron box in the base of the fireplace. A stone concealed the face and for years this was where his grandfather had kept his money and the land deed and the things he'd treasured, the vault of the Bank of Marquez, not a very big bank, but an honest one run by the truest man Marquez had ever known, a Spanish immigrant who'd married a native San Franciscan with English roots. He moved the rock, opened the box, and took out the Kline file.

Back inside he laid the file on the dining room table and opened a beer. If Katherine had been home she would have tried to stop him and maybe it was the rum and tiredness, the thrumming of his nerves, but the file and the grainy face looking up from a poor photo seemed to have a presence that he could feel. It disturbed the space in the house, but, of course, that was all in his head. It was the emotion of the day and accepting that Kline could be in California. He turned the pages and didn't need to reread words he remembered. A few witness statements. Photos of torture executions. He looked at the wavery ink lines of his own handwriting in the year after he'd left the DEA—or more accurately, been offered the chance to extend his leave of absence into resignation. A polite way of saying something else, and yet, he hadn't challenged them. He'd taken it because he'd bent their rules enough to where they could have done more.

He remembered the urgency with which he'd interviewed people, chasing leads, coaxing the frightened to talk, the long drives, always armed, gun lying under a newspaper on the passenger seat, watching the headlights behind him, the cars that passed on the other side of the road. A particularly hot night in Texas came at him now, boiled up through the rum and he remembered the feeling of paranoia. Was he inviting it back now? He turned another page. He should show Ruter this photo, he thought, a concrete telephone pole with two men chained to it, one Federale, one DEA agent, a very good friend he'd talked to that same night. A chain was around their necks, ratcheted the same way, hands bound, feet bound, gut slit. The knife had been wired to the concrete pole by its hilt. It hung above the head of the DEA agent, Ramon Green. He touched Green's image, whispered, "He's here, Ramon. I can feel him."

His voice echoed off the oak flooring in the small living room. They die but you take them with you and you keep them alive by remembering. No alcohol-fueled melodrama, he thought, but touched the page near Ramon's head again. What a terrible thing that had been. Could he explain someone capable of this to his team? He turned another page now and read through his attempt at a chronological bio on Kline. He'd made a trip to Thailand and wasted his money. At the time he'd had an FBI friend who'd kept him informed. He didn't know what they believed now. His last attempt had been rebuffed.

The Feds had learned that Kline was the son of Christian missionaries, Elizabeth and Henry Kline from Dayton, Ohio, who were kidnapped and killed in the late sixties by communist rebels in Indonesia. He stared at a photo of the parents. You're lucky you didn't see how the boy turned out, Henry. You wouldn't have liked it much. He'd even gone to Dayton, gone a couple of weeks believing he could find clues to Kline's hiding places in the family history.

The FBI believed that Kline had been sold or traded for weapons as an infant. Then until he was a teenager there was nothing. The year he turned sixteen a lurid story circulated in Indonesia of a young man with white blond hair who'd cut the throats of eight men in a jungle village. Villagers believed he could see at night. Allegedly, that young man had been allied with a communist guerrilla group and the FBI had spun it into a story, a bio that had gaps they couldn't fill. Somewhere around his twentieth birthday he disappeared. He turned up in Africa with a new name and was out of politics and working for drug traffickers. His move to Mexico had coincided with the years when cocaine was the drug of choice in America. Was he still operating from there?

He read on and then flipped the file shut. It had articles, it held analysis, some from classified government papers, the kind of thing they'd arrest you for in today's climate. He'd leaned on people to help him, he'd called in favors. Everything in the file he'd pored over god knows how many times. He finished the drink and it was nearly 1:00. He'd communicate with the Humboldt detective tomorrow, swallow his pride and call Ruter, set up to meet him.

He left the file on the table, then lying on the bed, the top blanket wrapped around him, eyes closed and the roar of the ocean in his ears again, felt a presence near him, pushed that aside, and thought about his last conversation with Katherine. The distance, the lack of spark. He heard the floor creak out near the kitchen and lay quiet, opened his eyes again. The sound had been distinct, not the house creaking as the night cooled, but someone inside, weight on the floor. He reached for his holster on the nightstand, lifted the gun slowly out, rested it on his chest over his heart. Then a scuffling, something moved on a counter, and he slid the blanket off, very quietly opened the nightstand drawer and removed the tiny flashlight Katherine kept there. He rose and heard the hinges of the old casement window in the kitchen squeak as he stood up.

He'd had poachers follow him home before and the house had been burgled. You could come unseen at night up through the brush and trees on the downslope. The last burglar had jimmied the deck door slider—it was old and you could lift it right out of the track. Marquez had cut a broomstick to block the slider, but only used it when he was going to be away.

He moved to the bedroom doorframe with the gun and flashlight. It got quiet out there and he had the feeling that whoever was there had just heard the floorboards squeak. A minute passed without any sound except an owl outside and he eased forward two steps, touched his heel down, rolled his weight forward very slowly, eyes adjusting to gray-black, looking for any movement at the end of the hallway. The faintest sound from the kitchen and he took another step and remembered that as he'd read the Kline file he'd opened the kitchen window for air. Another three steps, each one very slow, and now he was close and ready to come around the corner.

He knew a weapon might be aimed where he'd appear and got ready, visualizing the kitchen layout. It was small, Mexican pavers on the floor, a little rectangle and then the counter looking into the dining room. His guess was that anyone in there would press up against the refrigerator. Whatever was there was waiting, staying very quiet. He hesitated a moment, listening, holding his breath, then quickly crossed the opening to the kitchen with the flashlight held out but not on yet, his gun up, tracking. He clicked the light on movement on the counter and lowered the gun as a big raccoon went out the kitchen window and dropped down, no longer hurrying as it crossed the moonlit deck. A torn box of Triscuits lay on the counter.

He turned on the ceiling light, cleaned up the counter, and locked the window, feeling relieved and coming down off the adrenaline spike. It made him smile; it changed the night a little. He looked at the file on the dining table, walked around and opened it again after turning out the kitchen light. Moonlight reflected off the photos and he stared at the faces.

Marquez closed the file again, then took it off the table and slid it onto a chair so it wasn't prominently in view. He didn't want it in the moonlight anymore, wanted its presence diminished, wanted it where it was less important. He looked out on the deck again for the raccoon, then walked back down the hallway and lay down again. The file was a ghost net for him, the information and memories of Kline floating like the pieces of net that broke loose from fishing trawlers and rode undersea currents for years continuing to trap fish. You wanted to think it was over. You wanted to think he was gone, dead, or in prison somewhere. But it's not over. He's here.

8

Forty minutes south of San Francisco Marquez left Highway 1 and drove through fields of pumpkins out to a broad stand of eucalyptus trees along the bluffs. Fog shrouded the high branches of the trees and under the canopy the road was wet and dark. Droplets ticked onto the hood as he parked. Bailey's black Suburban wasn't there yet, but Marquez walked out anyway along the abandoned road to a concrete bunker built during WWII and waited, leaning against the yellowed concrete. Ten minutes later, Bailey waded through the ferns wearing cutoffs, sandals, and a gray sweatshirt. His ponytail was tied with colored rubber bands, the loose hairs at his forehead carried beads of water from fog.

"Starter motor went out. I had to hitchhike up and walk out through the fucking fields. I saw you go by, but it was like you had wheel lock, dude." Bailey held his hands up as though he had a steering wheel tightly gripped. His neck was rigid, his eyes staring straight ahead, smirking.

"I guess I was thinking so hard about what you've got for us."

The team had written Bailey off as a panhandler trading poaching tips, a virus in the system after he'd burned them once. But he'd also given them a couple of good leads. Marquez watched him open a pack of Camels, taking his time, milking the moment.

"You're going to like this," Bailey said. He pointed at the ocean with his cigarette. "A dude I know wants me to run him up to Point Reyes in my boat to pick up abalone he's got stashed in a cove up there. He's got something like five hundred ab in urchin bags sitting on the bottom of a cove near Elephant Rock." Bailey gave Marquez a serious stare. "This one is going to cost more."

"What's it worth, Jimmy?"

"Five grand. You give me the word and I'll tell him it's a go, this morning. Otherwise, he's asking someone else."

"When does this run happen?"

"Day after tomorrow."

"We're a go, but I can't go five grand. The state is a tightass, Jimmy."

"Hey, man, the state wastes money for a fucking living."

"That's its day job and this poaching fund is more like fun money. We can go two grand."

"Not happening."

"I can try my chief again. If you want I'll call from here and you can listen."

"Whatever, but I'm not doing it for nothing."

Marquez rang through to Chief Keeler's voice mail. He had to leave a message, that was no surprise—Chief Keeler never got to the department before nine. He watched Bailey draw hard on the cigarette, staring at him, something close to hate in the back of his

eyes. He exhaled, blowing a stream of smoke, then flicked the cigarette past Marquez, bouncing it off the crumbling bunker.

"There's no respect, man," Bailey said. "I'm just a tool to you
people."

"I'm not trying to rip you off," Marquez said.

"And I need some operating cash."

"I'll get you fuel money."

"I mean, like right now. Two hundred bucks."

Marquez got his wallet out. Bailey was agreeing to the two
thousand without saying it and needed to save a little face by
demanding fuel money immediately. He had two hundred in twenties that was meant to go a long way, but he folded it, extended his
hand, but didn't let it go.

"Who's the diver?"

"A dude named Mark Heinemann."

"He berths at Pillar Point?"

"Yeah, his boat's the *Open Sea.*"

"Is he a friend of yours? Do you hang with him?"

"Sometimes. He thinks you people are already watching him,
because I made up some shit about seeing people I thought were
wardens. He listens to me, man."

"Who's he selling to?"

"That's another trip. A dude comes around and talks to you if
you're interested, but then you have to call a pager number."

Marquez placed Heinemann now, a stocky, bowlegged, dark-
haired man in his early twenties with an older boat. They'd wondered
about Heinemann before.

"We were chilling on my boat and this freak was on the dock
looking for him and then took him up to a car near the sportfishing
shop," Bailey said.

"What type of car?"

"Some kind of four-door."

"What kind?"

Bailey shrugged, didn't know the make. "The main man told him they'd waste him if he didn't keep it cool with them, but that they'd treat him real fair if he did. I would have shined it on, right there."

"What did the man look like?"

"Don't know."

"Ask him, okay?"

"Is that like part of my two grand? If I don't come up with a description of these freaks you aren't going to pay me when this is over?"

"You're going to get a thousand upfront and you're going to give it back if there's no abalone at Elephant Rock. If there is, you get the second thousand the next day. But we need the buyer."

"The problem is I can't fucking ask a bunch of cop questions so Heinemann starts wondering about me." He smiled. "I can't stick out like you guys do."

Bailey's face looked pinched, the gray skin prematurely aged by sun and wind. Marquez looked down at him, remembering all the things he didn't like about him. He looked hungover and wasted, but his eyes glittered, so maybe he'd popped something to get going and maybe that's what made him talk a little loose this morning.

"What else did he say?"

"I don't know."

"Try to remember."

"Sorry." Bailey gave a tight smile, eyes distant, something different about him today. "We'd done a bong and some beers."

"You were toasted?"

"Yeah."

"What about the guy that came down the dock?"

"Definitely an ex-prison man, kind of a mix of Mexican and I don't know what else. Asian from his eyes, a stir-fried dude. Black hair, black eyes, stare right at you type of number, the way they

get fucked up inside and want to mess with people all the time."
Bailey lifted his ponytail off the back of his shirt. "Got a tail a little
shorter than this," making scissors out of his fingers to show. "Guy
was maybe five eleven and pretty buffed."

"Get something we can turn into a drawing and it's worth
money." Marquez paused to make certain Bailey registered that.
"We'll pay for it separate from the Elephant Rock ride. Get me
something I can work with, Jimmy, and I'll make it worth your
while. Could be worth a grand if we can get a clean description.
But if you make something up, you could be looking at charges."

"Fuck, man, you don't change. You're never going to lay down
any trust."

"That's right, the deal is I don't want to have to trust."

"I don't get that, man." Bailey shook his head and played it
out until Marquez looked bored.

"Talk to him and get a better description," Marquez said. "Get
something I can work with."

"Think I'll pass, dude."

"If it's good enough, we'll come up with a bonus."

Bailey shook his head. "You bust Heinemann, you can ask him."

He knew if he pushed Bailey now he'd get a promise of a
description, but his gut told him that Bailey would just make
something up if he heard any more money talk. It would be better
to wait a day and keep working him.

"Walk me through the order of things," Marquez said, after
giving it a rest, switching back to the abalone now, and Bailey
went with the change.

"We pick it up at Elephant Rock and take it to Sausalito. So
we'll leave here like midday or so, go to Elephant and I'm not sure
what time yet, but like real early the next morning we pass it off
onto another boat in Sausalito and Heinemann gets paid. He's
going to split from there and I come back to Pillar alone."

"What dock in Sausalito?"

"Down near the engineers' dock. Like right in there."

"Okay, we'll be there."

Marquez waited the usual fifteen minutes after Bailey walked away, then started back toward the truck. Halfway back he heard a car alarm and started running. He knew from the pulsing sound that it was his rig. He punched in Roberts's number on his cell phone as he reached the asphalt and saw one of the windows in the king cab had been popped out and lay broken on the ground. He killed the alarm as she answered. Both storage bins had been jerked out from behind the seats.

"Bailey shows up late to the meet, doesn't have a car, and this happens. Throw cuffs on him," Roberts said.

"Try to find him and run the plates on any vehicle that comes off this road. You should see him cutting across the fields. He was on foot unless he had a ride waiting or he's with whoever broke in."

"I'm on it; I don't see him yet. I'll call you back."

The glove compartment door hung by one hinge. He cleaned the glass off the seat and backed out, smelling urine as he drove away. He realized someone had pissed on the carpet behind the passenger seat through the opening left where the window had been. His laptop, binoculars, night vision gear, tactical vest, and files were gone, including the criminal history package on James Allen Bailey, the drug peddling charges. Marquez reached under the passenger seat and felt the laptop components and the relief that came with finding them. All they'd gotten was the IBM shell. The memory and hard drive were under the seat. The CD with everything relevant was still there.

Roberts phoned back as she got on the access road. "I see him cutting through, going toward the highway," she said. "And there are papers all over the side of the road. I see your plastic bins. I'll go get him."

"Let Bailey go."

"You're kidding."

"No, someone may be watching him. I'll see you in a few minutes."

When he drove up she was out in a pumpkin field gathering papers. Some of his clothes were in the shoulder ditch. She'd found two pairs of pants, socks, his tactical vest, camping gear, Bailey's criminal history file, and a fair amount of loose papers Marquez would have to sort later.

"We ought to go pick him up," she said. "I really don't get letting him walk away."

"We know where he lives and we know where he berths. There's nothing we can do right now but question him, and he'll deny any involvement and then blow off making this boat ride with Heinemann."

"Don't you think that was all bullshit so he could get his friends into your truck?"

"We're going to play out the hand."

"I don't understand, Lieutenant. He just ripped us off for several thousand dollars and he's walking across a field. What are we doing?"

The SOU had thirteen vehicles it rotated through. Most had steel toolboxes with hidden locks, bolted down to prevent theft because the team was often parked in remote areas. But in the past month he'd switched vehicles several times, and again last night, switching the jeep for the black Nissan pickup, and as a consequence he was using plastic bins. It had just caught up to him.

They searched the fields, shoulder, and ditch, but didn't find anything more. When they quit searching he assessed what was missing, hoping it was a run-of-the-mill theft. What they'd kept were things they could sell and they'd dumped everything that was obviously law enforcement, including his tactical vest. He called Chief Keeler and told him what had happened as he drove south to Pillar Point with Roberts following. Air rushed in the broken window and the truck stunk of piss. He drove into Half Moon

Bay to buy something to clean it and kept talking with Roberts.

"I don't like it any more than you do, and I don't like Bailey, but bracing him isn't going to help us. If we'd seen a vehicle pulling away, then we could have done something. But we didn't and we've got to know about Bailey's lead."

"His lead is bullshit. He's playing us for saps."

"Let's get a cup of coffee and take a look at Heinemann's boat."

They parked well away from Pillar Point Harbor, then eased up in Roberts's van, walked the last quarter mile, quietly angling for the shops. He pointed out Bailey's boat, the *Pacific Condor,* and Heinemann's *Open Sea,* three berths down.

"Bailey told me Heinemann thinks we're already watching him."

"Another lie. His little criminal mind has been trying to think of ways to get more money out of us and he hit on the fact that you always park there to meet him. Then he got some other part of Team Bong to help him."

Marquez pointed out the apartment they'd used to watch Pillar Point in the past. They could still borrow it and would have an SOU warden here when Bailey pulled out with Heinemann the day after tomorrow. If an excuse came from Bailey before that, then Roberts was almost certainly right. He could see Bailey now; he'd made it back to his boat and was working shirtless in the morning sun.

"What's going on now," Roberts went on, "is his friends are headed up to San Jose to sell the equipment and then they'll bring his share back to him. Meanwhile, he's setting up to scam us out of more money. It blows me away. I'll bet you dinner he burns us and there aren't any abalone hidden at Elephant Rock."

"Make it a lunch and I'll take the bet."

He'd felt a difference in Bailey last night on the phone and then again this morning. Bailey had something that made him bolder. He was down there working on his boat because he thought he was going to Elephant Rock, otherwise he'd be sleeping off last night. He believed in what he was selling, maybe not all of it, but enough.

Marquez looked at the *Open Sea,* checking for Heinemann, thinking over what Bailey had told him about the meeting Heinemann
had with the buyer.

"You're going to lose, Lieutenant. No way is a guy like Bailey
going to help us out," Roberts said.

"I'm making a different bet, Melinda. I'm betting he's going to
sell out a friend and you're betting he won't."

9

"We've got a couple of guys down the street," Alvarez said, from where he was parked watching Li's house.

"How long has the family been home?"

"About an hour and until a few minutes ago all the people stopping by have looked like relatives and friends. Now, we've got this pair, both male, one white, one Hispanic, sitting in a car down the street. How long until you get here, Lieutenant?"

"I'm coming up from Pillar Point with Roberts. We're just south of San Francisco but there's some traffic."

"These two circled the house once and parked a couple blocks away."

Marquez had made the decision to leave two wardens, Alvarez and Shauf, in position to watch Li's house. He'd gotten a search warrant, and yet had hoped they'd be able to let the family mourn, hadn't wanted to invade their privacy today. But neither was he going to let Li move abalone out of the garage.

"You're sure they're watching the house?"

"Ninety percent sure. Do you want me to go ahead and give the Oakland police a heads up?"

"Not yet."

"Good enough, we've got it under control anyway. Hey, what happened with Bailey? We heard you got broken into."

"Yeah, while I was meeting with him. They got everything fenceable, laptop, camcorder, all the night vision equipment, binos."

"Bailey?"

"Probably."

"What are we going to do about it?"

"I don't know yet. We'll see what happens the day after tomorrow."

"That's when he runs up to Elephant?"

"That's what he says."

He told Alvarez about Bailey's tip, the abalone supposedly stashed at the bottom of the cove at Elephant Rock, and they talked fifteen minutes on their phones about Bailey while Marquez thought about Li. Marquez didn't have any illusions about Bailey and felt embarrassed about the break-in, that he didn't have the equipment secured.

It took another half hour to get to Oakland. When Marquez exited the freeway Roberts was less than ten cars behind him. She followed him to a small park not far from Li's, where Alvarez was already waiting for them. Shauf was watching Li's house. They walked out across the sunburned grass and put some distance between them and the gangbangers hanging around the fringes of the park.

"They've gone inside," Alvarez said of the two men. "They walked up the sidewalk and we taped them. They aren't family."

Without waiting to be asked, Alvarez handed Marquez the camcorder and Marquez turned his back on the street and played the video. It had been shot at the outer range of resolution, but he could still make out facial features. One man looked something like Bailey's description of the man who'd been down on the dock at Pillar Point. Black-haired, a face made of hard-angled planes as though constructed from flat pieces of sheet metal.

"What about the car?"

"Rental and we're getting a name, right now."

"How long have they been inside?"

"Ten minutes."

Marquez was aware that they were making a series of assumptions here. They had nothing on the men other than they were visiting the Li family. But they might also be doing an ab count at the garage freezer or threatening Li.

"We've got the warrant," Alvarez said. "If he let these two in the door he might be happy to see us afterwards. Maybe today is the day to talk to him after all."

Marquez took in Alvarez for a moment. Brad wore ragged jeans, sandals, a loose faded Hawaiian shirt with a surf shop logo and was growing a small goatee again. It occurred to him that Brad was dressed a little like Bailey.

"We want Li to talk to us," Marquez said, "but nothing we're going to say will make him believe we can protect him. We can't watch his back and we can't convince him that we *can* watch his back—I know him well enough to say that."

Alvarez's phone rang. He answered and motioned that they needed to go. As he hung up, he said, "They're out."

Marquez was on the phone to Shauf as the men drove away. He picked up the gray car as it turned a corner three blocks ahead of him. Alvarez trailed and Shauf and Roberts stayed with the house. The car drifted through downtown Oakland, not pushing it, not in a particular hurry. They drove down Broadway, moving slowly in the right lane, the only car to brake and stop as a light turned yellow. At Jack London Square the men parked in an under-

ground garage and walked across the plaza to one of the bars along
the water. When Marquez entered the bar he saw a third man talking
to them before moving toward the door alone. Marquez phoned
Alvarez from the rest room, describing the third man.

Marquez took a table in a corner of the room. He ordered a beer
and a fish sandwich and could only see the back of their heads, but
found something familiar in the Hispanic. He couldn't put his finger
on it, though, and he asked the waiter for a newspaper, anything
he could read, and the waiter came back with the *San Francisco
Chronicle* sports section. The A's had lost again, Giants had won
10–3, and the men at the bar ordered another round. He heard one
order vodka and lime and read how the Giants got their runs as he
watched. He was certain they were eyeing the estuary, watching the
boats through the big windows, while keeping an eye on him, and
on everyone else in the room. His phone vibrated and Marquez
spoke quietly, leaning over, back turned.

"Number three is in the Barnes and Noble browsing books.
Are you sure he connects?" Alvarez asked.

"No, he may have just been talking. It may have been a
chance encounter."

"Do I stick with him?"

"At least until these two move."

The men downed their drinks, put money on the bar and
stood, giving Marquez a clean look at their profiles. They went out
the door, and when he was outside, Marquez hit speed dial for the
Marlin, got Hansen, and laid out what he thought would happen
next. The pair moved toward a boat that was slowing to dock. He
read the CF numbers off to Hansen and heard him call them to one
of the *Marlin* crew. A few minutes later the men boarded the boat
and Marquez watched it pull away, while Alvarez crossed back to
the bookstore to check on the browser.

"It's going to depend which way they turn," Hansen said, "but
if it's a fast boat we might have a problem, if they kick it up when

they clear the estuary. Who are they?"

"We think they link to the buyer we're looking for."

The next call was Alvarez saying the browser had left the bookstore and he didn't know which direction he'd gone. Marquez scanned the crowd up toward the Boatel and out on the plaza.

"Check the garage," he said.

"Already on my way there, Lieutenant."

Marquez took a call from dispatch. They'd run the numbers on the boat and it had come back as a rental from a marina up in Stockton, which made sense. It had an offshore design, yet looked decked out as a river boat. He relayed the information to Hansen.

"Bad news," Hansen said. "He must have hit the bay and got around the islands before we came up from the south and that means he's clicking along. I can run the docks and sweep toward Richmond but he's not in sight on the bay. We're scheduled to check the San Rafael Bridge anyway, so it's no problem. But if I were you I'd beat him back to the marina in Stockton, or get a uniform over there."

Marquez hung up with Hansen. Alvarez reported that he'd located their browser again, but that the car was gone from the garage. Someone had picked it up and they'd missed it. The browser had bought himself an ice cream cone and Marquez knew they'd been burned. Good chance the browser was a decoy and they missed the whole dance step. He made a decision now and gave Alvarez the address of the Stockton marina.

"Call you when I get there," Alvarez said. "What are you going to do?"

"Talk to Li."

"You're going to knock on the door?"

"I think we have to."

Half an hour later he was asking for Tran Li and showing his badge at the front door to an older woman. Li turned the corner of the hallway and came into view and Marquez had the feeling he'd anticipated the visit. He wore slippers and shuffled on the old oak floor. His left arm was in a sling and he looked as though he'd aged years in the night. His eyes looked through Marquez, then showed recognition and he said something to the woman in Vietnamese. As she moved away from the door Li motioned him in. He led Marquez to the door off his kitchen that led to the garage and his hand scraped over a light switch. He opened the old freezer and gestured at the abalone, but still hadn't said anything.

"I'm very sorry," Marquez said. "I can't think of anything harder."

"This is what I take." He slowly pointed at the contents.

"You had two visitors earlier who weren't part of your family and I need to ask you about them."

"This abalone for a friend's wedding."

After Li had lost the abalone case three years ago Marquez had made the point of calling him up and going to lunch with him. He'd wanted to try to cut through the cultural gap and communicate what the state was trying to do, because he'd seen the shame on Li's face as the judge had told him he was guilty of robbing the people of California. He'd realized that Li hadn't really understood what the judge meant. He knew also with the boy's death they weren't going to push the charges against him, but neither would they let him go. He was their link. Marquez had been on the phone to both Keeler and the Mendocino DA's office this morning, trying to get permission to negotiate with Li. He'd work hard on Li to get him to reveal his buyer. Li had to come across.

Marquez reached into the freezer, moved abalone around and did a rough count. He cut a finger on a shell and pressed the cut against ice, watched the blood dilute in water and felt uncomfortable. The timing was wrong, the moment wrong, though fifteen years ago he knew he would have barged in here, badged and busted him. His perspective had changed, although the urgency had only increased. A faction of the public had grown weary of trying to save species, of competing with animals for space and the right to make a living. Fishermen were baffled by overlapping regulations and laws that inadequately struggled to juggle competing interests. He thought of the divers they'd busted whose tag line was the same; leaving the courthouse steps they'd toss a last jibe, make the comment there was more than enough abalone and the Gamers drove trucks, didn't dive, didn't know. Even beyond the mask of grief it was in Li's eyes that he still didn't see a crime in taking the abalone.

"When is the wedding?"

"Now only two weeks. Everything I take is here. You take it now."

Marquez had done the rough count. Maybe a tenth of what Li had taken was here and he didn't think he needed to argue this for long with Li. He thought he could explain fairly fast.

"We've followed you for over a week, Tran. We have videotape and a strong case." He let a beat pass. "You have a prior conviction within a three-year time frame, which is bad in California." Li stared past him and Marquez heard someone in the hall, then the older son looked in. He moved into the garage as though he needed to protect his father and the suffering in the older boy's eyes was unmistakable. Marquez turned toward him. "I need to talk with your father alone, and it's all right, we're just talking. Nothing is going to happen today." He studied him, gauging how much was boy, how much was man, whether he ought to sit in on the conversation because there was a real possibility he knew what Li knew. "Unless you can tell me something about the two men who were here earlier."

Joe Li looked at his father, then back at Marquez. He spoke in rapid Vietnamese and his father answered quickly. Marquez had the feeling the boy was arguing they should talk with him.

"We want to work with you," Marquez said while looking at Joe Li. "But you're going to have to help us." Tran shook his head, said something in Vietnamese and as his son left the garage Li murmured in barely audible Vietnamese, speaking to himself, as though responding to voices only he could hear. Marquez waited and then spoke softly, explaining where they stood in very frank tones. He made no threats but repeated that he had to know today who the men were.

"Did these men threaten you?" He waited. He could smell the abalone in the garage. "Did they tell you they'd hurt you and your family if you didn't cooperate? You want to talk to me, Tran, because I'm going to try to get the DA to work with you." It was the third time he'd said it but still wasn't getting any acknowledgment. "Did they come here to warn you?" Li shook his head. "Have you dealt with those two men before?"

Li's fingers worked on the cuff of his shirt. "We're going to arrest them and they'll go to prison. You want to be on our side when it goes down." The statement sounded like hollow cop talk and he knew as he said it, he wouldn't get through to Li today.

"I go to prison and my wife and son move to Colorado. After prison I go there."

"You don't have to go to prison." Li shook his head in disagreement and Marquez couldn't remember a suspect arguing his way into prison. "You can work with us to take them down."

"You arrest me and take everything."

"I'm not going to arrest you, today."

"Yes."

Marquez didn't know whether he meant yes he should arrest him, or yes, he was acknowledging he wouldn't be arrested. There was a vacant emptiness to his eyes that made it pointless to try to reach him today and he regretted knocking on the door. They'd lost whatever shock value they'd have and had gotten nothing in return and Li's resignation would only deepen.

He moved out in the hallway and toward the front door and gave Li a card with phone numbers for Sacramento headquarters and Chief Keeler. He'd give Keeler a heads-up call now and looked at Li standing like a ghost at the end of the hall, then softly shut the door. When he started down the steps he heard a voice call, "Officer," and stopped, recognizing the son, Joe, who was standing behind a fence screening the backyard.

"I'm here," Marquez said.

"I heard them tell dad they'd kill me next. That's why he won't say anything. They said there was nothing any police could do to stop them. They aren't afraid of you."

"No one is going to kill you, Joe."

"My dad says they would." A door opened in the backyard and Marquez heard a woman call for Joe. "I have to go."

"Don't be afraid, we'll take them down. But I need your help."

There was no answer. He'd already gone.

10

Toward dusk Marquez returned a call from Ruter. It sounded like the detective was having trouble breathing. "Give me a second," Ruter said, and Marquez heard him coughing, heard something knocked over and Ruter swearing before coming back on the line. "Sheriff's orders are to lose weight, so I've got a treadmill in my garage and I'm out here with my cat. My wife is in there watching TV with a bag of cookies, but I'm not supposed to eat anything except carrots. But that's not your problem. I've got a tape of an interview with Davies we made this afternoon that I want you to hear parts of. I can play it for you over the phone, right now, if you're okay with that. I want to know if this is the guy you thought you were dealing with."

"Okay, go ahead."

"Hang on a minute." Marquez held the phone wondering what had happened that made Ruter willing to pick a phone up and call him. "Okay, here we go." He heard the whine of the tape and then

Ruter's voice, its pitch made higher and tone more mechanical by the recording equipment, asking, "Did you force Danny Huega onto your boat?"

"No, he took a ride with me because he wanted to talk."

"What about?"

"His friends."

"He got on your boat because he wanted to talk about what friends? Mutual friends?"

"I told him Stocker talked before he died and he'd better come see me."

"You were playing him?"

"Same as you goofballs are playing me right now."

"Did you tell Danny Huega that you killed Stocker and Han?"

"Sure, and I told him the same thing would happen to him, that you and your partner weren't smart enough to take me down. I told him he'd better get his ass down to my boat and talk to me."

Ruter clicked the recorder off. "Marquez, when he called Huega, Huega called me right after and said Davies had just told him he'd murdered Stocker and Han. We wired Huega and told him not to get on the boat under any conditions, but he did anyway. We were ready to arrest Davies right there, but Davies must have guessed what we'd do and got him on the boat, ran him out of range, then stripped the fuckin' wire off him."

"That's how you got the jump on finding Davies that night."

"That's right, as soon as the boat started out of Shelter Cove I was on the phone. Okay, here we go again. It'll be me talking first." Marquez heard the tape recorder whine as it started up.

"Are you saying you killed them?"

"No, I didn't kill them, but I was there when they died. There were three men, but only one did the real cutting, a tall man. When the knife work started, Stocker kept saying Huega's name over and over. He was trying hard to give the right answer, but there weren't any right answers that night."

"The killer was a tall man?"

"Yeah, about six foot three. You could see Stocker's eyes bulge and the tall man, he made it go slow."

"You watched this?"

"Yes, sir."

"From where?"

"From the brush off to the right. I'll take you up there, Ruter, if you can handle the distance. It's about half a mile, but we can rest along the way."

"Cut the shit."

"I followed when they led the prisoners out across the grass, then maintained a forward position near the edge of the clearing."

"You watched two men chained to a tree get murdered?" Davies didn't answer. "Without trying to stop it?"

"I was outmanned and unarmed."

"Did you think of making noise or throwing something?"

"Sure, I thought of a lot of stuff."

A long silence followed and someone cleared their throat, then Ruter asked Davies to describe everything he'd seen from the point he'd heard yelling, a man calling for help up the creek canyon. Davies thought that had been Peter Han.

Marquez tried to reconcile the story Davies had told him with what he was hearing now, Davies telling about hiking up the creek at midnight and arriving at 3:00 A.M., following the voices up the canyon and seeing them marched across the clearing, chained to the tree, and questioned by the tall man who'd knelt near them and asked his questions in a voice too low to hear. Ruter clicked the recorder off again.

"You hear what's missing," Ruter said.

"No gunshots."

"He wasn't there."

"He's doing a pretty good job of winging it," Marquez said.

"I know. Think about it. Here goes again."

"We saw you force Huega onto your boat," Ruter said on the tape. "Did you pull a gun on him?"

"He got on willingly. What happened was I told Danny I had photos to show him, pictures I took myself up at Guyanno before the lieutenant got there."

"Is that Lieutenant Marquez you're referring to?"

"Yes, sir, the lieutenant is the only pure play here."

"We looked at your camera and didn't see any pictures of Ray Stocker. Where are these photos you showed Huega?"

"They're gone, but here's the deal. I switched memory cards before you got there and taped the other one to my leg. I didn't want to take a chance on you and your partner's honesty and I already knew I'd have to talk to Danny Huega because I knew you two would come after me."

Ruter cut to Marquez. "He had night vision equipment stored in a day pack. There was a Canon digital camera in there and when we looked at what he had stored there were photos of the abalone table and the campsite. He may have switched the memory card just like he said." He paused a beat. "Is this the guy you thought you knew?"

"He's much more aggressive than I've heard him." Marquez thought about the description of the killer Davies had given. It wasn't much. A tall man, on the thin side, long head, hair that reflected the moonlight. "Maybe he's feeling the heat."

"He's going to feel it like a Tomahawk missile up his ass. Okay, here we go again."

The tape made a high-pitched whine and as it started again Marquez tried to put himself in the interview box, tried to picture Davies as he was pulled off his boat under the glare of the Coast Guard searchlight, being brought in and interviewed after pulling a wire off Huega and torturing information out of him.

"What were the photos of?" Ruter asked.

"Close-ups of Stocker's wounds."

"Why did you want to show him those?"

Now Davies hesitated for the first time. You could hear a chair scrape.

"I figured they'd come for him, too."

"Did you figure that or did you know Huega was afraid you'd kill him, too?"

"I haven't killed anybody."

"Why did he need to see the photos?"

"I wanted him to see what they'd done."

"Why?"

"I told you already. I knew they'd come for him. All three of those guys were working together and I wanted to get the truth out of Huega before he got wasted."

"What truth?"

"Information for the lieutenant."

"Lieutenant Marquez?"

"Yes."

"Did you get it?" Davies didn't answer and Ruter repeated the question and waited. "I asked if you got the information."

Ruter stopped the tape again. "He never answered that and there's no record of any call made from either Davies's cell phone or from Huega's, so we don't think he alerted anybody. But he may have used another phone to call whoever they were selling this abalone to. I think it's a good bet he got phone numbers out of Huega. But we didn't get any further with him on this line of questioning, so I'm going to skip ahead to where I'm asking him about injuries to Huega. He had a crushed left cheekbone and a skull fracture most likely the result of blows from a blunt instrument. Here goes."

"Did you hit him in the face?" Ruter asked Davies.

"No, sir."

"Where did you hit him?"

"Around the ribs because I was off balance. He dropped the gun and slipped down on the deck."

"Is that when you decided you had no choice but to kill him?"

"I was done with killing a while ago."

"When did you last kill anyone?"

"In the navy."

"When you were a SEAL."

"Yes, sir, but not in the line of duty."

There was a long pause and Marquez knew Ruter and his partner must have been debating whether to pursue that statement. But they did the right thing, he thought, continuing on.

"Tell us what happened after you disarmed Danny Huega."

"I hogtied him with a chain, then asked him questions."

"And did he answer them?"

"He was scared by then."

"He had a crushed cheekbone and a fractured skull. Do you want to tell us he swam in and then hiked ten miles?"

"He made it to Gitchell Creek is what I heard."

"You hit him with the iron bar. You stood over him on the deck and beat him and then floated him in and carried him up the beach, right? You relied on your SEAL training to move him without drowning him. In effect, you delivered him. You did what they couldn't do. It took your skills to pull it off."

"He swam in."

"You're fighting a war to save this abalone, but things went too fast with Huega. It got out of hand and you knew you'd hit him too many times, so you decided you had to get him on the beach whether or not these other people ever came for him. You anchored as close as you could, put dive gear on, used floats to keep his head up, and then dragged him across the beach and up to that four-wheel drive track at Gitchell Creek. When you got back to the boat you called the number he'd given you, told the voice on the other end exactly where he was."

"You ought to be a uniform deputy or mowing someone's lawn, sir. You're not cut out for this work. I'll talk to the lieutenant, but not you two."

Ruter broke in again. "We'd appreciate it if you'd sit down with him, Marquez."

"I'll give it a go."

"You hear how he goes in and out, that yes, sir, no, sir, shit."

"Maybe, a little."

"Something there, I think." Ruter was quiet, thinking about whatever that something was. "Listen to a little more tape and then I'll tell you our problem. I'm skipping ahead one more time. Here goes." Marquez listened to the electronic noise as Ruter fast-forwarded, had the wrong spot, backed the tape, apologizing, finally finding what he wanted.

"There's a moral abyss that if we cross we never return from," Davies said.

"Did you cross that abyss with Huega?"

"I won't answer any more questions without the lieutenant present."

The tape clicked off and Ruter cleared his throat. "He's right, he didn't kill Danny Huega. They're putting the time of death ten to twelve hours after we picked up Davies. We'll have to kick him loose in the next couple of days. I can drag it out for three days max, but he's got a story of Huega attacking him on the boat and having to defend himself, you know, blah, blah, blah. And he's right, Huega got on board voluntarily. Bottom line is Davies didn't kill him alone."

"Huega had a fractured skull and broken cheekbone?"

"Pulverized. Multiple blows. Injuries that preceded death by approximately six hours."

"I can come up tonight."

"I don't think I can set it up for tonight. How about tomorrow?"

"We've got a surveillance that could eat up the day."

"When will you know?"

"I'll call you in the morning."

"You hear how off he is, don't you?"

"I hear something I haven't heard before."

"I hear two voices. There's a hardwire problem," Ruter said.

Marquez didn't hear two voices and didn't say anything in response.

Ruter asked, "What about this description he gave. It rang bells for you, didn't it?"

"Yeah, it did."

"All right, Marquez, we're taking this Kline idea more seriously. Are there photos of him?"

"I've never seen a good one, but the FBI may have them now."

"I'll call them. How about if we talk in the morning?"

After he'd thought over the conversation with Ruter and the recording, he called Maria. Katherine's sister had picked her up from school, she'd stay with her cousin tonight and her aunt would drive her to school tomorrow.

"How's it going, Maria? How was school?"

"I'm fine."

She didn't really sound fine. If anything, she sounded sad.

"What'd you have for dinner?"

"I wish you and mom would stop bugging me about what I eat. Do I bug mom because she's fat?"

"She's not fat."

"She's got that little pooch belly. I'm never going to look like that."

"That's nothing."

"Whatever. I don't want to look like that."

"Your mom looks great."

"Only to you."

"We're talking about you, right?"

"I don't want to talk about me and I can take care of myself. Besides, I have to get off the phone now. Lisa wants to use it."

"Ask Lisa if she can wait a minute."

There was a long pause. "I'm totally sick of everyone talking to me about food. I have to go now, I really do."

He let her get off the phone, yet wished he was sitting next to her talking to her right now. He had an uneasy feeling that he hadn't had before about the eating issue and sat in the darkness thinking about it and began to worry for her, and for the distance forming between them. He thought about the gaps in the conversations with Katherine and the way they didn't seem to mesh anymore. Thought of five years ago when Maria was a giggly ten-year-old and how easy and uncomplicated life had seemed then. Everything had changed and moved; it was hard to accept the difference.

11

The ocean darkened and the horizon fog went from purple to black as night fell. Marquez stopped in Half Moon Bay and picked up three chicken tacos and a large coffee to go, then drove to the condo they'd borrowed to watch Pillar Point Harbor. Shauf and Alvarez were waiting there. After he'd pulled into the lot and gotten out, he took another call from Ruter. He put the tacos and coffee on the roof of the Explorer and leaned back in to get the phone.

"We can do it tonight, after all," Ruter said, and Marquez hesitated, thinking about it before answering.

"See you in four hours," he said.

Marquez called Shauf and Alvarez rather than walk up the two flights, told them the situation and was backing out of the parking space before remembering the tacos and coffee were on the roof. The coffee bumped off a side window and splashed onto the street, but the tacos hadn't slid off yet and he dropped them on the passenger seat, thinking he'd stop for coffee again somewhere up the road.

But he never did. He called Ruter when he was a half hour out and checked in with the team again. They'd placed a GPS transponder on Bailey's boat after he'd gone to a bar in Half Moon Bay. Tracking the boat with the GPS unit should be easy, but Marquez wanted visual surveillance and had called the Coast Guard about a helicopter flight. It was a funny thing; they'd found that poachers were used to the orange and white copters and didn't associate them with game wardens. He bit into one of the cold tacos as he listened to Ruter go on about Davies and it occurred to him he'd have to give Petersen a heads-up that he'd be getting into Bragg later tonight.

Davies was in the interview box alone, his eyes tracing the walls, when Marquez arrived. He held out his arms to show Marquez the cuffs.

"They're trying to charge me for Huega's murder, Lieutenant."

"Were you at Guyanno when Stocker and Han were killed?"

"No." Davies stared back at him. "I came up with that to scare Danny, but it turns out he was there."

"Huega was?"

"Yes, sir."

"How do you know?"

"We were selling to the same people."

"Selling abalone?"

"It was the only way to get close to them. I've got the money, I've been holding it for you." When Marquez didn't respond, Davies repeated, "It was the only way." Marquez thought he saw sadness before the steady intensity returned to Davies's eyes. "I didn't kill Danny. He swam in and I watched him start down the beach." Davies wiped the side of his face on his shoulder. His forehead carried the dull gleam of oil and he was unshaven. According to Ruter, he'd refused to eat or drink. "And he was fine then."

Marquez wanted to keep the questioning on Huega being at Guyanno during the murders, but went with the shift now.

"Somebody knew where to find Huega," Marquez said. "But you were the only one who knew where he was. What explains that?"

"Somebody was keeping track of him, but, hell, you know, around here you just listen to the police radios and they were buzzing that night. Any fool can keep track of what these cops talk about."

"They think you set Huega up."

"Look, the fat man out there listening had Danny ready to testify he'd seen a knife like the one used at Guyanno on my boat. I mean, he was cutting a deal with him, Lieutenant, as in dirty cop, and Danny was going along because they had him on a dope dealing charge and they were trading that with him. Anything I did, I had to do." Marquez had heard this self-righteous rap from Davies three or four times now. He felt the long, fast drive up, the two cups of coffee he'd had getting briefed by Ruter when he'd arrived. The coffee made his nerves vibrate and his stomach sour. He knew Ruter was convinced of Davies's involvement and was frustrated that he couldn't bring charges or get Davies to confess to assisting the killers. Davies was admitting to being in contact with these poachers and selling abalone to them, but wouldn't take it any further than that, even when they hinted at immunity from prosecution. He's not giving me the numbers either, Marquez thought. So why'd Davies want me here? Just to confess he'd sold abalone? That seemed small in light of everything else.

"You're thinking I'm a head case, aren't you, Lieutenant?"

"I'm thinking this is the time to tell me what you really know."

"Danny got into dope with them and that was the part that went bad on him. It was more than just abalone. They've been running dope for growers up in Humboldt and selling it to these same people buying abalone." The crow's feet around Davies's eyes, the wrinkles that lined his mouth, whose cause Marquez had put down to sun and wind, he now saw formed in part by anxiety. "They took out Stocker and Han because those two had cheated them. They were already looking for Danny when he got on my boat."

"You sound like you're sure of that."

"They asked me where to find him after Guyanno. Stocker, Han, and Danny, they were rotating their diving so two of them are out every day the weather permits. They'd been going at it for seven weeks, trying to pull a hundred abalone a day, about five grand worth. That was their goal, but their deal was another five bucks each if they delivered it already shucked, so Stocker started looking around for a place no one would pick up on him. Danny said they'd been beating their average for seven weeks, so I figure they'd been paid a quarter million so far. Some of that cash they used to buy dope, and then they sold the dope to the same abalone guys. It was all a big circle and they were making it big time. That's why they couldn't keep quiet about it. They used the Lost Coast for some of their dope smuggling and that's why I ran Danny up there, so he could show me where."

"And did he?"

"We never got that far. He pulled the gun and we got into it and then I found he was wired up."

Marquez had heard the gun story, the fight on the boat Davies had described to Ruter. Skepticism must have shown on his face because Davies reacted now.

"You don't believe me?"

"Tell me what Huega told you about Guyanno."

"Do you think I'm in with them?"

"No."

"But you think I've fucked up."

"You're in a fucking mess, I'm sure of that. What happened? Were they robbed?"

"Okay, look, this is what Danny told me. He'd been drinking in town with Stocker and Han and they were all going to party a little more that night and dive in the morning."

"When was this?"

"The night they were killed. He left his truck near the bar and

rode up with Stocker to the campground, figuring to get his truck
the next morning because they were going out early anyway. He
was in the cab of Stocker's truck because he didn't have a sleeping
bag. Danny said after they'd gone to bed, he smoked a joint and
listened to the radio while lying on the truck seat. He went to sleep
and he wasn't sure what woke him up. He didn't hear their car,
didn't see headlights, but he thinks it was yelling that woke him up,
maybe Stocker yelling. There was no one in the campsite and then
he heard screaming farther up the trail. They were putting all their
attention to Han when Danny got near enough to see. Han broke free
and ran and they shot him, then dragged him back and he saw the
man with the silvery hair bend over him. He said Han's screams
carried down the canyon. It was Han they really wanted to hurt."

"He saw it all?"

"No, he took off, got his ass down that trail, rolled Stocker's
truck out of the lot and started it before the road bumps up. The
truck is somewhere up in those dirt roads in the mountains along
the Lost Coast. Huega's ex knows where he hid it. So you know
they came down, saw the truck was gone and put it together. The
next morning I met you there and by the afternoon they'd called
me looking for Huega."

"Why didn't you tell the detectives?"

"Because their minds are already made up."

"And you've been making up stories," Marquez said.

"I've been fucking with them because they're stupid. They
don't get the imperative, you know? They don't get it."

"You told the detectives earlier that there were three men. Was
that coming from Danny Huega?"

"Yes."

"Let's get the detectives in here."

"Bring them in and I'm done talking."

"Then give it to me slowly, everything you can remember
Huega saying. Start with the time. What time of night was this?"

"I never asked him that. They probably closed a bar. He went to sleep smoking a joint, he probably didn't even know the time."

"Describe the men one by one."

Marquez took notes and the account didn't vary much from Davies's earlier telling. Two men had guns, one had a ponytail and the other was smaller, slight of build, wiry. The third man had come behind them, but he couldn't read any of their faces. The third man was the tall one, the one running things. He'd had an accent of some sort and had stepped into the moonlight not far from where Danny Huega was holding his breath. Davies grinned at that thought. "Danny said he walked like he was floating across the grass. He had hair that reflected the moonlight and Danny saw a blade, but that's about it. He didn't even say what color he was either, just the hair and the way he came out of nowhere."

"Dealing with these poachers have you ever heard a description of a man like this?"

"No, I've been dealing with Mexicans and with a white guy whose face you'd want to forget."

"Describe his face."

When he did Marquez knew they had their first link. It was the pair in Oakland, the white with the hatchet face and the Hispanic who was vaguely familiar. He was sure if Davies saw the video he'd recognize him, but he wasn't sure he wanted to show it to him.

Ruter opened the door and Davies stopped talking. Marquez listened to the detectives try to get him to say more, but Davies was done and Marquez left the room. Around midnight, Ruter came out and they stepped outside.

Marquez felt like the whole encounter had been disjointed and strange, but that Davies had mixed in truth. Either Huega or Davies had been at Guyanno during the murders. There was some indefinable thing he could feel, some truth mixed in. Ruter believed it had been Davies, that Davies was wobbling and close to confessing. He'd seen this before.

"That's why he asked for you," Ruter said. "He wanted to confess to you, not us. Then he got a little more spine while you drove up here. If you'd been twenty minutes away, he would have confessed. He was right on the edge." Ruter pounded a fist into his palm, "But dammit, we can't hold him."

"What happens now?" Marquez asked.

"We'll have to kick him loose until we can tie him in."

"Let me know when he's back out there."

"Oh, I will. Hell, he'll probably call you. You're the only pure play, remember?"

When he got on the road Marquez called Petersen, told her he'd pick up a couple of beers for himself and whatever she wanted to drink and meet her in Fort Bragg. They met on Elm Street and walked down the old road alongside the Georgia-Pacific property, between the blackberry bushes and down to Glass Beach where for decades earlier in the past century the citizenry of Fort Bragg used to dump its garbage into the ocean. Over the years the broken china, glass, and metal had been worn by the ocean, the glass rounded like small stones that glittered now in the moonlight. They sat on a rock and Marquez handed her a mineral water and opened the beer, a bottle of Indica from the Lost Coast Brewery.

"What do you think about Davies now?" she asked.

"I think he's got a private agenda he mixed up with ours."

"What do we do with him now?"

"Nothing. He's a suspect."

"At least Ruter is talking to us," Petersen said. "He's opened up to you."

"Yeah, we're tight now." He saw her white teeth in the darkness. He listened to another wave break and his head was buzzing in a way that made him wonder if he'd ever sleep tonight. "This is what I think probably happened. Davies gave Huega to the people who'd killed Stocker and Han. Maybe that was about abalone or maybe it was dope, but the bottom line was money. Some deal went sour and Davies delivered to gain credibility with them. If it's Kline, he'd need to do that. He made comments to Ruter about crossing an abyss there's no returning from."

"Or he was there and he killed Huega."

"That's what Ruter thinks."

"Ruter can count me in on that one, too. Either way, I guess you don't have to defend Davies anymore."

"Is that how I've sounded? You think the detectives are right about that?"

"Definitely."

Marquez opened another beer. He wasn't sure yet what it meant, but he knew what had changed tonight. Any connection he had with Davies was gone.

12

The *Pacific Condor* floated on a darkening sea, its rust stains lost to the fading light. Bailey was at the stern, Heinemann in the cabin. From the cliffs Marquez and Roberts watched Bailey finish a Coors, then crumple the can and send it spinning like a coin across the water.

"Jerk," Roberts said. "That was for us."

"He's making me thirsty."

They lay in low scrub brush and dry grass and it had been hot with the sun on them all afternoon. Now the fog was on its way in. Melinda's face was flushed, her eyes bright. It seemed to Marquez that her anger toward Bailey had grown steadily.

"Don't let him get under your skin."

"Except that can is more litter in the water now. The guy is a dock toad and so far we're watching a party boat. That's about his sixth beer."

"They're waiting for twilight."

He couldn't hear what she said next but he could feel the pulse of the air compressor on the boat. Bailey had turned it on when he pulled this last beer from the cooler. They watched the sun redden, the black jagged face of Elephant Rock smooth with shadows, and Roberts was right, the clock was running down. He glanced at her. She looked cold now, apple spots on her cheeks.

The cabin door opened and the bow-legged, black-bearded Heinemann came out. They watched his white-foaming splash as he entered the water, trailing an air hose, a hookah spooling from the compressor at the stern where Bailey worked as tender and kept watch, operating the davit, swinging the boom out and waiting, while underwater on the floor of the cove Heinemann used the air hose to inflate pop-ups, urchin baskets with floats. Two bobbed to the surface and in steady succession six more, and they were both quiet on the cliff until Heinemann's head broke the surface. He lifted his mask and hooked the first basket to the boom as Marquez refocused the camcorder, the light-enhancing feature turning Bailey's hair white as the first basket swung toward the boat. The urchin basket bulged and was edged in a way that said hard abalone shells were pushing at the fabric, not the small forms of urchins. Marquez videotaped and listened to Roberts's careful recording of the facts as the baskets were lowered into the hold.

Within ten minutes the anchor rose and the *Condor* turned south toward San Francisco. They hustled back up the trail and Marquez drove as Roberts talked to the Coast Guard and tracked the boat with the GPS locator. So far, it had gone as Bailey had said it would. He listened as Roberts let the rest of the team know and then talked with Petersen who'd swung in behind them. He felt upbeat. It had gone well. They had good footage; they'd have Bailey's testimony and if Bailey was right about Sausalito, they might get all the way to the buyer tomorrow. The *Marlin* and the Coast Guard would help track the boat the catch was transferred to and he hoped that would take them all the way home.

"Signal good?" he asked.

"Perfect."

The Kline file lay on the seat between them, Roberts's Gatorade on top of it. She picked up the Gatorade, wiping at the ring the bottle had left, as though somehow the file was sacred to him and she was worried he'd be upset. Earlier, he'd asked her to take a look at it, but so far she'd only thumbed through it as a curiosity. She tapped it now.

"How come there aren't better photos?"

"The FBI has better photos."

That got her more interested. The FBI added another level of credibility for her and he knew from talking to Roberts that she'd once considered an FBI career. She'd told him about being younger and imagining she'd be like Jodie Foster in *Silence of the Lambs*.

"What's the closest you got to him?"

"There were a couple of times. Once, in Mexico, when I was still DEA, we were up in a mountain pueblo—this was a joint task force with the Mexicans where we'd set up surveillance ahead of a wedding. A man invited to the wedding was the Mexican equivalent of a district attorney. He'd made a name for himself prosecuting drug traffickers and we'd heard the Juarez cartels were either going to buy him off or shut him down. We had our own reasons for wanting him to survive and keep doing his job, so we were trying to help the Mexicans protect him until he prosecuted a couple of cases we were very interested in. Two days prior, we'd been tipped that the cartels had hired Kline to take him out. The DA had come to this wedding with his daughter, a beautiful girl, maybe twelve or thirteen."

The last sentence came out like it felt, a stand-alone truth, a side fact until you knew what had happened and he paused, drew a slow breath, having never really gotten over this one. There were times driving along a freeway or a road anywhere, times when his mind drifted to her and for reasons in himself he didn't understand he'd calculate how old she'd be if she was alive still. He pictured her face easily as he talked to Roberts.

"The DA went to the ceremony at the church, then made a bee-line with his daughter for their car. He'd made his appearance and was avoiding the party. We'd asked him to avoid the party, and he was okay with it." Marquez glanced over. "I'm talking about a small church, crowded, old wood doors, stone steps, everybody spilling out after the ceremony. I was well up the slope on one side of town and I could see them walking across the plaza. It was a high desert kind of cold with a wind blowing and kicking up dust. A man came out of a side street and at first he seemed to be headed away from them, then turned back and raised his hand to get their attention. He called to them. Not in a hurried way, but I focused on him, and his face was hidden to me. I started down as soon as the DA took a step backwards, looked like he was trying to shield his daughter. Then it went fast. We think the man asked the DA a question, got the wrong answer and shot the girl through the forehead while her father had an arm around her. There was a delay, maybe fifteen seconds, time enough for more questions, and we got a shot off."

"You?"

"No, I was running down and Kline drove past me. Another agent shot at him but missed. Kline didn't kill the Mexican prose-cutor and the man didn't quit his job, but he lost his guts to pursue the traffickers. I heard there were other threats against his family and he folded up after that."

"Resigned?"

"Yeah."

"Who wouldn't?" Marquez didn't answer and she returned to Kline. "It's not like we have much to go on. Not like there's much proof about him being here, Lieutenant. What does the FBI say about him being in California?"

"I made one call and so far I haven't had a call back from the Feds."

She turned quiet and he didn't begrudge her skepticism. In fact, he respected it. He wanted SOU wardens who were skeptics. His theory of Kline being here could turn out to be a fantasy. He hoped it was. Roberts was young, unafraid, and strong. She was an expert markswoman, had a black belt, ran marathons, and had been scuba diving since she was ten. She had the shoulders of a swimmer and grew up in a generation where the young women pumped iron the same as the men. What she hadn't tested herself against was the absence of morality and he'd wanted to communicate Kline to her without overdramatizing, but felt like he'd failed. It was better left alone now.

At 10:27, the *Condor* passed under the Golden Gate Bridge and angled toward the north bay. It berthed in Sausalito as Bailey had said it would and Marquez got set up with the local police and the rest of the SOU. Roberts went for food while he talked to the Sausalito police, letting them know they were on location and as far as he knew the bust would still be early morning.

When Roberts got back, they ate, then moved down to a position on a docked boat. They'd trade off every four hours through the night, and she was asleep now, her head on a coil of rope, a blue plastic tarp hiding her body like a blanket. Sodium lights strung along the dock hummed and swung in the wind and the shapes of Bailey and Heinemann flickered through the pale light of their rear cabin window. Across the bay, the skyline of San Francisco glowed with a hazy brilliance and as the night deepened and quieted he listened to the water lapping at the dock and faint strains of music carrying from the *Condor.* He watched Bailey come out, pee off the boat into the water and he was near to waking Roberts to change shifts when a light came on in the boat berthed next to the *Condor.*

Earlier, he'd scanned the boat, the *Emily Jane,* hadn't seen anyone on board and had decided it was a fishing vessel. He lifted the camcorder and with the infrared hooked in he easily read the heat image of a man, then picked up a second individual and swung back toward the *Condor,* saw both Bailey and the diver out on the deck, the cabin door ajar, a shaft of light falling across the stern. A winch engine coughed and started and Marquez reached and shook Roberts's shoulder.

"We're on."

She came awake quickly, asking, "What time is it?"

"3:30."

"Bailey lied."

Marquez punched in the numbers for the Sausalito police and then Alvarez's cell phone. It would take Alvarez and Petersen at least twenty minutes to get here from the motel in Corte Madera and urchin baskets were already moving. They weren't going to get here in time and the Sausalito police said their first car wouldn't get there for ten minutes because they had officers assisting the CHP on a vehicle pursuit. He watched Bailey as the dispatcher told him the suspect car had crossed northbound on the bridge then dropped into Sausalito on Alexander Drive. It had since sideswiped three cars and the driver was on foot now with officers in pursuit. Sounded exciting, but it wasn't going to help them here.

Marquez repeated their situation and counted three men on the *Emily Jane,* then got off the line with the dispatcher. He had no problem taking down both boats with Roberts, but it would be safer with backup. He decided to give Sausalito as long as possible to get here.

"They've almost got it," Roberts said.

They heard the *Emily Jane*'s engines kick on and diesel smoke wafted across the dock as Marquez tried the *Marlin,* but as he feared, they were between shifts and docked at the Berkeley marina. He talked to a sleepy warden, asked him to find Hansen.

"Okay, we have to go," he said. "Get yourself ready." He slipped his tactical jacket on. STATE GAME OFFICER was written in large green and yellow letters, but he didn't think there'd be any confusion either way. He picked up his flashlight and looked at

Roberts crouched near the railing, her eyes shiny and alert. "I'll walk down, identify myself and order the *Emily Jane* to shut its engines down. They're going to pick up on me right away and as soon as they do, click your light on. Then get out on the dock. Let's look like as many people as we can while they're trying to make a decision. Bailey knows to do whatever we tell him, so he should be easy. We'll board the *Condor*, confirm it's abalone, then ask Heinemann to step down on the dock. I'll hold the other two in place and back you up on Heinemann. We're going to want to handcuff him before we move on the others, and in the meantime hope the Sausalito police get here. When they get here or after we have Heinemann under control we'll board the second boat. Not before. We clear on that?"

"Got it."

He looked in her eyes. It was her first SOU bust. "It'll unroll fast," he said. "Remember, when I click my light on, let them register me first, let them start thinking it's one guy, then we'll hit them with another light. All we have to do is hold them." But now, he saw a police unit slow to a stop up in the parking lot, lights off. Two officers got out quickly and then looked confused about where to go. They started one direction and stopped, as if afraid they were going to make a mistake. He pointed them out to Roberts. "I'll go get those two. Wait here."

He made his way back to the officers and led them down to wait behind a fish wholesaler's shed. Roberts would come in with him and the officers would follow. He worked back to her, adrenaline running now. "Let's go, but let me lead."

Marquez started the walk, his shoes making a quiet rhythm on the dock. He saw them pick up on the sound, then clicked on his flashlight and Roberts did the same. He held his ID chest high and said, "Fish and Game, gentlemen," as he reached the *Condor*. "Who's captain of this boat?" Heinemann pointed at Bailey. "Captain, we're going to board your boat and look at what you're moving."

The Sausalito cops started toward them. Marquez had hoped for four Sausalito officers, but the pursuit in town meant the two would be the only backup. That was okay, except he could feel a problem starting. The lights went off on the *Emily Jane*. Two of the men disappeared in the darkness, though they had to be in the cabin. Marquez moved alongside the *Emily Jane* searching for the third man as Roberts boarded the *Condor* and called, "Abalone, Lieutenant." She'd opened an urchin bag and he knew she was doing a quick count so she could arrest Bailey and Heinemann.

Marquez searched the *Emily Jane* with his flashlight, yelling to the men on board that he was Fish and Game and to shut their engines down and come out. When nothing happened he knew they had a problem. He saw the boat was only held by one mooring line and looked for another on board, figured he'd tie it off. He watched for movement, called out again, "Shut your engines down, now, gentlemen."

The third man must be hiding around the starboard side. Marquez didn't pull his gun yet, but he freed the clasp now so he could pull it easily, and behind him, he heard Bailey coaxing Heinemann, making a point to be heard. "Come on, man, it's fucking Gamers. We've got to roll with it."

Roberts was back on the dock, telling Heinemann and Bailey they were under arrest when a squat man appeared on the stern of the *Emily Jane* and walked toward Marquez holding his hands up, talking as he got closer.

"Hey, man, what's up? What's the problem?"

"This is a bust, come down off the boat." Marquez shined his flashlight on his badge while the cops kept their lights on the boat cabin. "Fish and Game."

"Okay, Fish and Game, what's the problem?"

"The catch you're transferring from your friend here."

Roberts had handcuffs out and Marquez kept his eyes focused on the boat cabin, looking past the man getting off the *Emily Jane*.

The other two had to be lying down inside the cabin. Where else could they be? There was scuffling behind him and he turned to see Bailey pounding down the dock. He'd broken free of the officer who'd gripped his arm and had run. One of the Sausalito cops was chasing and Heinemann used the moment to break in the other direction, knocking Roberts down as he passed, straight-arming her at the collar and springing toward the *Emily Jane*. Heinemann scrambled aboard as the man who'd climbed down had a knife out now and was slashing at the mooring line. He'd all but cut through it by the time Marquez got his gun out, disarmed him, and had him facedown on the dock with his arms out. Marquez called to Roberts and then slid the knife away with his foot. He turned to check Roberts's position and the cops chasing Bailey.

Roberts had leapt on board the *Emily Jane* and the boat had clunked into reverse, engines gunning, snapping what remained of the mooring rope. Marquez yelled at her to jump, but she was trying to handcuff Heinemann and didn't hear him above the diesels. He had to make a decision and left the man lying on the dock and went for the *Emily Jane* before it left with Roberts.

When he jumped he caught just enough rail to hang on, hoist himself over, and then aimed his gun at a man who stood under the deck light holding a sawed shotgun on Roberts. Marquez ordered him to drop the weapon, but the man didn't flinch, didn't move the gun from Roberts.

"Drop it, now," Marquez yelled. "It isn't worth it. You're surrounded. Lay the weapon down."

Marquez was within fifteen feet before the man said, "Not another step, fucker."

His grip on the shotgun was tight and Marquez knew he was thinking about emptying a barrel into Roberts and swinging the gun his way.

"You might kill her, but I'll empty a clip into you before you can get to me. Drop the gun," he yelled over the engines.

"There's a man coming up behind you, Lieutenant," Roberts called, and Marquez registered him without taking his aim from the man with the shotgun. "He's got a gun."

"Fucking right, I've got a gun," the man yelled, and Marquez couldn't risk turning to look at him. "In the water if you want to live." Marquez figured he must have jammed something in the wheel to keep the boat going straight. "Hey, pig, you listening to me?" He fired a burst and Marquez heard the bullets whang off metal above his head. "Go, now—now, or you're gone. You're both dead fuckers if you don't jump."

"We're going to jump," Marquez called to the man in front of him. "Tell your friend to hold steady and no one will get killed." He still held his gun on the man and kept moving toward Roberts, said quickly to her, "We're out of here. Jump now and I'm behind you."

"Not before you, Lieutenant."

He pushed her backwards, shielding her body as he did. Roberts disappeared over the rail. He heard a splash and took a long look at the man with the shotgun, kept his gun on him as he climbed over the rail, started to turn to look at the other man and heard, "You look at me and I'm blowing your head off."

He looked anyway before falling away from the boat. Their eyes met and he had the face forever, then was backwards into the darkness.

13

Marquez kicked his shoes off and surfaced, treading water while still holding his gun. What he didn't want to do was lose anything more, and what he felt was humiliation and anger. Fear of getting shot had left him as he hit the water. Now, he was cold and the heavy ballistic and tech vests dragged at him. The boat was moving away and they'd have to fight the current and swim to shore. He managed to holster the gun and started swimming toward Roberts. Chest-tightening cold was already working on him. He yelled to her. She yelled back and he couldn't make out the words. He saved his badge, managed to get it in a pocket and then let the tech vest slide and peeled his shirt, wrapped his shoulder holster around a forearm and got the ballistics vest off.

Then he swam steadily toward her. They had to get to the Coast Guard and the *Marlin*. They had to reach shore. The *Emily Jane* was running fast without lights and when he checked again he had to find the moon's reflection on the wake and followed that to the dark shape of the boat sweeping toward the Golden Gate. Roberts waited for him. She said the cold was no problem and they angled for shore, Roberts leading.

The dock lights drifted away and the current tugged them toward the Gate. They landed well south of the docks, coming ashore near the main part of town, Marquez's big frame rising out of the bay like some sort of Godzilla, algae slicking off him as he climbed the seawall rocks and then up onto the sidewalk alongside Bridgeway. They walked down to a hotel that seemed to be the only place open and as Marquez walked in shirtless the night clerk started dialing 911. He showed his badge and they borrowed a couple of sweatshirts carrying the hotel logo.

Marquez called the Coast Guard first, then the *Marlin*. He heard Hansen talking over the roar of the *Marlin* engines and knew he was up on the flydeck and the *Marlin* was running full out.

"We've got them on radar," Hansen said, "but they're flying, and I mean flying. What have they got on that boat? It's doing better than fifty knots. The Guard is going to have to run these guys down, but they'll get them. Hey, what happened out there? We heard you went swimming, again."

"We were outgunned and they said jump."

When he hung up with Hansen, he called Brad Alvarez, who was at the Army Corps of Engineers dock, talking with the Sausalito police. They were still looking for Bailey.

"We need a ride. We're at a hotel," Marquez said.

"What's the name of the hotel?"

Marquez had to look at his sweatshirt before he could tell him. They waited outside, both of them still shaking from the cold and thanking the night manager several times when he walked back out and handed them coffee, insisting the sweatshirts were on him. Marquez held the coffee, stood there waiting, embarrassment and disappointment coloring his thoughts. They had the bust they'd needed right there and they looked like Keystone Kops. Jump on a boat and then jump in the water. Bailey was going to say he ran because he got scared, he thought. He'll still want to get paid. Bailey will say he panicked, thought there was going to be a firefight. Roberts, who'd been quiet, finally said something about what had happened.

"It was my fault and I'll resign tomorrow."

"No, you're not, and we're going to find that boat."

"I just didn't want him to get away. I'm really sorry, Lieutenant. I could have got us killed, but I thought we could stop the boat."

"You keep underrating these people, Melinda."

"I know and I blew it. I'll ask for a transfer."

"Don't do that, you belong here." Alvarez's white Cherokee came toward them. Marquez touched her arm and said, "We'll sort it out."

"I messed up, Lieutenant. I don't want to pretend it was anything else."

She'd be pulled from the team tomorrow if Keeler got word of how it went down and Marquez decided he'd send her to Fort Bragg this afternoon because Keeler would be here in Marin this morning visiting an old friend having surgery at Marin General. The chief would want to meet, and knowing Keeler he might want to question Roberts.

With Alvarez they found the only place open to get hot coffee and food. Alvarez turned with a wry look, "Of course, you guys probably prefer surf 'n' turf."

Marquez stripped the wet pants and put on dry clothes and shoes when he got to his truck. He left on the hotel sweatshirt. He'd just finished changing clothes when Chief Keeler called. It was 6:00, which probably meant someone had called Keeler about what had happened, though he didn't know who that could have been.

"Have you got any more equipment left to lose?" Keeler asked.

"Not a lot."

"What is left, your vehicles? Something is wrong here. I'll be down there by 8:00. I want you to meet me at Marin General in the surgery waiting room. I'd like it if you wrote your report first and brought a printed copy." Keeler didn't wait for him to say he couldn't get it done in time. "You may hear from Chief Baird before I get there."

"About this?"

As SOU patrol lieutenant, Marquez had direct access to Fish and Game's top law enforcement officer, the chief of patrol, Gordon Baird. Each new state governor typically appointed a director of Fish and Game and a handful of deputy-chiefs, but the chief of patrol earned the rank and carried the real responsibility for law enforcement. The director's was a political office. Marquez didn't talk with Baird often, though every day he copied Baird his e-mailed reports. He heard Keeler's long sigh, as though he was too old for these types of problems.

"The FBI called off the Coast Guard pursuit of the boat you're after."

"When did that happen?"

"Over an hour ago."

"Why?"

"That's all I know, right now."

"Backed the Guard off the *Emily Jane?*"

"Did you get water inside your head? Yes, they asked the Coast Guard to cease pursuit."

"What are you talking about, Chief?"

"I'll have a better explanation when I see you."

Marquez debated calling Baird and got as far as dialing Baird's home number after Keeler hung up. He stared at the numbers on his screen as his thumb touched the call icon. Baird already knew Keeler was on his way down here and would want him to hear it from his deputy-chief. He pressed the call button anyway, then killed it before the phone rang at Baird's house, his hand trembling as he tossed the phone down. Why in the hell would they do that? What possible reason? He watched Petersen's headlights swing into the marina parking lot. She got out and walked over.

"You okay?" she asked.

"No."

Petersen smiled. "I've been working with the locals here, trying to run down our friend Jimmy."

"Anything?"

"Not yet." She pulled at the torn cuff of red fleece coat that had long ago faded to pink. "I think he got a ride out of here, John, maybe even by boat. A couple of fishermen went out about an hour after things went bad."

"We'll go looking for him at home later today. I've got to meet with Keeler first."

"Do you want us to keep searching for him?"

It had been three hours since Bailey had run, but dawn wasn't far off, the sky already white toward the east. Maybe daylight would compromise his hiding spot, which was really what Petersen was asking about. It was 6:10.

"Okay, give it another round. I'm going down to his boat and see what I find on board."

Marquez watched her drive off and then walked down to the dock to board the *Condor*. He recovered the GPS transponder first. He dropped that in his pocket. They'd impound the *Pacific Condor,* move it to Yerba Buena, and try to put heat on Bailey when they caught up to him. They couldn't charge him but they could question him and they didn't need a search warrant to go through his boat.

Marquez started at the stern, worked his way through the equipment there, opened a cooler that was tied off to the deck and found a couple of Coors talls, an empty Doritos bag floating in the water, and a seven-inch abalone lying on the white plastic bottom underneath it. When he lifted the abalone out and turned the algae-stained shell he could still smell the mineral brine of the sea. He let it slide back and opened the hold, thinking it was more likely that Bailey'd had a car parked somewhere near or a ride waiting for him. Petersen, Alvarez, and the Sausalito police had gone building-to-building around the dock. They'd checked bushes and walked the area. He used a flashlight to look in the hold and saw another basket down there, one they hadn't had time to transfer, and he winched it up now, counted forty abalone.

He lowered the basket back into the water in the hold and checked the rest of the deck before going into the cabin. Once inside, he pulled on latex gloves and began a search for evidence, anything he could hold Bailey with. There was a full baggie of marijuana and a couple of roaches. There was a large McDonald's bag packed with fast-food trash in a corner of the cabin and the smell filled the space when he opened it and rooted through it. He found a piece of abalone shell with a hole drilled in it on a leather shoelace and turned it in his hand. An odd design had been etched on the smooth green shiny part of the shell, a pyramid shape with what looked like the letter H on one face, a beach thing, maybe, worn around the neck. Was the H for Heinemann? How long had Bailey known Heinemann? He dropped it in an evidence bag and went methodically through the storage compartments, the emergency equipment, life preservers, a flare gun, a fire extinguisher, a ship-to-shore radio, bottled water. There were a couple of coats and he searched the pockets, found a handful of Mexican pesos in one, which he counted before putting back in the coat. He came to a locked cabinet and said quietly, "Too bad you locked it, Jimmy." He searched the pilot's section for keys, then decided to walk up to his truck and get something to open it with.

He came back with a small pry bar and ripped the cabinet door off, feeling a base satisfaction as the hinges tore out of the aluminum and the door fell on the cabin floor. Inside, he found a red metal toolbox. The upper tray carried a couple of screwdrivers, pliers, a tool for stripping electrical wires and a roll of electrical tape. He lifted the tray and underneath was a gun with a taped handle and a box of nine millimeter shells. He moved the gun with the screwdriver and saw that the serial numbers had been filed and burned.

"What have we got here, Jimmy?"

He knew Bailey would say he'd bought it or won it from some-body in a bar, that he didn't do the serial number work, didn't even know about that and kept it on board out of fear of poachers, particularly since he was working for the government. If he got the right judge, and there were a few of them, he'd get nothing more than a lecture.

"Marquez, who are you talking to in there?"

He turned at the voice, something familiar in the timbre, stepped out of the cabin and saw Charles Douglas. He lifted a gloved hand in recognition, but didn't say anything yet. Five years ago, Douglas had been an FBI special agent, but he'd probably advanced since then. He'd had the moves of a guy on his way up. They'd worked together briefly on a child-kidnapping case Douglas had been assigned to. Four kids had disappeared at random out of California coastal towns and the FBI came up with the idea they were looking for a lone male boat owner. Douglas had requested Fish and Game's help. As far as Marquez knew the kidnappings had stopped, but the case had never been solved. He figured Douglas was here as the emissary from the Bureau because they'd worked together before.

"Did they send you to explain it away?" Marquez asked.

"It was my call to back the pursuit off."

"Then you're just the guy I'd like to talk to."

"Let's go sit down somewhere we can talk. Let me buy you a cup of coffee. There's a little place, Flora's, Floradito, something like that, I'm sure you know where it is." He pointed down the water. "Why don't you meet me down there in fifteen minutes?"

"See you there."

Marquez put the tray back in the toolbox, shut the lid and was still thinking about it. He slid the dope into an evidence bag and dropped the bag in his pocket. He took another thirty seconds in the cabin. When he came back out he climbed off the boat with the toolbox and evidence bags in hand, then set them down as he peeled the gloves.

Douglas was already outside his car in front of Flora's when Marquez drove up. The deli faced the bay and had tables outside that were damp with dew and splattered with gull guano. Flora's did its true business at lunch and through the afternoons when the weather was good, but also sold coffee, bagels, and pastries to the early crowd. They carried their coffee outside and gulls wheeled overhead looking for food as they cleaned a couple of chairs.

Douglas looked unchanged. He was black with Cherokee blood and especially proud of the Cherokee. He was a history buff and could tell you anything you wanted to know about the Cherokee tribe. He'd come through 9/11 and the partial reorganization of the Bureau, and looked just as confident as the last time Marquez had seen him.

"Since when does the Bureau give free passes to poachers?" Marquez asked.

"I'm going to explain what I can."

Of course he was. He was here to explain and the only problem with that was the FBI was as stingy with information as a politician with the truth, and it was the Bureau's habit to always make their investigations more important than any other—9/11 had given them another magnitude of throw weight, but as near as Marquez could tell, it hadn't made them more competent. More busy, definitely. Under the direction of the Coast Guard, the Department of Fish and Game had done numerous patrols with the *Marlin*, checking bridge abutments at the Golden Gate, Bay Bridge, and Richmond/San Rafael, as well as watching the bay. Calling off the *Marlin* probably felt like calling off one of their own. There were stories floating all the time now about boats loaded with explosives, bridges targeted, the deeper fears of nuclear bombs delivered with cargo ships. The *Marlin* now carried automatic weapons, .308's. But the terrible new possibilities didn't cancel out his own job and he hoped Douglas wasn't going to throw terrorism at him.

"I'm going to tell you more than I should," Douglas said, his face showing the heavy burden the Feds carried. It had no effect on Marquez though, and if anything, it made him think less of Douglas, though he'd always liked him. Saying he was going to tell him more than he should probably meant he was going to lie, so maybe the Bureau really did have a live operation they needed to protect. "We're close to capturing an individual we've been after for many years. He's responsible for the deaths of five people in law enforcement that we know of and he's suspected of being behind the killing of a judge in Houston and a DA in Arizona in '97. There is an individual on the *Emily Jane* who's in our employ as an informant and who has dealings with this individual's organization."

"So Kline is here." He saw Douglas had been prepared for that, which must mean he's talking with Ruter.

"I can't name names."

"Are you involved in the investigation of the diver homicides?"

"We're assisting."

"Okay, well, we're looking for a large market poacher who's buying up north coast ab and it could be Kline. Are you telling me he's our buyer?"

"I can't tell you what I know yet, but I may be able to in the next day or two. I've got to get cleared first."

"How close are you to him?"

Douglas looked down at his coffee and picked up the cup, then immediately put it down again. He got out his card and wrote a couple of phone numbers on the back.

"These are private numbers you can reach me at. The top one will get me day or night."

"Where's the *Emily Jane* this morning?" No answer for that either and if you're a Fed long enough, you turn into one, Marquez thought. You start thinking your questions and thought processes are better and you begin to walk among the anointed. He took the card and pocketed it. "How about you call me when you're able to talk," Marquez said, as he stood up.

"Don't leave yet."

"I learned not to underrate him. He'll make the reality fit your fears. Thanks for the coffee, Charles, and it is good to see you again."

"I'd like it if you stayed and talked."

"I'd be doing all the talking, but give me a call if that changes." Marquez took four steps and turned back, looking at Douglas's face. "How'd you know to find me here?" Douglas didn't answer. "I guess that says it all. I'll see you."

14

Marquez stopped at the Sausalito police station on his way to the hospital to meet with Chief Keeler. He knew and liked the police captain, a frank and genial man named Jim Gerhardt. Sausalito police worked out of brown painted trailers that sat on a grassy hump of a hill at the end of Locust Street, trailers they'd inhabited since their former station had flooded nearly a decade ago. Marquez parked between two boats on trailers and wondered if Gerhardt would have stayed if he could have looked into the future and seen himself in a trailer park this long after the flood.

Gerhardt was at his desk. "I won't take much of your time," Marquez said, and watched him drop his reading glasses and slide his chair back.

"I'm sorry about last night, John. We got there as quickly as we could."

"I short-noticed you."

"You couldn't help it." He frowned. "We've searched town for this Bailey and your wardens seem to think he's gone, but you're not here about him, are you?"

"No, I'm here because I just met with the FBI."

Gerhardt nodded, reached across his desk, his big-boned wrist pulling free of his sleeve as he picked a card from a holder. He squinted at it, holding it a distance away, before fumbling with his glasses again. "Special Agent Charles Douglas," he said. "He was here with another agent this morning. He wanted to talk about the sequence of events last night."

"Did he say why?"

"He couldn't discuss it."

"The FBI called off our pursuit of the *Emily Jane* and I think they probably watched the whole thing here last night. They had the *Emily Jane* under surveillance and we stumbled into that when we showed up with Bailey."

"They didn't say a word to me about being in town with any surveillance team."

"That was my next question."

Marquez handed back the card, thanked him again for backing them up last night, and then drove to the hospital to meet Keeler. A couple of red-tailed hawks circled in the late morning sky above the parking lot and the air was clear and cool as he walked toward the entrance. Inside, the air was humid and rich with chemical odors. People had surgeries that saved their lives and children got born and many good things happened in these places, but he associated hospitals with some of the worst memories of his life. He moved quietly in here, asked at the desk where the surgery waiting room was, and when he walked in, Keeler was alone in the large, empty room.

There were gurneys in the corner and a couch arrangement where Keeler sat. From behind, he looked like an old valley rancher on horseback, hands folded into his lap as though holding reins.

He sat straight-backed, a legacy of Marine Corps training. He'd thinned at the shoulders in the last few years and his waist bulged where his uniform shirt was tucked in tight. His white hair was cut short and neatly combed. He wasn't far from retirement now, and lately had been talking about hanging it up next spring and working on his almond orchard behind the old farmhouse he'd bought and was restoring outside Davis. He was also refurbishing an aluminum-skinned Airstream camper and had plans to go all over the United States with his wife, Clara. The chief turned at the echo of footsteps in the empty room.

"How is he?" Marquez asked, meaning the chief's old friend who was in surgery.

"It's worse than they thought." He touched his abdomen. Marquez knew it was some kind of cancer. "I've lost three of my oldest friends in the last year and a half to cancer. I hate that. I hate it that they had to close him up and they're going to tell him they can't do anything for him." His voice dropped to a rough whisper. "Goddammit, I hate it." He touched his face, pressing fingers into his forehead, looked at Marquez and said, "You know, I can remember him like yesterday when we were no more than twenty-one. He was the one the girls always went for." He shook his head. "Tell me what happened last night."

Marquez walked through the sequence of events but left out telling Roberts to get off the boat. "I'd like to try to find the *Emily Jane*," he said. "They berthed somewhere up north."

"You want to pit your unit against the FBI?"

"No, sir, but we can't stop doing our jobs because they're after somebody. They owe us a lot more information, Chief."

"Why do they owe us if we walked into their operation?"

Marquez was unsure how to answer that. The Feds had wiped out a bust after he and Roberts had to bail off a boat at gunpoint, yet he also knew Keeler's respect for the FBI was almost unquestioning. He'd brushed with the chief on this subject a couple of times before and had learned that saying anything openly critical of the FBI was something Keeler saw as unpatriotic. Yet he could also sense an opening here. Perhaps because of the circumstances of the morning, perhaps because of the risk Roberts and he'd been in or a conversation he'd had with Baird while driving here from Sacramento this morning.

"Chief, I need the *Emily Jane*. We can find it without approaching anybody on board."

"Should we tell the FBI to cancel their operation?"

"No, sir."

"Then what are you saying?"

"There's a reason we crossed paths. We may be looking for the same people."

"We may be, in which case we're lucky the Feds are on the case." Keeler looked at him quizzically. "Are we leading back to your ghost killer?" Marquez shrugged. He'd already pushed the Kline idea far enough without evidence and Keeler didn't care for speculation. "Officially, there's no way I can let you do that."

"I understand."

Marquez watched a nurse walk through carrying a clipboard, smiling at them as she passed. He let Keeler think and was quiet. It was a foundation belief of Keeler's that no one should ever get away with endangering a peace officer, and he was counting on that.

"Did this FBI agent say anything to you about abalone poachers?" Keeler asked.

"They have an informant aboard the *Emily Jane.*"

"They didn't tell Chief Baird anything this morning. They apologized for having to intercede, but that's all."

"I think that's because we're after the same man."

"If you're right, they've got a lot more resources to go after him. In that case we should stand aside."

"They don't know the coast or the people that live along it the way we do and it's my judgment that we can't afford to wait."

"We're not going to deliberately cross them."

Then what are we going to do, Chief? Are we going to watch? Call them up when we have a lead? Marquez listened to the hospital noises and let Keeler weigh his own risks. The doors opened, a surgeon came out and then walked over to Keeler. He sat down on the edge of the couch and told the chief more about what they'd found and talked about other forms of therapy, but was candid that the odds were poor. The chief took this in quietly, then asked questions about what kind of care his friend—a widower and without immediate family—would get. What could be arranged? What could he do? The surgeon outlined generally what would happen, then slowly stood, said he was sorry, again.

Marquez walked out of the hospital with Keeler soon after. Keeler was thinking about his request, but it was no longer the right time to ask. He got Bailey's toolbox and the evidence bags he'd gathered out of his truck and showed Keeler the nine millimeter, its handle wrapped with electrical tape, then put the box with the gun in the back of Keeler's Isuzu after asking the chief if he'd drop the gun at the Department of Justice in Sacramento. He stood at Keeler's window, talking with him a little longer before Keeler drove away without answering whether they could look for the *Emily Jane,* or not.

Now, in the sunlight in the warm cab of the truck Marquez felt the long night like two heavy hands on his shoulders. He was sliding down the backside of adrenaline. He closed his eyes, reclined the driver's seat, and felt the sun on his face. Had to doze, had to rest a little before going on. He thought of Katherine, her dark hair falling at her shoulders, the bright light in her eyes when she laughed. She was due back today. He'd have to call Maria this morning. Then he let the fatigue take him and closed down.

He woke to Petersen tapping on his window with her cell phone. He'd been asleep about forty minutes and looked at her groggily, before it all flooded back. He opened the door and sat up.

"How'd you find me?" he asked.

"I always know where you are. You know, we used to wonder if you ever slept. Are you ready to get going?"

He drank from a water bottle. He needed coffee, food. They drove tandem to San Francisco and left her 4Runner parked on Gough Street. By 2:00 in the afternoon they were walking down the Pillar Point dock to where Heinemann's boat was berthed. A light wind was blowing off the ocean, the soft air smelled of salt, and you could feel autumn. Gold light hazed through thin fog at sea.

Marquez climbed aboard and knocked. The *Open Sea* carried a sleeping berth and they knew there was a girlfriend. When a curtain moved and the fingers of a young woman's hand showed he held up his badge, and then a blonde wearing shorts and a very thin cotton shirt opened the door.

"We're looking for Mark Heinemann."

"He's not here."

"Do you know where he is?"

"Up north, but I don't know when he's coming back."

"Can we come in and talk with you a minute?"

"If you want, but I don't know anything."

They established that Heinemann was her friend and that her name was Meghan Burris. She sniffled and touched her nose in a way that said cocaine. Without prompting she elaborated on her relationship with Heinemann. They weren't a couple, but they were going out together. She wouldn't be here right now if it wasn't for the cat, and she pointed at the striped tabby watching them.

"We're working an investigation we hope Mark can help us with," Marquez said. "We're also looking for a Jimmy Bailey. Do you know him?"

"Yes."

"Have you seen him today?"

"Nope." She crinkled her nose. "I guess I'm useless. I have to get going anyway."

"Have you ever heard Jimmy Bailey talk about abalone?"

"I'm a vegetarian."

Petersen smiled broadly behind her and rolled the cat on its back, scratching its belly. Meghan made it clear now she only knew Mark Heinemann from school at UC Santa Cruz and staying on the boat was just sort of a fun thing to do. She didn't believe in hurting animals. Marquez gave her his abalone rap anyway, the problem, what they were up against, needing the public's help to save the species.

"We think Jimmy Bailey may be involved with poachers and anything you tell us might help Mark, because we know they've been out on the ocean together."

"Mark wouldn't ever poach, but there were these kind of freaky guys who came down to Jimmy's boat."

"Tell us about them."

She described the men they'd videotaped in Oakland outside Li's house, the hatchet-faced Caucasian and the black-haired, buffed Hispanic that Bailey had claimed came to meet with Heinemann. There'd been another man but she'd only seen him at a distance. He'd never come down to the dock.

"One of the guys that came down here wouldn't quit staring at me so I left."

"If I opened a calendar, could you show me what day that was?"

"Oh, I already know. On this Saturday it will have been three weeks. It was definitely a Saturday because I didn't have school and I had to drop my car off that day."

Marquez opened his pocket calendar. He marked Saturday August thirty-first and glanced at Petersen, knew from her look she read Meghan as telling the truth, or what she thought was the truth. "See, Mark was down helping Jimmy with his engine and when one of them showed up, it was like Jimmy pretended he didn't know they were coming, but he did. He always acts like he can fool everybody."

Marquez nodded. He tried to gauge what her reaction would be to what he was going to say next.

"I'm going to tell you some things that you might not like to hear, but that you need to know. We saw Mark bring up urchin bags filled with abalone near Elephant Rock up in the Point Reyes area yesterday. He was with Jimmy Bailey on the *Condor* and they took their catch down to Sausalito late last night. We broke up a transfer to another boat there, but that boat got away. Mark ran to that boat during the bust and there's a warrant for his arrest now."

"Oh, so you came here to trick me. That's nice. Boy, does that suck. You said you weren't after Mark, but you are. No wonder I can't stand cops." She brushed her nose with the back of a finger, let her hand fall slowly. "So I'm supposed to be the stupid girlfriend."

"Not at all." He made up a reason now. "We think Jimmy Bailey tricked your boyfriend. It's Bailey we're really after," Marquez said. "Let's go back to the night of the thirty-first again, what you heard in the conversation on Bailey's boat."

She hesitated, then spoke. They'd been drinking daiquiris on the *Condor*. Jimmy and Mark were smoking. She'd had one daiquiri, didn't smoke, and the Hispanic guy had straight rum. Bailey told her she had to split for a while because they were going to talk private business. Mark pretended like he hadn't heard what Bailey had said. Mark wouldn't look at her and she'd been real angry when she left the boat. She'd gotten into a bad fight with him later that night and they'd broken up, for the second time, she said.

Petersen spoke up now, telling her they were going to check Heinemann's boat for anything Bailey might have asked Mark to hold for him. She asked Meghan if she had anything private she wanted to remove first, deftly explaining that they didn't need a warrant because they were deputized as customs agents. Petersen went through everything, found nothing, and they questioned her more, then gave her phone numbers to call. Marquez knew her first call would be to Heinemann.

As they walked away, Marquez said, "That story about Bailey had the ring of truth."

"Yeah, it did."

"We'll borrow the condo and I think we'll watch her."

"Do you want me here?"

"Yeah, I think you and Cairo."

He called Cairo as they drove up the highway a few miles to check out Bailey's house. Bailey leased an avocado-colored stucco ranch house in an old subdivision. The house had a small lawn of dead Bermuda grass and a white concrete path to the front door that ran like a freeway through a desert. Neither Bailey's black Suburban nor any other vehicles were in the driveway, but Marquez knocked on the door anyway. He looked in through the living room window at brown shag carpet, a few pieces of furniture, a widescreen TV.

"We're going to hear from his lawyer next," Petersen said from the porch steps.

"That's right, and then he'll surface."

As they drove away from Bailey's they talked over how to make the surveillance of the girlfriend worthwhile. There was no way they'd get a warrant for Meghan Burris's phone records, but they had an application in on a cell phone number of Heinemann's they'd gotten from Bailey. If Burris called him they wouldn't get real-time notification, though he'd made that request as well, but would get a location, an area to work. He dropped Petersen in San Francisco.

Late in the afternoon, Marquez crossed the Golden Gate and drove home, talking on the phone with Keeler as he walked in, telling him about Heinemann's girlfriend and his plan with the team.

"I dropped the gun at DOJ," Keeler said, "and I've thought more about the FBI. We don't want to interfere with anything they have going on. I don't want you to go up the coast."

"We go up the coast all the time."

"Don't go near the *Emily Jane.* Is that clear enough?"

He hung up with Keeler and called Shauf and told her to stick in Fort Bragg. He wrote out the report he hadn't finished earlier, talked to Petersen again, took a run to clear his head, and at dusk showered, made a sandwich and drank a beer as he went over his notes of the last twenty-four hours. He put on music, an old Gram Parsons, then tried Maria's cell phone and left a message. She was probably out with her cousin, he thought. Katherine was due in late and had declined his offer to pick her up at the airport, said it was easier to take a cab, and it left him sad and then he tried not to think about it and went back over all his notes, worked the sequence of events on the calendar, again, because sometimes things fell together.

Near midnight, he went to bed and when he woke again it was to the front door opening and footsteps. He reached for his gun, but pulled his hand back as he heard a suitcase drop and the door shut and lock. He heard her footsteps in the hallway and felt both surprise and unexpected happiness.

"It's me," Katherine said, leaning over him.

"Bonfire."

"I missed you."

Her hair cascaded down around his face and he slid his fingers along the nape of her neck and then pulled her on top of him and kissed her. He took her in his arms and touched the ghost streak of white hair at her right temple, traced her spine with his fingers, then the curve of hip and ass and long thigh muscle, as Katherine's hands slid along his belly and over his chest and face. He took her shirt and bra off and felt the warm heat of her. Then she was smoothly against him and he was in her and for a little while there was nothing else in the night.

15

He woke before dawn and lay on his back, not moving yet, not wanting to wake Katherine. Her face pressed against his chest and he felt the slow rise and fall of her breathing, the quiet exhale. He smelled last night's sex, the shampoo she used in her hair, felt the warmth of her and was afraid if he moved he'd lose the feeling of having her here again. But when he closed his eyes his cell phone beeped somewhere on the floor near his head. It must have rung earlier and probably it was the ringing that woke him. He slid an arm slowly down alongside the bed, fingers grazing the floor, finding the phone as Katherine shifted.

Five minutes later he was making coffee and talking to dispatch. It was 5:10. There'd been a call to Fish and Game during the night, a message left that Marquez listened to as he poured coffee.

"Hey," a man's voice said, "I don't want to give my name or nothing, but I know who those guys killed up at Guyanno Creek were selling to. There's a whole bunch of guys in on that." He cleared his throat. "I'm not leaving my number, man, but you can reach me through this one." Marquez listened carefully to the numerals again, moved the pencil swiftly from one to the next comparing them to what he'd written down the first time he'd listened. The message concluded with, "Leave me a way to get ahold of the warden that was up there at Guyanno and I'll call him back."

Marquez clicked off, laid the phone and pencil down, the phrase "the warden that was up there at Guyanno" still chasing him. It was an easy thing to know. The place had been crawling with police and the story of what had happened had gone out from there. It was unusual to get a request for a particular warden, but you could explain that away with the murders.

He turned to Katherine's footsteps and then held her as she pressed against him. He ran his hand down her bare back, the smooth skin there, the curve of her rump.

"I need your help today," she said. "Do you think you can be there when I talk to Maria?"

"I don't know yet, but I'll try. When do you want to do it?"

"After school."

"All right, but I'll have to call you, Kath. Depends how today goes."

"This is the kind of thing, John." She tensed and pulled away from him, from his inability or unwillingness to say absolutely he'd be there, and when she turned it was as if suddenly she was self-conscious of her nakedness and no longer comfortable around him.

He watched her go down the hallway, heard the shower running a few minutes later. He called Petersen while Katherine showered and dressed. Nothing had happened during the night in Pillar Point and Petersen sounded tired, said she didn't feel well. It was too early to call the number from the tipster and he folded the paper and walked back to the shower to talk with Kath, try to explain what was going on with work and why he couldn't commit to the afternoon yet. They had coffee together. Katherine said she had to go get Maria to drive her to school, then would head into the city to Presto. He watched her car disappear, walked back into the house, made more calls, and read through a fax he'd gotten on Heinemann. At 7:30 he called Ruter.

"Has the FBI taken over the cases?" Marquez asked.

"It's a joint investigation. What's it to you?"

"They stepped in on one of our busts." Marquez had made the decision to try to talk to Ruter. He figured they could help each other. "They had an informant on the boat we're after and I get the feeling from talking to them that it ties to Guyanno Creek. Have you asked them about Eugene Kline?"

"Yes."

"And what did you get back?"

"Nothing, so far."

"Ask again."

"Thanks for the advice, Marquez, but I get enough already. I've got to go."

He had a conversation with Chief Keeler after hanging up with Ruter, Keeler telling him he was invited to lunch with Chief Baird and the director of Fish and Game, Jay Buehler, and he needed to be in Sacramento at 12:30 and not be late. He took a call from Petersen as soon as he hung up with the chief.

"Girlfriend is on the move," Petersen said, and her voice was lighter now. "She went to Starbucks and now she's at a laundromat. She could wash all her shirts in half a load, but we also made a stop at Rite Aid for quarters, soap, and face cream. I think we're spinning our wheels following her."

"Let's go a day with her."

"If she orders a hamburger for lunch should we take her down?"

"Yeah."

"Come on, John, that was funny."

"I've got more on Heinemann. He was busted on campus at San Diego State four years ago for peddling dope. He'd been masquerading as a student but wasn't enrolled. He got away with a suspended sentence and a fine, but that puts him in San Diego while Bailey was still living there, and I'm wondering if those two go back a little further than Meghan Burris thinks. No way is he really enrolled at UC Santa Cruz as she seems to think. Why don't you check that today?"

"Sure, it'll give us something to do while she's getting her astrology charts read."

Marquez crossed the bay. The paint on his black Nissan pickup had faded to gray in places and the seat cupped around his back in a way that was always a little too tight, but he liked its reliability and unassuming lines. It was old and didn't stand out. Park it in a beach lot and no one noticed it. He parked on Webster Street in Oakland, three blocks from Li's shop and threaded through the morning sidewalk crowd. Next door to Li's place was a large Asian market with a steady traffic of early shoppers this morning, but Li's shop was empty. Li sold herbs and various other incidentals, things he bought in bulk from liquidators, or odd items like disposable cameras past their expiration dates, a mix of stuff he gathered and then moved out again at a slight profit. As Marquez had guessed he would be, Li was in his shop. He could see him at the rear though the door was still locked.

Li wore a black silk shirt and the hospital sling for his collarbone had been replaced by a red scarf. Marquez watched him through the glass as he shuffled forward. He had to be hurting terribly inside, but they needed to talk today, and it was the conversation they'd had three years ago after the Santa Rosa trial that Marquez was relying on now. They'd sat at a booth in a chain restaurant and Li had painted, in fragmented sentences, images of the Vietnam War, telling how the Cong officer had executed his parents, how his family came from China originally and how the Vietnamese on either side didn't like Chinese immigrants. He'd been conscripted and escaped and described watching American fighter jets low and dark overhead, the screaming noise they made as they came in off the water. He knocked over a glass in the restaurant as he told of the bombing of Hue, the decayed pale blue plaster of his father's high-walled office falling, and American soldiers, one with a face and hair like yours, he'd said. He made it out with the boat people, married in a refugee camp and waited his turn to come to America.

Li stood a moment looking at him, then opened the door. He looked down at the worn wood floor of the shop, gesturing for Marquez to come in, waiting for him to pass by, letting Marquez lead the way to the rear office because he was a police official. Marquez knew that Li had given his sons American names to protect them. He remembered Li saying that, describing the birth of his older son, Joe, born an American in an American hospital, and how he was raising his sons American and the things he was buying. "I buy computer games, CD burner, stereo TV," as though these things were talismans that would protect the boys. They dressed like the American kids they were and spoke English with their friends, wore high-topped tennis shoes. He'd talked about them going to college and his own business expanding, and temporarily left the abalone problem in the courthouse. It had been Marquez's impression that it was through his sons that Li felt connected to this country and something of that had to be gone now.

They sat at the table, what served as his office behind the counter, the cash register at the very rear of the long rectangular space. The walls were high and old, white paint fading toward yellow, cigarette smell permeating the air.

"I can't tell you more," Li said. "I go to prison, okay. You arrest me, okay. I understand."

Marquez showed him the photos they'd had made of the two men who'd visited Li. "These are the men that came to see you." Li shook his head. "That came to your house."

"I don't know those men."

"We videotaped them and had these prints made. Have you sold them abalone?" Li shook his head but Marquez felt an energy building inside. He didn't want to violate Li's grief, but he had to know, had to sway Li over onto their side. There was no one else, no other real lead left. "These guys came to threaten you and now we're going to give it back to them. We're going to threaten them, but we have to know how to find them."

He watched Li's eyes, knew this was the moment he'd go one way or the other. "Phone only good one time only. They change all the time."

"Show me the number."

Li got a piece of paper from a drawer.

"Let's try it anyway," Marquez said. "If they answer, tell them you have five hundred abalone you hid in a friend's freezer and you need to sell before we find it. You can tell them we've been here several times and we're threatening you. You need the money. You'll sell cheaper, okay? These buyers will be suspicious, but they're here to get abalone and they may try to work out a way to do a deal. So we're going to give it a go. I'm going to punch in your phone number and we'll see if they call you back, okay? Can you do that?"

"They say they will kill my other son if I tell you."

His eyes were dark, shining with sadness, liquid, not understanding how he could be asked to risk that. He shook his head, made as though he was going to rise and leave the table.

"We won't let them kill Joe and we'll help with the move to Colorado."

Li had told him about the move, that it was all set and Marquez's idea was that Joe and Mrs. Li leave early, even if it was for an extended visit and he had to help Li make the rest of the arrangements himself. He wondered if Keeler would go through the roof, but he didn't see another way to keep it moving here. It was a route, a way to do it, and Li could plea-bargain out by cooperating. His gut turned asking Li to risk another son, but he was confident that if they got the boy and his mother out of town today they'd be safe. He started calling the number on the piece of paper, watching Li as he did.

Maybe you pay for all cruelty somewhere. It should be that way, but he didn't know what else to do with Li other than to force him to help.

It was hard enough to get a county DA to go after poachers when they had the whole ring. Spending money prosecuting abalone cases didn't get district attorneys re-elected. It was hardly a hot-button issue.

Tell most people that white abalone was the first ocean species humankind could genuinely claim bragging rights to extinguishing and they'd shrug. Big deal, extinctions happened. Talk about managing resources and they'd agree with you, as long as it didn't cut into their lifestyle too much. Where was abalone in the scheme of things? It wasn't an African elephant, an orca, or lion. Not much glamour in an abalone and there never would be.

A century ago, abalone had been so plentiful along the California shoreline that all you had to do was wade in a foot or two and pick them up. Shellmounds attested to how plentiful they'd once been. Their shells had become a source of jewelry and inlay. Japanese had set up factories and shipped huge quantities home for food. Diving came after the easy stuff was gone and we're down to the end game for a species that has survived for a million years.

Marquez looked at Li and knew he didn't have the right to offer this man—who'd raked through ab beds for a week—taxpayer money to help move out of the state. And he didn't have the right to promise Li he wouldn't be prosecuted.

When the pager beeped he punched in the number for Li's shop and hung up. Within a minute, or maybe no more than thirty seconds, the phone rang. Li picked it up and sweat started on his forehead. Marquez listened in on the conversation. The man talking on the other end was smooth, quiet, and very clear.

"If you've got more abalone to sell, then stay by your phone and I'll call you back in half an hour," he said, and hung up.

Now it was very quiet in the shop and Marquez couldn't get Li to talk and sat silent himself. He smelled ginger and an herb he couldn't identify. The front door opened, bells tingling, and one of the older women who'd been at the house when they'd presented the search warrant came toward the back. Li called to her, his voice tight with anxiety, the pitch rising, maybe warning her off in Vietnamese. There was a rapid exchange and then she was closer, standing at the half wall separating the office area from the shop, wagging a finger at Marquez before turning and leaving.

A half hour passed. Forty-five minutes and he felt Li's nervousness grow. Then the phone rang again. "Yes, hello," Li said, and almost immediately instructions were given. Li made rapid notes, his gnarled hand agile across a piece of paper. Marquez held the phone to Li's ear while he wrote with his good hand. "Tonight," the voice said. "11:00." Marquez heard it very clearly, then a slowly delivered warning. "If anything is wrong, if you're not there, if anyone is with you, if we see anything, then it'll happen just like we told you."

"Yes."

"So you want to be really sure, because we'll wait and we'll do what we said. If you're lying and they're telling you they'll protect you, they're wrong. What'll happen is we'll wait for your kid as long as it takes, and I bet you know about waiting. I think all you gooks are born knowing how to wait. Same thing, my man, and you got to understand the people who hired me, they leave it open. They're good for the money and they just want the job done eventually. You don't want that to happen."

"This abalone is stored at a friend's house."

"Okay, you be sure now. Don't let the Gamers suck you into this."

The line went dead. Marquez tried to talk it out with him and explained how they'd deliver more abalone to him this afternoon

in an ex Webvan truck. The lettering was still on the side; he'd recognize it. Shauf would handle the drop with Alvarez's help. They'd
help Li load his Toyota.

"We'll be there with you."

Now, he got Keeler on the line and talked over protecting the
family, getting the chief to agree they'd move Joe Li and his mother this afternoon, leaving out the Colorado part for the moment.
He called Shauf as they finished.

"I have to go to Sacramento to meet with Baird, Keeler, and
Buehler, so you'll need to handle the delivery here," he told her,
"and I'll call you on the way back. We're going to get a step closer
tonight. We're going to make it happen."

"How's Li taking it?"

"Not well, but he's tough." She was silent. "We need him."

When she still didn't say anything, he said he'd talk to her
later and hung up. He knew she didn't think this was right or
moral. But he didn't see any other way because they were losing.
They were running out of time.

16

When he left the afternoon sunlight on J Street and entered the cool conditioned air, Marquez found Chief Keeler and the director of Fish and Game, Jay Buehler, at the far end of a curving concrete bar. The place was new and hip, but conservative enough to draw the political shakers. They served cosmos and martinis and the bar had tall cabinets of cherry wood and expensive cognacs on high shelves in front of mirrored glass. Keeler, who avoided bars whenever he could, looked uncomfortable this afternoon. In the nine years Marquez had known him he'd never seen Keeler finish a drink, though he'd stand at a Christmas party with a rum toddy or glass of champagne in his left hand. The single time Marquez had asked, he'd replied "I had an alcoholic father," as if that was all the explanation anyone would ever need.

Jay Buehler was single at fifty-five, balding, graying, and known locally for late nights and young women. He was a lawyer first, a successful one, a charismatic rainmaker in a firm that had played and won in the political casino of California politics. Unlike his predecessor who'd worried constantly about the SOU making a politically embarrassing mistake, and who'd pored over reports with anal intensity, Buehler worried more about being left out of operations and missing out on the fun. He liked having a covert team, liked the excitement of busting bad guys for a good cause and had managed to get the SOU budget temporarily doubled to more than three million a year by regaling legislators with stories of car and boat chases, stings, and midnight apprehensions. The current budget was well below half that and Marquez's conversations with Buehler often included a schedule of house committee meetings where Buehler had wrangled appearances he wanted Marquez to make and plead the SOU case for more money. It was the legislature's habit to have the SOU's patrol lieutenant periodically testify to the efficacy and value of the covert unit.

The meetings had been shorter this year. The state was out of money and Marquez's team had been cut to five wardens and himself. Buehler had taken the cut as a personal insult, but it didn't seem to be on his mind today. He came off his stool and gripped Marquez's hand with vigor. "Thanks for coming up," he said, as though there'd been a choice. Marquez caught his own face in the bar mirror as they turned, saw a big man, middle years, harder eyes than he would have wished, a face shaped by wind and sun.

A waiter distributed menus while Marquez recounted the blown Sausalito bust, Buehler interrupting with questions about the leap from the *Emily Jane* and the swim to shore, Keeler listening closely, some intuition telling him something was missing in the account. Buehler stirred his drink with his finger, signaled the waiter, then looked back at Marquez from under heavy white eyebrows.

"What's the situation with this Jimmy Bailey?" Buehler asked.

"He burned us and we haven't caught up to him yet."

"We don't know where he is?"

"No."

"Well, his lawyer does, and the lawyer was in touch with the department this morning. He's threatening a lawsuit and claiming he'll go to the media. He wants Bailey's boat back and the rest of the money he says we owe him. He's got some balls on him. His story is Bailey ran to save himself from being shot and didn't think there would be any issue with that because he's on our side and working for us."

"Where did he go when he ran?"

"Oh, he wouldn't tell me. He had to talk to the director of Fish and Game, and then he was very coy." Buehler looked at Keeler from under his eyebrows. "As near as I can tell we have to give him back his boat."

"I pulled a gun off the *Condor* that DOJ is looking at, right now," Marquez said. "Maybe that'll buy us time or a way to hold him when he surfaces."

"That's what your chief told me, but you see the problem we've got if we hold his boat."

"Sure."

"We're going to cut a deal with this lawyer."

"You don't mean pay him?"

"Bailey was in our employ and we're not charging him with anything. We don't want the lawyer going to the media. No, of course, we don't need to roll over but we can't hold his boat indefinitely and maybe it makes sense to give it back. See where he takes us. We can stall but only so far."

Marquez thought it over, didn't say anything.

"Let's talk about why you're here," Buehler said, and Marquez knew the prelude was over. Despite the conditioned air he felt sweat prickle on his spine. He didn't want the FBI's heavy hand over him. Before they knew it they'd be getting three sets of papers stamped just so they could set up surveillance in a harbor. "We've had very direct inquiries from the FBI that we believe you should know about. They've asked for and we've provided the names of the members of the SOU."

"You're kidding, sir."

"I'm not. We also got asked for information through the DFG liaison to the California antiterrorism unit here in Sacto even though nothing in this has anything to do with terrorism." Marquez knew that by nightfall the FBI would have photos and be building a file on the team. He picked at the food, no longer hungry and very surprised the Feds had been given that information. No doubt the line was that they needed to know for the safety of Marquez's team, in case there was another overlap, but his gut said the truth lay somewhere else. He watched Buehler drink a full glass of water, diluting the scotch, and was glad it was Buehler, not him. Marquez didn't miss walking out into hot afternoon sunlight and needing to take a nap to metabolize alcohol. But he was roaming a different country of the mind now, in many ways a worse one, about Katherine. He focused on the table again. This FBI request only reaffirmed his certainty about Kline's presence. The waiter returned and they ordered coffees after the dishes were cleared, both Buehler and himself ordering double espressos, the chief ordering black coffee. "How old are you, Lieutenant?" Buehler asked.

"Forty-six."

"I'm ten years older than you and I was too young for it, but what I'm leading to are the similarities between this post 9/11 gear-up and the way the FBI responded to the Cold War communist threat in the fifties. They spent a lot of money and threw a lot of agents at the problem and our enemies just adapted. They're in the process of making the very same mistakes. Their real problem is their ability to get inside these organizations; it always has been. Now, I don't know what they've got going with this individual they say they're trying to apprehend, but I do know they hold the power right now. Trying to fight the Feds this year is like wading up a fast, cold river. We'd only get so far. They have their good years and their bad ones, and right now everything is running their way."

When no one said anything Buehler folded the credit card receipt and stood up. "Let's go, gentlemen." They stepped outside and Buehler clapped Marquez on the back, telling him not to worry about the FBI getting their names. "If we can't trust them, we've lost anyway." Marquez watched him get in a black Mercedes convertible and wave as he drove off. He turned to Keeler.

"You were quiet, Ed."

"I didn't want to do anything that would interfere with him hearing himself."

Marquez smiled. "What's your take on the Feds?"

"They do have something they're afraid you're going to interfere with and they plan to keep track of your whereabouts. If they had their way your team would be wearing mountain lion collars."

"They're protecting poachers."

"I won't argue with that, but don't start preaching at me. Buehler's correct, we're not going to fight them and win."

Twenty minutes later, Sacramento was a skyline behind Marquez and in his rearview mirror the windows of the taller buildings reflected orange and red in the late sun. He crossed the causeway and rode through Davis in a stream of cars running fifteen miles an hour over the speed limit and still jockeying with each other for better position. He called Katherine. Maria answered, giggling, her teenage voice carrying relief at having her mom home, setting aside her war with her for a few hours. She put Katherine on.

"I'm on my way in," he said.

"I'll handle it alone, John." Her voice got quieter. "Maria and I are going to dinner together."

"You're sure? I'm only an hour away. I've got something happening tonight, but not until later. Or tell me what restaurant and I'll come there."

Kath was silent, keeping her distance, still upset over this morning, then saying she had to get off the phone as though talking to a business acquaintance. A profound sadness welled up from deep in him after he'd hung up, and he drove without taking any calls, letting the phone ring through to voice mail until he was coming through the dry hills above Vallejo and could see the bay in the distance, a milky haze above it, the sky red behind. He thought about the fragility of the connection now with Katherine, how the smallest thing said could trigger all the anger and an immediate turning away. She'd flown home and driven to find him and he'd failed her the next morning.

He listened to his messages, gassed the truck, and got back on the freeway. He talked with Shauf, Petersen, and Alvarez, and when he got into Marin he was still on his cell phone, finalizing how they'd track Li tonight, using all the team, bringing Roberts back down from Bragg, and still it wasn't enough wardens if the other side was smart. He drove through Marin and checked for Katherine and Maria at the Indian restaurant that was one of Maria's favorites, but didn't see them and didn't know what he would have done if he had. He bought a burrito and coffee and ate as he crossed the bay again and hooked up with the team in Oakland.

Two lights were on in Li's house, both downstairs. At 10:20 the garage door opened and Marquez rang through to the hands-free setup they'd installed in Li's truck. Li took three or four rings to answer and his voice was nervous and high-pitched.

"They call already."

"We're right with you. Leave this phone open now like we talked about."

"Yes, I know."

Marquez brought the SOU up behind and ahead of Li now. They floated him in a bubble and he listened to Li answer the phone with his own heart thumping hard at the poacher's voice, the clipped instructions to Li, the racial condescension as the man asked Li, did he understand. Li went east on I-80 and exited into Emeryville, crossing under the freeway and running up the frontage road on the bay side and then making a U-turn as the frontage road passed the base of Berkeley. In the darkness away from any streetlight and out along the road to the Berkeley Marina he eased to the shoulder and parked. It could go down right here, Marquez knew, a car pulling up behind Li, a casual transfer of coolers. No big deal, a little business, nothing more than that and over in seconds.

"Can you believe that?" Petersen asked, her voice soft and quiet. "If the *Marlin* was in port the crew could walk up and be our backup."

Li wasn't a mile from where the *Marlin* regularly docked, but the boat was on patrol. Marquez called Hansen, let him know where they were, that they were waiting. He talked with Li again, reassuring him. Then Li's phone rang, sharp and hard and loud in the truck. New instructions came and Li got on the freeway eastbound again, took the 580 cutoff and headed north toward the Richmond/San Rafael Bridge before reversing himself at the toll plaza. The caller said get off in Point Richmond, then directed him to the tunnel and ran him out the empty road toward Brickyard Landing and the marina there.

Marquez remembered a rock quarry filled with water, a dirt road running through the low humped rockbound hills behind the marina. It was another way to approach Brickyard, but after thinking about it he discarded it, and drifted the SOU in, one, then a second car down the long open road past the shoreline park and around the curve. To the left was a condo project built into the low rounded hills, and to the right, the harbor and the dark water reflecting the marina lights. The first warden turned up toward the condos, would have to talk to the guard at the gate.

Li had parked near Brickyard Cove Marina, and Marquez drove the road now, was the only car to follow Li's truck and anyone watching was watching now. He brought Petersen in behind him as Li got out and walked into the marina parking and stood where they'd told him to wait, away from the boats at the lot perimeter and under the lights. Marquez scanned the shingled and wood-sided buildings surrounding the marina lot. The metal-roofed condos across the street were quiet, a few lights on, no one visible outside, glass faces staring across the water. He drove past and parked, nodded to Petersen as she joined him and slipped her hand into his, walking side by side with him, leaning into him as they ran their ploy.

They walked out slowly along the dock, Marquez wearing a billed cap, an old leather coat, Petersen's hand firm and strong holding his hand. They passed a line of houses with boats docked out front as Alvarez reported steadily through an earpiece Marquez wore.

"I really am going to miss you," Petersen said, making light of it, though he knew that was her shyness. She was tender and made her way in the world with joking and humor, even with those they'd just busted. It was the innate mark of her gentleness. "I'm so used to seeing that big old scarred head of yours."

"You make me sound like an old elephant."

"In a way you are."

"I'm going to miss you, too. I really am."

"Roberts will tell you how to run things."

"Bet on that."

"John, how come you never had any kids? I mean, you were alone so long before Katherine and Maria."

"I had girlfriends."

"Yeah, I was one of them. You know what I mean."

"I thought I told you once."

"I don't think so."

"There was someone who I thought I was going to be with forever and she got killed on a trip we made together to Africa. This was a long time ago and we were pretty young and stupid about where we camped. I got drafted at the tail end of Vietnam, but never shipped out, and when I got out Julie and I went to Africa. Do you see Li still?"

"Yes."

"We were going to travel for a year and were doing it on next to no money and camped near a game preserve in Kenya. I went into town for supplies one afternoon and came back and she was gone. When she didn't come back that night I got to the local police and their first reaction was she'd gone off with another man. I found her two days later by driving around with one of the locals and watching the buzzards. She'd been raped and shot, then dumped in the grass less than a mile from where we'd camped. The animals had already gotten to her and it was the hardest thing of my life. I had a real hard time accepting it. When you're young you think everything has got to work out the way it should."

"Who killed her?"

"They suspected elephant poachers, three men they held for a while and then released. I had their names and I went to find them later and planned to kill them. But I found I couldn't do it because there hadn't been enough proof it was them. Turn toward me, face me like you want to be close to me and tell me what you see on the silver-gray boat down at the end."

"At the very end of the dock?"

"Yeah."

"Nothing. No, wait, there is somebody moving around. You are good at this, you know that."

"Hug me like we're a couple."

"No, hug me, and tell me you'll come visit after the baby is born." He held her and thought he could feel Julie with them on the dock. "God, I'm sorry, John."

"Long time ago, now."

"He's out of the boat and heading down the dock." Marquez talked into his wire mike. Shauf was sitting partway up a flight of

wood steps at the condo complex and couldn't see any other players
and there was no confirmation yet the boat man was coming up to
meet Li. Alvarez waited near an old railroad siding at the curve.
Neither could see anything happening but could get there fast if it
went down. "He's watching us, John."

"We're looking at the ocean. Tell you what, let's sit down here
with our backs to him and look out at the water." They sat down
and a few minutes later Marquez turned his head as though he
was just talking to Petersen. "He's hiding in the shadows, hanging
out about halfway to Li," he said. "Looks like he's thinking it over
and may be talking to someone, could be waiting for somebody."

They waited and looked out on a bay that was flat and quiet,
the water a smooth charcoal color under the dock lights. He felt his
pulse in his fingertips. He willed the man hiding in the shadows to
approach Li.

"How long do you think he'll watch?" she asked.

"Until he's sure."

Marquez called Li now, told him to pull the mike slowly from
his ear after they'd finished talking. Told him to get out and look
around. Told him there was a man sitting in the shadows thirty
yards to his right. And Shauf reported Li getting out, Li standing
with his hands on his hips, Li moving out in front of his truck,
looking around, and then walking back and getting inside, starting
the engine, headlights coming on, and then the man was up and
moving toward Li. He came around to Li's window and there was
a conversation and Li's truck rolled slowly forward with the man
trailing, looking down at the dock again, checking the road behind
and the haze of lights at the condo complex. The coolers packed
with abalone the SOU had loaded in Li's truck began to move
down toward the man's boat. In the distance Marquez made out
the lights of the *Marlin* as it cleared Angel Island.

"Fifty-four feet of stainless catamaran coming fast," he said,
"subtle as a Doberman." They got slowly to their feet and he watched

Hansen slow the boat down and then he turned with Petersen as Alvarez and Shauf rolled into view. Li and the man had made their second trip down the dock each carrying one end of a cooler, seemingly oblivious to the people moving around them, and that didn't feel right. They came back up the steps to the rear of the Toyota and when Marquez raised his badge the man hesitated as though he might run. But there was nowhere to go and the team closed around him.

"Mark Heinemann," Marquez said, "it's good to see you. We've been looking all over for you. The bad news is you're under arrest."

17

Marquez paused, taking in Heinemann's now earnest face, the styled haircut he must pay real money for, razored lines at the neck, hair that wanted gel to complete the look, making him the best-looking diver along the coast as he dropped off the back of a rusted urchin bucket. They'd driven him to the Richmond Police Station, borrowed an interview box, got him a token Pepsi, and listed off the probable charges, including boat theft, all of which seemed to baffle Heinemann as though it had been someone else and not him, his frowning puzzled look saying this wasn't the movie he'd been cast for. There'd been some mistake, which he was willing to help get cleared up. The old Vietnamese guy at Brickyard Landing, well, he didn't even know him, in fact, had only offered to help him move the coolers because he happened to be on the dock and the Vietnamese guy had asked. Heinemann worked it so hard that Shauf couldn't hide a smile and covered her lips with her hand.

"The owner of the boat you stole is very unhappy and looks like the wrong guy to rip off," Marquez said. "He's big, looks mean, I'd be careful."

"I didn't steal his boat."

"You found it?"

"Look, warden, or whatever you are, man, they dropped me at Marina Bay. They told me what I was going to do tonight, okay. I do it or they mess up my girlfriend. That's the way it's been since Sausalito. I've been on a boat with a bunch of fucking Mexican divers, working off what they say I owe them."

"Who are they?"

"I got tricked into all this by Bailey. I'm not going to bullshit you and pretend I wasn't involved but I didn't know what was going on."

"Who are you working for?"

"I don't know. Like I said, it was all Bailey's thing."

"Where'd the *Emily Jane* dock?"

"Eureka. Then they moved me to another boat and said I owed them, if you can believe that. But I never owed anything. It was bullshit and I didn't tell that Vietnamese guy I was buying any abalone. He made that story up when you guys got there. Obviously, you were watching the dude already."

"They threatened your girlfriend so you cooperated with them."

"Yeah."

"Where are these Mexican divers from?"

"Baja."

"How many divers?"

"Four, and me."

"What's the name of the boat?"

"*El Gordo Burrito.*" Heinemann laughed, but it was more of a bark, and not really a big dog bark, more like a guy who was nervous and a little scared. Vain guy and not too bright was Marquez's take. "I don't know the name of the boat. If we weren't diving, we were below deck like some sort of sweatshop, man."

Marquez didn't know what to do with that. It was farfetched, but could be true from the way he was talking. It was too off-the-wall to make up and would explain Heinemann disappearing.

"Was Bailey ever on that boat?"

"Fuck if I know."

Back to attitude. Other than this story about a dive boat and threatening his girlfriend, he'd given them little since they'd hand-cuffed him in Point Richmond. He'd sung a David Bowie song as they'd driven him here, and then listened to the charges, including abetting in the assault of a peace officer, as though he was listening to a waiter recite a menu. And he hadn't asked for a lawyer yet, which might mean he wanted to try to deal his way out.

"They'll kill my girlfriend if I started telling you a bunch of shit I don't know about anyway," Heinemann said. He took a drink of Pepsi and the brown soda dribbled down his chin before he could wipe it with his elbow.

He's not lying about being afraid of whoever he was diving for, Marquez thought, then asked, "Are you in college?"

"What?"

"Are you enrolled at UC Santa Cruz?"

"No, well, I mean, I plan to."

"Your girlfriend thinks you're going to school there. You lie to her, why wouldn't you lie to us?"

"She knows, man. Meghan knows what's up."

"She lied to us?"

"I'm not saying she lied."

"Someone lied."

"What's the big deal about a fucking college?"

"The big deal is you keep coming up in the middle of these lies. You want us to believe you, but you don't come across very believable. Tonight, you're caught with a stolen boat buying illegal abalone and what you did in Sausalito could bring felony charges. You're in a bad way, Mark. This story about working on a slave diving ship—why did you owe them for Sausalito if you held up your end? You picked up the abalone and transferred most of it to the *Emily Jane.* You got Bailey to use his boat."

"Bullshit, I got Jimmy to do anything."

"We're getting this from Bailey. He's going to testify against you. He's pissed off you burned him."

"Fuck him, he's not pinning any shit on me. I've done one thing here, man. I dove for money. I needed the bucks to repair my boat and I'll tell a judge that."

"That's not the way Bailey tells it. You want to read the transcript?" There wasn't any transcript, nothing to show him, but Heinemann's hesitation said he may not have been in contact with Bailey. "We might have a copy with us." Marquez looked at Shauf, said, "Mine's gone to the DA, what about yours?" She shook her head. "Okay, I guess we don't tonight, but I'll get you a copy. I don't have a problem with you reading it; I'll drop it by your cell, if you want."

"It was Bailey that got me into this. He offered me five bills for the Point Reyes dive and helping move it in Sausalito. But that was all and you already know what happened. You ask Meghan if she's seen me since. I've been like a captive on a slave ship, man, and then they brought me out for this bullshit tonight."

"Another problem I have," Marquez said, "is that you and Jimmy go back a ways. What I'm hearing is you two were working together in San Diego a lot of years ago, so it makes it hard to believe he sucked you into this."

"I was never in San Diego."

Marquez reached out and shut off the recorder. "I'm going to let you take that back," he said. "But you've only got about three seconds to decide."

"I got out of all that. I put that behind me and Meghan will tell you I've been thinking about going back to school. I don't deal drugs anymore. That was a bad phase of life."

"You berth three down from Jimmy at Pillar Point and you want to tell us that's coincidence."

"I thought we were talking about ab diving. I'm getting fucking confused."

"We're talking about all of it."

"I don't deal drugs anymore. If you think I'm in with Jimmy on that, you're wrong."

"Convince me about you. I want to believe we're not wasting our time talking to you but so far it seems like we are. It's getting late and you keep repeating the same story but you don't explain away the inconsistencies, so it's looking like you're blowing smoke at us."

"I'm just telling the truth, man."

"About a diving slave ship? Come on, Mark, give us a break."

"I'm not shitting you."

"We found your girlfriend's pickup at Marina Bay here in Richmond, but you say you were dropped off by boat. Do you want to say Jimmy drove it up here? Maybe Meghan gave him the keys and we should arrest her? That what you're saying?" He stared at Heinemann. "No answer? Okay, maybe we ought to bag it and get some sleep, let you get in there and meet your cellmates." Marquez glanced down at a sheet. "Twenty years in prison. That's what I get when I add up what you're charged with. You're way past abalone but you don't seem to get that we can make it swing one way or the other."

"Man, you keep changing subjects. I can't fucking keep up."

"Okay, tell us about the *Emily Jane,* and this is your last chance."

"I just ran for the boat. Your warden had her fucking knee on my back when they pulled guns on you."

"Tell us about the men on the *Emily Jane.*"

"I don't know about them. They never let me in the cabin and they dumped me on a dock in Eureka and then I got on the other boat."

Earlier, Heinemann said he'd run to the *Emily Jane* because that's what Bailey had said to do if anything went wrong. Marquez looked over at Shauf. "I'm going to find a bathroom," he said. "When I get back we'll wrap this up." He paused before going out the door, looked at Heinemann. "Tomorrow isn't the same for us, I want you to understand that. Tomorrow, every day after that you can talk to your lawyer instead of us."

"Whatever."

"Whatever?"

"Hey, man, Fish and Game is a fucking joke. You think I'm risking something happening to Meghan or me?"

Marquez threw cold water on his face in the bathroom and ignored the sidelong look of a Richmond cop. He walked back in as Heinemann was telling Shauf how easy it was to poach and not get caught. He was in his head swimming underwater somewhere with a light stick when Marquez cut him off.

"Why'd Bailey run?" Marquez interrupted.

"You tell me."

"Is Meghan Burris in on this too?"

Heinemann avoided the question. "Everything that happened to me I got forced to do."

"How many times are you going to tell us that?"

"As long as you keep asking the same questions."

"Who's buying the abalone?"

"Ask Jimmy since you said he's talking to you."

"He's talking to them, also. He's convincing them it was you that fucked up. Maybe when you were on that boat with the Mexicans you were wondering, what's going on, why am I not hearing from my friend, Jimmy? Should be hearing from Jimmy, right? Isn't he the guy to get you off that boat? You're not hearing from him because he put it all on you. Who'd they get Meghan's name from if it wasn't Jimmy?" Heinemann rubbed the back of his neck like a mosquito had bit him and Marquez knew they had an opening. Heinemann really was worried about his girlfriend. He studied Heinemann's face, thinking about how he could bring the image home. "The divers who got killed up north were selling to the same people you and Jimmy have gotten involved with and you're right to be scared of them. I was up there at Guyanno Creek; I saw those two. Do you know how they died?"

When Heinemann didn't answer, Marquez asked the question again.

"Stabbed," Heinemann said.

"Stand up. I want to show you what happened to them."

"I don't need the bullshit."

"It'll stay with you better if I show you."

"You hit me, I'll sue your ass."

"Nothing like that is going to happen."

Heinemann was visibly uncomfortable and squared his thick shoulders, showed a stance that said I can take care of myself and Marquez pressed two fingers low against Heinemann's abdomen, just under his belt, enough to make him nervous, enough to make him feel sexual vulnerability and Heinemann's eyes went to Shauf.

"Fuck man, what are you doing?"

"With the divers up north, these guys that got chained to a tree and killed, the knife cut was just above the pubic bone. He'll push the knife in and not too deep, at first. I've heard that arouses him, but I don't know if that's true, or not. Only you and he will know that, because he'll be pressed up against you. Good chance he'll be talking to you, maybe asking you questions, telling you it can be okay still, that everything can work out if you've got the right answers. But then, after you've told him what he wants to know, he'll push the blade in further. Not enough to kill you yet. We used to hear terrible stories about him making promises not to kill as long as you don't scream. If you can take the pain and not cry out, he's going to stop. Just don't say anything. Just listen to him. Your blood will run down into your crotch and your scrotum will shrink back as your gut burns. You'll watch his eyes change as he breathes into your face and you'll know he's not going to let you go."

Marquez brought his fingers up Heinemann's abdomen. He pushed Heinemann back against the wall with his fingers up under his breast bone. "The blade will rip up through your gut. Those divers up at Guyanno are no different than you. They messed up and he made an example out of them and when he's done here, if we don't get him first, he'll wipe all his tracks and move on. That's how he's managed to survive and stay ahead of the FBI. And they're not trying to bring him in, either. They're way past that. They want to corner him and bring enough firepower to make sure it's over." Marquez dropped his arms to his side and stepped back. "Your best chance is to help us. I'm not kidding you, I know this man."

"Then what do you need me for, if you know him?" Heinemann smiled like it was nothing. "Hey, I haven't seen any freaks and I'm not really involved in all this shit."

"He's tall, fairly thin, but not in a way that would make you think he's weak."

"Never seen him."

"The day the man came down to Bailey's boat there was another man up in a car Bailey said you went up and talked to."

"He went up."

"He said the man wanted to get a look at you and that makes sense to me." Marquez let a minute pass with only the hiss of the recorder, then dropped it on him. "Bailey works for us as a paid informant. We gave him two grand for this ride."

"Bullshit."

"He was," Shauf said, and slid over a report with Bailey mentioned as a paid informant. It was dated over a month ago, Bailey's name highlighted, Keeler's signature, DFG stationery. They waited as he read, studied, and stared. Then, he changed, and Marquez saw it happen, saw his face pale, saw the difference.

"We're going to leave you alone for five minutes and you think it over," Marquez said. "Do you want more proof Bailey works for us?"

Heinemann shook his head, and they only made it as far as the door. "Yeah, I want to make a deal," he said. "And, yeah, I met him and you're right about the guy. He's fucking weird."

"I'm going to show you a photo," Marquez said. "I've got a file." He heard his own voice as strangely calm. "But I've got to get it out of my truck."

He walked out to get it and his footsteps echoed in the corridor. The cool air of the night brushed his face and he crossed through the pooled light on the asphalt and heard the voices of the dead as he reached for the file, the promises he'd made.

18

Marquez opened the file, and the photos of Federales and cartel operatives had an almost quaint aspect, faces yellowed and cracked, haircuts dated. Half of those pictured were dead. Heinemann shook his head and Marquez flipped a page, smelling stone dust from under his house on the paper. He was still trying to get a better read on Heinemann, trying to get a sense of what made him roll over—or whether he really had—or was this another game. It was his experience that the vain often had a hard time seeing things for what they were.

He flipped another page and the face of Kline was there, features blurred, but the long head and heavy bones clear enough for Heinemann. Taken in Mexico City eleven years ago. He'd paid three hundred dollars for it and had tried to get the FBI to validate the photo, tell him it was Kline, but they'd turned him away. The photographer had been an expatriate American who'd refused to take pesos and Marquez remembered his argument with him regarding the grainy, fuzzy quality of the photo. Heinemann said nothing, and Marquez only paused long enough for him to get a quick view of each image. It didn't take long to go through the file. He thought Heinemann had hesitated, yet he hadn't said anything, had let him keep turning pages.

He prompted him now. "Did you get anything?"

"I don't know, maybe."

"Nothing jumped out at you?"

"Jumped?" As if the word was odd, frustration at being trapped, probably. "No, nothing jumped."

"Okay."

Marquez shut the file and without asking, Heinemann reached for it and he let him take it. Heinemann flipped the first page, asking, "What about computer enhancement?"

"What about it?"

"Couldn't these faces be aged up to today?"

"You'd know him, you'd remember him."

Heinemann flipped through again, Marquez watching, his senses keyed in. The file was a jacket with photos, all the paperwork removed, and now Heinemann's eyes lingered on the Mexico City photo. Flipped to the next page, then flipped back and touched the photo with his index finger.

"If anyone, maybe this guy," and Marquez felt his throat tighten and a floating lightness in his head. "It was dark. We were in the backseat of a car."

"Where?"

"In the harbor last month like you heard."

"Pillar Point?"

"Yeah."

They were ready and Shauf slid a Day-Timer across. "When?" Marquez asked.

"You mean the exact date?"

"Yeah."

"I don't know if I can remember the exact date."

"Your girlfriend says you're good at math. She says you could be a professor if you wanted." If you weren't moving dope and raping the ocean, if the day was a little longer or you taught night classes. "We need dates," Marquez said quietly, and could tell Heinemann was wheeling through the possibilities, was in a room with two game wardens and trying to figure out how to get out of here without getting charged, trying to figure out where to stop talking and start dealing. He was trying to calculate what exact dates were worth and what he gave up by pinning it down, what the risk was. He was most worried about Roberts, about getting charged with assaulting a peace officer, because he'd made an earlier comment that the longest prison sentence ever given for poaching abalone was three years. He wasn't worried about abalone poaching. He wasn't intimidated by anything they'd threatened regarding abalone.

Marquez watched him study the Mexico City photo and felt his pulse pounding in his ears, saw a red haze around the light in the room and was back with Ramon and a good friend, another DEA agent named Brian Hidalgo. Brian stood in the room now next to Shauf, pointing a finger at Heinemann and rubbing his own scalp making fun of Heinemann's haircut, then turning back to smile at him and asking, "Remember that plane going down?" They'd watched a drug smuggler's plane shot down and a ball of orange light rising from the desert plateau become a column of black smoke and spread in the cold wind until it was gone. Marquez shook it off, Hidalgo vanishing. Heinemann played with the calendar pages, stalling for time and Marquez caught Shauf's eye. Heinemann knew the answer and she gave the faintest nod of agreement.

"It was around the end of August," Heinemann said. "Yeah, pretty sure it was like Saturday the thirty-first, but it's not like anything happened that night."

"Saturday the thirty-first, what time?"

"Almost dark, sort of twilight. This guy in the photo might be a guy I met up in a car up in the parking lot." Heinemann leaned back and folded his arms. "So you really want this dude?"

"You would have noticed something else."

"About him?"

"A physical characteristic."

"It's not like I was paying that kind of attention."

"We're nowhere without it."

"I just picked him out of those shitty photos."

"That's not good enough." Marquez caught Shauf's confused look. He needed more proof, needed to be absolutely sure. Heinemann could be feeding them this date and the car story by pre-arrangement. He could have worked it out with Bailey and Meghan Burris. "You went up to this car and what got said."

"He told me what would happen if I messed up, like if I talked to anyone like right now. But it was weird, because it was Jimmy's deal."

"No, it was yours, that's why he wanted to see you. Bailey was just the hired ride."

Heinemann shook his head. His voice got quieter. "It was all Jimmy's."

"We've been paying Bailey and you keep saying he's the guy behind it all. If that's true we want you on our side of the table, but you'd have to have proof."

"I could get him to talk."

"That might work." Marquez gauged him. "You'd have to testify, too."

"I know."

"If what we're doing here, right now, proves out, then we'll want to talk about the next step, but listen, we're going to step outside again."

Marquez walked out behind Shauf. He faced her in the hallway and realized his hands were shaking.

"He's picked out Kline," he said.

"I get that, so why mess with him?"

"We need it to come from him, not just pointing at my photos. I want him to dig a little deeper because he'll be more committed to us if he does."

When they walked back in Marquez started slowly. "Think of it like this, we're telling you to wade into the ocean and just keep swimming out to sea. I want to see you swim out far enough to where I know you need us. You want a deal that keeps you out of prison and I want a confession in return. Dates. Times. Methods of transferring abalone. I want you to identify this man in a way that makes me certain. It's like a password for me."

"I don't know if I can."

"You're blocked on it, so we'll come back to it." Marquez reached and touched August thirty-first on the Day-Timer. "Let's back up. Start at the beginning, again."

He didn't say anything for a long time and then started. Bailey had gotten him involved by saying it was a one-time diving deal for the two of them. Two other divers that Bailey knew had already gathered the abalone and it was up in the cove near Elephant Rock. All they needed to do was pick it up.

"Who were these other divers?"

"Jimmy was the one in contact with them. We were working off GPS coordinates when we got up there."

"Up to Elephant Rock?"

"Yeah."

"You were reading the coordinates?"

"Yeah, I'm pretty good with GPS."

"Who were they?"

"The divers?" Marquez nodded, could feel this was the moment and exhaled slowly. Now he didn't want to put any pressure at all on Heinemann. Let Heinemann make his own decision. Let him come to us now, let him put it together his own way. Let him see we're sanctuary. We're your only hope, Marquez thought.

"It may have been those divers at Guyanno Creek," Heinemann said.

"That's convenient," Shauf said, and shoved her chair back. "A couple of dead divers."

But Marquez knew now. He got it. Shauf stood up like it was over, Heinemann trying to sell them Stocker and Han because they were dead and couldn't be questioned. Marquez calculated time now, Bailey's call and the urgency of it. He knew it could be, but shook his head. "We have a problem with that," he said.

"Well, fuck it, then. You guys don't believe anything."

"They're dead so we can't question them and it doesn't hang because they had their own operation going."

"Whatever." Heinemann shook his head like he was disgusted.

"Two dead divers," Marquez said after a quiet thirty seconds. "Two guys who've already got a pile of five hundred shucked abalone."

"Yeah, and they were going to shuck the ones we picked up, but they got wasted first. That's why Jimmy got the call. That's how it all happened. Jimmy knew one of the divers. The guy's name was Orion."

Marquez nodded. They were partway there. Heinemann hadn't gotten the name Orion from the newspaper articles.

"When they got killed you're saying Jimmy got a phone call to go pick up some abalone."

"Something like that."

"How would anyone have known where to find the abalone? Stocker and Han picked it, right? They left it on the bottom of the ocean. So who knew where to find it?"

"GPS," Heinemann said.

"You had coordinates?"

"We made a few trips like that. Like I said, I'm good with GPS."

"How many trips? Write down where you dove." Marquez handed him a notepad, watched him write, saw he was writing actual coordinates. He picked up the word Albion, saw Salt Point and couldn't read the other two yet. He had Heinemann say aloud where they'd dove. Shauf had left the room; now she came back in and they formalized the written confession. Four trips out with Bailey and transfers like Sausalito. This gave them probable cause on Bailey and Shauf went to work on the warrant. They'd bypass the DA's office in San Mateo County and go directly to Judge Maynard. Maynard was sympathetic to what they were trying to do and had once told Marquez that he was cleared to fax a warrant request anytime.

Marquez continued with Heinemann. They went back to August thirty-first, what had happened that day, and Heinemann's tone changed as he recounted how it had gone.

A man had come down to Bailey's boat just before dusk. There was no one else around and he'd seen him come down the ramp. He got on the boat and he obviously knew Bailey, put a hand on Bailey's back. Meghan had gone for more potato chips and they were drinking beer with him when she came back. The dude's name was Carlo.

Marquez copied a description, asked questions they could turn into an artist's rendering, told Heinemann he'd have to agree to sit with an artist, but knew already it was the Hispanic in the Oakland video. They'd get a photo made from the video, get a package of photos together for Heinemann to pick this Carlo out. In his mind's eye he saw the man getting on board, saying hello to Bailey, his fingers coming to rest lightly low on Bailey's back, fingertips brushing Bailey's spine, palm flat on the muscle as he told Heinemann since he was new to this he was going to get to meet the boss.

"So Bailey already knew this man?"

"Yeah."

"Did he ever say where he'd met him?"

"Not really."

"San Diego?"

"Man, how come you've got to tie everything together like this?"

"This Carlo led you to the car where the other man was?"

"Yeah, I was alone in there with him in the backseat and he told me not to look at him."

"So you did anyway." Heinemann smiled, obviously proud of how smart he was. Marquez knew he'd taken a good look at the man in the car. "Think about his face."

"His neck," Heinemann said.

"What about it?"

"A scar like this thin red line across his neck, like he'd been cut."

"Okay, you got it."

"You can barely see it."

"You saw it."

"That's the guy?"

Marquez nodded.

"I haven't seen him since," Heinemann said.

"Not after Sausalito?"

"I've seen nothing but these Mexicans. We've been diving at night with light sticks and these guys don't even speak English."

"What was the name of the boat?"

"*Coronado.*"

"And you got on in Eureka?"

"It was really Crescent City."

He explained how he'd been moved to another boat when the *Emily Jane* docked in Crescent City. He'd been told there was a full-blown manhunt underway and his only safe route was to get on this other boat. He'd had the feeling they were going to pull guns if he refused, so he'd gone along.

They questioned Heinemann another hour and then returned to how he would contact them when they released him, how the logistics would work tomorrow. They decided he'd call Bailey first and worked out the deal Marquez would present to the DA tomorrow.

"As long as I don't have to get on a boat with them, I'm cool with it," Heinemann said. "I'll do what you want as long as I get to go home, man."

"You've got to dance the dance and we'll dummy some charges and put that out to the press, theft of the boat, abalone poaching, but we won't leave you alone with them."

"How do I know you won't make the charges real if things get fucked up?"

"You've got our word."

"I want something in writing."

"Nothing goes in writing until we see how you move out there. We'll set up your release for tomorrow afternoon and we'll have your girlfriend's pickup wired and ready."

After Heinemann was taken to a cell, Marquez walked out with Shauf. The warrant request had been faxed off, but they wouldn't hear from Judge Maynard until early morning. The night had changed several things. They had a positive ID on Kline. They had Heinemann moving to where he'd testify against Bailey and they had a tie to the Guyanno divers. He felt like they were close to catching a real break.

Marquez drove home feeling better about their chances than he had in a month. He slept soundly for once and woke with a clear head.

At dawn the sky was scalloped with high clouds that burned and twisted in the winds aloft. He threw out an opened beer that he'd never taken a sip of last night and flipped through the mail, checked for messages from Katherine or Maria, then made coffee and sat outside with the newspapers before getting in his truck.

When he drove down the mountain he was thinking of Heine-mann's story of imported Mexican divers. They'd heard whispers of something similar last year. Mercenary divers. Travelers. The scarcity was driving prices up. Market poachers were becoming more sophisticated and exploitative. One study he'd read predicted

that one-third of all animal life would vanish from earth in the
next fifty years as habitat succumbed to the encroaching demands
of a swelling humanity.

Alvarez called as Marquez passed the new houses on the south-
east flank of the mountain, saying Bailey's black Suburban was in
his driveway and a porch light burning.

"Then we can knock on the door."

"How far out are you?"

"An hour, but the traffic isn't bad."

"It's always the opposite of the economy. It's going to get
lighter and lighter."

"I'll carry that happy thought. See you down there."

Alvarez was the finder on this search, the designated locator of
all evidence. Anyone else who found anything would point to it
and wait for Alvarez. He'd also do the initial videotape, prior to the
search. That way, only one warden would be required in court later.
Alvarez had picked up the Turbo Twin and had it in his truck. If
Bailey didn't answer the door and Marquez felt they needed to they'd
take out the lock with the Turbo, which would be Marquez's job
because of his size. He thought over what they knew about Bailey
on the ride down, what they'd gotten back from NCIC on the drug
charges Bailey did a year of state time for in '94.

When he got there Marquez parked at the mouth of the driveway, blocking the Suburban's exit. They took positions on either
side of the front door and Marquez knocked hard. Ten seconds later
he knocked again. When he'd been DEA they'd never let it go this
far because with drugs, evidence could be flushing down a toilet in
the seconds that were going by, and that was on his mind now,
thinking that if they could catch Bailey with drugs, anything, that
was a way to hold him in jail. But he'd also decided on the way
down that Bailey was capable of more than he'd ever thought and
he could be going for a gun. He waited half as long and then
knocked again and picked up the Turbo, counted to a slow five

and grinned at nothing as he swung it into the lock. He heard part of the lock bounce off the wall on the other side of the room and the door slapped against the wall.

"State game officers, we're coming in." He saw Bailey coming down the hallway, hair wet from the shower, a towel wrapped around him. "We've got a warrant to search your house, Jimmy."

"You wrecked my door, motherfucker. I was in the shower, I would have opened it."

"Maybe you're taking too long of a shower."

"Fuck you."

"Someone is going to go with you while you put some clothes on, then we're going to ask you to wait out here in the living room."

Bailey let his towel drop and looked at Roberts and Shauf.

"One of you ladies want to come with me? My clothes are in the bathroom."

19

They started in the kitchen and there was almost nothing in the cabinets, a few liquor bottles, soy sauce, a lot of empty shelf space, three Coors cans in the refrigerator, milk, soft drinks, moldy cheese, a package of English muffins, and then something that caught Marquez's eye, three Dannon yogurts. Bailey wasn't a yogurt eater. He'd been there for a couple of Bailey's breakfasts, pre-packaged Danish, or donuts from the convenience store, a couple of cigarettes and coffee. In the freezer was a bag of ice, two frozen TV dinners, a salmon tail, and two abalone steaks wrapped in white butcher paper. The pale meat had been in there long enough to have ice crystals. In this context it didn't mean anything and he rewrapped it and put it back in the freezer.

"Anything, Lieutenant?" Cairo asked, and Marquez glanced over him.

"A little bit of abalone, but it's old."

Bailey wanted to call his lawyer, kept asking to every minute, or so. It was Marquez's habit not to let suspects make any calls until after the team had completed a search. There was always a chance they'd make a call and tip someone else off before key evidence was found.

Cairo was in the living room, emptying out a TV cabinet filled primarily with old magazines. Bailey sat on the couch near him making his request every few minutes, Cairo in flip-flops and shorts, but wearing a tactical jacket. He looked like an armed junkie rooting through Bailey's stuff.

Marquez thumbed the liquor bottles. Gin, vodka, cheap scotch, Jim Beam. Bailey had flipped the lawyer's card at Marquez. Alberto Cruz, a name that was vaguely familiar, though he didn't read anything into it. He wished he could confront Bailey this morning with Heinemann's confession, but it would have to wait. He let the liquor cabinet door fall shut and Cairo came slowly over. The house smelled like dust and cat piss. The carpet was probably original.

"He occupies this place, but he doesn't live here," Cairo said. "This isn't a home."

He turned to Shauf's footsteps. "One of the bedrooms is locked," she said. "We need him to open it unless we're going to use the Turbo again."

"Jimmy, there's a locked bedroom. Have you got a key for it?"

Bailey didn't answer and Shauf went down the hall to the bathroom. Marquez walked down, tried the bedroom and then leaned in the bathroom where Shauf had lifted the tank lid off the toilet, looking for drugs.

"There's yogurt in the refrigerator," Marquez said. "Yogurt isn't his style, but we haven't seen anybody else staying here."

"Back home we'd run him in for yogurt." She was Texan. "But out here I think it's legal." She clicked open the door of the shower and he smelled the draft of mildew. She reached for a shampoo bottle. "Look at this. Did you know he washes his hair?" She picked up a blue disposable razor, turned it in her hand and asked, "What do you think?"

He opened the medicine cabinet. Aspirin, Advil, Band-Aids, strictly ordinary stuff until he emptied the rest of the medicine cabinet and found two prescription labels that were for people named Crawford and Ulrich. When he set these aside the cabinet was empty. The mirrored door swung loosely, too loosely, and he looked at the screws holding the cabinet to the studs, but they were secure and rust had bled from one.

He walked to the end of the hall now, opened the garage door and stepped into the cold darkness, fumbled for the switch, found it, and clicked on a four-foot fluorescent hanging from rusted chains. He hit the button for the garage door opener and it banged into the front of Bailey's Suburban after rising three or four feet. It slapped against the bumper, came back down, and he hit the button again, heard Bailey's muffled yelling from the living room where he must have seen the door hitting his car.

"You fucking Nazis."

A disassembled car motor sat on yellowed newspapers in one corner of the garage, looking like it had for years. He saw dive equipment and moved toward it, knelt to examine the scuba gear. A yellow wetsuit, flippers, a mask, gloves, booties, and scuba tanks. They lacked the dust of everything else in here. He picked up an underwater dive light and tested it, shining the light on the back wall where an old workbench, stained with oil and with an iron vise mounted on one end, stood on wooden 2 x 4's. Above it were shelves, paint cans, jars of screws, relics of the landlord he guessed. A few suitcases were stacked in a corner. He looked at the rafters, the weak light, and walked back out to the living room. He needed better light.

"Jimmy, I need you to back your truck up. Do you mind doing that or do you want me to?"

They let him back the truck up, then Marquez asked him to come into the garage and over to the dive equipment. He picked up a wetsuit and turned to face Bailey.

"How's that eardrum of yours, Jimmy?" Bailey claimed he couldn't dive anymore because of a blown eardrum. "This is yours?"

Bailey shook his head.

"You're storing it for somebody?"

"I sold it to a guy. I'm letting him store it here with his motor."

"What's his name?"

"Shit, I don't remember."

"You've grown some balls, Jimmy. You don't even seem like the same guy."

"You seem like the same asshole, dude."

Overhead in the gap between ceiling joist and roof rafters were pieces of lumber, mostly long pieces of trim, warped and checked and dried too long. There were pieces of copper pipe, heating duct, and angle iron. He scanned the workbench, then pulled the plywood away from the wall to see what was behind it, and now was looking at unfolded white waxed boxes with a Mexican label for abalone. He counted, turned to Bailey.

"Forty. When did you go into the shipping business?"

"Excuse me? My lawyer says you're going to pay for every lost day while I don't have my boat."

"You tell him next time you talk to him that all his hard work has paid off. You're getting your boat back and he ought to send you a bill. We're going to have to open that bedroom door now. Do you want to do it for us or do you want to ask whoever is in there to open it?"

Marquez could see he'd guessed correctly, though Bailey didn't say anything until they'd walked down the hallway and Bailey had leaned against the door. Then he spoke quietly, "Hey, it's me," he said, "you gotta open up." He turned back to Marquez. "She must have split."

"I'll go around," Cairo said. Bailey didn't know it, but they'd had the perimeter covered since getting here. That was another old habit carried from his DEA time. No one had gone out the window, but a few minutes later they heard Cairo's feet land on the bedroom floor. He opened the door and a shade sucked tight against the window as the draft blew in. "The window was wide open," Cairo said.

Marquez turned. "Who was in here, Jimmy?"

Bailey was too quick to answer.

"A chick I met last night. She freaked when you started knocking and I told her just to stay in here."

"Where's her car?"

"She rode with me."

"She walking down the street, right now?"

"I guess."

"You guess?"

"She's got her phone. She might have called a ride."

"What's her name?"

"Karen."

"Karen what?"

"Fuck if I know."

Marquez studied the rest of the room. A mattress lay on the floor. A couple of blankets and a sheet were rumpled near the bottom. A beanbag ashtray with butts and a couple of roach ends sat just off the bed and the room smelled like cigarette smoke and sex. Marquez moved toward the bed and stripped the blankets, first one then the other with Bailey watching.

"This is like maid service, Jimmy. We're making it easy for you to wash your sheets. Think of it as an opportunity." Bailey didn't respond. He pulled the bottom sheet and checked the seams, then lifted it and looked underneath, frightened the spiders but didn't see anything. Meanwhile, Cairo went through the closet, pulling clothes out, checking the pockets of the pants and shirts.

"How long have you been out of the house, Jimmy?"

"We're filing suit today to get my boat back."

"Seventeen thousand lawsuits a year in California and hardly any of them go anywhere. Seems like everyone is suing us this week."

"You're going to get your ass kicked."

"Are we?" Marquez paused, looking in the faded blue eyes. "Wouldn't be the first time."

Bailey moved into the hallway, muttering, slamming the wall with a fist, a move Marquez interpreted as a signal. Alvarez followed Bailey outside. Cairo picked up the beanbag ashtray, said he was going to take it in the kitchen and look through it more carefully. Marquez held a finger up, meaning don't say anything, mouthed "follow my lead."

"We're done in this room," Marquez said. "But I want to take another look at the kitchen. Let's go top to bottom on the kitchen again."

"You got it."

Marquez pointed at the door, signaled that Cairo should leave and shut the door behind him, which he now did. Then it was quiet in the room and Marquez waited, heard a faint scraping, a foot, knee, elbow, something moving to a more comfortable position. He'd seen a tiny piece of insulation on the closet carpet, but no ladder or anything to climb on, so it must have been done while they were knocking on the front door. He looked around for something to stand on. There was a dresser but it looked heavy to move, so he quietly opened the door again, walked out to the kitchen and got the broom he'd seen earlier.

Cairo came back with him. Marquez stood in the closet and with the broom handle reached overhead, lifted the access hatch, and slid it to the side.

"You may as well come down, so we don't have to climb up and get you."

Feet dropped through the hole, then legs, and he helped her

down. She wore panties and a T-shirt, and once on her feet she dusted insulation off her shoulders. She shook her hair and looked defiantly at Marquez.

"Did you like that?" she asked.

"What were you doing in the attic?"

"That's a stupid question if I've ever heard one."

"Why hide? Mark wouldn't care, would he? Have you talked to him yet?"

"Are you going to guilt-trip me now?"

"I'm asking."

"In case you haven't noticed, I'm not exactly waiting by the phone for him."

"You haven't heard from him?"

"No, and if you'll excuse me I need to use the bathroom."

20

Meghan Burris came out of the bathroom wearing cutoff jeans and a tube top. She walked straight out the front door and Marquez followed her out on the off chance he could reach her. They'd allowed Bailey to leave the living room, something they wouldn't ordinarily do with a suspect, and Bailey had gone to his Suburban. There wasn't anyone they knew about that Bailey could call to warn that his house was being searched and Marquez wanted to send a message to Bailey's lawyer, wanted the lawyer to know they were confident and coming after his client. They were building a case. Send a signal they didn't need to confine Bailey; they already had him.

Meghan Burris's blonde hair carried a purple streak that ran down the center of the back of her head and a lacy tattoo snaked its way down her lower back and under the waist of her pants. She turned to face him as he called her name.

"You already searched me when you helped me down. Do you want to do it again?"

"Why don't we talk before you get with Jimmy?"

"Why do I have to talk to you?"

"Let me tell you what we're seeing. Give me a few minutes. It might be worth it to you."

She looked over at Bailey who was in the Suburban on the phone, motioning for her to come get inside. When she turned back toward Marquez instead, the driver's door swung open and Bailey called her like he was whistling a dog home.

"Meghan, come here." When she didn't, Bailey hustled toward them, the phone still pressed up against his ear. "Don't even fucking have a conversation with him."

"You don't tell me what to do, Jimmy."

"I'm telling you to get in the truck. We're leaving." He reached for her arm and pulled her onto the driveway before Marquez caught his wrist.

"Go finish your phone call, Jimmy."

"You're really the big fucking guy, aren't you?"

He let go of Bailey's wrist, answered, "Tell your lawyer about it." He didn't hear what Bailey said as he turned away. Marquez moved out on the lawn with Meghan. He knew she didn't like anything about law enforcement. That radiated off her and had when they'd visited Heinemann's boat. But he also felt that there was probably a tipping point with her, a point where survival would kick in and it would be more in her interest to help them. He knew he had to rattle her cage a little and after Bailey backed off he turned to her. "You don't want to go down with Jimmy."

"Like I would even know how to poach anything."

"I'm not talking about poaching."

"Anything else you found is Jimmy's, not mine." She meant a little bit of cocaine near Bailey's bed that had been dumped into the carpet and left a white streak in the dirty brown shag. They'd debated trying to do something with it as a way of holding Bailey. She hooked her thumbs in the front of her shorts and her eyes turned with a different challenging light. "You don't really have anything to say, do you? You just want to get him and you want me to help, and now you think you're going to scare me."

"Does Jimmy have you selling drugs on campus?"

"No."

"We saw you do a couple of deals. Are you doing that on your own?"

"This conversation is over. You are like total bullshit. All of you people are."

"We followed you after the conversation on the boat because we need to find Mark Heinemann."

"So you can mess up his life."

Marquez nodded toward Bailey. "He's working with some bad people and you're going to have to choose which side you're on. There's not going to be any middle ground."

"Ooh, pretty scary. I'm so worried now I can hardly think. Look, do you really think he talks to me? It's real simple, okay. He took me to dinner and we got high and he was real sweet last night so he could bring me back here and fuck me since Mark is gone. Do you want to write that down or do you already know about stuff like that? Now, he's hung over and you kicked his door in and tore up his house and he's an asshole again. So do you really think he talks to me? Get real. I'm out of here."

She turned and started toward the Suburban. "Don't leave just yet."

"What, are you going to threaten me now?"

"No, I'm not. I'm going to give you a phone number you can reach me at."

"Why would I want it?"

"The people Jimmy and Mark are messing with are as bad as they come. I've been twenty years in law enforcement and not all of it Fish and Game. I've come across one of these people before and I promise you that Jimmy and especially Mark don't have any idea who they're dealing with. They're way over their heads." He handed her the card at an angle Bailey couldn't see.

"I wish I'd stayed home last night," she said, then walked to the Suburban and got in the passenger side.

She slammed the door and Bailey backed out of the driveway, turned and flipped him off, mouthing "fuck you" from behind the window before driving away. Roberts would follow on the off chance he'd lead them somewhere. Marquez watched the rest of the team filter out of the house and looked at the warped garage door, the avocado paint peeling off it. What did they have on Bailey? Forty cardboard boxes. Heinemann's story, which would need some evidence to be worth much.

What they had didn't add up to much yet. He watched Alvarez messing with trying to close the front door, running crime tape through the lock bore hole and trying to tie it off on the porch. Bailey's lawyer was probably already drafting a letter saying his client had been right there willing to open the door and never got the chance. Where was Bailey getting the money to hire a lawyer like Alberto Cruz? The blown-out front door would sound like macho bullshit to Keeler and in combination with the lost equipment, he knew it was going to get rough with the chief soon unless they came up with something.

"Hey, Lieutenant, how do you want to leave this? It keeps blowing open." Alvarez grinned at him. "What did you guys do in the DEA when you kicked in doors?"

"Throw a chair behind it and go out the back door."

He'd leave two wardens down here and take the rest north for the Heinemann release. He'd sit down with Heinemann this afternoon. Marquez talked through all of it now with the team before they split up.

On the drive north as he was coming through Pacifica he took a call from Petersen. There was a light wind off the water and he watched a line of pelicans above the surf as they talked.

"Will we get any help from her?" Petersen asked.

"I don't think so."

"No?"

"Meghan's pretty tough. She uses her sex like a cutting knife. You could try her, but I can't connect with her."

"That type usually talks to you."

"Not this one."

Marquez heard another woman's voice, then Petersen's name called out loudly, not her alias either. It made him smile. She'd already told him she was in line to get a sonogram, sitting in a waiting room listening to the chatter as she waited for her appointment.

"I've got to go, John."

"I can hear. Good luck with the sonogram."

"Do you want to meet me in Richmond or in Marin?"

"I'm going through the City first. I'll call you."

He slowed at a stoplight and lost the pelicans. Forty minutes later he was in San Francisco, a strange nervousness turning in him as he parked and walked down to Presto.

He could see Katherine behind the zinc counter, her smile loose and easy as she joked with one of her employees, and then her expression changed as he walked in. The smile stayed but her eyes clouded and she lifted a hand to wave hello before saying, "Just a minute, John. I've got to do one thing in back."

Marquez looked around at what Katherine had made here, the smooth limestone, the tall doors that folded like an accordion, tables with a couple of solos working laptops, the sunlight slanting in across the stone and onto the counter where a young guy was working the espresso machine and a woman with purple hair and a ring in her nose was taking orders. He looked through the glass at a plate of sandwiches cut in triangular shapes, little panini, she called them. She'd made a place that felt good to be in. It was easy to be here and he wondered about making a different life himself, something that fit better for both of them. Take a round table in the sunlight, drink a coffee and read a newspaper, take a long run along Stinson Beach and not worry about the Klines and Baileys of the world. He could get a different job and it wouldn't be so hard with Katherine. She came out from the back office now and then around from behind the bar, leaning toward him and kissing him, her face flushing as she did.

"I was coming through and thought I'd stop and see you."

"I have to walk down to the florist. Do you want to come with me?"

"Sure."

They walked in the sunlight down the sidewalk and she told him about her conversation with Maria and how little Maria had eaten yesterday. An orange, less granola than you'd feed a pigeon, half a banana.

"Not a whole banana, John, half a banana because she said a whole one would make her vomit."

"How much weight do you think she's lost?"

"She won't get on a scale with me around and she claims she has never felt better."

He'd gone on the Net and read what kind of problem anorexia was with teenage girls and young women, and that's what Katherine was talking now, although Maria had yet to see her regular doctor. Now, he asked the question he'd been carrying around.

"How much do you think is caused by you and me?"

"I don't know. I'm sure it figures in, but she's the one with the problem."

"What do you tell her about us?"

"Lately, that I'm discouraged. She needs to know the truth. She doesn't need any more bombshells." Katherine slowed to a stop and looked at his face. "The truth is we've been separated five months and not much has changed. We're still arguing."

"We may always argue."

"What do you think I should tell her?"

"That we're trying to work it out."

"I don't see you trying very hard, John."

"I'm here to see you, right now."

"Unannounced and on your way to somewhere else. Our marriage has never come first. You were too used to being on your own when I met you." Her eyes glistened and she shook her head. "You're one of the best people I've ever known and I don't want to fight with you, but you're never going to put us first." Tears started and she wiped them away angrily. "I think I've done all I can."

"Why don't you move back in and I'll resign as patrol lieutenant. I'll find another line of work."

"You can't do that." She shook her head. "I have to go to the florist. I have somebody coming right now that I have to meet." He stepped forward and put his arms around her. He felt her break and her chest heaved with quiet sobs. "I feel like my dreams are gone," she said, and he couldn't hear the rest. He wiped her tears and she took hold of his face and pressed hers against his and he felt her hot tears on his skin. "John, John, this is so hard for me, but I don't know if we're getting anywhere and I'm really afraid."

"Move back in with me."

"I can't."

And for the first time he realized the marriage might end. She reached up, touched his lips with her fingers, then turned and went down two doors and into the florist shop. He walked back to his truck and everything he was doing felt diminished and less important than it had an hour ago. He started the truck and dropped down toward Lombard, driving slowly, his thoughts clouded in confusion at what he couldn't seem to grasp. He took a call now from Alvarez.

"Bailey dropped Meghan at a house in Santa Cruz and came back to Half Moon. He's at a bar. We're with him?"

"Stay with him."

"You all right? You sound funny."

"I'm good. I'm on my way to Heinemann."

He was on Lombard running toward the Golden Gate Bridge with a desperation to make things right with Katherine, but with a new uncertainty and wondering what to make of it. He sat in the center lane on Lombard until he noticed a white sedan that he thought he'd seen earlier when he was on the sidewalk with Katherine, a government Crown Vic hanging three lights back now but pacing the pack he was in. Marquez changed to the right lane and then turned right at the next corner, dropped down to Chestnut and turned left into boutique and tourist traffic that moved at no more than twenty. He went two blocks and then saw the flash of the sedan's white side as it turned onto Chestnut.

He ran out Chestnut and started toward the bridge again. He passed cars, bumped well over the 45 mph limit and went wide of the toll booths, then stayed in the right lane crossing the bridge. On the other side, he exited into Sausalito, down through hills dry with the fall and drove along the water. Halfway through town he picked up the Vic behind him. He phoned Petersen.

"I think I've got someone following," and described the car to her, two occupants, one male, one female. He named a shopping center in Corte Madera and a trick they'd used before, and as he came through Sausalito and got on 101 again he drove north to Corte Madera.

He parked in the wide lot, talked to Petersen, gave her his location and told her he was going in for a coffee to go from Il Fornaio. Then from inside the restaurant he saw them turn into the lot. Two older women in front of him were slow ordering as they kept talking about a book called *The Smoke* they'd each just bought copies of. They'd heard the author read somewhere and kept talking about him while the guy waiting to take their order was standing around. Marquez was close to walking out, unable to wait much longer. He needed to make sure Petersen had seen the car turn in, but couldn't call from inside. Finally the women ordered. He got a large black coffee and called Petersen as he walked out.

"I've got you and them," she said.

"They just picked up on me."

"Yeah, I'm rolling toward them."

He got to his truck about the time Petersen blocked them from backing out of their parking slot. He pulled up behind her as the driver of the Vic was already honking for her to move. Petersen got out as Marquez got out and the passenger door opened on the Crown Vic. Both occupants were young, clean-cut, and fit, the woman's black bangs like a crow's wing, her sharp dark eyes locked on his face. The male had sideburns that ended well up his ears and hair cut like a golf course green. His clothes had the look and he opened his door, leaned around and jabbed a finger in Marquez's direction.

"Hey, buddy, we're trying to back up."

"You just got here. Why don't we talk first?"

"Move your vehicle, please. We're late."

He shut the passenger door and after a few seconds the woman in the driver's seat honked again, but she wouldn't make eye contact when Marquez walked up along her side. She wouldn't look up. She already knew they'd blown it and Marquez flipped his badge and then pulled out his phone. He watched the agents as the number rang through.

"Douglas here."

"Marquez."

"What can I do for you today, John?"

"I've got two of your finest trapped alongside a curb in Marin."

"Put one of them on. Put Harkin on."

Marquez looked at the agent getting out of the car, his face reddening with anger. "Harkin will call you back on his phone because we're taking off, but maybe you want to explain?"

"Why don't you come here for that?"

Marquez hung up and looked at Agent Harkin. "Call home. Your dad is pissed off."

21

"What if I can't get ahold of them?" Heinemann asked. "What if they won't deal with me anymore? What if I call the number and no one answers?"

"You go find Bailey and tell him you're back. If you can get Bailey to talk to you, we have something."

"Basically, you want me to try to burn Jimmy."

"Basically, what we want is to get to the people buying the abalone. Let me make an analogy to the heroin trade."

"Come on, man, give me a break, ab ain't heroin."

"Bailey is like a poppy grower to us. We're after the real traffickers, the people who move the product. But, yeah, you'd be in a courtroom testifying against Bailey."

"I wouldn't be any good in a courtroom."

"We talked about this yesterday. If you're getting cold feet, say so. If you want to think about it more, that's fine. I can get someone to walk you back to your cell."

But he didn't seem to need to and late in the afternoon they watched him drive away from Richmond in Meghan Burris's Datsun pickup. A GPS transponder had been magnetically attached to the engine block and tied off to the alternator so it wouldn't drop loose on a rough road. Another was buried in the cab. Security people at PacBell would monitor the pin registry of Heinemann's cell phone, allowing them to identify the phone number of anyone he talked to. The cab was wired for sound so they could listen to phone conversations.

Heinemann made the first phone call now. It was sooner than they'd asked him to, his nervousness obvious in a break in his voice, and Marquez worried about that. He'd watched Heinemann closely as they'd handed him the keys to his truck, had watched him cross the parking lot, all confidence gone from his face. The worn engine of the Datsun pickup had coughed blue smoke and Heinemann had the phone in his hand before he'd reached the highway.

Now, he was on the Bay Bridge, moving slowly in traffic. He'd turned on his radio to some station called Alice that Marquez recognized because Maria listened to it. He'd changed channels, then turned the radio off again and Marquez talked to him now.

"You doing okay?" he asked.

"What do you mean?"

"I know how it feels to be waiting for the call back."

"Yeah." Heinemann was quiet and then asked, "Should I call Jimmy now?"

"If you're ready, but you want to be yourself."

"I'm not nervous, at all."

"Remember, if it doesn't feel right we can back out."

Heinemann made the call to Bailey. They had a mike clipped to Heinemann's collar so they could hear the conversation, could hear Heinemann's breathing. Bailey faked concern that he'd been in jail, saying, "Dude, those assholes were at my house. I know what it's like. You didn't say anything to them, did you?"

"Fuck, no."

"You gotta hang."

"No problem. Hey, have you seen Meghan around the dock? I'm heading home, I'm done with this shit. You got me in way out of my league, man."

"Haven't seen her, but I've been like laying low except for the Fish and Game pricks kicking my door in."

The team drove ahead and behind Heinemann's pickup. A laptop was set up on Marquez's passenger seat, its antenna picking up a satellite signal. They didn't have the real-time capabilities of the CIA or FBI, but as long as Heinemann worked with them they'd be able to keep track of the Datsun. Marquez listened to the next phone call as Heinemann drove past Candlestick on 101.

"You made bail," a male voice said.

"Yeah, I had to put up my boat."

"What did they charge you with?"

"Stealing a boat, commercial trafficking in animal parts, a whole bunch of shit. I get arraigned in a couple of days. I didn't give them anything. It was fucking hard to get out and my attorney says I might have to plea-bargain."

Marquez shook his head. That wasn't the line they'd fed him and he shouldn't have said anything about a plea bargain, and yet, it was ordinary enough.

The man on the other end grunted. "What's this lawyer's name?"

Heinemann tripped up now, getting confused, giving one name, then pulling it back and saying the lawyer was named Grimwald.

"Grimworld?"

"No, like John Griswold." Heinemann spelled it out and it was the wrong name, didn't match the card they'd given him.

"Your girlfriend is with us and we're going to meet you on your way home. You give me your lawyer's card when I see you."

"What do you mean Meghan is with you? She has nothing to do with any of this."

"It's just how it worked out tonight and she's like us, she wants to see you."

"I did what you told me, but they must have had that old Chinese guy set up."

"We know that and everything is cool. Don't worry so much. I'm going to give you directions you need to remember, so maybe you want to write these down. You want to make this meeting. You don't want to fuck up any more than you already have."

"Why do you have Meghan?"

"Don't worry about it, she's having a good time. She likes to party."

"This isn't right, man. She doesn't have anything to do with this shit and I did what I was supposed to do."

"We're going to talk to you and I want to know about the people that interviewed you, the game wardens, who it was and then you and your sweetheart will be together again."

"It doesn't have to be so heavy."

"It's not heavy. You just fucked up, that's all."

"There were two of them. One was a big guy with kind of short blond-brown hair. He's like six-foot-three or something and the other was a blonde woman and stocky."

"I want names."

"I don't have them. He's a lieutenant, I guess. She called him Lieutenant."

"You're starting to sound stupid, kid."

"What's the big deal with the names?"

Good, Marquez thought. Hit back at him. The only chance of keeping this going was Heinemann pushing back.

"They offered you a deal, didn't they?"

"Sure, and I strung them along. That's why the charges are still hanging. They think I'm going to do something for them."

"Oh, yeah, what's that?"

"Look, all I want to do is get back to my boat and then we can meet or whatever. If you want me to dive a couple more days, that's cool." The man didn't say anything in return until Heinemann asked, "You there?"

"Keep driving south and go through San Jose. At 7:00 call this number."

He recited a number, had Heinemann read back what he'd written down, then hung up. Marquez cued his radio, talked to the team before calling Heinemann. "It's over," he said, "a no go. We're going to have to find out whether they've really got Meghan Burris and we may have to ask the locals for help."

He took a call now from the phone company. They had a cell number on the caller, a name and billing address. He called Heinemann.

"We're done, Mark. They know something is up. Do you have other numbers to call Meghan at?"

"Yeah, her house. She shares a house."

"Start making calls."

"And then what? Keep driving south like he said?"

"We'll play the game until we know she's okay. Are you good with that?"

"Yeah, totally."

"But you've got to do just what I tell you because it may get complicated, and we'll probably have to ask for help taking them down if it turns out they have her."

"Yeah, I know."

Marquez called the CHP, gave them a heads up they might have a problem they'd need help with. They drove past San Jose and toward Morgan Hill. Heinemann made the 7:00 call and got instructions to exit the freeway fives miles up the road. He drove east into dry hills that climbed toward a reservoir and a park. Beyond that was ranch land, a lot of it steep terrain, hills of rye grass that folded into ravines dark with scrub oak and brush, all of it dry as kindling this time of year.

Shauf and Alvarez went ahead, their headlights cutting the dark a mile apart. Marquez followed, reading the GPS on Heinemann's truck and relaying the info.

"He's off the paved road. He's on one of the dirt roads in those hills. When he slowed down someone must have been there on the road and directed him."

They found the cutoff, a cattle rancher's dirt track, a chain cut, a gate that swung open when Alvarez pushed it. Marquez looked up at the black outline of the hills and couldn't see headlights, but GPS said he was up there, back about two miles. This was someone's ranch. He reconfirmed the readout with Alvarez looking over his shoulder, double-checking him. The blue glow showed the Datsun had stopped and they debated their next move. Then it started moving again and accelerated rapidly, then stopped again, and he wondered if there was a problem with the GPS transponder.

"What was that about?" Alvarez asked.

"I don't know."

Nothing more happened for several minutes, then a flicker of light showed way up in the hills and they backed away and then a van came down the dirt road and ran through the gate without slowing. It hit the asphalt, turned back toward 101, and there was only Roberts and Cairo on that end. Marquez talked to them, told them to follow initially but to ask the locals to move in and help pull the van over if they couldn't get a CHP response.

"There are at least two men and probably armed. We're going up to look for Heinemann."

They turned up the dirt road, dust kicking up behind the truck as they climbed. The road was well graded but steep and Marquez had to sit in second gear and take it slow as they wound through the ravines. As they crested a ridge and could look out toward the darkness of the Central Valley to the east, the readout showed they should be close. But he didn't see the vehicle and kept going up until the road flattened on an open shoulder of the mountain. He checked in with Roberts while studying the screen. Heinemann was about a half mile back, according to the GPS readout.

"We've temporarily lost them," Roberts said. "We called the CHP and the sheriff's office but they left 101 before any backup got here. They headed west on Springer Road and we had to give them room and we lost them around a curve. They're here somewhere. There are some rural properties out here. We'll have to go house to house."

"You need local deputies for that."

"10-4."

They drove back down to where the readout said the transponder was and Marquez shined a flashlight off the side of the road, standing on the edge in the loose soil left after the road had been bladed. His light only shone partway down the steep ravine. He looked for marks and then saw broken grass and walked down to a gash in the dirt and realized the Datsun had rolled end over end. It had started straight and then the tracks through the grass ended and the next mark was where the front end of the truck had dug into the slope. He called back up to Alvarez.

"Stay up there and I'll check it out."

"Should I call anyone?"

"Not yet. They may have dumped the truck. Heinemann may have told them it was wired."

The dry grass was slippery and he dug his heels in and still slipped several times. He kept checking ahead with the light, could see where the ravine bottomed well below, but there was brush there and the truck must have carried into it, because it wasn't visible. He was finding parts now, glass, the hood folded like a discarded napkin, and he hoped Heinemann was in the van and had confessed to the GPS and the wire, and someone got the bright idea to lose the wired Datsun down this ravine.

Now he reached the brush and could see tires and realized that the rusted cab had collapsed. He smelled gasoline and heat from the engine and fought his way in through the brush. He leaned over, broke a piece of greasewood off and tried to shine the light in the driver's side. He smelled blood before he saw it and then a hand that he knew wasn't Heinemann's. He climbed over the truck to the passenger side and when he got the light positioned it took him a moment to reconcile what he was seeing. Meghan Burris's head was lying between her shoulder blades, pinned by the crushed truck cab. She'd been nearly decapitated, perhaps had gone through the windshield. He figured he'd seen enough over the years, but he had to turn and take a deep breath before cuing the radio, relaying the situation to Alvarez. They searched the slope for anyone else, wondering if they'd find Heinemann thrown from the truck.

They didn't find him, and from the road learned that Roberts had hooked up with the sheriff's deputies and was checking the houses along the stretch where they'd lost the van.

"How many houses?"

"Approximately ten," she said, "and one of the deputies is saying there's a dirt road that they might have taken but he thinks only the locals know about it."

They took it, Marquez thought. "How far does it run?"

"He says ten miles. They've already got someone on the other side, but no luck so far." She anticipated his next thought. "It picks up a paved road that works its way out to the coast and we're looking at how we can intercept. Cairo is already headed out there."

He waited with Alvarez for the fire department unit and then went back down the slope with two firemen. He gave a statement to the police from up on the mountain and much later, after Meghan's body had been removed and searchlights set up with detectives combing the area, the conclusion was that she'd made the ride down the slope alone.

They'd lost the van and before midnight Marquez pulled the

team back, told them it was time to find a motel. He checked into a Best Western and tried to sleep, but most of the night his mind churned with images of what had happened, fragments of the phone conversation with Heinemann. He rebuilt the chain of his decisions. Was it arrogance that made him send Heinemann back out there thinking he could fool someone like Kline? Had Heinemann watched her die or was his body up there somewhere? They'd do a daylight search. He'd leave part of the team down here. At 5:15 he got up and showered. The light was off in Alvarez's room when Marquez checked out. He'd call the team from the road and started north in the darkness.

The next call he got was near dawn and from Ruter. "I hope it's not too early," Ruter said, "but you seem to be a morning guy. I've got abalone for you that came out of Huega's girlfriend's house and don't tell me I was supposed to have called the DFG. This thing is a cluster fuck now. Your old friends at the DEA are involved and the FBI has taken over like you said they would. They send me for coffee."

"How much abalone?"

"Two hundred ten shells. Some big ones, too. How fast does that stuff grow?"

"About an inch a year and they can live thirty."

"It's in a county freezer."

"You should have left it alone."

"The DEA dumped it on the concrete to get to the dope stored under it. They didn't seem to be in any hurry to put it back and I figured you'd want it. I'd like to compare notes with you, Marquez."

"You took your friendly pill this morning."

"No, I'm figuring out what you told me in the first place. We need each other."

There was something else in his voice that Marquez could hear but not identify. Ruter was asking him to drive up today, but he wasn't doing it because he'd found abalone.

"I'll have to call you back," Marquez said.

When he talked with Ruter next it was nearly noon and he'd made the decision to go north to Fort Bragg tonight and was past Santa Rosa already. He called Petersen and they decided she'd sit down with Ruter, too. In the late afternoon when Marquez dropped down through the steep wooded country to Shelter Cove, Petersen was already parked in the lot and was talking to Ruter. The sky had smoothed and whitened to bone and wind had raised whitecaps. Ruter's eyes were watering with the wind and he wanted to go inside the bar, find a table and talk.

They went inside and got a table. Ruter told them his problem. "I met with the FBI a few days after the Guyanno killings, but they didn't want me talking to anyone."

They both knew Ruter wouldn't have said anything about the FBI anyway.

"They came to see me on the pretense we'd trade notes. They had a lot of questions about how you happened to be at Guyanno Creek and they photocopied my case file, including the notes you gave me. But on the whole, they treated me like a county hick." He smiled a cynical hard smile that his eyes didn't back up and said, "I'd almost rather deal with you."

Marquez leaned back against a wall done entirely in wine corks that had been cut in half and glued. The wall was ten feet high, twenty long, with a small patch left to do. The cork deadened the sound in a room that was already too quiet and Ruter kept his voice low and told them what the Feds had said about Kline, confirming that he was very likely operating off the north coast.

"They gave you his name?"

"Yeah, Marquez, I don't know why they told me when they wouldn't give you a straight answer."

"They know I have a personal interest."

"Could be."

"I take it they gave you a description."

Ruter nodded. "A photo." He took it out of his coat and laid it on the table and Marquez heard Petersen shift for a better view. But he could see it wasn't recent, was maybe a few years after the one he'd gotten in Mexico City. "They're also looking at Davies. Dope trafficking is part of this, too, at least as far as Huega was concerned. The DEA took his ex-wife in for questioning." Ruter shook his head ruefully. "I'm up to my ass in Feds."

"And what can we do for you?" Marquez asked. "You've got more info than we do. What's changed since we last talked?"

"I want to solve these cases," Ruter said, "but the Feds want me to gather information and pass it on to them. I know if you get close to him you're going to try to take him down and when you need backup I'll bring an army."

"The killings bother you that much."

"From the time I was a kid I wanted to be a detective. We had a neighbor who was murdered. He'd played minor league baseball and taught me to pitch when I was ten. He wasn't even thirty yet and was like a big brother to me. Someone killed him over a small gambling debt. I didn't get my badge to be a gofer for the FBI."

"You don't want your cases taken away."

"No, I can't stand it, and I know you're not going to stop looking for him."

"How do you want to proceed?"

"By communicating more."

"Good enough."

Then they were silent and didn't have enough in common to have a second drink together. Marquez laid a twenty on the bar.

Outside, the light carried the pale gold of late summer and the wind was colder with the sun setting. There were high cirrus, waves churned against the shore rock, and Marquez wondered if they were going to see a weather change. Rougher weather would make it harder for abalone poachers. He stood in the parking lot with Petersen and Ruter and then said he was going back into the bar to get a coffee for the ride back to Bragg. He used the bathroom, splashing water on his face, which he seemed to be doing a lot lately. He gave the bartender two bucks for lukewarm coffee.

When he came out Petersen was in her truck on the phone and Ruter was waiting for him near the bumper, lingering there. "Something else I want to ask you about and I didn't want to bring up inside because it's not necessarily related to anything," Ruter said. "But I'm going to run it by you." He paused, looking past Marquez at the horizon as if the subject was embarrassing. "I just want your opinion."

"Sure."

"I've had an old black cat that's been with me forever. Bad breath, bad temper, but I love this cat. I built a cat door into our kitchen door and she'd go out in the middle of the night when she was younger and bring back a rabbit as big as her." He showed with his hands. "Lately, she'd just sit out in the night and I think it made her feel like a hunter again." He bit down on his lip and looked at Marquez's eyes. "Someone killed her last night out near our front gate."

"I'm sorry."

And he was. He could hear what it meant to Ruter.

"I got her the day I got my badge and she was my good luck. She'd always wait up for me and you know you get home late at night sometimes. I named her Hero. Aw, Christ, this isn't your problem."

"How'd they kill her?"

"Looks like a knife. Most likely a neighborhood kid, some sick little fuck. But I've thought about Davies and that's why I'm telling you. We've pushed him pretty hard and I'm wondering if you can picture him doing something like this, but maybe that's having the Guyanno cases on my mind. It's probably an old case, someone with a grudge against me, or a kid like I said. That's not something you'd associate with this Kline's network, is it? There's no reason he'd take an interest in a county cop, is there?"

"Someone was trying to get inside your head."

"That's right, and they did it. That's why I wanted to run it by you."

"A knife?" Marquez asked.

"Yes, and that's why it's got me wondering."

"It's not the Davies I knew, but it doesn't seem that I knew him very well and I can't think of why Kline would try to get to you. Unless you've brushed next to something they have going on. But your cat, that's got to be someone that knows you."

"Or has watched me."

"There is that possibility." Marquez reached out and put a hand on his shoulder. "I'm sorry," and Ruter shook his head, his thoughts private, and he walked away looking like a man temporarily lost in himself. Marquez saw Petersen had gotten out of her truck and was walking over, wanting to talk again before leaving, and probably wondering what that was all about. Marquez raised a hand, waved to Ruter as the detective drove away. He guessed that Ruter's theory of a neighborhood kid was probably right. Some kid in a bad space trying out a knife or trying out the feeling of killing. Petersen leaned against his truck and looked uncomfortable.

"What was that about?"

"Someone killed his cat last night." He told her what Ruter had told him and she was quiet, absorbing it, saying she was sorry and then, "In the bar Ruter acted like a man who'd had a religious conversion. All of a sudden he's a Kline believer. I know you kept a file on Kline, but has the FBI really looked that hard for him all these years and not nailed him? No one can stay hidden that many years."

"You wouldn't think so."

"You're not afraid of him, are you?"

He looked at her and wondered what had happened to their conversation of the other day. Maybe she hadn't taken him seriously because she didn't believe he could think about Kline in a clearheaded way. She probably figured his worries were overblown and assumed as Ruter had, that Davies had killed Huega. Now, something in the bar conversation with Ruter had changed her and that surprised him.

"Kline almost took me out when I was looking for him and I still don't understand how he found me. I still think about that at night. Yeah, there's something off the planet about him."

"I've never seen you scared of a criminal. I don't know what to do with that."

"He'll go down this time."

"That kind of male bravado doesn't usually come from you."

"If we find him, it'll be us or him."

"Oh, that makes me feel better."

"You're not going in the line of fire, Sue."

"You think that's why I'm asking? Because I'm pregnant?"

"No, I don't."

"I may as well turn in my equipment today."

"Take it easy."

"Then don't lay this male bullshit on me."

"It's not bullshit."

"It's not? Okay, Lieutenant, see you back in Fort Bragg."

She went to her truck and he turned his back as her engine gunned. Her anger left him feeling lousy and he sat in his truck sipping the coffee, then shaking off the feeling and calling Roberts to see if anything more had turned up. He checked his voice mail, surprised he still hadn't heard anything from Keeler after the confrontation with the FBI yesterday. As dark closed in, he started for Fort Bragg and his phone rang as he climbed the steep road up from the cove. He stared at the screen before answering, somehow had known he'd hear from him.

"I've got a lead you want," Davies said.

"Go ahead."

"It's got to be in person. Where are you at?"

"Shelter Cove."

"You want to meet me in Fort Bragg?"

"All right."

"They're after me."

"Who is?"

"I don't know who they are. Call my cell when you get into town. I don't want to wait anywhere public."

"I'll call you," and Marquez hung up first.

22

Five miles from the cutoff that would take him back to
Fort Bragg, Marquez crested a rise, saw a long line of brake lights
and in the dip below, flashing lights of emergency vehicles and the
highway patrol. The driver of the car in front of him was out of his
vehicle with a foot up on his rear bumper. His head turned toward
Marquez's headlights and he squinted, face scrunched as if to say,
don't you get it, buddy, we're not going anywhere soon. A half hour
later the traffic was still at a dead stop and he'd learned that it was a
logging truck that had jackknifed and there was a fatality. He called
Petersen, thinking she might have to meet Davies and keep him in
Fort Bragg until he could get there.

"It must have happened after I drove through," she said. "How
come you talked down to me like that?"

"I wasn't talking down."

"You were patronizing me."

"I wouldn't do that, but if you want to say being pregnant is the same as not being, then we're not on the same page."

"I'm not saying that."

He didn't understand the intensity of her reaction, but knew she was serious and apologized again, although the apology didn't sit that well with him. He swallowed his pride, did it anyway, and then checked the action below. They had something like a 988 Cat with log forks and a top clamp moving logs off the roadway. The operator looked experienced and maybe they'd get the road open soon, but there was no way to know for sure and he told her about Davies's call.

"He wants to meet tonight in Fort Bragg and claims he's got information."

"That he couldn't give you over the phone?"

"He wants to talk in person, says he's being followed."

"Yeah, by little people in his head."

"I'm wondering if the Feds are tracking him."

"I think we should write him off. Skip the meeting tonight. He's trouble and he hasn't been straight with us."

"You're right, but I want to keep a conversation going. How about checking Noyo for his boat and then call me back?"

"This guy makes my skin crawl, John. He's up with two murder victims at Guyanno, then he's dumping Huega off his boat after torturing him and you still want to meet with him. I don't get that."

"He's not all smoke. He's had contact with our abalone buyers."

"You don't know that, but if it's true, what's that say about him?"

"It says he's got his own agenda."

"I'll check the harbor and call you."

There was a part of him that completely understood taking Huega up the coast and questioning him. He knew the feeling, but had never given into it. Davies was sure he'd been set up by someone and Marquez didn't think that part was an act, though he knew he was the only one who believed that. He hung up with her and saw the first cars crawling through down below. An hour later, as he drove through Leggett he took a call from Katherine.

"Where are you?" she asked.

"Up near Fort Bragg."

"That's four hours away, isn't it?"

"Almost."

"We had a funny thing at Presto today, John."

"What was that?"

"A couple of men came in after you left. They ordered cappuccinos and then just watched me."

"Were you behind the counter?"

"For a while and then I went in back because they made me nervous."

"Did you talk to them?"

"I tried to but they stood off on one end of the bar. Sara was afraid they were going to rob us, that's how weird it seemed."

"What did they look like?" She gave him a description now and one sounded like the black-haired man they'd videotaped with his friend outside Li's house. The other she described could be the prison-buffed Hispanic Meghan Burris had told them about. The man who called himself Carlo. She described a thick white scar on his left forearm and he heard the huskiness in her voice, knew she'd been affected by it, and wondered how they'd found the coffee bar. Had he been followed by more than the FBI the other day? He asked her to walk through a description one more time. "They sound like a couple of guys we've been after. I've got a videotape I'm going to show you."

"You mean they followed you here?"

"They may have, but I don't know what it means that they came in and stood at the bar. Whether they're checking it out or sending a message. Did they talk to anybody?"

"Just to order coffees."

"I'm sorry and I'll do something about it."

"Do what? What can you do?" He didn't have an answer for that yet and she continued. "I went up to the house today and got a couple more things. I took that light that I like."

"Did you think about what I said the other day?"

"I'm thinking about everything." Marquez didn't have anything to say to that. "The deer ate your last tomatoes," she said after a silence. "I guess they got up on the deck." They were welcome to them. "And Maria said she saw your hawk this afternoon."

"Maria was with you?"

"Yes. She says she can tell the hawk from the others."

With Maria he'd nursed an injured redtail back to health. For a long time it stayed close to the house, roosting in the redwoods alongside the driveway. They'd raised mice and it was a hard lesson for Maria to watch the hawk swoop down and take a mouse. He hadn't expected the bird to make it, thought it would end up sitting on a roost someplace like the Lindsay Museum in Walnut Creek. But the hawk had recovered and he and Maria made a game out of spotting it flying up on the mountain.

"I'll have to talk to her."

"You won't tonight. She's already in bed." He pictured Katherine's little house in Bernal Heights. She'd planned to rent it out long-term and he was going to make improvements to it over time. He knew how hard it must have been for her to move back there and remembered how excited and happy she'd been the first year up on Mt. Tam. Katherine went on, "We had a fight after she left the dinner table and headed straight to the bathroom. She thinks I lurk outside the bathroom door every time she goes in there."

"Were you outside the door tonight?"

"Am I going to get it from you, too?"

"I'm asking."

"You know, John, you're one person who doesn't get to judge me. She looks like a famine victim but thinks she looks like a fashion model."

"We'll get through to her. Regardless of what happens between us."

"I think we've already had this conversation."

He hung up with Katherine and drove into Fort Bragg thinking over the conversation. But there was nothing in this one he could draw from. He'd made the offer to leave Fish and Game, find another job, and that didn't ring true for her. She didn't believe he'd do it, he guessed. Or maybe she was already further downstream from the marriage than he realized. He knew something was going to have to give; they weren't going anywhere this way.

When he hit a stoplight he punched in Ruter's number, because that was the way they'd left it, that he'd communicate whenever he heard from Davies. Ruter's voice was slow and it sounded like he'd had a couple of drinks.

"He called me, too," Ruter said. "I think he wanted to hear my voice after killing my cat."

"Did he say anything?"

"That Huega, Stocker, and Han, all dealt drugs, and that it's common knowledge up here. He knows we found dope at Huega's ex-wife's, and says Huega moved dope at night out of some of these coves where they used to ship timber. Davies says the dope is going to the same people buying abalone."

"Wouldn't surprise me."

"Where I'm headed is I think this is looking more like a dope smuggling operation than an abalone poaching ring."

"Then you know more than you're telling me."

"They pulled half a kilo from the ex-wife's house."

Marquez listened to more on the dope smuggling theory, Huega, Han, and Stocker moving dope by boat for growers in Humboldt, the spin the DEA had put on it for Ruter to keep the detective out of their hair. Marquez knew because he'd been there himself, knew what lines they would have fed Ruter. Huega, Han, and Stocker putting into these secluded coves at night, dope ferried out to their boats and then transferred to the main buyer, the DEA on the edge of a big bust they'd been working for a year. He could hear it, but his problem was a poaching ring. The dope smuggling would go on forever up here. All you needed to know about the war on drugs was that prices had dropped steadily over the last decade. Match that fact with the basics of supply and demand and you had your answer.

Ruter changed subjects. "Here's a story about Davies you might not know. Last Christmas, Davies walked through a restaurant parking lot with a Zippo lighter, firing up the American flags everyone was running around with on their cars. He'd set five or six on fire by the time they grabbed him. He then told the arresting officer the flag isn't the country and people are getting confused. He said the founding fathers would have cleaned their rifle, not flown colored cloth."

"Where was this?"

"Fort Bragg."

"He's right, I guess."

"You're a funny guy, Marquez."

He heard liquid pouring, a glass placed on a hard surface, ice tinkling. "Then there's one other idea I'm going to throw out there. In this one Davies isn't the bad guy. He's being used by an unknown party. I can't tie anything together; I'm just throwing it out there because you're the guy to keep kicking that around. Call me after you meet with him. I'll keep my phone next to me."

"Yeah, okay."

A few minutes later he talked with Petersen and she said Davies's boat wasn't at Noyo. She chuckled but not with any humor. She really didn't want any more to do with Davies. "Maybe he spotted people hiding up in the trees when he docked," she said, "or a black helicopter hovering overhead. They're probably chasing him down the coast and he's just barely staying ahead of them."

"I'll call him."

"I wouldn't. If you ask me, we should let him go. He isn't worth it and he's never been who he says he is. But he's sure got your number, doesn't he?" She hung up quickly, still angry, he thought.

23

Davies's voice had an echo chasing it and was hard to hear. "I was waiting down at Noyo and saw your warden come through. A couple of the guys watching for me picked up on her, instead. One might have followed her."

"Watching for you?"

"Yeah, that's right. They've been on me." Marquez heard the thrum of the boat engine, waves hitting the bow. "I'm heading south. Can you meet me at Albion?"

"That's as far as I go tonight."

"I'll be waiting there."

Marquez started south on Highway 1 and called Petersen. "I talked to him and he says you might have been followed out of Noyo. Where are you now?"

"At the homeless shelter in Fort Bragg. I got ahold of Peggy and dropped the abalone off with her. Hey, John, hang on a minute."

"You see somebody?"

"I don't know, maybe, hang on, um, yeah, could be, but I don't know. I'm going to make a turn here." He heard a faint squeal of brakes, and knew she wasn't going to say anything until she had gone several blocks. He could picture her face, her truck moving slowly past the old buildings, the street empty at this hour. It was more than a minute and then she said softly, "Could be."

"Head down the highway and we'll trap them. I'll drop in behind them."

"How far away are you?"

"Almost to Albion."

"All right, I'm on my way."

"Let's keep the line open."

They kept talking and she lost track of the car as she left Fort Bragg. Now, she said nothing was behind her for a couple of miles.

"I'm slowing down," she said. "You must be close."

"I'm here, I see Davies's van. I'm going to park and find him."

Marquez found Davies sitting on his haunches on the moonlit gravel between two trailered boats, smoking a cigarette. Albion Harbor was empty and quiet, the dock dark, and Marquez had a good view of the access road and a view of the highway. Petersen would click her brights once as she crossed the bridge.

"The devil always gets what he wants," Davies said. "He knows our weaknesses."

"Good for him. How do you know you're being followed?"

"When they impounded my boat they buried something in it at the Coast Guard base. But I can't find it."

"Who did?"

"The Federal government."

"Why not the county detectives? Why the Feds?"

"I've been in their shit and they know it."

"You've been in the Feds' shit?"

"Yes, sir, and they want to keep watching me. I think they're after your man."

Marquez stopped on that. Davies had to have come to that on his own because there wouldn't be anybody telling him. There wasn't anyone in law enforcement associated with this who'd say a thing to Davies about Kline.

"Federal agents came down and questioned me after Ruter let me go. They were waiting when I picked up my boat. They questioned me about Stocker and Han. I guess they thought I had more dealings with that pair than I did."

The orange glow of the cigarette dropped to the gravel and Marquez could only make out part of Davies's face. He could see the shine of his eyes as Davies stood.

"They asked about Guyanno. They want to know what I've seen out on the water, whether I'd seen any illegal abalone sales."

"What did you tell them?"

"I lied to them." Davies was silent a long minute, then shifted his stance on the gravel, facing Marquez. "You're a good man, Lieutenant. No doubt about whose side you're on, but there's a real firefight coming."

Marquez had known men like Davies before. They could be harsh and discriminating in their judgment of others, but if they told themselves you shared a worldview or values similar to theirs, then you were not only safe from their violence but protected by it.

"What did you want to tell me tonight?"

"I'm going to lay some stuff on you; I've got a confession to make, but it involves some lying I've done to you, too. I'm ashamed of that but it's been for your own good. Truth is I killed Ray Stocker, but not the way anyone thinks. I was selling to these same poachers trying to get close to them. I'd been dealing with a man named Carlo. I sold to him three times and I've got the money for you. Each time I'd meet him on the side of a road. We'd talk by cell phone and the deals would go down real fast after he'd park. I knew that's how he was handling Stocker, too, so I did something to Stocker that was wrong and put him in jeopardy.

Have you done things you regret later even though you thought
you were doing the right thing?"

"You've got a new confession every time we meet."

"This is the real deal."

After Ruter had surprised him with the information on Davies's
navy record, Marquez had done a complete around the world on
Davies, gone through NCIC and California Law Enforcement
Telecommunication System, though he'd never made inquiries
with the navy. He hadn't found any record of arrests other than a
disturbing the peace five years ago and the Guyanno bar incident
with Stocker. He must not have been arrested for the flag burning.

"You put him in jeopardy?"

"Yeah, I broke into Stocker's truck and pulled a cooler out of the
back, cleaned out most of the abalone, left it two deep and filled the
rest with ice. See, they were doing deals where they'd hand over
the coolers just like I was and get paid and usually they'd come back
to drink at Hadrian's. I'd been following them and couldn't get too
close, but I'd been doing it myself. I didn't know they were taking so
much ab though. That part I didn't know, but you can understand
why I couldn't tell you. You'd have come down on me, but I've saved
all the money, Lieutenant. I've got it hidden away to give you. Anyway, they'd been building up ab and I knew they were close to doing
a deal, so I looked for an opportunity and took it when it came."

"You set him up and now you're getting pangs of conscience?"

"I thought I was helping you, but I didn't have any idea they'd
get wasted. That changed the whole outlook."

Marquez took the conversation back to setting up Stocker and
Han. He listened closely now. The short sale had gone down four
days before they were killed. Davies had jimmied the door on
Stocker's truck while it was parked at a bar. Inside were four coolers
packed with abalone. He'd bogused two of them.

"I'm gaining their trust," Davies said.

"The buyers."

"The big man. He knows I want to do more work."

"He's got a purpose for you."

"I haven't forgotten what side I'm on, Lieutenant. I've just messed up, that's all."

"You don't know what kind of mistake you're making. Maybe we ought to lock you up in a cell for a week. Take your confession and figure out charges."

Davies acted like he hadn't heard. "When I went up to check on Stocker and Han that morning at Guyanno Creek I knew something had happened because they hadn't been around for a couple of days. I wish I'd come clean with you that day."

"You should have."

"You know, that Han bought me drinks one night. He wasn't the asshole Stocker was. He didn't talk up his story too much."

"You're not going to bring them back."

"It's the devil getting his way."

"Lose the devil talk. If you're telling me you've compromised yourself for these people, then tell me everything you've done to try to get close to them. But either way, and I've said this to you before, you don't belong anywhere around this. Go visit relatives in the Midwest, sail your boat around the world, but get out of here."

"I was expecting more from you tonight, Lieutenant. You've disappointed me, man."

Marquez didn't know exactly what Davies meant. "You're telling me you're trying to avoid people you think are Federal agents and asking my help?" Marquez pulled his badge. "Why do you think I carry this?"

"I can get you to them, Lieutenant. The Feds know it and they don't want it to happen."

"If they didn't, they'd pick you up." Marquez saw Petersen's truck go past on the highway. He watched Davies light another cigarette and wondered if anything he said could be trusted.

"I guess I don't carry any weight around here. I'll see you, it's time to go."

Marquez watched him get on his boat and heard the engines fire. He talked to Petersen, told her he'd follow her back to Bragg, running a mile behind her in case she got picked up again.

"What does Davies want from us?" she asked.

"He wants redemption, but not the kind we can give. He needs to sit in a booth and talk to a priest."

24

The next morning the sky was colorless, the gunmetal ocean broken with whitecaps. Marquez left Petersen in Fort Bragg and started south, checking Noyo and Albion for Davies's boat, continuing south along the coast past Salt Point all the way to Jenner and the mouth of the Russian River before turning inland. He carried less hope this morning and leaving the coast drove slowly up the river canyon, thinking over what they had, wondering if there was more they could do to find Heinemann. He figured he'd set up another meeting with Douglas today to talk about Davies. An hour later, after he'd reached 101, he took a call from Keeler.

"Tran Li is on his way here to headquarters. He says he's driven all night to come see you. He was in Reno when I last talked to him, and I called you afterwards but couldn't get you on your cell phone. I could hear casino machines in the background, so I think he was telling the truth. What do you think this is about? Where are you?"

"In Marin but I'll head your way."

Two hours later, Marquez parked and spotted Li's truck parked down the street from the Resources Building that also housed DFG headquarters. Li was sitting erect in the driver's seat with his eyes closed. Marquez rapped lightly on the glass and didn't get any reaction, knocked a second time and saw the clouded awareness in Li's eyes turn to sadness and his hand fumble for the door handle. He got out wearing a puffy down vest that made him look smaller. He'd shaved his head, his face was gaunt. Grief and guilt were overwhelming him. As they rode up the elevator Marquez guessed Li had been fasting.

"My son talked to me in a dream and says I help you."

Marquez nodded.

"I have a man's name who bought abalone from me in Oakland. He has a business there for a long time. You can go talk to him."

"Can you prove he sold to you?"

"No."

He led Li to a conference room, then let Chief Keeler know. Keeler came in as Marquez sat down across from Li with a notepad and the little Motorola recorder he'd used for years. He stood the recorder upright in the middle of the table between them and Li shook his head. He folded his arms.

"No sound recorder."

"It's for me, so I can listen again later. Not for evidence."

"Not for this time, okay?"

Marquez reached and clicked it off. He lay it down on its side and knew he shouldn't have put it in the middle of the table. He'd made Li nervous. Li told him about a man named Billy Mauro who had a fish distribution business in Oakland on Second Street. Li repeated Mauro's name several times and Marquez stopped the conversation and got a phone book. He looked up fish wholesalers and found Billy Mauro's Fresh Seafood and had Li confirm.

"You took abalone to him."

"When my wife take kids to school she go by there and my sons carry the abalone in."

Marquez remembered Alvarez speculating the wife was moving the ab. He'd get a kick out of being right.

"She carried it in the trunk?"

"Yes, then she drive inside Billy Mauro's business."

"And your sons helped unload?"

"Yes. I count before and he pays me at my store."

But that didn't explain how during the nights they'd had the house under surveillance, nights when Mrs. Li's old diesel Mercedes had sat on the short driveway or on the street, abalone had been loaded into the trunk.

"How did you move the abalone to the Mercedes?" Li ignored the question and Marquez repeated it, and when he still didn't get an answer he wondered about the Mauro story. "I need to know how you got the abalone into the car."

"Why this so important?"

"Because we were there outside your house watching and we never saw it moved."

Li smiled suddenly, a competitive light flaring momentarily in his eyes, like a welding spark that burns bright and quickly goes out. "My sons carried the abalone in the school backpacks."

And now Marquez could see it. His first thought was that they couldn't carry enough abalone in their backpacks and then remembered the kids often went back inside the house again taking their packs with them. He'd only been there twice in the early morning himself, he'd have to ask Shauf and Cairo and Alvarez, but the time he had been there the older boy, Joe, had gone back into the house and his brother had been moving around in the backseat doing something which at the time he'd read as a kid fidgeting, but he was probably dumping abalone into garbage bags, unloading the backpack. Because Maria was always running around with a backpack that was too full and heavy, as were her friends, he'd come to take it as a norm and could see how they'd been fooled.

"They'd empty their packs and go back into the house for more?"

"Yes."

Marquez moved his notebook and laid a box on the table. It was one of the cartons from the Mexican supplier that they'd taken from Bailey's garage. He turned the red lettering so Li could read and watched Li move his hand for the first time, his fingers touching the lettering. "Yes, this name."

"At Mr. Mauro's?"

"Yes."

"Who else is selling to him?"

"I don't know."

"Do you know where he sells the abalone?"

"He ship it everywhere. When my son dies Billy Mauro comes to my house and gives money for Joe Li for college education. He is very sorry and he beg me to say nothing to police and the other men warn me not to speak. They know Billy Mauro so he do business with them."

Then he's doing business now, Marquez thought. He'd have to move the team around.

"Why don't you stay in Sacramento tonight," Marquez said. "We'll put you in a motel room."

"No, I go back to Colorado."

"We may need to talk to you more tomorrow. You need sleep. You can rest in the motel. No one except me will know you're there."

Li would start the long drive back to Colorado if he didn't talk him into staying. Li had that kind of determination. God knows, they'd followed him enough to know what he was capable of, but this was grief and an insomnia and need to be moving that Li probably wasn't even aware of, and Marquez put the effort in now to get Li to follow him to the Best Western where he usually stayed himself. He checked him in, paid for the room, and walked Li down to the door and got a cell phone number from him, gave Li his and said he'd have more questions tomorrow. He'd told Li he wouldn't have to testify. But if they took this Billy Mauro down that could change, though he didn't want to say anything about that yet. He'd have to find a way to keep Li out of it.

He drove back to headquarters and the chief was working on papers at his desk when Marquez walked in. Keeler didn't look at him but asked him to sit down, which was usually a bad sign. He kept his focus on the papers while Marquez talked about what he'd gotten from Li.

"That might be the break we've needed," Keeler said.

"I'll check it out."

"Not before we have a conversation about you. Only two things are keeping you out there as patrol lieutenant: your past record of success and the personal fondness of the director for you. But neither Chief Baird nor I will protect you any further, and, frankly, I don't know how much longer Director Buehler will either. This confrontation with the FBI was completely unnecessary and the way you handled it was, in my view, adolescent. Did you block their car?"

"Yes, sir."

"Had you already guessed they were Federal agents?"

"A guess isn't worth anything."

"What's the answer?"

"I'd assumed they were."

"So you thought you'd confront them. They asked you to move your vehicle and you refused."

"I asked to see their badges and by then I was on the phone to Douglas."

"You'd better be careful here, John. You'll have only yourself to blame, so if you have any questions when that time comes you can get all your answers at home. You'll hurt the SOU, as well, if you go head-to-head with the FBI. They've asked for our cooperation and they say they've passed on all the information they can without compromising their sources, which as you know better than anyone here, is another way of saying they can't risk revealing anything at this point. Now, they want you out of the picture."

"Douglas asked for that?"

"No, it was way over his head, and I can tell you you're gambling everything you've worked for because you don't like the Bureau's style. They won't talk to us, so you're going to show them up by exposing them."

"Chief, they—"

"Don't argue with me and I don't want to hear any explanations. There's nothing I can tell you that you don't already know. If you want to take your career down and ruin the unit you built, then I don't have time for you." Keeler's face reddened. "I've never taken you for a damn fool. Shut the door on your way out."

25

Marquez drove past the Best Western motel before leaving Sacramento. He wanted to see Li's Toyota parked in the lot and know that he was still here. He'd meant to talk more with Keeler today about Li. He would have done it on the way out if the conversation hadn't gone so downhill. With the death of the boy and with Li cooperating Marquez hadn't done anything to see that charges were at least filed against Li, and he knew Keeler expected that at a minimum.

An hour and a half later he was back in the Bay Area, Keeler's words ringing in his ears as he was escorted down a hallway in the FBI building in San Francisco. Douglas was waiting for him, his face hidden by an ancient computer monitor.

"Is that you, Marquez?"

"It is."

"Give me a minute."

Marquez took a chair and looked around the tiny space. At least Douglas had it to himself. A photo in a gilt frame showed Douglas with one arm around his wife and the other around two sons who looked about twelve and fourteen, sturdy, cheerful-looking kids, and Marquez remembered the last photos he'd seen when the boys had been much younger. On the wall to his right was a letter of commendation from the director, and on the desk a small triathlon trophy won that Douglas used as a paperweight.

"You're winning medals," Marquez said.

"It was handicapped for age. There was a big difference, let me tell you." He slid his chair over, pride on his face that the paper-weight had been noticed. His face looked like smooth rock this afternoon. "Have you had lunch, Marquez?"

"You want to do this over lunch?"

"It's not going to be any easier up here."

"All right, let's go eat." Marquez reached down to his side and lifted his laptop. "I brought this. We got a little shaky footage down near Morgan Hill the other night that I want to show you."

"Is this where the girlfriend got rolled down the hill?"

"Yes."

"They doped her up."

"That's what we're hearing. We lost a van we were following, but we got a few murky shots I want to show you after lunch."

They walked to a Japanese place that Douglas said was cheap and not far away. The sky was ragged overhead now, but the side-walk was sunlit. They talked about baseball and the 49ers, what they had coming up, tried to reconnect in some way as they walked to the restaurant. But the sports talk didn't get them anywhere and they sat at a small maple table now in a corner of a room that filled with light every time the sun moved from behind clouds. Marquez ordered a small plate of tuna sashimi, a bowl of rice, miso soup, as though the soup could touch the emptiness inside. He felt like a diplomat on the losing side of a war, waiting to hear what the terms of surrender would be. Ready to protest but knowing his words would fall on deaf ears. It wasn't his career in jeopardy that had made him call Douglas. It was the threat to the SOU, the way Keeler had laid it out.

He ate and looked at Douglas, again, his smooth dark face, sturdy build, winning a triathlon, thinking that Douglas must work hard at it. It took a particular discipline, a strength of mind more than body. He wasn't in bad shape himself, but nothing like that. He knew they weren't that far apart in age and that when they were kids there couldn't have been more than a handful of black agents with any hope of a career path like Douglas had going in the FBI. Things had gradually changed and Douglas had had the guts to go after that change.

"What do you think of Mueller?" Marquez asked, keeping the conversation on the FBI for the moment.

"Good director. Sorry we lost him out here."

"Do you want to go east yourself?"

"Not as bad as you want to ship me."

"I'm having a hard time figuring out what the Bureau wants from us."

"Communication."

"Like talking to God."

"That's because you keep asking me to tell things I can't."

"You had two agents tailing me and I don't get an explanation."

Douglas smiled suddenly. "Take it as a compliment, Marquez."

"Yeah?"

Marquez picked up his chopsticks, ate the sticky rice, and the food did something good for him. He asked about Douglas's wife, his two boys, and found that he liked him still and could separate him from the Bureau. But he wouldn't let Douglas buy lunch, didn't want to owe him for anything.

Then they were back in Douglas's office. Marquez booted up, showed Douglas what they had. Shauf had managed to get photos of the van. She'd picked a spot ahead of them on the road out toward Gilroy and caught faces in a streetlight. He knew already that the photo quality was too poor to enhance. He wasn't asking Douglas for help with that, just wanted to see his reaction to the passenger's face, because he had a nagging sense he should know.

"This is who rolled her down the hill?"

"Yes, and the van was stolen."

"I recognize him," Douglas said, "and I'm guessing you do too. You've got Eduardo Molina there. He's using the name Carlo. He had plastic surgery just like the boss. That's why you had trouble recognizing him. He also caught a customs agent bullet in '95. It almost killed him. When's the last time you saw him?"

"I haven't seen him in fifteen years. We were right there with him on an Oakland street and I didn't recognize him."

"I've seen that footage, and, yeah, they really did a number on his face. He's been with Kline all those years. He's your confirmation, Marquez. You've been looking at him."

"I guess I'm slowing down."

"That'll be the day."

Douglas was flattering him now, so there must be a reason. Marquez could tell he was calculating. He watched Douglas fold his arms across his chest.

"We appreciate what you do out there, Marquez."

"Yeah, how's it helping you?"

"I know you think we're protecting poachers and we know Kline is doing a lot of buying, but frankly we don't know where he is, either. If we did I wouldn't be sitting here and you know that."

Douglas stood and came around his desk. "I'm going to bring another agent in and she's going to show you something we've got for your SOU. Call it a gift from the Bureau to make this go a little easier. Your chief tells me you've wanted these for a while. Do you want more coffee or anything?"

"No, thanks."

Douglas went to get the other agent, introducing her as he

brought her in. Elaine Hempel. She had a firm dry handshake.

"Elaine knows tech like you wouldn't believe." He felt Douglas studying his face as he prepared to continue. "We're at a point where it's going to make more sense to coordinate our efforts. We've talked to your chiefs about this."

Marquez watched Hempel open a box and lay out telelocators on the desk. She handed him one. He knew the model, made by a Canadian company. He'd looked at them several times with the hope of buying sets for his team. They'd even got a couple as demos to try out, but they hadn't had the money to buy this year. Telelocators went for two grand each, were an inch by an inch and a half in size. You carried one and you could be tracked real-time anywhere.

"These are a gift," Douglas said. "Not a loan. We appreciate what you're up against. There are ten, so that covers your whole team, right?"

Marquez nodded. Easier than trying to watch us, he thought. He hid his bitterness and picked up one of the telelocators, turned the black plastic in his hand, liking the small size.

"You let us know your operational intents on a daily basis and we'll respond to the viability," Douglas said. "We'll handle overall coordination and risk assessment. We'll determine what contact is made with Kline's organization. At the end of the day they'll all go down, Marquez. Kline will go down."

"What do you mean let you know our operational intents?"

"You can shut down the individual divers all day long without a problem, but we'll handle Kline and Molina. You don't touch or make contact with anyone in his organization without clearing it with me first."

"There's the Bureau I know and love."

"Everything I'm telling you, I've talked out with your Chief Baird."

"Do you mind if I call him?"

"Be my guest."

Marquez got Baird on the line and Douglas put him on speaker-phone and made a point of saying he and Marquez had been to lunch and gotten things figured out. They were just now handing over the telelocators, and Lieutenant Marquez had a few points of clarification he thought his chief would want to listen in on.

"Go ahead, Lieutenant," Baird said.

"Do I take direction from the FBI, sir?"

"Only if your operation is overlapping."

"And how will we know?"

"Agent Douglas will coordinate."

Douglas held up a telelocator, and said, "the locators," so Baird understood.

"You know, sir, how remote the locations can be."

"You'll e-mail your daily report to the FBI, as well."

"Is that right, sir?"

"That's what we've agreed to for the duration of this operation."

Marquez didn't know what to say. "Any more questions for me?" Baird asked, breaking the silence that followed, and when there weren't any, said he was late to a meeting.

Douglas killed the speakerphone with a finger, and said, "We worked well together once before."

Agent Hempel handed Marquez the telelocators and briefed him quickly and efficiently on how they worked, how to get them up and running. She gave him her card in case he needed more help. But the word "together" didn't belong here. The Bureau had figured out how to use his team as another set of eyes. They'd done the army one better and come up with a new-age dog tag. They didn't care one way or the other about abalone and would share informa-tion only on their terms. Marquez picked up the box of telelocators and thanked Hempel for the demonstration.

"I guess we'll be talking," he said to Douglas and turned toward the door, his gut in his throat, his thinking clouded by surprise and anger.

26

When he left the meeting with the FBI he met with the team in a Home Depot parking lot off the frontage road in San Rafael. Their pickups and battered vans blended easily with the carpenter and contractor crowd and no one really paid them any attention as they parked off to one side, away from the rolling carts and foot traffic coming and going through the front doors. The parking lot was windy and vast and the faces of his wardens looked somehow more weathered and tired than yesterday. They wore their sunglasses and kept their distance, their postures quiet, an edge of wariness radiating from them as they waited for him to explain away their confusion and mistrust. He distributed the tele-locators as he talked, watched Roberts quickly drop hers on the driver's seat of her van as though she didn't want it touching her flesh. Alvarez turned his in his right hand while his eyes burned with the intensity and indignation of a man who'd just been robbed.

"What gives, Lieutenant?" he asked. "Are they going to tell us where to go and what to do?"

"They're not going to direct our days, but whatever Kline has planned they don't want us to get in the middle of. They'll let us know if they have a conflict with our location, or who we're following."

"Do we need to get their approval for a bust or surveillance?"

"Or even who we build a case against," Shauf threw in, and Marquez glanced at her, hands in the pockets of her jacket, wind ruffling blonde hair at her temples. He turned back to Alvarez.

"They're planning to take down Eugene Kline, but they don't know where he is and they're concerned we're going to inadvertently blow it for them. That's all I really know and my orders are to distribute these."

It was the fourth time he'd said it. He felt the same way as Alvarez, but he'd stepped back into his patrol lieutenant shoes. He'd deal with it a different way.

"We may as well all go home," Alvarez said.

"We're not going to quit, but we are going to stand down for a day while we get it figured out."

He heard the bite in his voice, felt his face tighten. They definitely weren't going to quit or let up. They'd improvise, adjust, find out what the FBI had going. He looked from Alvarez's skepticism to Petersen's quiet watchfulness, to the earnest face of Shauf, to Cairo's bemused eyes, Roberts's angry focused intelligence. The team had been larger three months ago. He probably missed Peter Chee most, for his clear reasoning.

"First they call off the pursuit of the *Emily Jane* and now we're reporting to them." Alvarez shook his head.

"They've got the money and the tech tools, maybe it'll help us."

"Right."

"And we'll adjust to it."

"They're pulling the strings. We're puppets now."

"Carry the telelocators and we'll see what the Bureau can do for us. We'll work the lead from Li, we'll stay on Bailey, and we've got tips to follow up on."

"Come on, Lieutenant, they just put a leash on us. By the time they get through analyzing each situation it'll be too late. They don't care about what we're doing; it's just shellfish to them. They're busy saving the world."

He could come down on Alvarez, tell him to get over it and forget the Feds, and he was close to it, but checked himself. Let them think it over tonight and they'd start focusing on the fish broker, Billy Mauro, tomorrow. He understood and felt the same frustration.

"We'll start working on Mauro and stay close on Bailey."

"Hey, maybe Bailey is working for them," Cairo said, "and that's how come he ran. He knew the Feds were there watching him. He could have gotten a ride out of there in a Fed car. Maybe that's how he disappeared."

"Bailey isn't working for them. They don't know much about Bailey other than his criminal history. They don't think he links to Kline. I asked."

"But what do you think?" Alvarez asked, and he knew they'd all been wondering. Bailey had been Marquez's informant. Only Marquez had worked him and Bailey had burned them, and now Alvarez was speaking for all of them. They needed to know what he really thought.

"I think he's being used by Kline and he ran because he expected a gunfight. Maybe Kline's people told him they'd take out Roberts and me and the Sausalito cops complicated the plan."

Marquez shrugged. He wasn't going to speculate beyond what he had already about Bailey's motives. He let it go at that and ended the meeting. Shauf would go back to the borrowed condo across from Pillar Point with Roberts, Cairo to Fort Bragg, and the others would stand down, take motel rooms, or make the drive home. He watched them go to their vehicles with an air of defeat and decided he'd get everybody together again in the next couple of days. He didn't think he'd said it very well, hadn't made clear that they would keep their autonomy no matter what. They'd figure it out, or at least he would. Law enforcement was all push, pull, a mix of failure and success and you did what you had to do to keep it going. They were at that sort of crossroads and his gut said the FBI was worried and that his Fish and Game team had been pulled into the mix not so much because they'd interfered or stood to, but more likely because satellite imagery and agents in suits driving Crown Vic's into small coastal towns and asking questions wasn't adequate. They need us more than they're worried about us interfering, he thought.

"I talked to Nick Hansen today," Petersen said—she'd lingered behind, was in her truck now with the window down. She smiled at a memory of the conversation, probably Hansen's dry humor, coming back to her. "He asked me if there was anything I want to know about the Golden Gate Bridge pilings. He says he can't even count the trips he's made out there and says he spends half his days on Fed patrols."

"We aren't going to work for them. I promise you that."

"Even if they sing their common cause, all for the greater good song? We're after the same guy and all."

"No way, no chance."

"What about the chief?"

"He won't cave."

"That's what I wanted to hear. Well, I might make a run all the way home tonight."

"You can drive with an easy heart now."

She laughed. "I'll come back down to Fort Bragg in the morning and check out that other tip." She put on her seatbelt and then looked puzzled, glancing back at his eyes as she started the engine. "I've got a question."

"Ask it."

"Does Douglas know this Kline said he'd kill you someday?"

"No." And there's no reason to tell him, he thought.

Marquez watched her drive off, made a couple of phone calls from the parking lot, then drove down to Tim's Treads, a tire store Alvarez said he was headed to. He found him in the small waiting room and they walked outside, looking at the traffic on the frontage road, Highway 101 across the fence beyond.

"They want control of us," Alvarez said.

"It's a telelocator, not an implant in your brain."

"You know they're using us."

"What I think is they need us. They have information that makes them believe Kline is here for more than dope smuggling and abalone. He's an enterprise, Brad."

"Like we're not up against it already."

"Get over it tonight and I'll talk to you in the morning."

He thought about Petersen's last question as he drove away. He'd been injured and sick the night Kline came for him, but how had Kline known he was vulnerable? He'd never have that answer and never stop wondering. He got ready to call Katherine as he drove away. It was a spur-of-the-moment idea, but early enough in the afternoon that maybe she and Maria didn't have a dinner plan yet.

He waited for her cell to ring and remembered crossing the border back into Texas and the old two-story wood frame he had rented for next to nothing and barely used. There'd been a single working bathroom, a bed, a place to cook. He'd had trouble getting out of the car and the house had been hot, dusty, the tap water running with rust that he'd thought was blood in his fevered state. He'd barely made it upstairs to the bed, forced a window open, left the lights off, was lying on his back on sheets that were drenched with his sweat when he'd heard noise in the yard, a car engine, someone down there, idling with their headlights off. He'd managed to get his gun, get into the attic space where he had access to the roof before the front door opened. Then he'd waited, shaking with fever in the dry attic heat, his breath rasping hoarsely, the gun slick in his hand, watching through the crack, watching and listening as he tried to quiet his breathing, tried to focus outside the fever.

A figure had entered the darkened room. He'd heard boots clicking like hoofs on the ancient wood floor and looked down on the figure whose shoulders were hunched and indistinct and whose eyes by some trick of reflected light were faintly red as the face turned upward.

"I will find you," said a voice that seemed to come from inside his head. "I'll hold your heart in my hand."

He'd heard liquid sloshing as the steps retreated, smelled gasoline as he'd tumbled from the attic, heard the whoosh as it ignited and a ball of bright light illuminated the room. He'd climbed out on the roof, slid on the asphalt, grabbed at old wooden gutters and fallen two stories as the gutter gave way and fire enveloped the house. He remembered hearing ammunition popping as the heat caught it, as the volunteer fire brigade strapped him on a board before sliding him into an old hearse converted to an ambulance. He'd had nothing left, not even his passport, and the hospital had called the DEA and verified he was who he said he was. He'd been ten days in the hospital and had come home to California.

"John," Katherine said, and her voice was light.

"I'm off this afternoon. I could pick up some food and the three of us could barbecue tonight." When she hesitated he knew it could easily be that she had other plans, and he felt funny immediately and wondered if he should have made the call.

"Where?" she asked.

"Either house. I can pick up food right now."

It was like dating Katherine, inviting her to dinner, hoping she'd agree, his pulse rising as he waited for her answer. The distance kept on hurting, same old sad story, a cycle he had to break for both of them. Either they went forward or called it, no way around that truth. It made him think of his sister living in London. She'd built a new life with a British banker husband, erased America from her head, and told him he'd never have a normal marriage because their childhood had been too much of a mess. Their mother had dropped his sister and him at their grandparents when he was nine and his sister was twelve. Their father had already left; mom was headed for rehab. She'd never really returned, had visited, but never took them home, and when he was thirteen and his sister a junior at Redwood High, their grandfather sat them down and told them their mother had died the day before in a train accident in India. For a long time he'd gone on believing she was still alive and he'd imagine he was seeing her on a street corner or driving past in a car.

Then in the summer of her senior year in high school his blue-eyed sister had graduated to heroin rather than college. She'd become rail-thin within six months. She'd moved out and he'd found her in a Tenderloin crack house a few months later, had told a pimp he was her brother and turned his back on a gun and carried her out in his arms. Darcey was why he'd gone into the DEA. Darcey was also one of the few people he'd ever seen beat heroin, or at least get to where she could live without it. The last long conversation they'd had, he'd told her he and Katherine were having trouble.

That night, he barbecued salmon and roasted potatoes in the fire, two of Maria's old favorites, though she said she'd stopped liking salmon as much and wasn't hungry for it at all tonight. She made them a salad and her own separately, putting only a few drops of olive oil on the leaves she planned to eat. She cut the end of a cucumber over the lettuce while Katherine lectured her. Maria's salmon sat on a corner of her plate throughout dinner and Marquez watched her feed it to the sink as her mom's head was turned. Then she got on the phone with her friends, after explaining that she'd actually eaten a big lunch.

"Do you see it now?" Katherine asked, as Maria talked to her friend in the back room and the two of them sat out on the deck in front of the dying embers.

"Yeah, I see it. Her weight is down."

"Way down. I'm taking her back to her doctor."

He drank a beer and they moved off Maria. He listened to the day's problems at the coffee bar, some of the complaints she'd fielded today, her expansion ideas. He questioned her more about the two men who'd come in, then showed her the video from Oakland and without looking very close or long she dismissed those men. He didn't push her on it because she didn't want to think that way tonight, and they tried to make it normal and sit out here like they used to and have it be easy and the way it used to feel, but couldn't do it. And yet, she sat close to him, curled in the chair, resting an arm on top of his, her fingers through his fingers, everything as fragile as glass. He held her hand gently and thought carefully about the chain of events with Heinemann while staring at the fire. When his cell rang he put the beer down and Katherine said she was going to get Maria and it was time for them to go. She got up slowly, her eyes averted as he answered the phone, figured he had to answer.

"I helped load two thousand abalone onto their boat today," Davies said. "We winched it over from a salmon trawler. The trawler dragged the catch underwater to the meeting. They had the bags hanging off the back of the boat in case they ran into any of your people. They were going to take a knife and cut the line. These people would take a knife to you, too, Lieutenant. I got some film for you if you want to meet tomorrow morning."

"What did you film?"

"Their boat and the guys that came in to pick me up. I bought this little video camera off the Internet that I hooked up to my boat cabin. I can run it remote control. If we sit down I can draw you the hull and give you a top-down view of their boat. I can meet you around dawn in Sausalito, unless you're done with me."

Marquez watched Maria walk out from the back room, saw the hall light go off.

"Or I'll meet you near that engineers' dock."

"I'll be there if you've got film for me."

"What did I just tell you?"

Davies hung up, not waiting for any more, a statement in that, and Marquez laid the phone down as Katherine walked out onto the deck again.

"We're leaving," Katherine said, and Maria was already out the door, not checking back to say good-bye. "She's angry at me, not you, John."

"I can be there when you take her back to the doctor."

"The doctor wants to talk to her alone, but I'll call you after."

Marquez put his arms around her and drew her close. He didn't kiss her but slid his hand under the hair on the nape of her neck and held her face against his. He felt her hold him, her fingers briefly on his spine. She straightened and he saw Maria standing in the front doorway staring at them, her hands pressed together in front of her, her facial expression one out of childhood. Maria's eyes found his and questioned, then she turned and he heard her feet go down the stairs.

27

When he left the house the next morning he called Alvarez and told him he needed backup for the Davies meeting and that he was picking his boat up. It was still dark when Marquez got to the marina. He used his headlights to see as he fumbled with the gate lock, then hooked the boat trailer to his truck, backed it down to the water, floated it, climbed on board, and clicked the blowers on before firing the engines. He hit the switch redirecting the exhaust through the drive to quiet the engine noise, but it was still particularly loud and deep in the darkness. He left it idling, tied off on the dock as he parked the truck and trailer, then carried his tactical vest and surveillance equipment back down. He poured coffee from a steel thermos as he motored out past the 5-mile-an-hour signs, smooth water rippling ahead of the bow. He had other uses for the boat today, but figured it would also work well for this meeting with Davies.

Now he followed the channel buoys, sipping coffee, looking at headlights crossing the San Rafael Bridge as he aimed the boat toward Angel Island and brought the speed up to twenty-five. The boat slicked across glassy water. The morning calm probably meant it would be hot today. He concentrated on the bay ahead and thought about how to approach Billy Mauro, refusing to let himself believe Davies's promise last night of having film to give him. The sky whitened overhead and the silhouette of the east bay hills was rimmed with pink light as he passed Angel Island.

When he tied off in Sausalito and came ashore, he didn't spot Davies and realized he hadn't really expected to. There were fishing boats on their way out and he checked the dock, retrieved the coffee thermos and sat on a concrete bench facing the water, drinking another cup though he hardly needed it. He watched the light change and remembered a crabber they'd busted here a year ago, the crabber's wife berating them as they'd lifted each crab out, measuring its shell, finding twenty-seven of a hundred were undersize while she kept telling them that they were destroying the industry, that they were the problem.

Across the bay, the sun rose above the hills and a finger of light colored the smooth harbor water. Davies was a no-show. No surprise, so get on with it, he thought. Their focus today would be on the Oakland fish broker, Billy Mauro. He called Alvarez.

"Let's get some breakfast. I'll buy, but I've got to dock where I can see the boat. Maybe one of those tourist spots farther down."

"Sounds good to me, Lieutenant."

Alvarez ate an omelet, Marquez scrambled eggs and toast. The big room was almost empty. A party of cheerful Germans was a few tables over talking in an animated way, but there was little other breakfast traffic. He called Shauf and Roberts, who were in Oakland scouting Billy Mauro's operation. Shauf had discovered that Mauro was well liked and well known along the waterfront. He had a dock location where he received directly from fishermen, but his office and production were in a corrugated metal building on Second Street. He shuttled two brightly painted vans, moving fish from the pier to the warehouse on Second Street, sometimes bringing the fishermen along to haggle price, then running them back down to their boats. But it looked to Shauf like most of the communication was by cell phone, a buyer meeting the boats, looking product over and communicating with Billy Mauro at his desk in the warehouse.

"So what's the plan here this morning?" she asked.

"We'll go see him." Because he didn't see any other choice. There wasn't time to set up surveillance. "Brad is with me. He'll hook up with you and I'm bringing my boat over."

He kept the boat's speed down as he crossed the bay. The only rough water was the wake from an empty outbound cargo ship flying a Chinese flag. He brought the speed up enough to plane after the cargo ship passed and now to his right as he passed San Francisco, the early sunlight reflected with the colors of copper and bronze and mirrored light off the skyscrapers of the financial district. He wore a Giants cap backwards and didn't need a coat this morning. Well before the estuary he cut his speed and tried Davies's cell phone once more before docking, didn't get an answer and didn't leave a message. Roberts picked him up in Jack London Square.

Mauro's business was sandwiched between a produce supplier and another seafood delivery business. Its street face was corrugated aluminum siding and two sliding doors sheathed with battered and dirty galvanized sheeting. A man stood out front hosing down the sidewalk and nearby street. A delivery truck with the company's logo, a blue and yellow fish with a smile on its face as it leaped from the ocean into a net, was in the building being loaded by two men in dirty white uniforms. They looked like they'd been working cleaning fish, and they paid scant attention as Marquez and Roberts walked in.

Billy Mauro was in his office on the phone and waved them in without knowing who they were. He seemed an energetic man, pointing to the phone, meaning that he couldn't get out of the conversation yet, but studying them, his round face quizzical. The room smelled like cigar smoke and Mauro in his short-sleeve white shirt looked like a middle manager from four decades back. He had the attentive eyes of a man used to solving problems and Marquez solved one for him, right now. He got his badge out and showed it to him. Mauro got off the phone soon after.

"I have a friend in Fish and Game," Mauro said. "Chief Wagner."

"He retired," Marquez said, "and died of a heart attack about five years ago. He was a good man, where'd you know him from?"

"Dead?"

"Yes."

"Really." Mauro looked away. He shook his head, the unlit cigar clamped in his teeth again. "What can I do for Fish and Game today?"

It was Marquez's plan to tell Mauro what he'd been accused of and if he reacted to that, try to keep him off balance and see what they could learn.

"Someone has accused you of buying illegal abalone."

"Ridiculous."

"Of course, but we have to follow up on these things."

The cigar came out now and Mauro laid it down on the desk. The wet end of it stuck to his finger and he had trouble getting his fingers loose.

"There are so many regulations now compared to when I started into this business. Not Fish and Game regulations, but for example the health department was just here yesterday. They want me to put Sheetrock on the inside of my building." He looked as though he expected a reaction. "It has been the same way for thirty years and no one has ever gotten sick eating anything I shipped." He shook his head at the absurdity and then reached down and picked up the cigar again. When he looked up again his eyes were cautious and distant. "I bring in Mexican abalone, but that's legal. I'll get the papers if you want."

"You bring it in boxed?"

"Boxed and frozen, by boat and truck. They're talking about a dock strike very soon so I have more than usual, but you can see it's all legal."

He pushed the papers across to Marquez. He used the cigar to point at the name, Carcenaros, the same Mexican firm Bailey's boxes were from. He could feel the change in Roberts, felt her tighten next to him as she put it together, and Marquez threw another brick through the window as Mauro looked for his papers.

"We have videotaped testimony from Tran Li. He names you as one of his buyers. We've showed it to the DA and it's enough to go on for commercial trafficking charges. We sent our last ab poacher to prison for three years and impounded all his equipment and boats. The middle men got longer sentences."

"He's lying."

"He drove a long way to tell us."

"Li is scared you'll trick him, so he's making things up he thinks you'll like. He's an immigrant. They're all afraid of the police. You know how it is. He stills lives like he doesn't belong here." Mauro looked for confirmation, for understanding. "But I've never bought anything illegal, never even once." He tapped his desk with an index finger. "Li is trying to cut a deal, right?" He tapped his chest lightly. "I've bought urchin from him, but never abalone." Shook his head for emphasis. "Never abalone." He pointed at the wall behind him. "Next door is my competitor. If you ask him what I say when people try to sell me illegal product, he'll tell you I tell them that I'll call Fish and Game if they don't get the hell out of here. Look." Mauro opened a desk drawer and removed a card that he handed across to Marquez. "Deputy-chief John Wagner," he went on, "I show them the card, tell them he's my friend and I don't buy anything illegal. Li is trying to save himself by placing blame on me. If you ask people you will find I've been in business as long as I have because I'm honest."

"I have to tell you that Li has made a full confession," Marquez said. "He feels he has nothing more to lose."

"As I said, I know the family, and losing their son was very hard. He's probably very scared of you."

"That doesn't cover it."

"Should I call my lawyer?"

"You could, but I think it makes sense to talk first. We have enough for a case against you, and you're right, it's your worst nightmare, a plea-bargain deal was cut with Li after the DA was sure our case was solid." He paused. "That was before Jimmy Bailey." He saw Mauro's face pale and then tighten high on the cheeks. "But we're not really after you. We're after the buyer moving product through you and we want all the places you ship to. If you can't give us that, if you can't contact them or they're gone, or you want to deny it all, then we'll put the charges together and padlock your building when we arrest you."

"This is all nonsense. I have bought fish from Li, but never abalone, and you have no proof of anything." He picked up the cigar again. "I am very legitimate." He pointed to an Oakland Chamber of Commerce commendation framed and hanging on the wall. "People know this about me." His face colored. "Enough of this." He picked up the phone, fumbled with a Palm Pilot and started punching in numbers. "We'll see," he said. "We'll see. You have no case against me and you're not going to bully me."

"We're not trying to bully you. In fact, we're giving you a chance to cooperate. Ordinarily, we'd stake out your place and build a case, but we don't have time and we don't think we need any more than Li has given us. I can show you the video. I can show the Carcenaros boxes we took from Jimmy Bailey's house when we searched it. But those are only pieces of the puzzle and your problem could get a lot bigger. You've got to decide whether it's worth letting that happen."

Mauro hung up the phone, pushed the shipping papers forward, again. "Look for yourself."

Marquez didn't pick them up again. This was how the game was played, the same papers used over and over. They could be dated from last December and still be in use today.

"Where do you ship the Mexican product?"

"Everywhere."

"Local restaurants?"

"Everywhere. Hong Kong. Washington, D.C. Paris. Everyone wants legal abalone. Come on, I'll show you the walk-in." Mauro got to his feet.

"All right," Marquez said. "We'd like to take a look at it and we'd like to show you the boxes we took from Bailey's house."

"No one is going to believe Bailey. No jury will believe him and whatever he says about me is a lie."

"Let's tour the walk-in."

There was a large prefabricated walk-in freezer and stacks of white boxes marked "King Salmon." Marquez opened a few and looked in at the salmon steaks. There was Chilean sea bass and gulf fish and shrimp, Hawaiian albacore, even urchins. The red epoxy floor was clean, the air chill, the lights a sterile fluorescence. Mauro said he ran a careful operation and reaffirmed there was no reason to have any misunderstanding. May as well get everything in the open and clear his name. The demand for abalone was very strong, he said, but it was Carcenaros that shipped to him and he didn't deal with anyone else. They were welcome to use his phone to call Mexico and confirm that he'd done business with them for years. There were workers here who spoke Spanish and one of them could act as a translator.

"What kind of business have you done with Jimmy Bailey recently?" Marquez asked.

"Urchin, but not much."

"We're losing a lot of abalone to poaching and we're going to do everything we can to stop it."

"You should."

They pushed back out through the walk-in door and Marquez nodded at four Hispanic workers sitting together on their break. His guess was these workers weren't overpaid.

"Have all your employees been with you a long time? When we separate them and question them, what will happen?"

They all looked at the workers and were making the men nervous. Marquez had seen two Hispanics loading the truck when they'd walked in and his guess was they were closer to each other than to the boss. They could separate them and break them down and his Spanish was plenty good enough for that questioning.

"I'm going to call my lawyer."

"Why don't you ask him about cooperating with us? Tell him we're willing to deal today only. Today is very informal."

Mauro walked to his office and they waited outside.

Roberts gave a crooked smile, showed a different side. "What do you think, do we have him boxed in?" she asked.

Marquez smiled, but he didn't know yet. He thought Mauro would roll over but wasn't a hundred percent sure. Mauro would play the percentages, he was pretty sure of that. He'd telegraph the situation to his lawyer without actually saying anything outright and he'd take his cue from the answers. He was on the phone now and that could be to his lawyer or it could be to poachers. That was the risk Marquez knew he was taking here. He'd done a lot in the name of expediency, lately. But they'd learned that both Bailey and Li had done business here and he had a feeling they were about to learn that Mauro was a practical man. After all, he'd tried to buy Li's silence and had gone to him immediately. Perhaps he'd reason now that Bailey and Li were coming at him from completely different angles and that would increase his vulnerability. They could hear the rise and fall of his voice, but not the words. They listened and waited.

28

Billy Mauro opened the door of his office and motioned them in. He dropped the shades that screened his windows from the work space and his forehead carried a light sheen of sweat as he sat down. He removed two 9 × 11 color photos from a brown paper envelope and slid them across facedown to Marquez, then pointed at a printer in the corner.

"I printed from e-mail attachments."

"Where did the e-mails come from?"

"After Li's boy drowned, I let them know I was putting my business up for sale on the Internet."

"Let who know?"

"The men you're looking for."

Marquez laid a hand on the photos but didn't turn them over yet, wanting a more complete description from Mauro first and guessing that the photos had some shock value. He watched Mauro slide a desk drawer open, then suddenly he had a handgun, but he was holding the grip with two fingers to show he wasn't pulling a gun on them. Roberts had already gone for her gun and had it out while Mauro laid his on the desk.

"No, no, officer, I'm just showing you the gun I bought after this. They threatened my family. I never would have done business with them otherwise. They watched my family and then came to me and said if I didn't work with them they'd kill my family. My mother is ninety and lives in a rest home and they got her name somehow, so what was I supposed to do? Call the Department of Fish and Game?" He tapped his computer. "Your department is less than four hundred people, I looked it up. Are you going to protect me with only a few people in the area? No, of course not."

"Maybe your friend the mayor could," Roberts said. "You should have called the police and us and you know that. You wanted to make money and you saw an opportunity."

Mauro's broad face turned toward her. "You don't have any children, do you?" She didn't answer. Mauro looked at Marquez. "What about you?"

And Marquez had a feeling they were getting something like the truth now. "You always have to fight back," he said. "Whether you'd called us or not, you knew it was wrong. But we would have had a setup here and eventually taken them all down. They never would have known you were involved."

"Okay, you say that, but look at these first."

Marquez read the expectation in his face and still didn't flip them over.

"Where's the e-mail?" he asked.

"Deleted."

"On this computer?"

"Yes."

"Let's get it back."

"I've never retrieved one. You'll have to show me."

"You're as bad as I am," Marquez said, and Roberts was already on her feet, coming around the desk to help Mauro scan through his deleted mail.

It didn't take long to find and open it and they didn't find any others from the same address. There was no text, only the attachments.

"Open the attachments?" she asked.

"Go ahead and we'll compare them to the photos."

She opened the first one and Marquez flipped the photos over, a feeling like a cold finger on his chest touching him as he looked at the first one. It was a shot taken at the killing scene at Guyanno. At the far left of the print, part of Stocker's arm showed along the left side of the photo. You could read a series of blue dots on Stocker's bicep and Marquez realized that the tattoo really was the constellation Orion as Davies had said. His eyes moved off Stocker and followed the image. There was the trunk of the oak and the chain around Peter Han's neck. Han's head was pitched forward, his eyes closed. He was the subject of the photo and Marquez wondered if that was because Billy Mauro had some Asian blood in him as did Han. Was there a racial angle? Did they think Han's murder would feel closer to home? He could make out a reflection of blood on Han's thighs. It glistened, hadn't dried yet, and he stared at it.

"Look at the other one," Mauro said, seeming to know what he was thinking and Marquez slid the top photo off and looked at the one underneath. Han was looking up at the camera. His left side was bleeding, but there was no knife wound yet. Han had his head pressed back against the tree trunk. He's trying to get enough air. He's wounded and he sees what's coming. You could see pain, fear, resignation in his eyes, but Marquez also saw something he thought was courage, defiance. He'd been shot, chained to the tree, and had known this was the end. Why Han?

"They told me this would happen to me. They called the day after Li's accident, so I went to Li and begged him not to say anything to you."

"Did Li see these photos?"

"No, no, of course, not."

"Did anyone come see you?"

"Yes, a man came and I have a video."

"Do you have sound, do you have his voice?"

"No sound." He pointed up at the corner of the room and when Marquez saw the tiny lens buried in the wall, he knew he should have seen it when he walked in. Looking around, you wouldn't expect something like that. "He was in the chair you're in."

Mauro put a CD in his computer and explained that the camera was activated from the desk and it burned a CD. He'd had it installed after he'd had a problem with a union rep. There'd been threats he'd been trying to get on tape and there was a sound system, but it was down temporarily. He played the CD for them now and they watched a silent movie.

Marquez didn't give any sign that he recognized the man and asked, "Have you had contact with him before?"

"On the phone. I recognized his voice."

"How often do they deliver?"

"Every few days."

"And what do you get for it?"

"One dollar an abalone plus the shipping costs." He added, "They pay in cash."

"How many have you shipped?"

"There's no record."

"Make a guess."

"Three thousand a week."

"How many weeks?"

Mauro shrugged. "All summer." The abalone was delivered, cleaned, and then shipped out whole frozen or cut into steaks. In Asia, a smaller three-inch abalone was preferred and Mauro explained that all of the smallest went there. The boxes were delivered separately and he didn't know how that worked. Had he dealt directly with Bailey? "Yes, very directly." Bailey had delivered weekly, driving a white panel van, but he didn't think Bailey was diving. "But with money it's always the same two men I deal with."

"When was the last time?"

He watched Mauro consult a Palm Pilot. He turned it so Marquez could read the screen and then showed a record of past calls and meetings, which he now downloaded and printed out for them. Marquez folded the printout, put it in his notebook. When it seemed they'd gotten all they'd get from Mauro, Marquez stood up.

"We're going to want to trap the two men here next time they call," he said. He walked over to the computer now and sent copies of the e-mail to DFG headquarters in Sacramento, to himself, to Chief Keeler, to Ruter, and to Douglas at the FBI. He blew off the urge to lecture Mauro, saw fear edge back into his eyes and thought of Mauro begging Li.

"What about my family?"

"We won't try to do a bust here. We'll follow them and then we'll link it to other evidence. We'll try to figure out a way that protects you. But when it all goes down you'll have to testify."

"I can't do that."

But you'll probably have to, he thought, though Mauro didn't have to be convinced of that today. And he was right to be afraid of these people. He looked at the face Mauro's camera had caught.

"What's this man's name?"

"Carlo."

Marquez nodded and studied Molina's face.

"When do you expect another delivery?"

"In the next few days."

"We'll be here for that one." When Mauro didn't respond, Marquez talked through how it would work. He took his time, slowing it down, getting a better read on Mauro. He explained how the bust would work, the partnership they'd be moving into, and suggested Mauro call his lawyer again. Marquez went outside to call Keeler. When he came back in, Mauro sat looking down at his desk. Probably wondering how else he could have played this, Marquez thought. Wondering if he should have talked at all. "These two men aren't going to hurt you or your family," Marquez said, but could see the fish broker didn't have any faith.

"I know they'll come here," Mauro said. "I know they will." He looked up abruptly. "I really don't think you understand how serious they are."

"So are we," Marquez said. "So are we."

29

Marquez ate lunch with the team at a Thai restaurant in Oakland, then talked an hour with Chief Keeler about the opportunity Billy Mauro presented. At the end of the conversation Keeler transferred him to dispatch to replay a message left earlier, a report of an unauthorized fishing boat left in China Basin. The caller sounded like an older woman—she'd refused to give her name and had hung up without revealing which pier. Dispatch obviously thought the woman was a crank, but the timing was too coincidental to the missed meeting in Sausalito so Marquez decided he'd go by China Basin and run the wharves there before pulling his boat out of the water.

He crossed the bay, cutting his Fountain powerboat's speed as he got close to the China Basin piers, then goosing it again as wake wash caught him from behind. The afternoon had turned sultry, high clouds masking the sunlight, and around him the air was heavy with the smell of bay mud. Ripples from his wake sloshed

against the creosoted pilings as he hugged the ends of pier buildings, checking each dock, easing his way along. He passed a large
wharf renovation sign, one that had been there long enough for the
lettering and the taxpayer money to fade away and then glimpsed
a white boat berthed beyond two ancient crabbers, a metal boom
arching over its stern. He brought his boat around, turned into the
shadowed water under the strings of broken windows and weathered
wood and saw white paint, black trim, a blue painted door, Davies's
boat, the *Opal*. The caller, who'd told dispatch that she lived on the
pier, had claimed that three men had gotten off the boat.

As he turned to dock at an empty slip, a gray-haired woman
on an ancient pleasure craft came out on her deck, called to him
that he couldn't dock there and he knew immediately that she was
the caller. He tied off and walked down to talk to her. An iron gate
blocked access to her gangplank and he showed his badge while
she studied his torn jeans.

"You're with Fish and Game?"

"Yes, ma'am." He handed her a card.

"I called the police this morning, but they haven't been out
yet. They told me to call the Port Authority and Fish and Game."

Skin disease, what might be rosacea had marred her cheeks.
She covered her chin self-consciously as she scrutinized the card.

"Your message said the boat came in late last night."

"Yes, it did. Very late."

She handed the card back and told him the boat arrived at
1:30. She'd awakened to the noise and watched from the dark of
her forward cabin as three men got off, leaving the boat tied with
only a bowline, so it banged against the dock all night. That was
why she'd called. The boat was going to damage the dock. She
pointed up toward the street, describing as best she could the van
that picked them up. Marquez looked at the concrete steps leading
up from the dock, then at the chain-link gate lying nearly flat.
They'd been carrying things but she couldn't tell what because the

dock lights were burned out. She thought she'd heard Spanish. He waited for her to elaborate and she didn't, but unlocked her gate and came out on the dock, touched his wrist, her fingers like a tiny bird alighting. "I'm sorry I'm not more helpful. Will you find the boat owner and ask him to move it?"

"We'll try to."

"They're not allowed to dock here."

"If we find the owner, we'll certainly tell him, but in the meantime I'd appreciate it if you'd call me at this number if you see anyone near the boat."

Marquez looked around and wondered what possible arrangement she had to live here. Something grandfathered, some debt owed. The few other boats looked like they were permanently docked. He excused himself, walked back down and wrestled with the stern of the *Opal*, pulling it over to where he could tie it off, then got a flashlight off his boat, put on gloves and entered Davies's cabin.

Three months ago he'd had a beer on the *Opal* with Davies. He'd heard a few comments about the dire world situation that he'd put down to beer talk, but wondered how those views played in now. That was a conversation he hadn't shared with Ruter yet—Davies's view of the Middle East, his certainty about the inevitability of a Third World War. Davies's dive equipment was missing from its usual spot and he searched the bins and storage lockers before returning to the wheel. The pilot license, navigation manuals, maps, log, and equipment were neatly in place. So were the emergency radios, the flare gun, everything thieves would grab if the boat were left open and unattended.

He saw no evidence of struggle or violence and touched things in a minimal way, economizing his moves, not believing the cabin would become a crime scene, but knowing there might be important evidence here. There was ground coffee in a filter, but no coffee made, then something he couldn't account for, a half-full Folgers coffee can, lying on its side in the trash, coffee grains spilling out across the wrappers underneath. He knelt and studied the coffee as though getting closer somehow would bring the answer out. They'd caught up to Davies, he thought. He'd been making coffee and had gotten surprised. Maybe Davies had dropped the can in the trash as a signal when a gun got pressed to his back. Marquez knew he should back out of the cabin now, not contaminate anything further. He stood slowly. He'd call the San Francisco police and see if he could get them to come out with their crime scene techs. Do that before calling Douglas. He walked out on deck, opened the hold and lay down, shone the flashlight beam on the dark water. There was little water in the hold, a foot or so, and he moved the beam back and forth until he was confident there wasn't anything there. When he closed the hold and stood up, the woman was standing on the dock looking at him.

"I remembered something."

"Good, I'll be right there." He shut the cabin door, climbed onto the dock and peeled his gloves.

"They'd all gone up toward the street and then one of them came back down and got back on the boat. I believe he threw something in the water. I heard a splash like a brick would make."

"Could it have been something bigger?"

"No, I'm sure it was small. He stopped as he was going up and then came back and threw it in."

A diver could check under the dock. He could dive himself. He looked down at dark oily water. Would they find anything in that mud? He wrote his cell number on another card and handed it to her, telling her his first name was John, and asked hers. "Corinne Mathews," she said, and he shook her tiny hand, grateful for her willingness to help. She was still watching as he backed his boat out. He gave her a wave and a smile, though he was very troubled by the *Opal*'s presence here. The bay was still flat and calm all the way out to the Gate. No sailboats this afternoon, some motor traffic but not much. Marquez got on the phone to SFPD before pushing up the throttle, angling the boat as they transferred him around. They wanted to wait to see if Davies showed up today and reclaimed his boat and he hung up thinking he might as well call Douglas.

Marquez had gotten his boat, a twenty-nine foot Fountain, several years ago at a Fed auction. The hull had been damaged during a DEA bust and the boat went for way under market value, and still it had stripped his savings. It took another ten grand to repair the hull, but he didn't think there was a manufacturer that built a better offshore boat and had figured it would help his team. He'd named it *Bonfire* after Katherine's nickname and when it had some engine problems three months ago he'd blamed it on the separation.

But it didn't have any engine problems this afternoon and he reached for the throttle and kicked it up. The Fountain carried two 502 Mercs. It blew through fifty and he raised the tabs, opened the throttle.

"Where are you, Davies?" he asked aloud. "What happened there last night?" And the wind tore his words away as the *Bonfire* ran for home.

30

Marquez's phone rang as he drove away from the marina. He'd been on the phone to Keeler, trying to reach an agreement about how to handle the Mauro situation and expected it to be Keeler calling back before he saw the screen read "Private Number." When he answered he heard multiple voices and his immediate reaction was that someone had inadvertently hit his phone number, perhaps an informant. The voices were male and the sound muffled as though from a cell phone in a coat pocket. He heard yelling now, someone saying, "Back up, back up!" Then another order in Spanish and several seconds of quiet followed by muffled voices, and one voice much clearer that he was sure belonged to whoever carried the phone, saying, "Okay, okay."

He thought he heard someone pleading, but it was distant like something you might imagine you hear in the wind, then three distinct pops that Marquez knew was the sound of gunfire, and the phone clicked off abruptly. The next call came in minutes and he stared at the screen unable to recognize the number and still wondering what he'd just heard.

"Lieutenant Marquez?"

It was another detective investigating Meghan Burris's murder and wanting to meet him in Pillar Point. For several days Marquez had tried to get back on board the *Open Sea,* Heinemann's boat. He knew it had been searched already—the detective told him they'd like to go through the boat cabin again today with Marquez present, the implication being that Fish and Game now could have a look.

Marquez got there in just over an hour and there was very little to look at. The detective, a freckled middle-aged woman, showed him loose papers with nothing coherent on them, an address book that Marquez thumbed, and a log she'd found in the boat cabin.

"I'm looking for anything with the name Mauro on it," Marquez said. "He's an Oakland fish broker and it's unlikely he knew Burris, but Heinemann may have dealt with him."

Mauro had insisted that wasn't the case, that he didn't know anyone named Heinemann and Bailey was always alone. The poaching angle he'd already talked over with this detective several times in phone interviews, but she went back through it pedantically now as Marquez searched the cabin. He left the *Open Sea* an hour later having learned nothing and walked past Bailey's empty berth. He met briefly with Cairo, then headed north, talking to Keeler at dusk as Keeler was leaving headquarters. Douglas had called complaining that the telelocator readings were static. Either the equipment was malfunctioning or most of the team was in one location all day.

"They aren't carrying them," Keeler said. "You tell them they're making us all look bad after we gave our word."

"I'll take care of it."

"Or I will."

Keeler hung up and Marquez called Hansen. He wanted Hansen's perspective on the FBI as an overseer, to hear what the FBI had him doing and what Hansen thought about the homeland security patrols he'd made for months. Hansen was onboard the *Marlin,* coming up from the south bay.

"Reminds me of my riverboat days in Nam," Hansen said. "It's just the times we're living in. The Feds have new information about every two weeks. They don't have any choice but to check it out and until they're comfortable again, they're going to run all of us. Tell you where our boat is at right now, we're passing the old naval yard south of Hunter's Point, and I'm looking at the abandoned crane that loaded the Hiroshima bomb. That says something about all of it, doesn't it? Hey, I saw one of those Fountains streaking across the bay this afternoon. Looked like someone familiar standing tall at the wheel."

"Where were you?"

"Berkeley pier."

"You've got some good eyes on you still, Nick."

"They're the only thing that's held up. I'll talk to you later."

Marquez got Katherine on her cell phone on her way home from Maria's doctor. She asked him to come over to talk about what the doctor had said. He headed to Katherine's house, making a call to Petersen as he drove.

Petersen had gone out to the campground at Salt Point chasing down a poaching tip and interviewed a woman staying in a camper there. Her husband was a retired Park Service ranger who'd become suspicious of a couple of divers staying in the campground. Last night he'd seen headlights after midnight and got out of bed when he heard voices. He'd copied down the license plate of a white panel van after he'd seen the divers loading coolers into it. When he'd turned his flashlight on them and demanded to know what they were doing, someone had struck him from behind. From the damage to his skull and the pattern of the bruising the hospital speculation was that he'd been hit with a hammer. He was still in the hospital and Petersen had gone there after talking with the woman.

"He's going to be okay," she said. "He was able to talk just fine, though they didn't allow me more than a few minutes with him. He'd written the license number on his palm with a pen, but he also fell on that hand and they cleaned it up at the hospital while he was still woozy. He didn't realize they'd rubbed the ink off. Both he and his wife say they can identify the men who've been camping at Salt Point."

"But they're gone now."

"Yeah, they'd dragged him into some bushes and his wife didn't realize what had happened until she woke and started worrying around three in the morning. She called the sheriff, and deputies found him. They've already got a composite worked up and tomorrow I'll take that around to the harbors and bars and see if I can find anyone that recognizes these guys."

"Be careful."

"Are you going to coach me in my last month?"

"I guess not. Let me know what you find out."

He ate dinner with Katherine and Maria and though the conversation was friendly the evening felt charged with tension. After dinner, Katherine walked him to his truck, and got in on the passenger side to talk. Maria had met alone with the doctor, who'd in turn talked with Katherine afterwards, telling her that Maria was definitely anorexic. She'd set targets with Maria and would see her again in two weeks. She'd also advised that Katherine avoid any more confrontations, because Maria had told the doctor that her mom was making it harder to get things in control.

Maria had eaten an adequately portioned meal tonight, then withdrawn to her room and homework and the music she downloaded off her computer, and the friends she kept in constant e-mail contact with. Katherine was quiet in a way he'd seen only a few times before. Something else had been said to her that he suspected had both hurt and surprised her.

"I suppose I'm a failure as a parent," she said. "Her father left when she was two and a half and maybe she never really got over that. So often things go all the way back."

"I wouldn't make excuses for Maria and you've been doing the right thing calling her on how she's eating. Her doctor has got it wrong."

"The doctor says it's healthier to work from goal to goal."

"You've been doing the right thing."

"You don't make a very good cheerleader, John, so knock it off." She paused a moment. "Maria told the doctor that you and I are divorcing. Have you said anything like that to her?"

"Never."

"I feel pretty disillusioned and I know I've said some things to her, but I've never said that."

"Maybe she needs us to reach resolution one way or the other."

"I know, and I've been going to a therapist, and when she asks me what do I really want I can't tell her. I don't really know. I'm sorry if that's hurtful."

"It's what it is," he said, though it stung him. "Better that you say what you feel."

"I guess I'm still really angry, but I can't talk about that tonight. I'm too worried about Maria."

Marquez walked back in to say goodnight to Maria, and told her what he'd told her when he and Katherine had separated. No matter what, he was there for her. He told her he wanted to help her get through this. He talked with Katherine a while after, and left the house wondering why they couldn't get their marriage together, why he was driving away. "What are the issues?" his sister had asked, when he'd tried to talk to her about the problems. There was the issue of Katherine believing he put his work ahead of the marriage. People that love each other get around work issues, his sister had responded. "You're not the first person to be on the road a lot of the time. It's ordinary. Your problem is somewhere else. You must make her feel second best. Maybe you diminish her." He drove home and thought about it on and off through the night. It was as though Katherine wanted the distance right now. She wanted him to change jobs, transfer out of the SOU and being constantly on the road, but she wasn't going to tell him directly. He put on music, an old Doors tape, turned the lights off, sat on the couch with the slider open, and then slept there, unable to move to the bedroom.

The next morning Alvarez was hosing the sidewalk in front of Billy Mauro's Fresh Seafood when a white refrigerated van with two men in it drove up. Marquez watched through binoculars. The truck slowed as it hit the bump before entering the building. He got a good look at the men inside, inwardly turning the surgery-altered face of one into a much younger Eduardo Molina. Hard eyes raked over Alvarez who'd turned away with his hose.

The van backed up to the loading dock and Alvarez moved back inside, took up his new job of cleaning fish. He activated the hidden video camera and taped the men getting out of the truck, watched them go into Mauro's office and shut the door. Marquez adjusted his earphones to hear Molina and Mauro talking. Molina wanted the van emptied now, but pressed Mauro to send one of his own vans to pick up a load of abalone coming into Pier 45 in San Francisco.

"I don't know," Mauro said. "I don't want to do that."

Molina continued as if he hadn't heard Mauro. His voice was low and very controlled, his English almost without accent.

"They'll look for your truck before they dock," Molina said. "So you park where they see you easily."

"I don't even know if I can get in there at that hour."

"If they don't see a truck they'll turn around and that's no good."

"What if Fish and Game is there? I never agreed to do any-thing like this."

"We're going to take care of them. You don't need to worry about them." Marquez heard a chair slide. "At three," Molina said, and Marquez slipped off the earphones and dialed the number Douglas had given him.

"We've got Molina in Oakland," he said, as Douglas answered.

"Let him go. Under no circumstances go near him." Marquez didn't respond, watched the white panel truck bounce off the curb and start down the street. "Do not follow him." The panel truck turned the corner. "Are you hearing me?"

"We're going to have to sit down."

"Marquez, you've got to let him go."

"He's gone."

"That's what has to happen." He exhaled. "Okay, let's meet right now."

31

He met Douglas in China Basin and they drove to a restaurant across from the ballpark. The Giants were on the road and it was easy to get a table where they could talk. Marquez ordered a turkey sandwich and coffee, his mind on Molina and the second man pulling away in the van.

"How'd you come up with Billy Mauro?" Douglas asked.

"We got his name from an abalone diver we busted, a Vietnamese immigrant named Tran Li who was delivering his catch there because that's what he was told to do. Kline is using Mauro to distribute and that probably means he's using other distributors, as well. Mauro runs their abalone through his plant and packages it in boxes from a Mexican shellfish broker he's got legitimate import papers for. There's an old problem where papers get reused over and over."

"Is this the Vietnamese diver who lost his kid up near Fort Bragg?" Douglas asked, and Marquez nodded. Douglas pointed a finger, said, "He's working for you."

"No, he's out, and the family has moved to Boulder to live with his wife's sister. He came back to tell us because he's haunted by the death of his son."

"Guilt?"

"And grief."

"We're pulling Bill Mauro in today. And those photos you e-mailed me are the real thing."

"The photos were all of Peter Han." Douglas nodded faintly in agreement. "Does that mean anything to you?" Marquez asked.

"Let's stay on Mauro. We'll bring him in and I'm going to have to ask you to back away from him until we know more."

"You've got a way of killing my appetite."

"Hear me out first." Douglas rubbed his forehead and leaned forward, elbows heavy on the table. "The problem is getting worse. Our informant, the one on the *Emily Jane,* the one you were after, had a gun stuck in his mouth last night by Molina. Molina told him to lose himself or die. He said they'd run him thirty miles off the coast and throw him in the water if they saw him again. He called me from Las Vegas this morning. He's out and he was our pipeline. I need every source you have, John. If Davies is talking secretly to you, I need to know."

"Then give me why."

"Kline was hired to do a hit here in the Bay Area. We believe it's supposed to be this week and we've lost track of him. We thought we had him yesterday, but the man we took down turns out to be a double. We're still holding the double and if you want a look, I'll take you to see him. It'll blow you away. Looks just like Kline and he'll show you his scar. He had plastic surgery in Mexico City two years ago. They shaved his head, peeled his scalp down over his face, modified the bone structure, and came up with a pretty good double. He says his eyes leak all the time and half his face is numb, but the money is good."

"So Kline knows you're after him."

"That's right, we fucked up. I'm going to give more today though I'm disobeying an order, so it stays between us, okay? I'm telling you because we're out of time. We have a contact in Mexico who's sure this hit is going to take place. It's someone within our judicial system and we've been over every case being tried in California and have come up with four candidates, including a DA and a judge here in the Bay Area. There are six murder trials pending this morning where the accused is a gang member and the killing was drug-related. Some of those gangs distribute for cartels. So it may be a payback, a debt owed, or he may be here to kill a witness. We don't really know—"

"That's too big a field," Marquez said. "You know more than that. You wouldn't put this kind of effort in."

"That's why this informant on the *Emily Jane* was so important. That's how we were keeping track of him. He'll do this hit unless we find him first." Douglas paused. He lifted a hand from the table. "No question he's taking abalone and moving dope. The abalone is a new gig, the dope operation he's had for years. We've been trying to work our way into that operation. Don't ask me why he got into abalone this round. We don't get it."

"It's better money than dope. That's why."

"We're seeing a lot more of Molina all of a sudden. You're seeing him more. He knows we know Molina and may be dangling him as bait to lure us. That's part of why I want you to stay away from Molina. Kline probably has countersurveillance on him."

Marquez flashed on a wedding party where the photographer and his assistant gathered the family for a group photo and killed them all. There was no morality in Kline, no real connection to humanity, only the continual question of what people could do for him.

"Your name has come up," Douglas said. "We got that from our informant and there's a chance Kline knows the names of all or part of your team. He may be tracking you, and you of all people know what he's capable of."

Marquez watched Douglas put ketchup on his hamburger, take a bite of it, dripping ketchup back on the plate.

"What do you know about Jimmy Bailey's whereabouts?" Marquez asked.

"Why?"

"We've lost him and he's doing business with Kline."

"We don't think he's a real player," Douglas said. "He's a low-level drug peddler." Douglas handed over a card now with a number handwritten on the back. "If you get the feeling you've got someone watching you, call this number."

Marquez suppressed a smile, but it struck him as comic and theatrical that if Kline came for him he'd get a chance to phone and call for help. He took the card and then before they finished talking got some insight from Douglas into the FBI's take on why Kline was poaching abalone. They believed he was laundering money by paying it out for abalone and then selling the abalone largely in Asian markets. Marquez said good-bye to Douglas on the sidewalk and mulled what he'd learned as he drove away.

He met with the team and gave them everything he'd gotten from Douglas, then talked it over with Keeler and sent three wardens back to Pillar Point and Cairo and Petersen to Fort Bragg. They'd stay on Bailey and wait for Heinemann and check out some recent tips. Marquez called Katherine and she invited him over. When he got to her house the front door was open and he could hear Katherine and Maria in a sharp exchange. It was the same thing again, the same pattern.

"I'm having dinner in my room tonight," Maria was saying. "I have too much homework."

"What are you having?"

"Tomato soup."

"What else?"

"Toast."

"That's not enough."

"I had lunch; I'm not hungry for anything else."

"What did you have for lunch?"

"A sandwich, and it's none of your business. I'm not having this soup anymore." Through the open deck door, Marquez watched Maria slosh a pot of soup into the sink and fling her toast into the garbage. She saw him and said, "I'm not eating anything tonight and no one can make me. I'm sick of this."

"Go to your room," Katherine said, "I'll talk to you there."

Marquez heard her door slam and Katherine stood with her hands on her hips glowering at him. She picked up the soup can, slammed it into the garbage, held up a little plate of peanuts, no more than ten scattered across it.

"Look at this," she said, "and I'm supposed to let the doctor handle it."

"Can you force her to eat?"

"I'll spoon-feed her like a baby if I have to. Her period has stopped and her bones are going to be as brittle as sticks in a few months. This is going to stop now and that stubborn little will of hers isn't going to prevent me from making her eat. I will not let her destroy herself because she wants to look like one of these emaciated godforsaken models. You could cut paper with the hip bones of some of those women."

"Didn't her doctor set a goal of a pound every four days?"

"It doesn't matter."

"She told me she's going to make that."

"Guess what? Anorexics lie. They deceive. It's part of the game. I've got two friends who started down that path twenty years ago and they're still skin and bones. They exercise constantly and they actually think they look good, but they look like they just walked out of Auschwitz and they don't fool anybody. That isn't going to happen to my daughter."

"You've got to give her a chance."

The conversation went down from there and he didn't end up

having dinner with Katherine. He drove home. That night he fell asleep in a chair on the deck with a blanket wrapped around him. He dreamt of Africa and his first wife, Julie, a morning out in the bush. He smelled the early morning coffee and the acacia trees and grass. They held tin mugs and crouched, smiling at each other, watching the black silhouettes of elephants move across a plain in the dawn. Julie sat close to him again in the night and he felt what he'd felt that morning, that the world was open and theirs to make and the life ahead was going to be grand. Her hand had slid under his shirt and around his back and he'd held her tight against him after they'd made love.

The sensation was so real in memory that as he awoke he felt as though he'd violated his marriage with Katherine. His face was wet with dew and his neck kinked from sleeping in the chair. He rose clumsily and a deer bounded away in the darkness downslope. He laid the blanket on the chair, walked in the house, and fell asleep again in the bedroom, a hand on Katherine's pillow, his mind still floating in the dream.

Later, it was a call from Douglas that pulled him back from his personal problems. It was early, a red sunrise, and Douglas said a male body had washed up at the base of cliffs near Daly City. A hang glider pilot who'd been scratching low along the cliffs yesterday had spotted a corpse but inexplicably had waited until midnight to call 911. The rough description was close enough to be Davies, and Douglas was offering Marquez a ride down.

"Unless you want to follow us," Douglas said.

"I'm going to continue south, so I'll meet you down there."

A Coast Guard helicopter was in the morning sky alongside the cliffs. When he met up with Douglas, another FBI agent, and local detectives, it became clear they wanted him there to help ID the body.

"We've got a way to get you down there," the detective said, "But I've got to warn you it may not be pretty. They don't always float and a lot of times the decomposition gasses will leave them standing on their heads and bumping along the bottom. Was this a friend of yours?"

"Someone we're looking for missed a meeting and his boat was abandoned."

"I got a feeling you're just the man I want to talk to."

The detective grinned, showing yellow teeth, and they walked out the half mile. Marquez belayed down on a rope that had been set up. Douglas came down the same way and the other agent stayed on top. The detective got lowered in a basket by the helicopter and then they were on the small beach, moving across the black rocks.

The hang glider pilot had launched and scratched his way north, trying to find enough lift to make a good day of it. He thought at first that it was a dead seal, and now, seeing the body wedged in the rocks, wrists tied and arms bound behind the back, ankles bound, and the head facedown and still hidden, Marquez could understand why. The pilot had bagged up his kite and gone home. Later, his conscience got the better of him.

The body was swollen with gas. They backed up for a wave that lapped halfway up the corpse and the detective talked. "The rescue people hate this. They want to come in, pick up the body and go, but they leave stuff behind when we let it happen that way. This one is naked, but we might find something down here in the rocks." He pointed at two exit wounds in the back without commenting on them. "I'll bet they had him take his clothes off before they bound him. Let's get him turned over."

They had to drag him back and then flipped him. His nose and eyes were gone and a small crab dropped out of his beard. A lot of his scalp and one side of his face had rubbed off. It wasn't Davies.

"Is this your man?" the detective asked.

"No, but I recognize him."

Marquez looked at Douglas and then at the body again, remembering the phone call two days ago, the muffled voices, the gunshots. Heinemann looked like he'd been in the water longer than that, but maybe, just maybe. He turned to Douglas.

"I need to talk to you about a phone call I got a couple of days ago and there's some information in my truck you'll want." He looked over at the detective. "We got him killed. We had him wired up and then lost him."

Heinemann's skin was the color of putty. He'd been stripped, bound, thrown overboard like a sack of garbage. That probably meant he told them everything first.

"He was working for you?" the detective asked.

"More like we were using him and he was using us. We've been chasing an abalone poacher."

"This is about poaching?"

"Yes."

Douglas cut in. "Let's go up top," he said, and to Marquez, "this was for you. He sent you a message."

32

Marquez pulled what he had on Heinemann out of the truck and waited as the detective copied the parts he wanted. When they got to the murder of Meghan Burris a light seemed to go off in the detective's head. He knew about it, more of the pieces connected for him, and Douglas took the conversation from there, his hands moving slowly in the air as he spun a story.

Marquez didn't need to hear it and walked back over to his truck. He dropped the tailgate and called Petersen back. There was a light wind off the ocean this morning, not enough to generate any lift for the glider pilots, yet air junkies were arriving and a few had unfolded their gliders out on the sandy launch area. He watched them as he talked with her.

"I've asked around about the two Salt Point divers," Petersen said. "One guy I talked to thinks they have a rented house in Fort Bragg and they've been diving north of town. I got a street name and thought I'd check it out."

"Do it, but take Cairo with you."

"He's down at Van Damme State Park checking another tip. There was a CalTip call last night that he—"

The clattering of helicopter blades drowned her response and he watched the body bag swinging in a metal basket beneath the hovering copter. They lowered the basket, slipped the bag out, and the helicopter rose into the fall blue sky and started up the coast. He heard Petersen clearly in the quiet that followed, about Cairo following up on a tip and finding nothing so far. She gave him the street name in Fort Bragg for the Salt Point divers and then said good-bye. He flipped the tailgate up and looked at Douglas, wanting to talk alone with him before leaving.

Beyond the edge of the parking area, out on the flat sand and dirt along the top of the cliff, four hang gliders had been unfolded and their keels rested in the sand. He watched one of the pilots sliding ribs into the bright-colored sail to draw the wing taut and saw the awareness of what was going on over here, heads nodding toward the police vehicles at one end of the parking lot. He couldn't look at the gliders without remembering the year that followed after he'd returned home from the hospital in Texas. After he'd exhausted his money and given up on finding Kline.

It had taken the winter to heal his body and the next spring he flew to San Diego and took a bus down to the Mexican border and began hiking north on the Pacific Crest Trail. In the week he'd lingered among the highest peaks of the Sierra, in Muir's Range of Light, he'd watched hang gliders circling with hawks as they caught thermals rolling up the dry eastern face from the desert far below. He'd watched the pilots negotiate the turbulence and trash air over the great mountain faces while he sat high on the rock trying to figure a way to move his life forward again. He remembered hiking in moonlight the hundred switchbacks up from the meadow and lying on the summit of Whitney under the cold brilliance of stars, trying to find the motivation to return to society.

He looked from the gliders back to Douglas, still remembering the Pacific Crest, how he'd moved in the early and the dusk hours, largely avoiding people, but encountering bear and deer and then elk as he got farther north. Near the Washington and Oregon border, as the fall closed in, he'd helped a woman with a badly sprained ankle, carrying her pack, assisting her back to a trailhead, and that ordinary act had been the catalyst that brought him home.

Now Douglas walked over to him. "We're going to assist on this one, but I'd like it if you gave us everything you know about or had going on with Heinemann."

"Sure, but I think you've got everything at this point."

"I'd also like a way to reach this Tran Li."

Marquez wrote down Li's phone numbers, tore the page out of his notebook, and said good-bye to Douglas.

"This one bothers you because you feel responsible," Douglas said. "But you're not. Heinemann got himself mixed up with these assholes."

"I wish it was that simple."

"Let him go, he made his own bed. Listen, I got a call on the way down here. Your Bailey is back in Pillar Point."

"Thanks for that. I'll go see him."

Forty minutes later, Marquez was in Pillar Point, standing above the docks looking down at Bailey scraping paint on his boat. He talked to Petersen again before walking down. She'd seen dive equipment in the driveway of a little asbestos-shingle house in Fort Bragg. An old Chevy Nova, pumpkin-colored, was parked out front, matching what the retired ranger had remembered. It was probably the right house. She hadn't seen any activity but had scouted several good places to watch the house from and was currently heading north to check a couple of other coves she'd heard these divers might be working.

Marquez walked down to Bailey, who wore nothing but a pair of shorts that hung loosely on his hips and wraparound mirrored sunglasses. He held a two-inch putty knife that he'd been using to peel paint from the cabin door with and cleaned the knife as though Marquez wasn't there, dropping a curled paint strip into a plastic bucket on the deck of the boat.

"We're working on a way to charge you, Jimmy."

"I haven't done anything wrong except use a shit batch of primer that didn't dry tight. This is going to be a bitch to repaint." Bailey's pupils were pinpricks, his eyes carrying a hardness Marquez didn't know he had in him. "I knew you'd come by today."

"You've done a pretty good job burning us, but we're not far from bringing it down around you. You could be standing in a lineup tomorrow."

Bailey flicked a large paint chip into the water. He scraped the knife blade on the top of the bucket and started on the door again, saying, "Did you drive all the way down here to dump shit on me again?" Bailey grinned at a thought, his chapped lips pulling back over his teeth. "If you go through my house again and you find another babe in the attic, you're welcome to her. You can use my mattress. I know that's what you were thinking last time and she was pretty fun when she was coked up."

"I found her in the truck after your friends rolled it down the ravine. The cab collapsed on her and snapped her neck. Her head was turned around."

"I never liked her face anyway, but she had a nice ass."

"What did you say?"

"I said she had a nice tight little ass. Too bad you got her killed."

"Did you get Mark Heinemann killed?"

"Last I heard he was up north."

"Heinemann's body washed up this morning south of San Francisco. I pointed the detectives toward you and said I'm sure you know what happened. I told them you'd played it both ways with us and we're trying to take you down on something new now. We've got someone looking at a six-pack of photos with your face as one of them. We hope he'll pick you out today and then we'll haul you in."

Bailey turned and wagged the putty knife at him. "You know, you're total bullshit. I helped you people and you've treated me like garbage because I got scared. My lawyer says you're frustrated by your own inabilities and that's why you come after me."

"The people I work with think you're a beach rat, Jimmy. They think you don't have much upstairs and the wind blows through empty rooms, but I think they underestimate you. You're a lot more connected and a lot smarter. You were dealing successfully out of San Diego for years and I think that's where you first hooked up with him. That's how come he's willing to hire you up here. You're a known quantity and you've got your cover all worked out. You look like a sunburned dock toad living on gin and tonics, but that isn't the case at all, is it? But, you know what, Jimmy? The fun is just starting."

"Dude, I know that, and I wish I was going to be there when it gets to you. I really fucking do."

"When was the last time you were in Mexico?"

"Fuck off."

"You're going to get on your new phone when I leave here, but that conversation isn't private either. It's closing around you, Jimmy. You think you're riding on a former relationship with the man, but you're way over your head. They'll come for you just the way they did Heinemann because you're a liability."

Bailey turned his back and farted loudly as he started scraping paint again. "That's the last word, dude," and Marquez walked away. He heard Bailey call after him, "Fucking asshole," but Marquez never turned again.

The call came from Cairo at two that afternoon when Marquez was crossing the Golden Gate after leaving a meeting with the FBI. He could hear the worry in Cairo's voice. Cairo had lost touch with Petersen and when he'd last talked to her she said she had a vehicle behind her that she was unsure of.

"The reception was bad. You know how it's okay along the coast for a while, then goes bad immediately after you turn in?"

Marquez did know. "What do you think she was trying to tell you?"

"I couldn't hear her well enough. I could hear her truck engine straining. I think she was on an uphill grade and pushing it."

"How long ago?"

"Twenty minutes now."

That wasn't a lot of time, but Cairo didn't spook easily. It must have been her tone. Cairo heard something, fear, maybe.

"When did you last try her?"

"Just before I called you."

"What about her telelocator?"

"It's not with her. I'm at the cold house. I just found it in the bedroom."

"I'm coming to you."

When he hung up, fear gripped him and his stomach knotted. But don't think like that, yet. Cairo is going to call you back and say she just turned up. Twenty minutes is nothing. She could be in the Burger King; she could be anywhere. Maybe she's lying above a cove with a video camera. He tried to hold that idea as he started north.

An hour later he had the whole team on the road headed to Fort Bragg and had called Keeler and Baird and asked for help from uniformed wardens and from the Coast Guard with a helicopter. He called the Fort Bragg police, gave them a description of her Toyota 4Runner and a physical on Petersen. When he got into Bragg, Marquez drove through town and continued north to where Cairo was.

The late afternoon sunlight had faded to an orange haze over the ocean. Cairo believed that Petersen had been somewhere in this area and Marquez left the coast highway and turned up Teague Ranch Road because he and Petersen had used spots up here on a surveillance a few years back. The road climbed steeply and he thought the steepest stretch would also have been the last place with clear phone reception. You could make calls from farther inland, but the reception sketched in and out on you and a lot of calls got dropped. The road climbed through grassland and hills that rose into coastal mountains, then folded back on itself and ran across forested slopes.

His radio crackled a couple of times and he talked to Cairo, then to Chief Keeler who let him know several uniformed wardens were on their way to help. The road entered trees and dipped as it crossed a creek bed, then climbed steeply up switchbacks to the next ridge and he turned around there because he could no longer see the ocean and reasoned that her purpose for driving up here would have been surveillance of the coves or bluffs below.

And then another idea occurred to him, of what she might do if she was being pursued and couldn't get through on a cell phone or radio. He drove slowly back down, remembering the places they'd used before, locations where you could get a vehicle off-road. He returned to the concrete culvert that carried a creek beneath the roadbed, parked and walked down to the dry creek bed, looked in through the culvert pipe. A circle of light came through from the other side, the downhill side. Cool air flowed down through with the faint breeze up from the ocean. The bottom was stained dark and powdery moss had dried well up the curve. He crouched and walked through the culvert and on the other side saw a turned-over rock, the raw soil underneath. He looked down the dry bed and saw tire marks against a boulder. He found marks from scraped paint, studied the color, then tried to get Cairo on the radio to tell him he was going to hike down the creek bed. Farther down, he began to put it together, found a second set of tire prints and realized it had been a pursuit. He paused at broken taillight glass, knelt and picked it up.

Petersen wouldn't wreck a vehicle to chase a jeep or anything else down a creek bed unless there'd been a very good reason for it. But this could be something altogether different, the paint color coincidence aside. Kids out four-wheeling and drinking beer, could easily be kids, he thought. He stopped at a gash in a tree, touched the blue paint left there, and looked at the V-shaped tire prints alongside the trunk, touched the grooves with his fingers. It was too violent. Someone had been chased. He tried Cairo again.

Where the creek dropped off a three-foot ledge, both sets of tracks cut into the topsoil, digging in as they made a hard turn and climbed away from the creek bed. They'd skinned the dry grass down to bare soil trying to climb up the slope. He climbed rapidly toward the ridge, having no trouble following the tracks. The driving had been rough. The lead vehicle had ploughed through low brush on the steep slope, tires tearing at the soil, and he guessed they'd been afraid of stalling and had pushed it hard, kept the engine revved. He neared the ridgeline, saw blue sky low at the tree bases and knew he was close to getting a wider view. At the top was a rock outcropping and looking down, he saw her blue 4Runner.

Standing on the outcropping, looking out on the ocean, he got through to Cairo and worked his way down to her truck while talking to him. The driver's window and the back were open and the truck was empty. Droplets of blood had spattered on the dash and on rocks outside the truck and he told Cairo they'd need dogs. He clicked off the radio, yelled for her, and tried to follow the blood, but it petered out quickly. He smelled gas leaking from the truck and saw where the suspension had hooked on a rock. She'd been chased. It was a gutsy thing she'd been trying to do to get down this slope. Without doing anything to disturb evidence, he tried to think it out. If she was injured, bleeding, and still trying to get away, she'd take off in the easiest direction, or take up a position with her weapon. The bleeding was concentrated around one area of rock. Why had she stood in that spot? Held at gunpoint? Told to stand there? Or she got out of the 4Runner hurt, but with something pressed against the wound, dazed and trying to stop the bleeding before trying to escape. She'd go down the slope, try to reach the trees and lose herself. That was the next place to look.

From below, it was easier to see what had happened. It looked like the right rear tire had dropped off the side and when the truck started to slide off it had bottomed out. With enough time she would have freed it and he took that as another sign that someone was right on her. She didn't have time to get the truck free and had gotten out. She must have been outnumbered or wouldn't have run.

He kept working his way down. Berry bushes grew in damp ground at the base of the outcropping and there was low brush in front of the trees. Then the slope dropped away and he searched in the trees and brush until he heard engines grinding above him.

By mid-afternoon, close to forty people and bloodhounds from Santa Rosa searched the surrounding terrain. Her car was dusted inside and out for prints and a cast taken of the other vehicle print. Marquez watched the dogs work the scent back up the hill, then went up to talk with the big-bellied man who was working them.

"This is as far as she went," he said. Marquez laid a hand on the head of one of the dogs. "My money says she got in the other vehicle," the tracker said. "Or let me put it this way, that's what my dogs think."

"Your dogs think she walked up here and no further."

"That's about the size of it."

"Got in a vehicle?"

"More than likely. She didn't walk any farther than where we're standing." He pointed at one his hounds. "They don't come any better than him and he picked up her trail immediately and this is where it stopped." Marquez had watched the dogs work. He'd seen the same thing. The houndsman picked at a tooth and turned toward him. "You ask me, they brought her up here at gunpoint and carried her away."

33

The search continued on the slope until well after dark and the decision had already been made to go out to the public. They put out a photo of Petersen and her truck and were already getting some response. A couple who'd been picnicking on a cliff above the ocean remembered seeing a white van turning up Teague Ranch Road, its tires squealing. But they didn't remember the 4Runner and couldn't say what time in the afternoon the van had gone up the road.

Marquez gathered the team together near midnight at the cold house and they walked through the search plan for tomorrow. Ten wardens would arrive in the early morning to help and he wanted to widen the search in the area where her truck had been found. They'd walk the whole slope, every inch. Pieces of broken taillights and samples of both paint colors had been taken from the dry creek bed and from the trees the vehicles had scraped, but he wanted to walk everything again. They'd find something they'd missed. He polled everyone for other ideas and then broke up the meeting.

Before sunrise the next morning he drove to the Harbor Motel where Petersen's husband, Stuart, was staying. Stuart had asked to go with them this morning and his motel door opened now as Marquez pulled in. He watched Stuart walk over.

"Just tell me she's alive," Stuart said, after they'd started driving.

"We don't know anything."

"Then tell me why anyone would abduct her. What do they want?"

He couldn't answer Stuart's fear or his own. As they drove through town Marquez's phone rang. He started into a U-turn before Keeler had finished talking.

"That was my deputy-chief, Stuart. A ransom note has been e-mailed to headquarters."

"What do they want?"

"My chief forwarded a copy to me. I'll plug in my computer in your room. We can read—"

"Oh, God, oh, God, she's alive."

"They're asking for two million to be delivered tomorrow to a location they'll provide in the next e-mail."

Stuart seemed stunned a moment, then talked as if he was alone, repeating over and over, "I can do it." His head turned abruptly. "Where does it go?"

"You won't have to come up with the money, Stuart."

Marquez raced back through town, phoning Alvarez on the way, asking him to let the rest of the team know. He pulled into the motel lot alongside Stuart's car. In the motel room he plugged into a phone jack and powered up the laptop. He clicked through the passwords into his e-mail with his heart pounding. Stuart stood over his shoulder and read.

She is alive for now. John Marquez delivers $2,000,000

tomorrow. Instructions to follow. Respond via Marquez at 12:00 noon 22 September.

Stuart adjusted his wire rims and folded his arms across his chest, then sat down on a chair. "You deliver," Stuart said, and unfolded his arms again. "They can trace this. The FBI can locate where this was sent from. They have that Carnivore technology and all kinds of stuff now."

Marquez glanced at him, doubted he knew a whole lot about that. He reread the e-mail. It had been addressed to CalTip@dfg.ca.gov. and had arrived in the middle of the night. It was lucky anyone had found it this early in the morning, but maybe the FBI had tipped headquarters to watch for an e-mail ransom demand. He knew Douglas had already read it and would be working on a response and wanted to talk with him about it, but wasn't sure he wanted to do that with Stuart in the room.

"How do they know your name if the unit is supposed to be covert?" Stuart asked.

"It may be someone I've come up against before."

"I wanted her to quit last week. I should have made her. Oh, God, this can't be happening."

Marquez tried to keep his voice calm, the tension out of his inflection. He laid out a scenario where they paid the ransom and got her back. When he'd finished, Stuart shook his head vigorously, his imagination already forming another conclusion.

"I think they got your name from Sue. You see, two million is the exact amount I got from a lawsuit settlement. I won a big case against a railroad and they know what I got and they're asking for it. It's somebody up where we live who knows what she does for a living and followed her here. The amount is too coincidental. It has to be that."

Or she'd found a way to keep Kline from killing her, Marquez thought. She had an idea and begged and argued that she had this net worth via her husband. Gave them facts they could check. He looked at Stuart, his dark hair receding to mid-skull, a delicate almost feminine quality to his features. According to Petersen they'd known within minutes of meeting that they were meant for each other.

"I don't care about the money," Stuart said. "Let's respond, right now. I know the FBI will be involved, but I want to give them a signal that I'll pay. Let's try to move the hand-over time forward. Let's suggest this afternoon. I have to make calls though. I need to go to my car and get a phone number, and I'll call my banker."

"Hang on a minute, Stuart."

Marquez's phone was ringing and when he saw it was Keeler's number he excused himself and walked out to his truck, sat there looking at a line of beige motel doors as Keeler explained what was evolving.

"How long will it take you to get here, John?"

"Three hours."

"We're going to schedule a meeting around that."

"You've spoken to Douglas?"

"Yes, and they want a response made from here, but they want to talk to you first."

"I'm on my way." He hung up and went inside to get the laptop and let Stuart know they'd call him from Sacramento. But looking at Stuart he didn't see why he shouldn't sit in. "I may have to talk you into the room, but why don't you follow me."

Stuart's white Camry sat uncomfortably close behind him all the way to Sacramento. He led him into the meeting and Stuart must have thought it out on the ride because he conducted his own defense for being there, arguing that they needed him to verify authenticity and for his knowledge of her habits, the things no one else could know about his wife. For words she might use to pass a message in the communication. Then, succinctly and without drama, he presented his theory about how the idea might have been hatched by someone who'd read the newspaper in Redding or learned of the dollar amount of the award by word of mouth.

Chief Baird deferred to the FBI and they made the decision to let Stuart remain in the room, on the condition that he left during parts of the discussion, which turned out to include questioning about whether Petersen's pregnancy could be via another man and the possibility she'd staged the event and run off with her lover. And they were interested in Stuart's money, that the amount he'd made on this last award was nearly the same as the demand. But Marquez caught Douglas's eyes and knew this part was an exercise. Douglas knew, they all knew.

Now, as they took a coffee and bathroom break, Douglas slid into a chair next to Marquez. He touched him on the arm, leaned over and said quietly, "You know what's coming."

"And we'll say yes."

"I don't know how yet, but we'll be there with you."

The door closed and the meeting started again. It was 11:20 now, forty minutes from the deadline. Douglas turned to Marquez after Stuart had been asked to leave the room.

"Okay, John, what's your guess? Where's this ransom going to deliver?"

"Someplace where he controls the access, someplace not too easy to get to." Marquez recalled how Kline had used an old mining area in Mexico. He'd bought off the local Federales, and the mines were in dry mountain country honeycombed with dirt roads, connecting shafts, and scattered entry points with rock overlooks. He went on, "Kline used to prefer the night, but I don't know how he operates anymore. You'd have to tell me."

"He still likes the dark."

"He'll ask for a hand delivery and take that person or persons hostage until he's sure he's away safely. We had a case where he snapped one of those neck rings the Colombians were making for a while around the neck of the wife who delivered a ransom."

"For those of you who don't know," Douglas said, "that was an explosive device that could be detonated remotely and blow the victim's head off at the shoulders."

"He won't relinquish control until he's sure. That's the bottom line," Marquez said. He could feel their eyes on him. The room quieted and everyone waited on his answer.

"Then why don't we insist on a wire transfer or something of that nature?" Chief Baird asked.

Douglas answered, "It's like John said, he won't give us the option." Douglas turned back to Marquez and asked the question he already knew the answer to. "Are you willing to deliver the money?" Marquez nodded. Douglas glanced at his watch. "Okay, I've got five minutes to noon. Anything else? Anybody, any last comments? John, anything?"

"Send it."

The e-mail was short, said they agreed to the terms but needed to verify she was alive. At one minute to noon Douglas talked to the FBI tech, confirming they were ready to go. He hit "send" and Marquez watched the antivirus icon appear and then disappear as the e-mail went. For minutes no one moved, until Baird pushed his chair back, stood up and then rested a hand on Marquez's shoulder. Marquez sat with the FBI agents for another hour, met briefly with Keeler and Baird, then drove home. They wanted him to wait there to be easily available.

Once home he checked e-mail every ten minutes. The house felt too small and the waiting inadequate. Then, shortly after 4:00 the response came to Marquez's mailbox, to an address he used outside the department, mostly for private e-mail. Petersen knew that address and he had to assume they'd gotten it from her. He read the new message then forwarded it before opening the Web site it gave. The message read: *$2,000,000 cash to be loaded in waterproofs and Marquez will deliver via Zodiac. Must have a*

range of 100 miles. Confirm Web site, confirm delivery terms
agreed. www.officerinview.net

Marquez clicked onto the Web site as the phone rang. Douglas.
The FBI was already looking at her. Petersen was naked and seated
in a chair. Her face carried plum-colored bruises, her arms and legs
were taped to the chair. The backdrop was black and he couldn't
read anything in it and realized she was trying to smile. They must
have told her she had to smile, and he couldn't distance himself,
couldn't separate himself as he listened to Douglas's analysis. He'd
brought this on her. Take anything and everything that he'd ever
done with Petersen, any of the busts, the surveillances, anything
positive they'd ever done together and she would've been better off
never having met him. He'd brought this to her.

"It's intended to shock us into compliance and confirm that she's
alive," Douglas said, "but it doesn't confirm she is. The signal is
bouncing but the Web site is transmitting real time. However, this may
be a digital tape they made yesterday. It doesn't tell us she's alive."

Marquez heard the front door open and he came to his feet,
startling Katherine as she came in.

"What do you make of the Zodiac?" Douglas asked.

"It allows him a lot of flexibility. I can run up on a beach or
out to sea and a hundred miles is a long swing."

"He knows we'll track you every which way, so what's he
thinking?"

"I don't know."

Katherine gripped his hand hard as she looked at the screen.

"I don't have to tell you she may already be dead," Douglas said.

No you don't have to tell me, Marquez thought.

"And there's no guarantee he's going to let you deliver and
go," Douglas continued.

"You sound like the guy I buy boat insurance from. After we
do a deal he makes sure I know what's not covered."

"You've got a family and we can make up an excuse. We'll get a volunteer, someone that shoots very straight and swims well."

"She's one of my team."

"He used this format three times last year and all of the victims were already dead." Marquez didn't answer. "I'm going to come see you and we'll write the response," Douglas said.

When he hung up, Katherine said, "John, you already know it's a trap. I understand wanting to save her, but you can't do this."

"I don't know any other way."

34

Katherine stayed through a meeting at the house with Douglas. She grilled cheese sandwiches and made coffee. Douglas told him the FBI would get a Zodiac outfitted, but Marquez shook his head, said Fish and Game had a boat. It was already on a trailer and had twin Honda engines, was reinforced, and most of all, it was familiar to Marquez. But how much cash would he carry and how would they get it in time? And how quickly could they close on his position if he needed them? Who was the officer in charge at the Coast Guard? He'd carry his Glock .40, a second gun would be on board, stun grenades, night vision equipment, a short laundry list of defensive weaponry. He watched Douglas's sidelong glance to the kitchen where Katherine cleaned quietly and was listening.

"This stuff will be useful if you have to abort," Douglas said, picking crumbs off his plate, wiping his hands, his eyes on Marquez's face. "But you'll be at their mercy at some point when you deliver."

"That's where you come in."

When Douglas left, Marquez told Katherine another Kline story he never had told her before, about Mexican military planes used to ferry cocaine and dope, and the death of a DEA agent named Brian Hidalgo, a sunrise, a haze at horizon and the sun's blood light and Hidalgo's body in the burned-out car. Spanish phrases, forgotten Indian dialect, words he'd lost returned to him.

"Kline tortured Hidalgo and inside twenty-four hours had started working his way back through our team. I shot the man who was supposed to kill me and the word we heard after was that Kline swore he'd get me. When I quit the DEA and decided to hike the Pacific Crest Trail, I think he did send someone for me. I'd crossed a junction near Kearsarge Pass in the southern Sierra and had camped at a place called Charlotte Lake, planning to hike down the trail at Kearsarge and resupply in Bishop early the next morning, but I met a man on the trail who said there were two men who'd camped for a while near Kearsarge who were looking for me. They'd showed him a photo and he'd recognized me. They'd told him they were there because my mother had died of a heart attack, but she died when I was a teenager so I knew it was bad. I stayed off-trail and I waited."

"You saw them?"

"Yeah, and I'm pretty sure they were Kline's people. I hiked during the night the next two days. I didn't get home until late that fall." She already knew the rest, but he said it anyway. "I hiked north to the end of the trail in Washington and you and I didn't meet for another two years. By then, I was trying to put it behind me."

"You should have talked more to me, John."

"If I could do it over again, I would."

"And now he's asking for you by name. You can't go, John. You just can't do it. Think about Maria and me. Ask yourself what you're doing. You're carrying the same guilt you had when I met you and now you're going to risk sacrificing yourself. This is crazy, really crazy."

"The Feds will be close by."

"How do you know?" He didn't and Douglas didn't either. "Maybe you want to die, John. Maybe then everything is even and you're with your dead friends. It's all even and fair again." Her face flushed and tears flooded her eyes as she shook her head. She stood and moved away from him. "You're going to go even though Douglas said he'd get an FBI volunteer."

"I think her only chance is if I show."

"I can't wait here and I can't be a part of this."

She stood and shook her head. Then she walked out the front door and he heard her car start, gravel kicking up on the driveway as she drove away. He watched her headlights hit the road.

Near midnight he checked his e-mail, found nothing, and opened the Web site again. Petersen's face had changed, the bruising had darkened. Some sort of necklace hung from her neck and he focused there, saw the iridescent green, the cut triangular shape and he was sure it was similar to the abalone piece he'd taken from Bailey's boat. He fought the terrible heaviness inside and reached for the phone to call Douglas.

"I recognize what's around her neck," Marquez said. "I pulled something similar off Bailey's boat."

"What's it mean?"

"Maybe nothing. It's abalone shell, so maybe it's a statement."

"Do you have it still?"

"No, it went back to Bailey. His lawyer got everything released before we had probable cause on Bailey."

"Is it the same shell?"

"It could be."

"Incoming," Douglas said, and Marquez saw the mail icon flash. He clicked to the e-mail as Douglas cleared his throat. "Are you reading?"

"Got it," Marquez said. "I'm reading now."

John Marquez, you'll be in Humboldt Bay at 7:00 a.m. tomor-
row. You'll need fuel for a 400 mile range. Money in waterproof
bags. Any surveillance and she'll be executed.

"The bags you carry will transmit position," Douglas said.
"We've got two fishing boats we'll get there before you arrive, but
why Eureka, Marquez?"

"It's been fogged in for two days and it's big enough to where
you wouldn't pick his people out as easily. The four-hundred-mile
range could mean he's going to burn a lot of time determining
who's following."

Marquez gave Douglas Katherine's numbers and then called
her as he drove down the mountain. He stayed on the phone with
her until he was almost to the boat. In San Rafael he hooked the
trailer up to the Explorer with the help of an FBI agent, then started
north with the FBI following and the SOU leading. Cairo and
Roberts would get into Eureka by dawn. Shauf and Alvarez were
heading to Shelter Cove with another Zodiac. The *Marlin* had left
the Berkeley marina and was already five miles north of the Gate.
He drove slowly up 101, towing the boat, taking the occasional
phone call from the team and Douglas. He talked to Kath again
and Keeler, then to Baird as he came into Eureka. It was cold and
the light flat this morning, the pavement wet, fog rolling in from
the bay. Foghorns sounded and a nervous energy burned in him as
he put the boat in the water and called the number they'd given
him, what the FBI had confirmed was a cell phone activated yesterday morning in San Francisco.

"I'm in the harbor. Where do I go?"

"All business, are you?" An Irish accent, he thought. "Leave
the bay and go south. Give me your phone number."

Marquez read it off as the boat bounced in the first swells.
"How far south?" The Irishman didn't answer and after the line
went dead Marquez positioned the phone where he could keep it
dry and still reach it. It was a satellite unit and he had backup in

case this one went down. The bags of money were near his feet and cabled to the boat. When he left the harbor he skirted the coast, passing the mouth of the Eel River and moving out to sea a little farther before Douglas called.

"We're with you, but keep your speed as steady as you can. How are you doing?"

"It's going to get a little choppy ahead, but I'm good."

"When you made the call they were in a car probably on Highway 101 near Santa Rosa. They didn't stay on long enough to determine their direction. In case you were wondering, he recruited out of the IRA, got a handful of ex-IRA working for him."

"Kline did?"

"Yeah, in the '90s."

"I heard the one I just talked to as Irish."

"So did we."

When he hung up with Douglas he wiped water from his face and sealed the Velcro at his wrists after putting on gloves. With the lack of sleep the cold reached him a little faster and there was more wind out here. He went south now for two hours and hit a patch near Cape Mendocino where the wind was cross and fog shredded through the rocks that the wind was trying to drive him toward. Waves pitched the Zodiac and it slapped hard on the water. At half-hour intervals, Douglas called.

"You're doing all right?"

"What are you, my mother?"

But he had a tightness in his chest and the cold seemed to come from inside out. Katherine's voice echoed in his head.

"Your chief is here with me now. We've got a copter inland, moving with you. You've got another thirty miles of fog and you'll hit blue."

Unless he turns me around, Marquez thought, or heads me out to sea. The reassurances were nice but meant nothing. He cut his speed and got off the phone with Douglas, called Shauf. Her father had been a fisherman up here. She'd gotten into resource management because she'd heard her father talk all the time about how the fisheries were collapsing. He'd railed against the bottom-raking industrial trawlers that took everything, and he'd had names for them, would point to a trawler and tell her that one is named the *Antichrist*. She'd gone through her childhood thinking there was a boat out there named that.

"I'm coming onto Punta Gorda," he said. "What's your guess?"

"Somewhere along the Lost Coast and we're already here. We're in the King Range on that main dirt road."

The Lost Coast was his guess, too, because it was empty, because you could follow one of the creeks to the water and pack the money back out through the mountains on foot, and because Kline had trafficked drugs out of Humboldt for years. Along an empty stretch of the Lost Coast, a quick execution after the money was handed over, but better not to think that way. Better to think it's going to work out. He swept past Punta Gorda, continued south, reached Shelter Cove and the phone rang.

The Irish voice said, "Where are you?"

"Still going south."

"Where the fuck are you?"

"Shelter Cove."

"Circle."

"How long? I'm burning through my fuel."

He circled an hour, half of it talking to Douglas, ate a dry roll and a Payday bar, drank hot tea from a thermos. He'd heard an edge in the Irishman's voice that said killing came easy to him. Another call came and they moved him farther south, then back north five miles before turning again. The thrum of the engines vibrated in his bones now. The cold ran deeper and he was close to Fort Bragg. More phone calls and the *Marlin* had him on radar, so did an FBI copter and a spotter plane and a fishing boat carrying FBI agents, so he knew it wouldn't be anywhere near here. He was through half his fuel now and ran on one engine only, conserving out of habit, crouching in the boat to loosen his muscles as the fog began to sweep back in the late afternoon. Two hours now since he'd heard from the Irishman, so maybe they'd called it off. Then the call came.

"Are you ready?" the Irishman asked.

"You're going to have to show her to me before I put to shore anywhere."

"Turn south, again."

"I'm burning fuel fast. I don't have much more range."

"It was Belfast in '85 when the lad carrying the ransom ran out of petrol and got his man killed, the stupid arsehole."

The line went dead, and the next call didn't come until after dark. Marquez was south of Fort Bragg about twenty miles, running with lights and GPS, but it would be much harder after dark to put in anywhere, dangerous with the rocks. The Irishman had him continue south another hour, then reverse and turn north. By then the sea had calmed and he rode half a mile offshore in a light wind. Douglas checked in.

"There's a boat three miles off your port side we're looking at. Nothing else close to you." Static and a bad connection, then, "We've got agents all along the highway." The SOU was there too, but Kline would know that the shore was lined with police. "They may run you all the way back north."

"Are you just chatting me up?"

"How are you doing?"

"I'm ready to get it done."

Near the coast at Van Damme State Park he got the call to turn shoreward and run hard toward the surf.

"You want me to run aground with the money and lose it in the ocean?"

"No, you arsehole, I'll bring you home." The Irishman barked at him about some kidnapping that had gone bad along the border in Peru, then cut back in, "North again, you fuckin' copper."

So he has me in sight, Marquez thought. Reading a heat signal if nothing else. Close in as he was the Sony Palm IR would work at this range. He was close to the surf, too close to rocks. He flicked on the boat lights and the Irishman said nothing. "You'll see a flash of blue light."

Several minutes passed, the Irishman still on the phone. "I see it," Marquez said, and turned toward the caves of Van Damme. "We're going to run you through the caves and she'll be waiting for you. You don't want to fuck up now and lose one of your own. She'll be wearing a hood and two men will be with her. You'll take a boat ride together."

Marquez saw the blue light flash again and moved closer, glad that he knew these caves, maneuvering the boat constantly to stay off the rocks. Hit the rocks and it's over. He eased inside the cave, the Zodiac engine an amplified roar. He swept his light along the rock and in a cleft saw what looked like a woman sitting with a hood over her head. A man yelled for him to bring it in close, yelling "faster, faster, come on, you fuckhead, in here and kill the engines," and now Marquez saw light in the water below, a diver surfacing near him, the man onshore still yelling instructions, holding an assault rifle on him as the diver boarded and Marquez fought the impulse to go for his gun.

"Don't move," the order came again, and then to the hooded woman sitting on rocks, "Raise your arm. Let him know you're okay," and when the arm came up he wasn't sure if it was Petersen's, but a second diver had the bow rope and was towing him over to the rock, the Zodiac rising with every swell, the sound drowning the man's voice.

Now it was the diver behind him speaking, telling him to put his hands out, patting him down as the other diver boarded. "Where's the money, lad?" And before he could answer a knife cut into one of the cabled bags and the diver yelled to the Irishman.

"It's here."

"Let's see her face," Marquez demanded. He didn't see the blow coming, but it was the diver behind him and he tried to rake an arm back to defend himself as his knees buckled. His hand caught teeth and he snapped a head back before sinking down. He didn't feel the second blow but felt his arms pulled back, handcuffs clicked on his wrists, then his ankles, and he heard faraway laughter as he rolled into the cold water and felt himself pulled forward, dragged along the sand, then a knife cutting off his shirt, and he was shoved and propped against a rock. The Irishman squatted near him on the sand, his voice low, a light on Marquez's face, the breath of the man on him.

"The tide's out, lad, enjoy the beach."

Marquez saw the woman pull the hood off. She wasn't Petersen.

"Where is she?"

"I hear she's the crew's favorite on a boat somewhere, but you can ask him yourself. He's coming to visit you here. If I was you, I'd be giving myself up to God."

"Where is she?"

"You're a fuckin' fool, lad."

Marquez watched the Zodiac motor slowly out of the cave with a single man guiding it. The rest had gone, however they'd gotten here. He knew it would take time, maybe too long, to sort out that the man at the helm wasn't him, and Kline had to be counting on that. The Zodiac turned out of the cave, the light vanished, and there was only the roar of the waves.

35

An hour or more had gone by and he needed to get out of the water, had to get above the incoming tide. They'd stripped his clothes down to his shorts, had taken a knife, a second gun, the telelocator off him. How long would it take Douglas to figure out that someone else was running the Zodiac? He'd get suspicious when the calls didn't go through, but when would they start searching the caves? Get up, he thought, get off the sand and on the rock as high as you can. He lifted his head, staring into the darkness, head throbbing and not thinking clearly, his body trembling with cold. He could make out the cave entrance but there was little light. Pushed off with his heels, dug them into the sand, used the rocks to help pull himself up and then fell again. Fought his way back up as a wave ran as high as his knees.

There'd been a rock ledge near here when he'd swept his light across. If he could find it, maybe there was a way to get onto it. Four feet higher would buy a lot of time and sooner or later they'd come here. He got to his feet, his back resting against the rock, breath coming in gasps. Had to get out of here, had to get high enough to last through the changing tide. Where was Douglas? What was taking so long? He pressed against wet rock, leaned into it, hopped sideways, working his way along.

She's on a boat, the crew's favorite, the Irishman said. Then she's alive. She's alive and can be found. He felt the gap in the stone now, leaned his head into the hollow. How deep was the ledge? No way to tell, and he tried jumping up and sliding onto the rock. Got partway onto the shelf and slid out, fell on his back on the sand, his shoulder striking a rock. He lay there, numbed. A wave touched his legs and he rolled to his side, got on his knees again, to his feet, tried again, fell again. On the fourth try he finally got enough of his weight onto the ledge. He rested and inched forward, praying there was enough room, that his shoulder wouldn't brush rock too soon.

But there was plenty of room. The shelf was deep and worn smooth by the ocean. Marquez slid toward the back and lay on his side, watching for light, moving his legs and feet to fight the cold, trying to keep his fingers from going numb as another half hour or more passed. Waves finished against the rock now, spray reached him, and where was the Zodiac now? Why was it taking Douglas so long to backtrack?

Then he saw light but not from a boat, something surfacing in the cave, another diver, he thought, and slid against the back wall. The light came closer, moved toward him, and he heard rubber, the snap of a mask, a man's hard exhale lost as a wave came in. The light had vanished and Marquez strained to hear, knew the diver was on the small beach where the Irishman had left him. Now he heard the tanks clank against rock, saw a beam of light working low along the water to his left and then quickly turned off.

"Where are you?" a voice said, but the light didn't come back on.

Afraid to leave the light on, Marquez thought. Looking for me and surprised I wasn't where they left me. The light scanned again, this time the beam reaching closer. He heard the air tanks clank against the rock again, the rip of Velcro, the man repositioning himself, and briefly the light was on again. When it clicked off Marquez got ready. The next pass would reach him. He brought his knees up, thought he'd try to kick out, drive his legs into the man's chest.

Then without warning, the sound masked by rough water at the cave entrance, there was a boat motor and a searchlight played along the walls. Marquez slid forward as the boat turned around. He heard a hard splash and the boat swept into the cave, its lights raking across him.

"Identify yourself."

"Marquez," he shouted. "Watch out! There's someone in the water under you! Don't let the diver get away, stay with his light!" But either they couldn't hear him or didn't understand. And then there were arms grabbing him and they struggled to get him aboard.

"Do we have her?" Marquez asked. "Do we have her?"

"No."

"Stay with the light, there was a diver," and a blanket was wrapped around him, a woman telling him they couldn't do anything about the cuffs yet as they tried to pick up the light outside the cave, and a search began along the beach.

"We'll find him," he heard the boat's pilot say, but he knew they wouldn't. He'd lost the money and they had nothing. He leaned over the side looking down into the dark water. Who was the diver? Was it Kline?

36

"You're a stand-up guy," Douglas said outside Marquez's house, and Marquez waited for the reason Douglas had driven up here. His heart had jumped when Douglas pulled into the driveway, afraid Douglas was here to deliver bad news in person. Marquez hadn't gotten home until dawn and this was where the FBI insisted he be, as though Kline would contact them again. "You probably came pretty close to buying it last night. Good thing you got on that ledge."

"What about the Irishman's comment she was on a boat?"

"Do you believe him?"

"I want to believe she's alive. How much money was in those bags?"

"$200,000. A lot of one dollar bills."

That brought a rush of anger in Marquez. He squinted against the sunlight, his eyes tired, his mind veering off from how Kline would react to the short money.

"Tell me. You shorted him, so what was your plan?"

"To be there, John, and I think you know that. He didn't bring Petersen; he wasn't ever planning to make a trade, which probably means he doesn't have one to make."

It was Alvarez who'd figured out that the man on the Zodiac had gone off the side wearing dive gear and swum to shore. The Zodiac steering had been locked and it had run out to sea drawing all but the vehicle surveillance with it. The FBI theory was that he'd floated the money ashore with him and met his ride.

"There was a last image on the Web site before it went down," Douglas said. "You'll see it soon enough. Her head was tipped back and she had a knife at her throat. The facial contusions were deeper, more colored. I'm told they took at least forty-eight hours to develop the color they had. It means that not all the images were shot the same day, but whether that's good or bad we don't know. I don't want her husband to hear any of this. He doesn't know about it now and doesn't need to."

"I won't be the one to tell him."

"How computer literate are you?"

"Not as literate as my fifteen-year-old stepdaughter."

"I hear you on that. The site is down, but he may come back up, and if he does and keeps the same sequencing going, it may not be a very happy ending."

"You're talking around the edges of whatever you have to say."

"What I'm getting to is, it's our opinion there's nothing more that can effectively be done. We need to let him make the next move, because we don't have one."

"I think the Irish bastard was telling at least part of the truth; she's alive on a boat somewhere. We can check every boat over sixty feet in California."

"And if you get close you may cause him to kill her. Better for your team to sit tight, hard as that is, and we're all over the boats anyway."

"I'm not going to have my team stand down."

"Then, if you find a boat, don't do anything except call me."

"We're going to come up with a list of boats."

"And we'll work together. Here, I brought you another one of these." Douglas fished a telelocator out of his pocket. "Don't lose this one."

He watched Douglas drive away and then turned to Katherine. She'd been here when he'd gotten home and he figured the FBI must have called her, must have alerted her though he hadn't asked. Now he talked to her about his fears for Petersen, his sense of loss and responsibility, the terribleness of having her taken this way. She touched his face, her fingers cool and smooth. She said he ought to get some rest, but what he did after she left was lay out how the team was going to check all vessels over sixty feet. Had to be at least that big, he thought, or at least they'd work from that point. He'd have to get Baird to lend wardens. He took a call from Stuart Petersen, and the conversation was very hard, Stuart saying repeatedly that they had to try to contact the kidnappers, go out to the media in a new way, that the FBI was stonewalling. Marquez could feel Stuart's hope dying. After he hung up he closed his eyes, thought back over each thing he could remember from last night.

Somewhere in the late afternoon he fell asleep, waking at dusk with a blanket over him and hearing Katherine and Maria talking, taking comfort from the murmur of their voices before closing his eyes again. An hour later he rose and walked into the kitchen. Maria was there alone, her mother was in the shower.

"What's going on, Maria?"

"I'm making dinner tonight." Maria hugged him. "I'm really glad you're back."

"Count me out on dinner," he said.

"Oh, you have to eat or you'll lose weight."

"I lost too much weight once. I wouldn't want to do that again."

"Maybe there's a message there for me."

He smiled at her sarcasm. You were only young and self-centered a particular way once and then life showed you otherwise. But he had a lot of tolerance for that. He hadn't been that fun to talk to as a kid, himself. "How much weight did you lose?" she asked.

"About thirty-five pounds. Some people on my undercover team were killed and I had a hard time with it. I felt guilty and unworthy, and there was suspicion thrown my way because I'd been the only one who'd made it. And I didn't handle that very well, couldn't handle my integrity being questioned. It made me very bitter and angry and I had to walk it off in the mountains and when I did, I didn't eat enough."

He told her more. He told her of a moment of change, of self-awareness that had happened to him, a dawn on San Francisco Bay, watching the sunrise from a boat. The light on the water had been particularly beautiful, like a thousand prisms reflecting that morning. Hoping he wasn't sounding too corny, he tried to tell Maria how he'd realized what he loved and what mattered and what it meant to embrace the positive.

But he could see that Maria had lost more weight. When they ate dinner an hour later, she cut a couple of small slivers off a chicken leg and counted out the string beans she put on her plate. She finished and asked to be excused.

"Mom, will you clean up since I made dinner?"

"Sure."

"Is it okay if I do my homework with the TV on?"

"Don't turn it on too loud."

She turned the TV on before going down the hall toward her room and Katherine got up quickly from the table. She walked over to the edge of the kitchen wall where she could see Maria's bathroom. When Katherine went around the corner he figured

Maria was in the bathroom and knew Katherine was listening. A few minutes later, Katherine was back.

"This is her routine now."

"Let me try to talk with her again tonight."

"She's going to tell you she's got to do her homework and right after that she'll say she's too tired to talk and has to go to bed. John, I know you can't possibly think about this right now. Was there any news at all today? Did they find anything in the caves?"

"No, but we're going back tomorrow."

At a little after 11:00 Maria came out of her room. Marquez was out on the deck with Katherine. Maria waved a hand good-night from the deck door and Katherine coaxed her out and hugged her, then stepped around her, leaving Maria with him. As she left, Maria said sharply, almost bitchily, "What was that about?"

"She loves you."

"She shouldn't try to control me then."

"You're the one in control."

"Tell her that."

"I haven't said much to you about it yet, have I?"

"Don't tell me you're going to start tonight?"

"Why don't you sit with me a few minutes?" She sat on the picnic bench and wouldn't look directly at him. "If we didn't say anything, we wouldn't be worth anything as parents. I told you the mess I got myself in. I let things go too far, sometimes. Maybe you're a little like that, too."

"Oh, so now we're alike."

"We might have that in common. You ate and then went straight to the bathroom, right?"

"So you're accusing me, too?"

"I'm asking you."

"Why would I want to throw up?"

"Maybe you want to control your body, because maybe the

rest of your life doesn't feel like it's under control." She didn't give
a sign one way or the other. "Mine feels that way right now, too.
What's going on in your life?"

Maria deflected the question. "Mom says you shouldn't be
leaving tomorrow and should do what the FBI says."

"Then I wouldn't be in control." That got the slightly crooked
shy smile that was hers only, that was there when he'd met her
when she was four. "But that's not really it, either, Maria. Sue
Petersen is missing and I have to do everything I can to try to find
her. I stayed here today and shouldn't have."

"Mom says she might already be dead."

"She might be, but if she's alive she's got to believe I'm looking for her."

"Well, mom is always wrong."

"She's not wrong about you." He paused a beat. "I know you,
Maria, the lying has got to be making you feel lousy. You've got a
problem here and you've got to face it, and if anyone has the will
and the strength to do that, it's you."

Maria didn't answer but something was happening. He saw her
shoulders shaking and tears starting in her eyes. When she looked
up the tears were streaming down her face and she cried silently,
then shook her head, sobbing, confessing something he couldn't
make out initially. Her voice wavered, talking now about problems
with her friends, feeling like an outcast, people ignoring her, calling
her a freak behind her back.

"You don't look like a freak."

"Everybody says I do."

"You don't. You were bringing your weight down and maybe it
got a little away from you and went further than you hoped. It's
the kind of mistake I would make."

"No, you wouldn't."

"The thing about friends is you only have a few true ones in a lifetime, and I wouldn't sweat the rest. If I hadn't been there last night, then I wouldn't have been Petersen's true friend."

"I don't have any friends."

"Talk to me, talk to your mom, start there. We're your friends. She's all over you because she loves you, but she'll back off when she sees you turn it around."

"I mean at school."

"You're beautiful and bright, Maria. You've got it all going your way and you're going to have to use that great will of yours to work this problem out. That's what got you into this and that's what's going to get you out. But first you've got to try to figure out where it started."

"I already know that."

"Then go back to where it started and unravel it. Take it a day at a time. Two good days and maybe a bad day, then three good days in a row. Four good days. I'm having a real hard time with Petersen missing, but I've got to keep on with the SOU team. And you've got to keep going forward with school and what you have going. I'll make a deal; I'll tell you how it's going for me and you tell me how it's going for you. Can we make that deal?"

She nodded and got awkwardly to her feet. He followed her inside. From the hallway she turned and looked back to him, her face a vulnerable cross between child and woman.

The next morning he made coffee and stood on the back deck as high clouds to the east streaked with color. He drank a second cup, calling everyone in the unit, talking over the plan for the day, then called Chief Keeler.

"Douglas told me yesterday that Kline doesn't experience ordinary emotions," Keeler said, his voice strained and raw. "He doesn't have any conscience, at least not in the way that we think of one." Keeler added that he'd been up since two in the morning, thinking about Petersen. "Nothing like this could have ever happened when

I started here thirty years ago. We couldn't have imagined it. Every decade or so a state ranger or warden would get killed by poachers during a confrontation, but nothing like this cat and mouse with poachers who have better equipment than us. That goddamned Internet has done more to help criminals than anyone else."

Marquez walked back into the house explaining why he was sending Alvarez back to check the Van Damme caves. The FBI hadn't done their search for evidence at low tide and he wanted to do that. He picked a list of boats off the table, heard Katherine and Maria moving around in the back rooms.

"I got a list of boats yesterday, Chief, everything longer than sixty feet that has docked at a California port in the last month. I'm going to head up the coast this morning."

"They asked that you remain available."

"I'll be back tonight and I'm available by phone." Marquez paused a beat, unsure how Keeler would react, but he seemed okay with it. "The last place they had me go was up north. We lost a full day yesterday."

Marquez hung up remembering a day years ago with Petersen when they'd been out at Point Reyes checking on an abalone bed. A tipster who was leaving her boyfriend but turning him in to Fish and Game first insisted he'd stripped it. Marquez had gone into the water and found the bed intact. Petersen had laughed when he'd surfaced and said the ab bed was there still. Then they'd sat in the warm sun along the beach and eaten sandwiches. She'd taken in the day and her fingers sifted the warm sand and they'd talked about what would come next and gathered up their lunch trash and headed on.

Marquez limped out of the house, one of his legs a little sore. He loaded equipment but was on the phone until after Katherine and Maria left. Now, he backed his truck around, registering that the new side window was the only one without dust. He saw a piece of folded paper under the windshield wiper just before taking off, and got out, picked it off the glass, and unfolded a lemon-colored piece of stationery.

"Thanks, John. I love you. Your daughter."

He read it twice because there'd always been a careful accuracy to her signings, usually finishing any card or note to him with "your loving stepdaughter," and he'd never asked her to pretend otherwise, although she almost never heard from her true father. Katherine had done the real child-raising and he'd helped out from the sidelines. With this current problem, Katherine had done the difficult part and he was just coming behind with some talk, and despite the note, there was no saying whether he'd made any difference with Maria last night. Still, he folded the note and put it in his pocket, meaning to keep it.

Three hours later, Marquez left the coast highway and started up Guyanno Canyon. The road was narrow and laced with the tar used to repair cracks. He wound up through the trees, remembering the day he'd come to meet Davies and what had changed since then. He'd talked to Ruter yesterday afternoon and Ruter had volunteered that Davies was still his number one suspect in the Guyanno murders and threw out an idea, that Davies had led Marquez down the coast to San Francisco, then ditched his boat before fleeing the country or at least California. Trying to make it look like something had happened to him.

"You still think this is about abalone poaching, but it isn't. I know you still don't believe me," Ruter had said. "I don't know about Peter Han. He may have been the equivalent of an innocent bystander, but Davies definitely came to kill Stocker."

"What more have you learned about Han?" Marquez had asked.

"Neither the ATF or DEA have any record of him, nor do the people we've interviewed up here. If he sold dope, the people he sold to aren't around. His background is sketchy, but we know he was hanging with Stocker and Huega."

Marquez mulled the conversation as he drove the canyon road, closing in on the campground now. Down to his left the oaks and bays grew thickly along the creek. Farther up the canyon he could see white sky above the mountains and the rock along the spine. It was beautiful country, yet the first story he'd ever heard about Guyanno Creek campground had been about a group of bikers who'd arrived late one night and then held hostage and repeatedly raped two young Swedish women who were on a trip across the United States, and he believed he could feel that same darkness now as he parked and stepped over the chain.

He limped up across the broken asphalt, stopping short of the creek trail. This had been a torture/execution, but what drew Kline here? What could two abalone poachers reveal to him and why were they worth so much effort? He might kill them for cheating him, but he wouldn't come all the way up here to do it. Kline would send someone like Molina to straighten it out.

He weighed the idea that Davies had led Kline up here and somehow participated in the killings. He shook his head in frustration. He was going down the wrong path again, it came back to the problem of what would motivate Kline to take these guys out. He tried to think clearly, tried to separate what he really knew from everything else, but his worry and anguish over Petersen kept clouding his thoughts. Why had Kline come to Guyanno Creek? Why kill these two?

He started up the creek trail and hiked to the clearing of dry grass and thistle, then crossed to the tree where they'd been killed. He touched the cut in the bark where the knife had been buried and where the chain had scraped as the men writhed. He saw the tracks of feral pigs, where they'd rooted the earth checking the dried blood at the base of the tree. Stocker here, Han there, and he touched where Stocker's back had been, thought of the photos of Han sent to Billy Mauro that they'd assumed had a racial slant. Maybe they'd been wrong. Maybe no one had bothered to take any photos of Stocker. He turned and looked across the clearing and saw the moonlit night in his mind's eye, heard Davies's voice in his head, the account he'd claimed that Huega gave him, Huega who'd escaped in the truck. He saw them marched across the clearing, Stocker cooperating, Han breaking and running at some point. What could Han know that Stocker didn't? He thought about that on the hike back down and called Douglas's cell phone when he got to his truck.

"We've talked about your informant on the *Emily Jane,* but was the FBI also selling abalone to Kline's network?" Marquez asked. "Were you supplying your informant with abalone so he'd be valuable?" He heard Douglas breathing quietly on the other end.

"I won't lie to you, we bought some abalone illegally that we then used. We did that on four occasions. Where are you that it's an issue this morning?"

"Guyanno Creek. What other ways did you try to infiltrate his network? Did you hire Davies?"

"No, and as I told you, Davies is a loose cannon and he may be the perp in the Huega case."

"Do you have any proof of that or does it just fit to paint him that way?"

"I don't need this from you and I don't have time for it. What are you doing back there anyway?"

"Trying to figure out what I missed." And it came to him now. Ruter had interviewed Han's landlord in Daly City and came away thinking the landlord didn't know who he was renting to. Han's live-in girlfriend had disappeared fast, and no one up here knew him. He'd showed up with cash and drugs and cultivated Stocker. He heard Douglas's soft exhale and then the pieces came together. "Han was FBI," Marquez said softly. "He was one of yours," and Douglas didn't answer.

"You need to come here."

"Not this morning, I've got a few more stops. Was he one of yours?" Douglas still didn't answer. Marquez finished, "I'll call you later today."

He clicked the phone off, laid it on the picnic table, and then watched it ring and ring. When it stopped, he picked it up and called Ruter.

37

Ruter was already at a table on the restaurant deck, his briefcase leaning against his chair near his right leg. He buttered a saltine cracker as Marquez sat down, and there were bread crumbs scattered across the tabletop. It looked like he'd already finished a basket of bread and seemed self-conscious about it, brushing away the crumbs as Marquez adjusted his chair.

"The cooler weather makes me hungry and at home my wife's there with a calculator adding up every calorie. There's no butter in the house. We've got this oily shit in a little plastic tub that tastes like cold motor oil."

Marquez nodded. His mind was on Petersen, and now Han, not Ruter's eating habits. When the waitress came over Ruter ordered a BLT, Marquez a turkey sandwich.

"I think Peter Han was an FBI agent."

Ruter's eyebrows went up, but he didn't say anything and

when a busboy landed a basket of bread Ruter handed the kid the butter ramekin. He pulled a piece of bread, tore it in half, and seemed to be contemplating the Han idea.

"Why would they keep that from us?" Ruter asked.

"Because they were afraid it would jeopardize their Kline operation."

Ruter nodded as if something in the idea made sense to him, and a new tension began to form in Marquez. He watched Ruter lift the murder book out of his briefcase, open it on the table, put on reading glasses, and then scan his case notes.

"Han rented that house in Daly City," Ruter said, "but a girl-friend lived there with him, a nice woman, according to the landlord, clean-cut and polite. Why I bring her up is she told the landlord that she was going to arrange a service for Han, said he had no immediate family, which would also fit. The landlord wanted to attend but he never heard from her. He tried to contact her, but the phone numbers she'd provided had been disconnected. I'm talking less than a week after Han is killed. She also never came back for her things." He stopped as another idea occurred to him. "Han's body is still at the morgue. Pretty soon, the county will have to deal with it, meaning no one has come forward to claim it. The Feds always take care of their own. They'd never let that happen."

"Unless he didn't have family and they felt they had to leave him there," Marquez said, and thought, or maybe he wasn't really there and they'd got the coroner to play along.

"Do you want what I learned about Han's past employer?" Ruter asked.

"Everything you've got."

"All right. Employer was Horizon Industries out of Belmont. You call and a rep will call you back and tell you they're wind-ing down operations, moving to Nevada for tax reasons. Listed as a California C corporation that buys and sells used electronic equipment. Been in existence since 1997. The man I talked with confirmed Han had worked there, mostly at a computer screen. He also said Han used to talk about getting a job along the coast somewhere near the ocean."

Their orders arrived and Marquez studied the turkey sandwich, thinking that what Ruter had on Han could fit with his idea. He watched Ruter pick up his BLT and hit it the way he'd seen a great white hit a seal off the Farallon Islands last winter.

"Tice," Ruter said, as he swallowed.

"Who?"

"Lenny Tice. The Bragg police call him Lenny Lice. He's a local lowlife, one of Stocker's friends. Tice suspected Han was an undercover drug agent. I interviewed him and he threw that on the table, so you're in good company." He chuckled. "He thought Han was one of your old gang, DEA." Ruter took another bite, wiped his mouth with the back of his hand, wiped his hand deftly on the napkin. "Told me he wasn't up for the dogs, the bullhorns, the long-haired undercover guys with their riot guns. Tice pointed us toward the dope at Huega's girlfriend's house and we waited to see who else would show up. That's when the DEA got brought in. You're saying Han was undercover trying to penetrate this Kline organization. Well, what did Douglas say when you called him? Which I'm sure you did before calling me."

"He wants to sit down."

"I'll call him, if you want. As soon as we get out to the parking lot."

Marquez handed the waitress a credit card and ten minutes later they were sitting in Ruter's sedan, Marquez listening as he looked out at the ocean. He heard Douglas ask, "Are you sitting there with Marquez?"

"Yes, but I'm asking you." Ruter picked at his teeth with a yellow plastic cocktail stirrer while Douglas hesitated. The FBI no doubt had a plan for how to handle any questions like this. Douglas wouldn't want to dig a hole for himself but he owed the investigating detective a straight answer.

"Marquez came to you with the idea, so put him on."

Ruter handed the phone over. "He wants to talk to you."

"What's the game we're playing here?" Douglas asked.

"I'm looking back at everyplace the SOU has been and who we had contact with and that has to do with Petersen."

"We'll talk and no bullshit, but not over a cell phone. That okay with you?"

"That's fine, but when?" Marquez asked.

"Today. Now what are you doing with CATIC?"

"I got a list of boats from them yesterday." CATIC was the California antiterrorism coordinating body set up after 9/11. All boats coming into California ports were supposed to go through a notification process and be boarded by a team before coming into port. Marquez had requested a record of all vessels sixty feet or longer docking in California in the last two months. From that he'd culled his list. "Nothing has changed since we last talked. If we find anything, we'll call you first."

Douglas relented. "He was one of the good guys, Marquez."

"I'm sorry."

"It hit us hard."

"I'm sure it did."

Marquez hung up and handed the phone back to Ruter, and told him Douglas had finally confirmed that Han had been an FBI agent. A half hour later he was at Van Damme State Park. There was a kayaking outfit in the parking lot getting their clients ready to paddle out to the sea caves. He looked at the expectant faces of the largely middle-aged group and wondered if he'd ever visit those caves again in his life. He didn't turn into the parking lot but into the camping area on the other side of the road and found Alvarez and Roberts looking glum, sitting on Alvarez's tailgate up near the end of the paved area, drinking Calistoga juices. Brad's hair was wet and he wore a wetsuit peeled down to his waist.

"We checked the caves and didn't find anything there, but up the coast we found a wetsuit, booties, a mask, and gloves. They were in the same area we checked yesterday with the FBI." Alvarez reached around and leaned into the pickup bed and slid out a large plastic evidence bag. "Nothing says it's theirs but you've got to figure. It's a wetsuit and gear and maybe you'll recognize it. Kind of an unusual color."

Marquez opened the bag and pulled the suit out. It was pale gray, same color as the suit the Irishman had been wearing. There was at least a chance of pulling DNA off the suit, but whether the Irishman was in any database, or whether that would do them any good was another question.

"Nice work. I'll drop this with the FBI this afternoon."

"Where are we going to take it from here?"

"We'll work the list on these boats, harbor to harbor. I'm going to divide the state up between us, but a lot can be done by phone first."

He carried the dive gear over to his truck and brought copies of the list back. He distributed the list knowing he was the only one who held any real hope that it might matter.

38

The ocean was gray-green at the horizon, the sky white and smooth overhead when Marquez left the coast. He followed a camper in a long line of traffic, taking two hours to get back up the canyon, past Boonville, and on out to Highway 101. He had a hard time with the slow traffic and sweat started on his forehead. He lowered his window, thinking they'd blown the ransom handoff, botched their best chance. They were running out of time, if they weren't already out. She couldn't die. That couldn't happen. He came around a slow line of cars and edged in front of the leading car. The young woman driving flipped him off as he accelerated away.

At 3:30 he crossed the Golden Gate and fifteen minutes later handed the evidence bag to Douglas, getting no answer of how quickly the Bureau could do anything with it. He listened to an agent recount to Douglas some vague new tip of a terrorist threat, some FBI-speak passing between them on how it was being handled. Always overwhelmed here, he thought. Making decisions based on priority and resource, and with Petersen they had nowhere to look, no current leads.

Marquez followed Douglas into his office and took a chair to read the files he was finally willing to share. Records of boats they'd searched. Their undercover operatives. A blown bust.

"It's unlikely we've missed a boat," Douglas said, as he handed over a marked list.

"It's one we've already seen. It'll be right under our noses."

"Is it? We have forty agents out there looking for Kline. Tomorrow, we'll have more. If you want to help us, focus on the divers and the things your team knows. Maybe someone will make a mistake there that leads us in, but you're not set up to board boats. Leave that to us and I'll let you know on this wetsuit as soon as I know."

Marquez drove home under the pale orange light ahead of sunset. Inside, he turned on the news, checking to see if anything was running about Petersen, if they were still putting out the information, but an airliner had gone down on approach to Heathrow with over two hundred aboard, including the U.S. Secretary of the Interior. Already labeled a terrorist event, all news was focused on the crash. He looked at the row of houses the jet had plowed through, listened to what was known so far, and then heated soup Katherine had brought last night and called Billy Mauro at home.

Mauro's voice was unnaturally bright. "I met with the FBI again today," Mauro said. "They want me to only talk to them, then they'll talk to you."

"Yeah? Have you heard from Bailey?"

"Not from anyone. I have a number for the FBI for you to call."

"Thanks, Billy, I already have it."

After hanging up, Marquez drank the soup and took a couple of aspirin. He lay on the couch with a blanket, the TV on low, throwing blue light in the otherwise dark room. Holding the lists of boats he called Shauf and Roberts who were up in the Fort Bragg cold house. They'd worked the phones all day and he crossed off the boats they said were no goes. He phoned Alvarez, who'd driven north and was in a Crescent City diner. Alvarez would take the northernmost part of the coast, starting up in Coos Bay, Oregon, early tomorrow morning, and work his way down.

Katherine wouldn't be coming up tonight, but he called them now, talked a while with Katherine about the note from Maria, the conversation last night. Then he heated more chicken soup and made some toast before moving equipment from the Nissan to the Explorer, figuring to switch vehicles tomorrow. Later, when he fell asleep it was on the couch, and near midnight his cell phone rang and he reached for it, afraid of the news it would bring. He looked at the screen expecting Douglas or Chief Keeler, then clicked off the TV and said hello.

"It was 7:55 A.M. when Pearl Harbor was attacked. That's when they came in. Not many people remember that," Davies said. "That's what time I made the first call to you from Guyanno."

"Where are you now?"

"Not far from you."

"Yeah, why is that?"

"I've done some things lately that are going to send me to hell, Lieutenant. But I had to prove myself to him to get inside. He puts you right to the test."

"Is she alive?"

"She was when I saw her, but it's not a good situation. She lost that baby and I tried to help her, but he had me deal with something else. That's his way of putting it to you. He knows how to do that like no man I've ever known. He doesn't leave you a way back, Lieutenant."

Marquez moved off the couch and across the cold floor to the kitchen. He found his shoes.

"What have you done for him?"

"He wants me to kill your wife and the girl and bring you in. I went by your wife's coffee place today. I saw your daughter there."

"Stay away from her."

"He's got a power about him, doesn't he?"

"We tried to pay the ransom. What do we have to do to get our warden back?"

"She was in a warehouse but I hear she's on a boat now. What I hear is you'll know the boat by the moon."

"Where is this boat supposed to be?"

"They're getting ready for something. I can tell. When he sent me out he said if I can't bring you to him, he wants me to bring back your thumbs and he's got people who'll run your fingerprint."

"Bring me where?"

"I don't know."

"You're lying."

The line went dead and Marquez called Katherine, then Douglas.

"Marquez," Douglas said, his voice flat, and Marquez could hear sirens and vehicle traffic. Douglas was on a street somewhere.

"I just got a call from Davies."

"Yeah?"

Marquez heard more sirens. "What's happened?" he asked.

"We missed him, Marquez. The hit was a Florida judge out here vacationing from Dade County. He was shot leaving a restaurant in San Francisco tonight. We didn't know. We didn't have any way of knowing. We thought it was a local they were after. We'd narrowed it to a couple of possible drug cases here, but this was it. This was the cartel hit. They're trying one of the Cardoza family in Miami next month. I don't know how we could have known. Christ, if we'd only known the judge was here we could have put it together. Kline will leave now. Jesus Christ, he came here and made the hit. I'm sorry, Marquez, what about Davies?"

After Marquez related the phone call, Douglas said, "I'll get agents to your wife's house and yours. Give me ten minutes. But I think he's just a crackpot, Marquez. I think he just likes making the calls. I wouldn't worry about it, but we're on our way."

39

Marquez called Katherine back and turned on the porch lights. He laid a gun next to his laptop and then clicked on the computer, which seemed to boot up too slowly. As he'd feared, the Web site was up again but had changed. A scene that maybe only he would recognize showed on the screen. It took him a moment to be sure what he was seeing, a yellowed photograph of a human skull on a stone altar ringed by candles, and at the center the DEA badges. There were wedding bands and photo IDs, driver's licenses, and the other proof Kline had laid out and photographed eleven years ago. It still reached across the years and shocked him.

He clicked out and checked for e-mail, found nothing, backed out, and his cell phone rang.

"There are three agents on their way to you," Douglas said. "Four agents are in Bernal Heights with your ex. Anything more from Davies?"

"No."

"Keep trying to call him."

A few minutes later headlights showed up on Ridge Road, disappeared in the dip in the driveway, then reflected through his windows. He saw two men in a white Suburban in the driveway. He opened the door and told them they were welcome to stay if they hoped Davies would show, but that he was taking off, which didn't make any sense to them. They tried to get him to wait while they called Douglas.

"Douglas has my cell number," Marquez said. "Tell him to call me."

When he got in the Explorer he threw his coat on the passenger seat and glanced behind him, making sure he'd transferred everything from the Nissan. A little more than a half moon was well into the western sky when he dropped off the mountain. He couldn't look at it without wondering what the clue about the moon and the boat was supposed to mean. He spoke the names of boats he knew as if hearing *Blue Moon, Full Moon,* or *Moondance* would bring the connection.

Marquez was near the base of the mountain, ready to turn past the bar on the corner when he heard a rustling behind him. He knew immediately someone was under the tarp covering the equipment, someone who must have gotten in when he'd left the truck unlocked earlier, when he'd been transferring what he'd planned to take. Marquez started pulling and Davies's voice was hard.

"Bring your hand back to the wheel or I'll shoot you. Drive to where you dock your boat."

"What's there?"

Davies climbed from the rear compartment and Marquez glanced at the rearview mirror. Good chance the FBI would pick him up or already had. Douglas would call, no question about that, and now he felt a cold gun muzzle press against his neck.

"Stakes are high, Lieutenant." They crossed lower Marin on the freeway and then drove through San Rafael and came up alongside a cop at a stoplight. Davies slouched back behind the passenger seat, his profile hidden by the tinted windows. "If you do the wrong thing, you'll get the cop killed," he said. "Take your hands off the wheel and you'll make your wife a widow."

"My hands are on the wheel, but I thought we were on the same side." They drove to Loch Lomond Marina, turned in, and were alone. "I need to turn around and line up the boat hitch. I've got to get out."

Marquez had a way he angled the Explorer, a way he liked to line up on the fence and another boat that had never been moved in the time he'd rented here. He purposefully missed this time, knew the trailer ball and boat hitch wouldn't be near enough to hook the boat trailer up.

"It's a life or death situation, Lieutenant, and I've got to bring you to him and we need your boat for that."

"I'm always missing with the hitch," Marquez said.

Davies's voice was low and very quiet. His face had been darkened with camouflage paint and he pointed the gun at Marquez's chest.

"There isn't enough time for this shit. Hook it up."

Marquez backed up, got out and attached the trailer hitch, then backed the boat trailer down until the Fountain floated. He did it all slowly and knew the FBI had his position from the telelocator. He got on board with Davies now, though the Explorer still idled, its muffler coughing as it caught water.

"Back up slowly," Davies said, and got on the boat behind him. "Keep the speed at twenty-five as we clear the channel. You can figure his people are watching."

Marquez went with it, hoping Davies was taking him straight to the boat. He looked at the Explorer sitting on the ramp with the driver's door open, headlights on and the engine running, and backed the boat around. They came under the San Rafael Bridge and out into the open bay, veering right of Angel Island through

Raccoon Strait, and above the engines he asked, "Out the Gate?"

"No, and cut your speed. Go under the Bay Bridge."

They crossed past the San Francisco waterfront, under the Bay Bridge, and down past China Basin. They headed toward boats docked offshore in a row in the channel. He saw an old transport vessel, maybe a hundred and twenty feet in length flying a Turkish flag, and saw the crescent moon on the flag.

"You try anything and he'll kill her," Davies said. "If the Feds came in with you, he'd kill her first. You understand, Lieutenant. It had to be like this. You want to call them this is the last chance. Go ahead if you want, but if they take us down before you get aboard, you won't get her back. He gave me until dawn to bring you and I said I'd do it. He wants you and you want her back, but you'll be on your own in there."

Marquez climbed up the ladder with Davies aiming at him from where the Fountain idled below, a second man above him, a small light guiding him. He could drop off the rungs and into the water without hitting the Fountain. More than likely he could avoid getting shot, swim away, and come back with the Feds. The boat wouldn't be leaving, but what about Petersen, what if they killed her in the time it took? And the Feds would be coming anyway. He looked down again. Davies was on the ladder now, the low throb of the Fountain engine gone silent.

As Marquez reached the top of the ladder, hands as big as his own grabbed him, dragged him over the last rungs, pushed him chest-down on the deck, and a man squatted near his head with a gun. He heard Davies's shoes clatter up the metal rungs, giving directions to the men and being ignored. They jerked Marquez to his feet, covered his head with a burlap sack, and he heard the hollow echo of their boots as he was led down a passageway and made to climb down a ladder before his wrists were bound behind him with duct tape.

"I'm with you, Lieutenant," and Davies from behind him slid

something metal into his hands. "Switchblade," Davies whispered. "Grip it and cover it."

A walk-in freezer door in the galley swung open and a heavy boot caught him from behind, low on his back. A rifle butt chopped at his shoulder and he stumbled forward into the compartment, bounced off the back wall and fell sideways. They ran duct tape around his ankles and left him, the door shutting, a chain rattling, a lock clicking loudly.

He uncurled his fingers from around the knife, turned it slowly in his hand, opened it and sawed through the thick layers of tape on his wrists. He pulled the hood off and reached down under his ankles and made a clean cut that didn't show from above. He tried the door, pushed gently against the chain on the other side and could only open it an inch. He slit the plastic wrap on a package of frozen meat, pulled the telelocator from his shoe and shoved it into the package. Then he sat down against the back wall and waited, marking the time, hours passing as his fingers worked the burlap hood, knowing he'd have to put it back on, knowing he'd have to wait until the last moment, past all fear, past pain if he was stabbed first. He'd have to keep his head when the hood came off. He'd have to face everything, gamble and wait. His breath was shallow and every noise he heard was Kline coming down the corridor. He'd have to lie still, then struggle, let him start before bringing the blade up. He thought, if Kline leaves the hood on, I've lost.

There were footsteps, muffled voices, more than a few, the chain rattling, and Marquez put the hood on, cinched it. The door swung noisily and he heard Spanish, orders given for the men to go up on deck and then the door closing. A fist crashed into one side of his face, stunning him, almost causing him to drop the knife. A hand slid under the hood and gripped his throat and held his head pressed against the wall while his shirt was torn open and a blade touched him, sliced skin and cut his pants open. And

Marquez held himself still as Kline's hand remained tight under his neck, long finger pressing up under the jaw, pushing him tight against the wall, Kline's weight resting on his thighs, his face close by, the blade low on Marquez's gut and stinging. But he kept repeating to himself, he'll want you to see, and then the blade poked at the hood. It cut through fabric near his eye and dipped into his cheek and Marquez barely reacted. Then he heard the hood fabric cut as the knife sliced through it and Kline's breath was on his face and the knife back at his gut.

"Look at me. This is your death."

And he saw the colorless skin, looked into Kline's eyes so near his and said, "Not yet, Kline, don't do it, and I'll tell you what you need to know."

When Kline hesitated Marquez brought up his right hand with the knife in a slashing move, catching part of his throat, punching the blade in and ripping forward as Kline recoiled, blood flowing down his neck. Kline lunged forward, trying to stab Marquez in the chest. The blade sliced skin as it went past and then Marquez drove him sideways, fought him, punching hard at him, grabbed the wrist with the knife, got the blade free pounding the wrist against the wall. And Kline still fought him. Blood pumped from his neck, and Marquez hammered his face with a fist until he stopped struggling. Then he reached for Kline's knife and held the blade at his throat.

"Where is she?"

Kline's eyes closed. His face grew very pale and Marquez lifted his weight from his chest, moved a knee off him, reached and shook Kline's face. When he did Kline went for him, fingers hooking to dig out his eyes, clawing at him, tearing into his cheek and Marquez drove the blade forward and down, hands gripping tightly, leaning into it, all his weight on it. He drove the hilt into Kline's chest and heard the blade scraping on the metal floor underneath before snapping off. He watched him spasm once and go still.

Then came gunfire and men yelling, stun grenades going off, screaming, more quick bursts of gunfire, and he pushed the door open to a gangway filled with smoke.

He ripped the last of the duct tape off, wiped blood from his hands and then raised them as an FBI team held shotguns on him. He made them understand who he was. He was ordered to wait on the top deck, yelled at to go up now, but he refused. They didn't have Petersen, hadn't found Davies, and there was fighting below deck.

"We've got a warden on board, kidnapped."

"Get the fuck up the ladder."

"I'll stay with you."

He fell behind them, went cabin to cabin, bullets whanging off the corridor walls as he advanced behind the fighting. Now there was a much deeper, deafening, metal-rending blast and the boat shuddered. He swung the door of an empty cabin, swung another and another, moved on as emergency lighting came on and the main lights died. He stepped over bodies, stair-stepped down another level and pushed a cabin door against the body blocking it. He heard more yelling now, men clambering up the stairs.

"Taking on water," someone yelled. "Taking on water fast! Everyone out, let's go, let's go."

Marquez kept pushing, throwing his shoulder into it, sliding the body blocking the door out of the way. Then he saw her. A chain held her to the metal frame of a bed and near her was Davies slumped with his back against the wall, dead, his shirt soaked in blood. He felt for her pulse, then checked Davies's pockets for a key, found nothing and looked at the bodies at the door. He rolled one over and saw it was Bailey, the other Molina, and realized Davies had fought them. He didn't find a key on either of them. The boat groaned as it listed, he had to get her out of there. He hammered at the bed with the stock of a gun, and began to break the bed apart, then lifted her over his shoulder, dragging a piece of metal hanging off the chain still attached to her arm.

The narrow gangway was empty. A single emergency light emitted a red glow near the stairs, and he worked his way toward them, a cabin door banging open behind him as the boat shifted further. He heard a staccato rip of gunfire, feet clanging on the metal stairs below, more yelling, terse hard orders given, a bullhorn, someone yelling in Spanish, couldn't make out what they were saying. He climbed the stairs, calling ahead, identifying himself, "Marquez. Fish and Game," and finally found help. A call was made to get a helicopter to get her to a hospital. With the SWAT team he got her into a basket and Marquez gripped her hand, touched her face. He watched her rise into the sky.

As they completed the arrests the Coast Guard arrived to help clear the boat, which was listing further to port. The fear wasn't that it would sink, but that more explosives would detonate. Marquez got off with the last group onto a Coast Guard boat. He borrowed a phone and called Katherine and after that he let go. Where Kline had cut him low on his abdomen was only a flesh wound but it had bled plenty and stung. He needed to get a bandage. He sat down and let a medic help him, looking back at the listing vessel as he did, registering the name *Bosporus* and spotting the *Marlin* now crossing toward them.

Douglas told him later that nine were arrested, four Mexican nationals and five carrying multiple passports, two that were wanted in Europe, America, and Mexico for murder and drug trafficking. Alvarez and Cairo recovered the Fountain drifting in the south bay and brought it back to its berth in San Rafael. His truck had been towed, but he located it that afternoon.

The FBI had lost two agents. Another died at San Francisco General late in the day. Marquez saw Douglas sitting with senior FBI personnel in the lobby when he came back to check on Petersen that night. Douglas's face was ashen, his eyes downcast, but Marquez caught a faint nod as he walked by and after he'd passed the group he waited out of earshot before going to the elevators.

He saw faces turn his direction and Douglas rose and walked stiffly from the group toward him, offering his hand as he got close.

"The boat isn't going to sink; they stabilized it," Douglas said. "There was another charge and if it had gone off, the boat would have sunk in minutes, taking everybody with it. Several people here would like to meet you."

"I'd like to get back on board the *Bosporus* tomorrow."

"I'll get you on. You want to get to that abalone."

"Yeah."

"Let me introduce you here."

"I'm going up the elevator first. I'll sit down with you after I come back down." He put a hand on Douglas's shoulder. "I'm sorry about the agents who were killed."

"We've got two in surgery."

"How are they doing?"

"We don't know yet."

Petersen was conscious and saw him come in. Stuart was at her bedside dabbing her forehead with a sponge a nurse had left him. She brought her hand up to push the sponge away, and he saw she was very pale, her eyes too bright, Stuart explaining quietly that she had a high fever, the result of a blood infection. They'd pumped her full of antibiotics and were confident she'd be okay in a few days, but the real loss was in her heart and Marquez could see the sad emptiness in her eyes. He'd already been told that what Davies had reported was correct. She'd miscarried in her third day of captivity. He talked to her now, took her hand, tried to make her smile. When she spoke the thoughts were in fragments, the effort at forming sentences evident, and a nurse returned and asked that Marquez leave soon. Keeler had told him earlier this afternoon that a doctor had said she wouldn't have made it another forty-eight hours without antibiotics.

"You were hard to find," he said, and leaned over her. She tried to smile and he touched her face. "I'll check in tomorrow."

"I'm really tired, John," she said, and then as he turned to go, she added, "He saved me, John. All the way along he had them fooled."

"Marquez saved you," Stuart cut in, but Marquez understood. He turned back and leaned to hear her last sentence, saw tears flood her eyes. "Don't let them wreck his name," she whispered.

40

Marquez caught a ride out to the *Bosporus* the next morning from the *Marlin*. Douglas was already aboard, wearing jeans, tennis shoes, and a T-shirt that read FBI in black letters across the back, a casualness of dress Marquez had never seen in him. Douglas's face bore the marks of the emotional ride of the last day and they were both quiet and stood on the main deck looking at the San Francisco skyline before going below to the cold storage where the abalone was. There had to be five thousand.

"What happens to it?" Douglas asked.

"We hand it off to charities. Why don't you take a couple home? Tenderize them, pound them, and then cut them into steaks. You'll find out what this is all about."

"I might take you up on that."

He knew what Douglas had on his mind and waited for it now, heard him clear his throat and suggest they go to the walk-in where Marquez had fought with Kline. They climbed back to that

level and followed the narrow passageway through the galley with
Douglas talking as he walked in front.

"You finally got him, Marquez." Douglas opened the door of
the walk-in and Marquez saw the arcing blood splatter dried on
the walls, the dark, almost black pool of blood at their feet. "Life
or death," Douglas said, and Marquez knew where Douglas was
going. "We recovered the telelocator in case you're wondering."

"Keep it. I don't want to lose another one."

Marquez stared at the pooled blood, his blood mixed with
Kline's. He waited.

"Did you really keep the hood on until he was holding a knife
on you?"

"Yes."

"How'd you keep yourself still?"

"I knew I had to."

"Man, that's unreal, that's just unreal." He could hear the edge
in Douglas's voice, Douglas working him. "How's it making you
feel looking at this now?"

Marquez looked at the blood and thought of his friends in
Mexico and silently told them it was done. He knew where Douglas
was going and shrugged, not giving away much yet.

Douglas asked, "So you struggled with him and you managed
to get control of his knife?"

"We wrestled."

"Rolled around on the floor?"

"Something like that."

"Was he losing strength from blood loss?"

"He was going to," and they looked at each other. "He might
have even bled out."

"They're telling me the neck wounds weren't fatal. They were
bad but not fatal."

"Is that right?"

"That's what they're saying. The other one was definitely

fatal. You wrestled and what happened? You get on top of him and all of a sudden you've got the knife in your hand?"

Marquez pointed at the floor where the struggle had left long streaks of blood, smeared by a knee, a shoe, an elbow. There were stainless shelves on either side with frozen food products sitting on them, bloody handprints on those where he'd stood as he got up off Kline's body.

"Yeah, I was able to pin him down."

"Was he still struggling?" Marquez looked at him and nodded. "But you had the upper hand by then. You must have seen how he was bleeding."

"Sure."

"And what were you thinking, or do you remember? Did you realize those wounds weren't fatal?"

"He made one more attempt, tried for my eyes."

"So you made sure."

Marquez stood silent with emotion sweeping through him, all the inner promises he'd made to the dead, all the years wondering and knowing Kline was out there still. Yeah, he'd driven the blade through Kline's heart and he'd known what he was doing, which was the question Douglas was asking. He'd pushed down until he felt the tip of the blade slide off a rib and snap on the metal floor. He'd crossed Davies's abyss.

"You're asking if I had a choice," Marquez said. The Feds had anticipated capturing Kline. Douglas had counted on questioning him.

"Maybe I am, but I don't want an answer. Or maybe you don't remember. Basically, you were defending yourself, trying to save your life." Douglas paused. "You're going to get asked a lot of questions this afternoon, but I can understand the actual moment being a little hazy. They say the knife went in and then was pushed through with great force and the tip snapped on the floor decking after it exited his body. The ribcage was compressed enough by force to allow the knife to go all the way through him.

You sliced a rib almost in half and buried the knife hilt in his chest, but then you're a big man. Still, you're going to get questioned about it." Marquez felt Douglas's hand on his back. "Let's go back up top."

"You go up; I'll be there in a minute."

Marquez stepped out of the walk-in and shut its door. He laid a palm on the cold metal door and knew he'd had a choice. He'd held the knife over Kline and brought it down into his chest with all his strength. Douglas was letting him know not to say or remember much about the fight, but that didn't feel right either. Marquez lifted his hand away, walked out the passageway and climbed the stairs into the sunlight. He stood at the rail looking out across at the City again, at the mare's tails of cirrus fanning from the west, thinking about Kline, just the things he knew Kline had done, the people he'd killed. He didn't hear Douglas walk over, but then felt a hand on his back.

"You answer some questions this afternoon and then it's over, Marquez."

"It all happened fast, but I had a choice."

"No, you didn't, and fuck him." Douglas pointed at the *Marlin*, Hansen clearly visible at the wheel on the top deck. "There's your ride. When they ask, you say you were rolling around fighting on the floor. Kline had the knife, then you had it and you don't even know what happened. You were fighting for your life. Or say nothing." Marquez didn't answer that, wasn't sure what he'd do yet, and Douglas moved the conversation on. "Where do you go now?"

"A bear poaching deal." The answer sounded hollow and out of place.

"Never ends, does it?"

"Not really."

Douglas offered his hand and Marquez shook it. "We owe you, Marquez. You take care of yourself."

"You, too."

He rode across the bay without looking back. He knew he wouldn't be able to lie about killing Kline and decided he'd say nothing. If they wanted to take it further, that was their call. The boat dropped him and he spent the afternoon with the FBI and their many questions about Kline, about whether Marquez had a personal score to settle. They read his silence as an admission and they brought Douglas into the room and walked through the sequence of questions again, let him know they'd put a lot of resources into finding Kline and had expectations about unraveling his network, following the tentacles back to the cartel and the murders of three American judges. Cases that had gone back years in addition to the new killing here in San Francisco.

He watched the nostrils of the man across from him flare as he insinuated that Marquez had murdered a suspect. They walked him through the sequence again, coming up to the point of holding the knife, to the point where if he'd seconded the empathetic voices in the room who suggested he was fighting to defend himself, he could have walked out easily. But he couldn't bring himself to do that and when they let him leave at dusk, he knew he'd left them to an internal debate.

That night he chopped oak kindling, split a log, and built a fire. He poured a scotch and sat on the stone bench near the fireplace and used a knife to cut the pages from his Kline file. One by one he fed them to the fire and watched the cardboard backing curl and burn and the photos color and smoke, then darken at the center and burst into flame. And he wept for his dead friends, tears no one would see that dried with the fire heat, tears he'd held back for more than a decade. He broke the ashes apart with an iron poker, poured another scotch, and then walked out onto the deck under the stars and knew that for him, it was over.

41

A few weeks later on a cloudless morning in October when the sky was a dark blue and the sunlight gold with the fall, Marquez drove up the coast to an abalone festival with Katherine and Maria. They turned off the coast highway onto an open grassy field above the ocean about a mile before Mendocino. A volunteer wearing a fluorescent vest waved them toward a parking spot at the end of a long row of cars. It was a cook-off, an annual deal put on by the Mendocino Area Park Association.

Blue cooking smoke rose in the clearing and pickups, cars, and campers were backed up to barbecues and grills. Beyond it all was the dark blue line of the ocean. They walked in and Marquez handed all but one of the tickets he'd bought months ago to Maria, then bought a couple cups of chowder and stood with Katherine in the sunlight as Maria wandered off. You handed a ticket over and got to taste somebody's abalone recipe and he watched to see what line Maria would get in. But she went first to the tables of beaded jewelry, T-shirts, and other fairground paraphernalia. She leaned over a table, a long-legged young woman wearing a tube top and jeans.

"Gaining weight," Katherine said.

"She's going to be okay, Kath."

And so were they, he thought, finding their way to some different space. It would take time but he was more patient with that now and knew they'd get there. He checked his watch, glanced back toward the entry gate. He'd had another conversation with the FBI yesterday and though the man he'd talked to didn't seem happy about it, they were going to treat his killing Kline as self-defense. They wanted him to sign something tomorrow and he'd agreed to.

Katherine slipped her hand into his and he moved closer to her. He scanned the crowd out of habit, took in the faces and saw the DFG table and the uniformed officer talking to a couple of women, probably explaining the habitat of abalone and the effort at sustainability.

"Here she comes," Katherine said, and they watched Maria walk back across with a plate of fried abalone. One of the pieces had a little American flag stuck in it.

"Try this," Maria said. "It's got this great sauce," and Marquez picked up a piece and bit into it. He reached for another and she pulled the plate back, her eyes lit with a wry humor he hadn't seen in a while. "Get your own," she said. "You've still got a ticket."

An hour later, Maria and Katherine were ready to leave and went on ahead to the truck while Marquez waited through the last of a line to use the remaining ticket. The cook was pounding abalone on his tailgate, then grilling it in strips on a barbecue. Marquez watched it cook, got served a plate and walked toward the exit. He looked back once, figuring she'd made other plans and had decided not to stop by. Then he spotted her. She was with Stuart and standing with another couple, people who looked like they were friends. Petersen wore a cap and stood a little back from the group and to the side. He could see Stuart laughing and judging from their faces it looked like the other man was telling a funny story. Marquez took a bite of abalone and lingered near the exit, debating whether to cross the clearing. But he was unsure whether to interrupt.

He'd talked with her plenty on the phone and had been to see her in Redding about a week and a half after Petersen had gotten home. They'd sat in her living room drinking tea while she told him how she'd find herself crying unexpectedly and how her mind would go blank at times. She was getting help with it, seeing a psychotherapist. He saw her face turn in sunlight, the cap that had shadowed her eyes coming off as the man with the funny story started talking to her. When she smiled that light quick smile of hers he felt a rush of warmth.

There were some things you never really got over, but you could get past them. Petersen put her arm around Stuart and looked out across the clearing and saw him now. Marquez saw her nod and held up his index finger, an old joke between them, signaling her that she was the number one warden. But it wasn't a joke today and he wanted her to know that. He held her gaze and smiled back at her, then waved and slowly turned away. It was time to go home.

Acknowledgments

I would like to thank the following people: California Department of Fish and Game Assistant Chief of the South Coast Region Mervin Hee, Captain Nancy Foley, Lieutenant Kathy Ponting, Lieutenant Adrian Foss, Lieutenant Keith Long, Warden Richard Vincent; without their help and guidance this book wouldn't have happened. My agent, Philip Spitzer, whose sensibility and undaunted enthusiasm I've relied on throughout. My editor, Jay Schaefer, for seeing the true possibilities in Marquez and then guiding me to write a better novel. Branch Russell, Lydia McIntosh, my brother and sister. Greg Estes, Paul Hansen, Tim Stokes, John Buffington, Tony Broadbent, David Hayden, good friends who waded through rough drafts and offered ideas that were often better than my own. I am deeply indebted to a crime fiction writer—who shall remain nameless here—for his extraordinary generosity, thoughtful advice, and the encouragement he gave when it mattered most. My daughters, Kate and Olivia, for their humor and patience, for enduring the "just give me another few minutes to finish this paragraph" that so often stretched into an hour. And especially to Judy, my wife, who never once challenged my idea that I could and would write novels, and whose support has never wavered.

JUST PUBLISHED

Night Game: A John Marquez Crime Novel
By Kirk Russell

In this gripping new crime novel, Marquez pushes the boundaries of
safety and politics when he takes his team of Fish and Game officers
on a dangerous operation in pursuit of bear poachers. A murdered student, a missing game warden, and threats to his own family draw
Marquez even more deeply into the tangled world of international
traffickers and offenders. At the center of his investigation is a wildly
attractive and highly unreliable woman, who sets some traps of her own.

ADVANCE PRAISE FOR *NIGHT GAME*

"Genuine evil and heart-stopping action are not reserved solely for the
gritty inner city, but flourish as well in Kirk Russell's rural California
settings in his second John Marquez outing, *Night Game.* This is a
series, and an author, to hitch on to."
—C.J. BOX, AUTHOR OF *TROPHY HUNT*

"*Night Game* is an engaging, harrowing, and at times heart-breaking
tale told with crisp, evocative prose. Author Kirk Russell guides us
through a world of ruthless bear poachers and organ harvesters, with
an unerring eye for how the marginalized mandate of wildlife protec-
tors opens up into a much larger story of who we are and how we
live. A bracing, convincing, and heartfelt read."
—DAVID CORBETT, AUTHOR OF *THE DEVIL'S REDHEAD* AND *DONE FOR A DIME*

"Kirk Russell writes with the clarity of a mountain stream. He has
captured a fascinating subculture and peopled it with characters deep
enough to drown in. The story flows through the brain with an exhil-
arating rush."
—NEVADA BARR, AUTHOR OF *HIGH COUNTRY*